PRAISE FOR
CLOCKWORK PHOENIX 2

Wonderfully evocative, well-written tales . . . Each story fits neatly alongside the next, and the diversity of topics, perspectives and authors makes this cosmopolitan anthology a winner.

— Publishers Weekly, **Starred Review**

Original tales by some of fantasy's most imaginative voices . . . each chosen for their unique perspective and stylistic grace.

— Library Journal

A collection worthy of serious attention. I expect I'll see several of these stories again, in a year's best collection or two.

— SF Revu

The best original genre anthology that I read this year.

— OF Blog of the Fallen

Sixteen unique voices that manage nevertheless to harmonize into a sort of choir of the uncanny singing in the key of beauty and strangeness . . . I highly recommend it, and look forward with great anticipation to *Clockwork Phoenix 3.*

— SF Site

PRAISE FOR
CLOCKWORK PHOENIX

Lush descriptions and exotic imagery startle, engross, chill and electrify the reader, and all 19 stories have a strong and delicious taste of weird.

— Publishers Weekly

I highly recommend the book to anyone look~~in~~ ~~~~ otch fiction irrespective of genre label~

ow

CLOCKWORK PHOENIX 3
New Tales of Beauty and Strangeness

Edited by Mike Allen

Copyright © 2010 by Mike Allen.
All Rights Reserved.

Cover Painting:
"Light of the Harem" by Sir Frederic Leighton, c. 1880

Cover Design Copyright © 2010 by Mike Allen and Vera Nazarian

ISBN-13: 978-1-60762-062-4
ISBN-10: 1-60762-062-6

FIRST EDITION
Trade Paperback Edition

July 1, 2010

A Publication of
Norilana Books
P. O. Box 2188
Winnetka, CA 91396
www.norilana.com

Printed in the United States of America

CREDITS

Also by Mike Allen

Poetry
DEFACING THE MOON
PETTING THE TIME SHARK
DISTURBING MUSES
STRANGE WISDOMS OF THE DEAD
THE JOURNEY TO KAILASH

Fiction
FOLLOW THE WOUNDED ONE

As editor:
NEW DOMINIONS:
Fantasy Stories by Virginia Writers
THE ALCHEMY OF STARS:
Rhysling Award Winners Showcase
(with Roger Dutcher)
MYTHIC
MYTHIC 2
CLOCKWORK PHOENIX:
Tales of Beauty and Strangeness
CLOCKWORK PHOENIX 2:
More Tales of Beauty and Strangeness

Clockwork Phoenix 3
new tales of beauty and strangeness

Norilana Books
Fantasy

www.norilana.com

CLOCKWORK PHOENIX 3

new tales of beauty and strangeness

Edited by

Mike Allen

ACKNOWLEDGMENTS

For this third volume of *Clockwork Phoenix,* the largest one yet, I have to acknowledge first and foremost the support of publisher Vera Nazarian, without whom none of these volumes would exist. As always, my wife Anita assisted me during all phases of this particular creature's assembly, and again, credit for the stories' unique arrangement should go to her. I'm grateful to Amal El-Mohtar, Michael M. Jones, and Cathy Reniere for their input and encouragement, to Anne S. Zanoni and Francesca Forrest for invaluable assistance with proofreading, and to all the contributors, some of whom had to patiently wait quite a while to see their finely crafted pinions bolted into the machine.

As we put this book together, Blair Grimm, a fellow Roanoke, Va., resident who had for years been instrumental in gathering the science fiction and fantasy fans here into a coherent community, passed away at the too-young age of 52. Last fall, having just finished exhausting cancer treatment, Blair selflessly helped a motorist free their car during the heaviest snow storm this region has seen in over a decade, and afterward died of a heart attack. The mourners at his funeral all spoke of his generosity, his gregariousness, and how he, like Will Rogers, never met anyone he didn't like.

This book is dedicated to Blair's memory.

In memory of Blair M. Grimm

CONTENTS

INTRODUCTION

Mike Allen

Everything.
    And then, nothing at all.

The cosmos spins its gears and stretches wings, the ticks of its constant grinding both too slow and too rapid to ever be detected. When it collapses to ash, everything within the dimensional tiers of its clockwork body burns to nothing.

Every pinion of this universe is a vane of time rooted in unfathomable past, grown up and out to form a spine that supports uncountable possible futures. And each of these feather-shafts fans out strands of temporal down that are themselves fractal branchings, mathematical quandaries of choices taken and not taken.

This celestial entity is vast and avian, at once bird and gear-spun egg, its shape incomprehensible to our eyes as its outlines distort and refract through higher and higher dimensions. Our linear brains can only grasp small portions of its living surface, trivial compared to the titanic and invisible feats of mechanics that bring this cosmic beast to life.

But that surface is all we can know — thus it is vital to know it. With more facets than a galactic cluster of diadems, each of these facades contains a new world that you and I may peer into as through a reading lens. And everywhere we look, the celestial clockwork meshed beneath the surface constructs a different face.

Here, bodies pile in graves, and here, bodies rise from them. Here beings that were once men walk against the grain of time with ease, while here time sweeps all before it in a relentless flood.

Here we spy upon winged machines, portraits in miniature of the universe that spawned them, sharing their dangerous wisdom with things of weaker flesh. Move our gaze here: now those wings bear madness, or the sadness of final peace.

Here above a vista of towers numerous as molecules we seek in vain for those who've hidden themselves in chambers deep beneath, until someone grows their own will to fly, soars in the sky just beneath us, tantalizing, so bright yet still so far out of reach.

Some of these surface denizens hop from world to world as easily as disrupting a dream. And some are like us, doomed always to stand outside the dreams of others, looking in.

And yet, all these teaming shards of consciousness amount to no more than figments and fragments, elementary particles bonded in a puzzle of gearbox bird and orrery egg.

Amid these wonders and horrors, you and I are no more than two uncertain strands, and the ends of our ropes are already burning. Every strand of time is a fuse, every event along its length the fuel that converts all our existence to ash.

The last surfaces we see are our own skins, peeling as we ignite.

And yet, like clockwork, like the inexorable heartbeat of the divine, a universe reduced to nothing has no choice but to crawl and crank and grind until its pieces restore themselves, ourselves still contained within it, recombined into something beyond the comprehension of our old lives, yet still enduring a rebirth. The light of new stars, the splitting of new cells, all background noise in the swell of the defiant raptor's roar.

We do not recognize each other when we return, and yet, here we are.

And once again, we have new facets to explore.

A new beginning.

THE GOSPEL OF NACHASH

Marie Brennan

1.

In the beginning God made the world, and on the sixth day he made creatures in his image. Male and female he created them, and they were the bekhorim, to whom God gave dominion over every herb bearing seed, and every tree bearing fruit, to be in their care. Mankind he formed from dust, but the bekhorim were made from air, and their spirits were more subtle than that of man.

Then the LORD planted a garden eastward in Eden; and there he put the man he had formed, and the bekhorim tended the garden, for they had dominion over all growing things. And he gave to each of them a duty, saying, Each tree in the garden you shall tend, and each of you shall have a tree, which shall be as meat for mankind, and for the beasts of the field. But of the tree of knowledge of good and evil they shall not eat.

Among the bekhorim there was one called Nachash, and to him it was given to tend the tree of knowledge of good and evil. And Nachash was saddened, for all his kindred had purpose, but he had none, for man and woman ate of every tree in the garden save his, and he labored without purpose.

He went therefore to the woman, who was called Chava, and said unto her, Yea, hath God said, Ye shall not eat of every tree of the garden?

And the woman said unto the serpent, We may eat of the fruit of the trees of the garden: but of the fruit of the tree which is in the midst of the garden, God hath said, Ye shall not eat of it, neither shall ye touch it, lest ye die.

But the tree was the tree of knowledge of good and evil, and Nachash knew of no death in it. And for what purpose did it bear fruit, if not to be eaten? Therefore he said to the woman, Ye shall not surely die, for in the day ye eat thereof, then your eyes shall be opened, and ye shall be as gods, knowing good and evil.

And when the woman saw that the tree was good for food, and that it was pleasant to the eyes, and a tree to be desired to make one wise, she took of the fruit thereof, and did eat, and gave also unto her husband with her; and he did eat.

And the LORD God was wroth with them, and expelled them from the garden. And the bekhorim he expelled likewise, for the sin of Nachash, who had beguiled the woman into eating. Their forms he altered in divers ways; but Nachash he cast down upon his belly, to crawl in the dust from which man had come. He placed at the east of the garden of Eden cherubims, and a flaming sword which turned every way, to keep the way of the tree of life.

2.

Thus were the bekhorim made wanderers in the lands outside of Eden, which were as a wilderness, full of thistles and thorns. For the LORD had cursed the ground, that Adam might labor with much toil to bring forth food from it, and for the bekhorim it was likewise cursed; that which was their dominion was now fallen into ruin. And the bekhorim lamented, saying, We are condemned; for the sin of Nachash we are condemned.

But he had sinned unknowing, for Nachash had not eaten of the fruit of the tree. Of good and evil the bekhorim were ignorant.

Now it came to pass that many among them sickened and became weak. In the garden there had been neither sickness nor death, nor any ill thing, but in the wilderness beyond there was much confusion, for no creature yet had knowledge of death. And the LORD God went to the tree of life and took from it a branch; and from that branch he formed a creature, shaped like unto the bekhorim, and breathed life into her, saying, This is my daughter, for she is created from me. And she was called Anaph, because she was born from the tree of life.

The bekhorim were then living in the lands west of Eden. Nachash lived not among them, but skulked and crawled at the edges of their camps, and whenever one saw him, that one threw a stone, to drive him forth. Yet one day he came within their camp and said to them, Send me not away, for I have had a vision, which comes from the LORD God. He hath shown me a wind out of the east, where Eden lies; and this wind bringeth a great mystery, which is the mystery of life and death. Follow me into the east, that we may greet this wind, and know the will of God.

But the people jeered and did not believe. They said, Why should the LORD show this vision to thee, for whose transgression we are all condemned? And in their hearts they were afraid, that if they approached the garden they would be struck down by the angels who kept the way of the tree of life.

Therefore Nachash went alone, journeying forty days and nights through the wilderness, until he faltered with weakness and thirst. He said, Though I can go no further, my faith endures; I will lie here in the dust, and await the coming of that which is promised. And in that moment he felt wind upon his face.

The wind was the coming of Anaph, who came as a storm and a whirlwind, driving all the dust before her. Yet when she laid her hand upon his face, her touch was gentle, despite that there was strength in it; and with her touch Nachash was revived, and opened his eyes. Before him he saw a glory so terrible he hid his face, saying, You are an angel of the LORD, and I am not worthy to look upon your face.

Look, said Anaph, and Nachash looked; and now she was as any bekhira, but he did not forget the glory he had seen. She said unto him, I am the wind that was promised, and I bring the mystery of life and death, which few will understand. Because thou alone has sought me, I will make of thee my first disciple, and to thou shall be given to understand more than all the others.

Nachash bowed his head and said, You honor me more than I deserve.

No honor, said Anaph, but a terrible burden, for the mystery of life and death is both cruel and kind. Thou wilt grieve for thy decision to seek me here, and be despised for its consequence. Yet I tell thee truly, all of this must come to pass, for it is the will of my Father the LORD God.

And Nachash did not understand, but bowed his head again, and accepted the burden Anaph lay upon him, which in later times brought much grief to his people.

3.

Westward she went with Nachash, him upon his belly in the dust behind her, until she came to a camp of the bekhorim. And when they saw her they were much surprised, for their kind were few in number, though not so few as man;

strangers had they none. Yet they welcomed her in; but when they saw Nachash in the dust at her heels they halted, saying, Here is one who is not welcome. For his wrongdoing we were expelled, though we are guiltless of his crime.

Guiltless you are not, said Anaph, for all your kind are kindred, and what tainteth the one taineth the many. Yet I say to you, be not wroth with him; all this was foreseen by the LORD God, from whom nothing is concealed, and nothing may happen without He permits it. You must allow him into your camps, for none should ever be exiled from among yourselves, however great his crime.

And they said unto her, Who are you to know these things, that are a stranger to us?

She answered them, A miracle hath come to pass with Chava and Adam. On the day I was created, so too was life created within Chava's womb; on the day I set forth on my journey, so too did her travails begin, the great pain which the LORD promised her. And when Nachash opened his eyes and beheld me, yea, at that very moment, she put forth new life, which is a son, and he is named Qayin. For a branch hath come forth from the tree of life, and the spirit of the LORD hath gone into it, and I am that branch, sent unto you.

But many among them believed not, for they did not understand the mystery she had imparted regarding Chava and her son. Neither did they understand Anaph herself, for they believed the LORD had turned his back upon them, condemning them to sickness and suffering.

She went therefore among them and found one, a mighty bekhor, whose body was grown weak, so that he could no longer lift himself from where he lay. And she stretched forth her hand, and when she touched him, strength grew once more within him. Thereupon he leapt up as if newly created. Then he knelt at the feet of the daughter of God and said, I know not who you are, but you have given me back my strength; for that I will follow you to the ends of the earth.

She said unto him, Follow me and you will bear that which you understand not, for this is the will of the LORD, that the bekhorim, his firstborn, should bear to mankind this mystery, which is for them. And he was called Koach, and became her second disciple.

She went then among the camps of the bekhorim, and wherever she found sickness, she had but to lay her hand upon the one who sickened, and that one became well. She performed great miracles in this manner, and some who witnessed her miracles followed her, even as Nachash followed her. They complained greatly of this, asking why he should go before them, who was the source of all their guilt. But Anaph told them he must be at her heels, for she had laid a burden upon him, and he must stay with her until he had delivered it unto its fruition.

4.

These were the disciples of Anaph: Koach, and Gidul, and Yofi, and Savlan; Ometz, and Yedida, and Tikvah, and Machshava. And Nachash was the ninth.

To these nine she taught many things, which were hints of the LORD's plan for the bekhorim. She therefore took them apart, and sat with them upon a hill, and spoke, saying, You are the firstborn creations of the LORD, the elder brothers and sisters of mankind. And it is right for the elder to teach to the younger, knowing things of the world which the younger has not learned. For this you will be rewarded.

I bring to you the mystery of life and death, which is to govern the world now the gate of Eden has been barred. On this day Chava has brought forth a second son, who is called Hevel, and in this manner shall all of mankind be propagated: in woman's desire for her husband shall the seed be planted, and in pain for their sins shall she bring it forth. And their days upon the earth shall not be without number; in time their strength shall wane, and when that hour comes their souls shall depart their bodies, going to their heavenly Father to be judged. But of that mystery none among the bekhorim may speak, nay, not even myself; for that is reserved to mankind alone.

Through me do they gain this gift of life, but you must bear it to them. As once you tended the trees in the garden, now shall you inhabit the wilderness without; to you the LORD gave dominion over every herb bearing seed, and every tree bearing fruit, to be in your care. You shall be of the trees, and of the waters, and of the airy winds, and of all things giving life. For you there shall be no weakness, nor any departure; you shall neither eat nor drink, save by your own desire, and the toil of mankind is not for you. Eternal shall your lives be, and this is the gift of the LORD to his firstborn creations.

So taught Anaph, and the disciples marveled at her words.

Then she laid the commandments of God upon them, saying, Remember always the day of your birth, which was the sixth day of creation; and celebrate it with your actions. Fear the name of the LORD, for it is fitting for the eldest to show respect by their fear. Give not your own names to those who might abuse them; names are holy things, and in them is power. Break not your oaths to any creature, for as light and all things came into being upon the word of the LORD, so too do your words call forth the thing which you swear; to render them false is to destroy that which you have created, which is an abomination.

These were the teachings of Anaph to her eight disciples, and to Nachash, who was the ninth, and first among them all.

* * *

5.

After Anaph had wrought many miracles among the bekhorim, and taught to them their holy covenant, she drew apart for a time. And Nachash stayed by her side, for he had been with her since she opened his eyes in the wilderness, and he bore great love for her. Recognizing this, Anaph said unto him, It is not good that thou holdest me thus in thy heart, for it will only make heavier the burden thou bearest. But Nachash said, It is only through my love that I was saved; though I am not yet redeemed, for I still go upon my belly in the dust. I will obey any commandment of yours, save that which commands me not to love.

Then she gathered together her disciples and once more imparted to them the will of God, saying, Chava hath borne two sons unto Adam, who are Qayin and Hevel; she will in time bear more, and daughters besides. But it is not fitting for a man to marry his sister, nor for a woman to lie with her brother; it is an abomination. How then are the generations of mankind to continue? I say to you, this is the gift the bekhorim shall bear to them, taken from the hand of the LORD. Two of you must go forth now to the place where Chava and Adam dwell, and give yourselves as wives to their sons. And before you depart I shall baptize you, and wash from you the gifts given to the bekhorim, that you may receive the gifts of mankind; human you will be, and bear sons and daughters to the sons and daughters of Adam.

When the disciples heard this, they were much disturbed. They went apart from Anaph to consider her words in the stillness of their hearts. But when the bekhorim heard what had passed among them, many were wroth, and the angry ones said, We are the eldest children of the LORD, and favored in his eyes: for us there is no toil or sweat, no sickness and no death. Why should we abandon these gifts to become less than we are? For Anaph said also that others must go:

until the numbers of Adam's seed grew so many that one might not be close cousin to all the rest, they must take their husbands and their wives from among the bekhorim, who thereafter would be human.

And even those who heeded Anaph yet questioned, asking, Is it not fitting that the seed of Adam should give something to us in return? This sacrifice is asked of us alone, whose numbers are few and unchanging; why should we not have compensation out of the multitudes of his children, to console us for those we have lost?

She answered them, saying, Consolation shall be yours, for when it is needed, you shall bear children, and not with the pains of Chava. As you bring life to mankind, so must they bring it to you; they shall be your midwives when that time comes, that your numbers may be restored. And this reassured many, but not all.

Her disciples then came to her again, and Anaph asked them for their answer. And Ometz stepped forward and said, I will be wife to Qayin, and Yedida followed her, saying, I will be wife to Hevel. To them Anaph said, Sorrows you both shall know, for hard is the way for those who first break the path; but you shall be rewarded for your choice.

Then she took them to the banks of the river, and there she washed from them the guilt of Nachash, so they were bekhorot no more, but as women. But she clothed them in green, in remembrance of their former natures, and thus they went forth to the place where Adam and Chava dwelt, and there gave themselves as wives to Qayin and Hevel. And Anaph said, Keep the memory of this act, as your tribute to Heaven, and to the Father who gave you life; that in future times others may go unto mankind and cleave to them as wives. But let mankind treasure that which hath been given to them, and mistreat it not, lest they lose that which they have received.

* * *

6.

And to the six of her disciples that remained, and to also Nachash, Anaph said, The final mystery is soon to come, which shall seal your covenant with the LORD. Truly I say to you, though you understand it not, this is the fruition of all that my Father hath willed for you; for I am born of the tree of life, and this is the fruit I give unto you. Take, eat; by this are you washed clean of the guilt of Nachash, and made holy again in the eyes of the LORD.

And the disciples did not understand. But Anaph drew apart with Nachash, and said to him in secret, This is the burden laid upon thee, that thou must understand more than all the rest. Unto Qayin thou must go, and counsel him; for the time hath come for the sons of Chava to make an offering unto the LORD. And he is a tiller of the ground, as his brother is a keeper of sheep, and from this will each make his offering: but unto Qayin thou shalt go, and tell him there is a fruit he must offer to the LORD.

But Nachash, fearing, said unto her, I cannot tell him of this offering, for in the silence of my heart a voice speaks, warning me that great grief will come of it.

Anaph said, And so it will. For it shall be as I warned thee: that thy greater understanding would be a burden, and thou wouldst be despised for it. Yet this is the mystery I bring to thee, that without death there cannot be life: whereas in the garden all was perfection, and neither life nor death were needed, here in the wilderness there must be both; and so I bring them. Through me did Chava bear her first son, and through me shall come also death, so that man's time upon this earth shall not be eternal, but only that of the bekhorim.

Then Nachash wept, for love abided in his heart, and so great was the pain that he thought this must be the death of which Anaph spoke. But death was not for the bekhorim. And he had promised her that he would obey any commandment, save the commandment not to love; and the bekhorim could not break their word, lest they commit an abomination.

7.

So he went forth, crawling upon his belly in the dust, until he came to the feet of Qayin. And to him he said, Go you into the wood, and you shall find there a tree, whose fruit is more pleasing than any that grow in this wilderness. Take with you your sickle, and reap from that tree, and offer its fruit unto the LORD. And Qayin thanked him and rewarded him, saying, For this gift I will give you a gift in return, that the first child my wife bears shall be yours to keep.

When Nachash returned all the disciples questioned him, asking, Where is Anaph, for we cannot find her. Then Nachash told them all she had said. Of the mystery they did not understand, but Koach saw the meaning of his words, and began to stamp upon his back, crying, Traitor. The others took up this cry, and threw stones at him, as they had in days past, saying, Traitor; thou hast betrayed our teacher, and because of thee she will die. And he lay beneath their feet, accepting their punishment.

At last Savlan halted them, saying, We must go find Qayin, and stop him, for he will slay our teacher.

In haste they went, and Nachash followed them, crawling in secret upon his belly, hidden by the grasses of the earth: but in haste also went Qayin, to the place where Nachash had told him the tree might be found. Together they came to that place, and there stood Anaph in the form of a tree; and Qayin took a jawbone, the sickle with which he reaped his crops, and swung it at the fruits of the tree; and they fell into his basket. But the blood of Anaph fell upon a stone, staining it red: which henceforth became anathema to the bekhorim, for it was the blood of their savior that made the stain within the stone. And a voice came out of the temple of Heaven, saying, It is done.

In that moment the tree withered and died. And the disciples, weeping, said, Where is the fruit that was promised to us? We have lost our teacher, the daughter of God; and in her place we have only desolation. And from the eyes of Nachash the tears fell unceasing.

8.

Then Qayin brought of the fruit of the tree an offering unto the LORD, and his brother Hevel brought of the firstlings of his flock and of the fat thereof. And the LORD had respect unto Hevel and to his offering: but unto Qayin and to his offering he had not respect. And Qayin was very wroth, and his countenance fell, for by his hand the savior of the bekhorim had died. But all this was intended by the LORD.

In the place of sacrifice, Nachash remained upon his belly in the grass, gazing upon the desolation of the tree. Then came to him one whose face he did not recognize, whose form was that of an angel, saying to him, For what cause do you weep?

Broken with grief, Nachash said, For the one who was my teacher and my love, who is now but dead wood before me; but truly for myself, who betrayed her, and who must now live with this pain until the day of judgment. For she brought death into the world, but it cometh not until its appointed hour, which lieth far off for me.

Unto him the other said, That need not be so.

Then he spoke divers things unto Nachash, of how the world might be changed; for if death were born untimely, then any creature might depart this earth and proceed to that which lay beyond. But Nachash said, Nothing lieth beyond, not for me, nor for any bekhor; for to mankind the LORD hath promised the paradise of the righteous, but to the bekhorim he hath promised nothing beyond this earth.

The other answered, You would end, and be no more; and be annihilated utterly. And to Nachash this seemed a thing to be desired, for it would bring an end to his grief.

He went therefore among his kindred, and again they drove him forth with stones. But many were angry, and to them he spoke, saying, Qayin hath killed our teacher; he hath slain the branch of the tree of life. To them we bring life, but to us they bring only death. And this perversion of the teachings the disciples did not hear, for they were occupied with their own grief.

To those who listened, Nachash promised a different covenant, saying, In this covenant shall the bekhorim be exalted, and not made servants to mankind; for we are first-born, and it is fitting that the eldest should have dominion over the youngest. From among them we will take our servants, and surrender none as their wives; to them we will give no gifts, but take that which is pleasing to us. And we shall have life eternal, a covenant sealed with blood.

He went therefore to Qayin, and to him he spoke, as once he had spoken to the woman Chava, but this time malice lived within his heart. He said, Why did the LORD have respect unto your brother and to his offering, and not unto you? Why should the younger be given the task of herding, that he might offer of the firstlings of his flock and of the fat thereof, and the blood which is pleasing to the LORD, while the elder toileth among the thorns and the thistles of the ground? For Nachash had hatred in his heart for Qayin, and this was the counsel given unto him by the one who found him in his desolation, that it should bring greater grief upon him.

Qayin went therefore to his brother Hevel, and walked in the field with him. And with the jawbone that cut down the branch of the tree of life he slew him, spilling the blood of his brother upon the ground, so that all the earth cried out. Then came the voice of the spirit of evil, saying, It is done; death hath entered the world untimely, and now man may die before his appointed hour. For Anaph had died at the time appointed by the LORD, but Hevel was the first to be murdered.

And the LORD said unto Qayin, Where is Hevel thy brother? And he said, I know not: am I my brother's keeper?

And he said, What hast thou done? The voice of thy brother's blood crieth unto me from the ground. And now art thou cursed from the earth, which hath opened her mouth to receive thy brother's blood from thy hand; when thou tillest the ground, it shall not henceforth yield unto thee her strength; a fugitive and a vagabond shalt thou be in the earth.

Thus was Qayin exiled from the presence of the LORD, with a mark upon him lest any should slay him; and this brought great joy unto Nachash, that he who spilled the blood of Anaph should suffer, and the gift of death should be denied him. But unto all the earth now that gift had been given: and so he went among the bekhorim who had heeded his words, saying, Remember this; slay their youths in the flower of their youth, before their appointed hour, in remembrance of the first murder. And this they did every seven years, on that night upon which Anaph was slain.

9.

But when half a year had passed after the murder of Hevel, a great wind sprang up in the lands about Eden, bearing a wondrous scent, as of blossoms and growing things; and all the wilderness came into bloom, though its glory was less than the garden of Eden. And the disciples went into the place of desolation, and there they found the tree that was dead now lived again, and upon its branches were a myriad of fruits. These they took and gave unto the people, and everyone who followed not the words of Nachash ate of them, and the fruit was the fruit of life. Then came Anaph among them once more, saying, This is my body, which hath been given for you.

At the sight of her all the people marveled, and her disciples fell at her feet. Six there were, for Ometz and Yedida had gone as wives to the sons of Adam, and Nachash came not among them now. And Anaph questioned them, saying, Where is my first disciple? and where is he upon whom I laid this burden, which was to betray me unto my death, that I might be born again? And the disciples said, Teacher, he is gone; he hath formed a new covenant, which is not a covenant with God.

And Anaph sorrowed, for her Father had foreseen all this, that Nachash would love her, and that his love would bring him to obey her; but upon her death it would lead him away once more, and into the path of evil. But of this Anaph herself had not known, and it grieved her.

Of the resurrection of Anaph Nachash had heard, for the wind bore her touch to him. But he could not bear to look upon her again, with all the blood of his guilt upon her hands, and so he went once more into the wastelands about Eden, which were as wastelands no more, but blooming in the spring of her return. Unto the gates of Eden he went, and the cherubims permitted him passage, and the flaming sword did not strike him; unto the tree of knowledge of good and evil he went, which had once been in his care.

And of its fruit he ate, and understood what he had done. He cried out then, and Anaph heard him cry, and bowed her head in sorrow; for upon his understanding, he went without hesitation unto the tree of life, and from its branches he hanged himself. For the gift of the spirit of evil unto the bekhorim was the gift of death, which to them brings annihilation, and Nachash was no more.

10.

And in after times those who kept the holy covenant were called Seely, which means Blessed, but those who kept the covenant of Nachash were called Unseely, and they kept his pact with Hell. And unto both was given eternal life, but iron is anathema unto them, for its mark in the stone is the mark of the blood of Anaph, who was the tree of life, and slain by Qayin. All this was known beforehand to the LORD God, who permitted Nachash entrance into Eden, that one among the bekhorim might understand what had come to pass. But when the day of judgment comes, then all the bekhorim shall cease to be, for on that day their appointed hour will come, and for them there is only life eternal, but nothing to come after.

TOMORROW IS SAINT VALENTINE'S DAY

Tori Truslow

Elijah Willemot Wynn: A Life • Chapter 7

Your Strangenesses are numberless
For each I love you all the more
It is not me that turns from you
But my unenchanting form.
          —Catherin Northcliffe, "The Mortal Lover," 1887

Merish song was attributed unique physical qualities even in folklore, and as with much folklore this has proved to have a factual basis. We now know that their songs move through the air as particles rather than as waves, penetrating and becoming stuck under the shells of moon-floating molluscs. A layer of tissue forms over the song-grain, and a kind of pearl is formed. What remains unexplained is the remarkable fact that shells containing these pearls

have recently been found on mortal shores, and when held to the ear have echoed mer-songs from over a hundred years ago.
      — Tony Peacock, "Defining Elemental Sound,"
          Modern Faery Studies, June 2008

A fter the lecture tour and all the controversy that bubbled in its wake, it was suggested to Wynn by his colleagues that he leave England for a time. Not surprisingly, he embraced this advice and made preparations to visit the Tychonic Institute in Denmark. Before he could leave, however, came the announcement that was to open a new door for him, one that would lead to so many captivating insights and the promise of lasting good relations between humans and merfolk. Had he lived longer, history might have followed a very different course. But whatever did happen to Elijah Willemot Wynn? Previous biographers have latched onto wild conspiracies, but in the light of cutting-edge new research, the facts speak for themselves. We are now entering a darker chapter in his life: the academic alienation and the increasingly bizarre theories leading up to his disappearance—but alongside that, the unorthodox personal life, and at the start of it all, New Year's Day 1880.

On that day, it was announced that at long last members of the public would be able to buy tickets for the Great Ice Train. Wynn was among the first to book his place. It was the moment he had dreamed of all his life: the journey to

the moist star,
Upon whose influence Neptune's empire stands[1].

---

[1] *Hamlet* 1.1.118-9. How Shakespeare knew of the mer-people's tidal migration to the moon remains a mystery, but these lines show that the Bard knew even more of Faery than we have given him credit for. *Hamlet* is not usually considered an elficological play, but in *Rosencrantz and Guildenstern Are Faeries* C.C. Temple uncovers a wealth of hidden references and makes a compelling argument for *Hamlet* as a *radically* Faery-based text.

The train departed on Friday the thirteenth of February—a
date now infamous in history. Horace Hunt, who was also on
that fatal journey, recorded it in his memoirs:

> We stood shivering in our thick coats on that
> desolate Northern platform . . . the train rose
> out of the water like a ghost. We stood, gaping
> idiotically at it—but not Elijah. He mounted the
> step and strode into the carriage. Emboldened,
> we followed—several slipped and fell on the
> frozen steps, but at last we were all aboard. I
> had followed Elijah into the first carriage.
> Directly before us was the captain's car, com-
> pletely filled by the intricate engine, pipes
> connecting jars and tanks of strange half-sub-
> stantial things. The sea glowed all around us
> . . . we gazed up through the ceiling to our
> destination and felt a queer tug as the Moon
> opened her pores. A watery clicking came from
> the engine; the enchanted molecules of unfrozen
> water thrummed through the sides of the train
> as it was lifted with all its captive passengers
> into the heavens. We were utterly silent, awe-
> struck by the sight of the Arctic sea beneath,
> the vast starry expanse above, all seen through
> the pipes and gears of ice in the glass-green
> walls of this glacier shaped so much like a train.
>   We gathered speed and were soon mov-
> ing faster than the fastest locomotive on Earth.
> The rattling was just as loud as any train at
> home, so loud that I thought the carriages
> would splinter and leave us in the void above
> our darkened planet. To be sitting on the thick
> silver fur that lined seats of ice with all that
> space and darkness in every direction was

beyond belief. I suppose I sat gaping at the
sublimity of it for some time, but I eventually
roused myself and had started to form some
great thought that might have changed the
course of philosophy and religion, when I saw
the Lunar surface was growing closer and closer
ahead—why was the captain not slowing us
down? He paid no heed to the shapes so frantically dancing in the engine's bulbous jars- the
smoke in one tank had materialised into a
tangling of cuttlefish which all turned jet-
black—the captain had gone as pale as the
Moon's face, staring as if he could not comprehend where he was . . . [2]

Hunt and Wynn were among a small handful of survivors.
Many were killed by great shards of ice as the train shattered;
many more when the wet lunar air entered their lungs.
Before Kristoffersen's successful refining of sailor's stone,
the only way mortals could survive on the moon was to receive
a kiss from a merwoman. An explorer of those early days
recalled "a row of sirens, lovely naked bodies with hideous
scaly legs and flat disk-like eyes, waiting on the platform to bestow their briny kisses of life"[3]. The
train crashed outside the city's dome, with no platform and
no waiting merwomen. As the moon was soaking up
seawater, however, several merfolk were appearing in
their moon-forms nearby. Some noticed the peril of those
still living and rushed to plant kisses on the men who
held their breath.

Wynn was reached by a young mermaid who had been
gathering sea-flowers for her garden, who

---

[2] Hunt, *Diary of a Man in the Moon*, 17.
[3] Ulysses Wright, quoted in *Early Accounts of Moon Exploration*, ed. S.
Bannerjee, 87.

> *Bedecked with microscopic nacre scales*
> *Outshined the galaxy's starry spray[4].*

Dizzy and bruised, he let her take him into the dome.

The city, until six years before, had been mobile, washing between moon and sea with the tides. Since the construction of the dome, the merfolk could enjoy the same permanence there as in their enchanted sea-palaces—but the moon-form of their city was then a tight cluster of palatial seashells and nothing more. This would remain as the centre of the new town, but the settlement that Wynn crashed in front of was at that time still a network of industrious, rough-cut hamlets and villages around a gilded heart.

Wynn's rescuer and her family lived in an isolated crater by the dome's circumference. He limped badly across the short distance, his feet lacerated by the fragmented train. Thus it was that he arrived at the setting of his most vivid passages: permanently crippled and leaving a trail of misty blood in the air.

> They are citizens of Melzun, a family of gardeners toiling to make this young city beautiful. They live in a hollow fringed by thick multihued polypi, surrounded by glimmering rock-pools and pearly boulders that serve as anchors to the long-tendrilled flowers that caress this strange, moist, salty air.
>
> At the bottom of the hollow, lined with living sponge, my pretty little saviour and her sisters laid out food in silver bowls. They eat lying down on their stomachs, which appears uncomfortable—but I think they are used to grazing on their bellies. We ate elongated mush-

---

[4] Northcliffe, "The Moon-Jewel."

rooms that reminded me of oysters, and some of the polypi from their garden—gelatinous and red; I was apprehensive of them at first but they were delicious, although it is impossible to describe the flavour; they tasted *bright*—and fruits rather like oranges, but turquoise, with a taste something like spiced rum. It seems everything that grows here takes on a subtle salty taste, but it is not unpleasant.

I spoke very falteringly in the mertongue, trying to somehow explain that I needed to find the RAEI [Royal Anthro-Elficological Institute] building. They insisted that I rest till I have recovered from the accident—they will take me to the town when I am better. So here I sit on a bed of slowly beating sponge, gazing out of this hole at the sky where sleeping nautili float weirdly in the starlight, writing this—though I don't know when I'll be able to send it . . .

(Letter to Robert Creschen, 1880)

His wounds healed well, "with the aid of an unpleasant, squirming unguent," though even then the long journey on foot to the gilt shell-buildings of central Melzun must have been painful. Wynn forgot his discomfort as they drew nearer, becoming wildly excited by the symptoms of mer-human cooperation he saw around him. Man-made streetlamps held blue mer-conjured fire and drew "silent fish on gossamer wings to kiss their own reflections." He was equally impressed by the old shell-buildings and the newly built ones in more human styles—in particular, the water-house, stocked with "great tanks of clean water that we mortals may drink, but securely sealed so no merman will touch it and dissolve." He got as far as the first step leading to the RAEI and stopped, enraptured, at the sight of an omnibus rounding the corner, "exactly like a

London 'bus, but with wheels encircled by delicate anemone fronds and pulled by a beast rather like an overgrown mackerel in the shape of a horse" (Letter to Nellie Bell, 1880).

The Institute, however, was a bitter disappointment, stuffed to the top with stuffy government scholars who squinted at fins through lenses and made futile attempts to render merish architecture on paper. They did not warm to Wynn, regarding him as an amateur and his ideas dangerous. He endured their old-fashioned methods and their comments on his lack of alchemical knowledge for a month, before deciding that he would make more progress living amongst the merfolk and observing the routine of their lives. He returned to the family that had shown him such kindness on his arrival.

Wynn reports that they were just as welcoming the second time, even building him some sort of room out of fine yellow coral in their now-thriving garden. Why they were so keen for him to stay and study them remains a mystery. It was there that he wrote his most celebrated works, uncovering a great deal of information on mer-culture in conversation with his hosts. Not long after his arrival, he witnessed the event that inspired a series of writings eventually to be collected in *Festivals and Rites of Passage among the Merfolk:*

> The youngest daughter sat at the heart of the house, her hair entangled by tentacled flowers that writhed from the limpet-starred ceiling and her face scintillating with fins plucked from countless scarab-like fish. She was given a bowl, into which her sisters placed various lunar fruits. She ate these sitting upright, an awkward position for her species to eat in. Her family stood around, holding censers filled with a bladderwrack-like plant that smelled, when burned, like a summer's sea-breeze, singing

songs that appeared to ripple through the smoke in colours never seen on Earth.

When she had eaten, she joined in the song, at which the woman of the house stepped forward with a silver tray holding fish-bones strange to the eye, as if they were of mercury, flowing inwardly while keeping their outward shape. The tentacles from the ceiling gripped the girl's arms as the woman pierced her back, between the spikes of her vertebrae, with these unearthly bones. The child cried out, and the air around the holes was coloured by red spray.

I observed the parents' own piercings, quicksilver spines which seemed part of their flesh, significantly larger than the girl's ornaments. After the ceremony, which ended with more singing and the drinking of a heady liquor made from pearls, the mother explained to me that they *are* a part of her. After piercing, one tidal cycle between mortal moon-form and elemental sea-form transforms the jewels first into a part of the merman's soul and then of his living body. From what phrases of their singing I could glean, I believe this is somehow connected to their longevity, an area which still demands meaningful research. A merman can live for an astonishing three hundred years, yet no established elficologist has provided a convincing study of this. I submit that my discovery of the piercing ritual is a possible key to understanding it.

(FRPM, first edition, 34)

The dig at the RAEI did not pass unnoticed, but by the time complaints were aired, Wynn had quite different matters on his mind. In his essays and books, he continued to call his favourite subject for observation "the youngest daughter of the house," but in letters to friends, as the years went by, the descriptions of her changed. From "my pretty little saviour," she was transformed into a variety of whimsical creatures, including "the bright pearlskinned flower-enchanting heart's light of this cold moon" (Letter to Catherin Northcliffe, 1882). By the time she was eighteen, he had a name for her: "Opal," which he claimed was wonderfully similar to the first syllables of her merish name (never recorded). It is hard to miss the Shakespearean connotations here, especially given her love of flowers and a curiosity about humanity that prompted him to travel to Earth and back just to bring her books—including the plays of Shakespeare. By all accounts she was a charming and innocent girl who loved to sing—Wynn would have lost no time in imagining her part in the favourite play of his youth and naming her after the "mermaid-like" Ophelia. Perhaps "Opal" herself embraced this association, uncommonly enamoured as she was of human poetry.

As her womanhood bloomed, so did their romance. This is largely documented in the poems of Catherin Northcliffe, who controversially gained the title of Lunar Laureate in 1885, and treated Wynn's adopted household as an idyllic writing retreat for some time. Two years previously, Wynn had written to her (then still in England) about Opal dancing,

> in a splendid squid-silk tent all sewn with dusky pearls. Since she came in on the last tide her arms are encrusted with the tiny peaks of silver barnacles that flare in the deep blue lamplight, like sequins or perhaps armour. Her tiny peacock-scaled feet twist in ways that jolt my eye, suggesting, in the corners of my vision, that they are not tiny at all. I never used to think of

my feet, and if I do now it is only to regret their condition. What must it be to have toes that are really the fleshy, scaly shell of a vast, unworldly tail-fin? There is a subject for you! A mortal, upon seeing a mermaid dance, yearning to have such legs, such power, such strangeness. I will await the poem, sealed in a mottled glass bottle, on the next tide.

(Letter to Catherin Northcliffe, 1883)

Northcliffe was captivated. Their correspondence from then on focused on little other than the merfolk and their culture. When she came to the moon she stayed with Wynn for long periods of time. The mermaid figures in her poems are doubtless almost all Opal. The mortal lovers are often a version of Wynn.

How far Wynn allowed the physical aspect of the relationship to progress is unknown. Some poems from Northcliffe's "Siren" cycle hint at bizarre debaucheries, but one of her unpublished poems, apparently narrated from Wynn's perspective, is far more frank:

A mortal maid and an undine
I spied amidst the coral ferns
And knew not if I greater yearned
To kiss the pink-lipp'd or the green.

"Twin cups of rarest love I see"
I cried—"I cannot choose my way"
Twin bosoms, scale and skin, laughed "Nay,
Love can full fill these vessels three!

Think you we two would willing part
That only one should take thy hand?

Come lay here on this lucent sand
And learn to share thy brimming heart.[5]

However, better-substantiated accounts of mer-human sexual encounters[6] are harrowing enough to suggest that Wynn would have reacted far more strongly than he did if the poems were true; they are clearly Northcliffe's fantasy, fuelled at once by her jealous desire to compete with Opal in Wynn's estimation and her own repressed lesbian attraction towards Opal.

It is far more likely that Wynn kept Opal at a physical distance, enjoying an idealised, non-sexual—yet always deeply passionate, in its way—romance.

But even that was no match for their ultimate incompatibility.

> My Opal has come back from the sea wearing living beads in her hair, bubbles of light clasped amongst her locks, winking red, yellow and mauve. I have seen this on other merwomen, a sign of yearning for children. I have been feeling not dissimilar pangs myself. But what can we do? I cannot carry her eggs in my belly and she could not nurture my seed in her womb. Oh, if I could only change that!
>
> (Letter to Robert Creschen, 1887)

Of course, he could not. But he grew obsessed with the idea, returning to the RAEI and bombarding its professors with wild new theories. A doctor there, one of the first to notice the adverse effects of the Lunar atmosphere on the human brain, kept notes on Wynn's behaviour, from his initial visit as "a pseudo-elficologist raving about how he would become a

---

[5] Northcliffe, "The Three of Cups," c.1886.
[6] As collected in *True Nightmares: Sex on the Moon* vols. I, II and III, ed. Jared Norman.

merman if we gave over our valuable resources to his lunatic scheme" to the letters the RAEI started to receive from Wynn after his return to Opal's family:

> He wrote again yesterday, saying he had undergone a version of the merfolk's ritual piercing. This, he supposes, would transform him over time into one of them, if we were to help him travel between this plane of being and another over and over again. It seems the mercury in those bones has only been fuel to his insanity.[7]

After several fruitless months of mimicking every aspect of merish life and repeatedly asking the RAEI for various forms of aid, Wynn went suddenly quiet. Very little is known about his activities over the following year; the next record of his movements that we have is a final letter to the RAEI in October, 1888, stating that he was leaving and knew he would find better help in England. What was he up to in the meantime? In all likelihood, he wrote: friends that he spoke to upon his return to Earth report that he mentioned a work-in-progress entitled 'This Too Solid Flesh,' the manuscripts of which are lost. Robert Creschen was one of those Wynn met, and though Creschen only gives a cursory mention of their meeting in his diary, it was not long after that he penned his first literary success, horror classic *The Mermaid Wife* (1894). If this work was influenced by Wynn's experiences, as it undoubtedly was, some disturbing conclusions about his final months on the Moon can be drawn from it. The passage wherein Creschen's fictional Wynn-figure, William Elverson, relates his misfortunes to the narrator is particularly chilling:

---

[7] Notes collected from the RAEI by Lucien Farrell, British Library.

"You think you know things, that the concrete
world and the aether are mapped in formulae by
your alchemists." He leaned close, gin and nightmares rank on his breath. "If you had seen a
shadow, a mere reflection, heard a whisper of
what I have, you would not set foot on that train.
Your eye would flinch from the sight of the moon
in the sky. The night and the sea would be
devilish to you, and you would not walk another
easy step in your life. She ruined my mind,
Crescent, and even that was not enough. She
wanted to spread her corruption into our race,
wanted to debase my humanity and my bloodline; she would have—good God!—shared me
with a merman so he could carry the demons we
created."[8]

Underneath Creschen's melodramatic association of merfolk
with demons, there is conceivably some truth in the suggestion
of a surrogate father, and it is not unreasonable to conclude
that such a demand would be sufficient to drive Wynn away for
good. Once on Earth again, he became much calmer, and
deeply absorbed in study.

And that is where Opal's story has ended—until now.
But in February 1889, something happened to change Wynn
completely. From then on his friends noted "inexplicable
strangeness, prolonged waking dreams, frighteningly alien
movements and utterances"[9] which increased until the time of
his disappearance. What was it that sent those first fine cracks
across the surface of his sanity?

What else? He received word of Opal's suicide—a
suicide we could not have known about until last year's
discovery of merish song-shells. These shells, holding songs

---

[8] Creschen, *The Mermaid Wife*, 149.
[9] Creschen, *Memoirs*, 624.

sung on the moon over a century ago, are currently stumping our scientists by washing up on Earth's beaches. One of these shells has just been dated to the thirteenth of February 1889: the day before Wynn's mental health took a drastic turn for the worse; the ninth anniversary of their first meeting. The song within the shell is English, which no other mermaids are known to have sung in. Now, her voice flies hauntingly across the years to us, and the song is all too familiar:

> *Tomorrow is Saint Valentine's day*
> *All in the morning betime,*
> *And I a maid at your window,*
> *To be your Valentine.*

> *Then up he rose and donned his clothes*
> *And dupped the chamber door,*
> *Let in the maid, that out a maid*
> *Never departed more.*[10]

The responses so far to this discovery have been speculative, tenuous at best.

What seems to be a echo, perhaps a sort of feedback caused by the metaphysical transportation of the song-particles, has been seized on by some scholars who claim it is in fact a male voice singing faintly alongside her. Isobel Cutter even claims that it proves her (already widely discredited) theory that Wynn succeeded at becoming merman, writing that:

> The fluidity between mortal and merish form
> needed to be activated somehow, and with no
> outside help his only option was astral projec-
> tion. To hear him singing a duet with Opal

---

[10] *Hamlet* 4.5.48-55, recorded in song-shell, Luna 13 February 1889, accessed by the author at the St. Ives Ocean Observatory.

seems impossible—unless, of course, he was successfully projecting onto the moon. North-cliffe's later work mentions a ghostly lover slowly becoming more solid—perhaps this is Wynn, at last becoming the merman he longed to be. His Earthly disappearance, in that light, is only logical—his Earth-bound self would have eventually become purely elemental.[11]

As discussed, Northcliffe is hardly a reliable historic source—her refusal to join the human exodus from the moon at the turn of the century and the subsequent brain-damage and physical decay she must have suffered renders her late work (what has been recovered of it) particularly questionable. But besides this and Cutter's flimsy science, the theory conveniently ignores the source of the song.

Here was a mermaid who had loved a man—who had been named after Ophelia by that man, maybe even driven mad by him—who knows what lasting psychological damage may have been caused by this passion for a man of the wrong species, and who could only ever fail to live up to her society's ideal of masculinity? The answer, then, to the question of *what possible reason she could have to sing one of Ophelia's mad songs* is woefully clear: unable to find him after his return to England, she chose to end her life in a way that she hoped would connect them. He had seen her as an Ophelia, so she would live out his ideal to the very end. We can imagine her wreathing herself in living flowers and walking, singing as she went, to the centre of Melzun, to the water-house with its tanks of clean water. We can picture her slipping quietly inside, opening a tank and climbing in and—singing still—closing the lid on herself even as she began to disintegrate, turning the fresh water to brine. Later, the tank

---

[11] Cutter, "Notes on a Late Nineteenth Century Song-Shell," Metaphysics Quarterly, October 2008.

would have been checked, found to be contaminated, and drained off outside the dome. And when the moon next released its absorbed water back into the sea, Opal's particles would have returned with it, nothing more than foam on the high tide.

CROW VOODOO

Georgina Bruce

Mortimer Citytatters is a midnight crow and a sinister spiv, but he knows what people want in wartime is a story. So he tells them: spine-chillers, bone-warmers, knee-tremblers, colly-wobblers, stories that drill your teeth, that perform open-heart surgery, stories that make the blind walk and the lame speak. It's a good all-weather business, combined with a spot of common or garden begging, that makes ends meet.

No one should trust Mortimer Citytatters, but Jenny is paying him to write letters to her sweetheart in the war. The crow writes scathing love letters, without a lick of sympathy in them.

Dear Robin, he writes in scratchy midnight ink, *Now that the nights have turned longer, I barely think of you.*

Robin reads them over and over, the black crow letters in the smudged envelopes that come every week. He reads them until the ink starts to wear away and the thin paper goes bald in thumb-sized patches. The letters are good: they have violence in them. They give him sleepless nights. *I danced with an American soldier. He had strong arms.*

Robin cannot stop thinking about Jenny's cold little body, their first time together the night before he shipped out. He must come home safe, he thinks, home to her. But Robin worries about how she is making ends meet and what Mortimer Citytatters might ask her to pay for the letters. Surely it cannot be so very much. *Tell me if it hurts, Jenny.* But he doesn't want her to stop.

Jenny could write her own love letters, but Mortimer Citytatters is a midnight crow and he has the cruel voodoo she needs. The letters are black crow magic, but if they keep Robin safe it can't be wrong, Jenny tells herself. She is paying for the promise of his homecoming, but she doesn't know how much. It costs such a very little, really, and it hardly hurts at all, the crow says.

Bombs fell near us. I could be dead by the time you come home. The tramps sit on legless chairs in the rubble.

Mortimer Citytatters keeps Jenny's account very carefully. It is a long time before he lets her see his sharp beak.

He names the baby Savage Citytatters, a good crow name and it will give her black hair when she grows up. He tucks her under his waxy black wing; she feeds on softened grubs out of his gullet. The baby doesn't cry much. Perhaps she is content to sleep in the humid feather bed and eat mushy grubs; perhaps it is nice.

When she can walk on her podgy legs, Savage Citytatters goes with her father to the City. While her father tells spells and stories to the war-dazzled punters, Savage collects rubbish in a little bag: used tickets, apple cores, bread crusts. The other crows call her *sweetling* and *hushling,* and give her cigarette ends to put in her little bag. Mortimer Citytatters calls her *darkling vane,* and sometimes, *Jenny's chicken,* which are special magic names a father should teach his child. In the evening they go home to the tarpaulin house under the bridge, and after doing her chores, Savage spreads the contents of her little bag out on the ground, and sees which things have power. Sometimes it is an apple core, and sometimes it is not. Paper is often good. This work is arcane and difficult, crows' work. Savage usually mistakes the things for what they are not, and the things get thrown on the fire.

Although she is small, Savage must work hard for her father. If she works hard, Mortimer Citytatters will stroke her black hair with his wing. Savage collects wood, and begs for matches, and makes the fire just warm enough. She has to find food. Sometimes it rains and there are big snails, or she makes a stew of apple cores. Once she found a bag of kittens, alive, that had been swept up the bank of the oily river; she roasted them with wild onions. She sweeps the floor of their home, which is always too muddy, and re-makes the deep nest. At night Savage curls under her father's black wing, and he tells her the crow stories.

Once, a girl, he says in his laconic black voice, *and that is the whole of it, came on a shuddering horse to a stop. They had pieces of moon, they were silver, and then there was the Very Old. The Very Old put the moon into the girl, into her belly, and the girl bled on the horse, so the horse galloped away. In the moonlight they didn't. In the sunlight they did. That is how it happens.*

Savage feels the story wake up inside her belly. She thinks this story was sleeping in her insides, and now her father has woken it with his telling. The more stories awake within her, the more she is crow, and the more power she can find in the world. This is why the stories are told, father to daughter. Savage curls up under the wing and feels a fierce love for Mortimer Citytatters that carries her off into sleep.

* * *

Jenny comes to the City to watch the girl and the crow. She doesn't tell Robin. He came home from the war, like the crow spelled, but broken and spoiled. So Jenny comes to the City alone and stands at the edge of the square, smoking her cigarettes one after the other. She doesn't want to come, but she must be punished, she thinks, the way some women punish themselves with knives and flames.

Savage Citytatters, she is thirteen and becoming more crow every day. She sees the woman watching and her heart flaps its black wings at her. Why does her heart fly to her? Like it is flying out of her chest, towards the woman, and Savage feels strange to herself. She wants something she cannot understand: to stand next to the thin small woman and lay her head gently on her shoulder, to softly take her hand.

Now she is old enough, Savage stays with her father when he tells crow stories, and there are punters come for the telling. Mortimer Citytatters takes a tooth from one man, takes a whole eye from a girl. They want things from the crow that only a crow can give. *They only pay what they can afford. We must make ends meet.* Now that there is something that Savage wants, she feels pity for the people who come for crow voodoo. She will not let her father know she is starting to like how it feels: the pity, the wanting.

Savage Citytatters can find things of power when she needs to now, and that evening before home she trails around with her little bag, collecting apple cores, used tickets, and paper, always paper, and like this she comes to the edge of the square where the woman watched all day. The woman is gone, and there are many pieces of rubbish here, but there is one powerful thing that Savage badly wants. It is a cigarette end, smoked down to the filter, squeezed tight between the woman's fingers and dropped, still smoking, to the ground. This special one Savage puts in the bag with the rest, with her father calling her to *come, darkling vane, come home.*

* * *

In Jenny's home there is work: drudgework and slow patient work, the work of marriage. Jenny knows they did a wrong thing with those letters, all those years ago, but it is she alone who pays. She only wishes she could bring the girl home with her, sit her by the fire, pull out her soft black wings. Jenny has lullabies, clean apron pockets, warm bread dough: all waiting.

When Robin came home broken, Jenny married him anyway. She fed him and put him to bed every night, and washed him, and cooked and cleaned for him, and held his hand to cross the road, and did her best to love him. He doesn't know to love her back any more, but some part of him remembers, for he often asks Jenny to read him the crow letters that brought him home. Jenny pretends she doesn't understand, says not to be so silly, there are no letters like that. But on this night, just this once, when Robin asks for the letters, Jenny opens the locked cabinet and takes out the shoebox from under all the piles of wedding linen that they hardly use, and she takes out the old thin letters.

Dear Robin, she reads, *a war goes on electric there are very flies in here I mean a man no girl no what is this sound I have under my wing.* Jenny cries tears on the scratchy crow ink, melting the thin paper completely away in the worn patches where Robin once held it with his finger and thumb. *You carry it on your back under water meadow grass fear no sky this sky is no good now why are you still flying.* These aren't their letters any longer, the spells have worn off them now, leaving behind the faded inky crow words without any magic left in them. Just nonsense. Jenny wants to put the letters away, but Robin holds her wrist, tells her to carry on. He closes his eyes, waits for the words again. *This boat is sailing swimming birds swim under the water fish fly in the sky the horse comes be on the horse you horses swimming away.*

When the letters are finally finished, Jenny feels empty, but Robin is full up. He doesn't notice Jenny's tears, but he says to her: "Remember how cold you were, little Jenny? And I said, *Stop if it hurts, Jenny. Tell me if it hurts, love.*"

In the night, Jenny wakes up in a silent bed, next to a cold husband. He has come undone at last: he is dead. Jenny lays her head on his chest and weeps on his blue cotton pajamas until they are wet and transparent, and Jenny's face is stone cold all on one side.

Savage Citytatters spreads out her collection of rubbish on the earth. Of all the cigarette ends, she picks out the special one, and this she puts in a little pocket under her soft downy wing. Of the other things she puts the apple cores in for the stew, and the paper scraps are good for thickening soup, and everything else she sweeps into the fire. Again she feels her heart beating its wings inside her chest, and she thinks of her father's grim beak. This is her first secret from him, the way her heart begins to spread its wings, and it is a dreadful bloody one at that.

Savage has never wanted anything before except to curl up under her father's wing and sail into sleep on his dark voice, telling the crow stories into her dreams. She cannot understand why the small watching woman has power, or why Savage must keep it secret, but nonetheless there is an electric thrill in waiting for her father to fall to sleep deep inside the nest, so she can conjure magic in the secretive dark.

When she is sure that the crow sleeps soundly, Savage opens her pocket and takes out the cigarette end. She puts it on her tongue, tasting the vile burning poison in it, and sits next to the hearth, slowly chewing, and spitting the juices into her hand. When she is done, she mixes the juices with a little ash from their fire and puts it on the jelly of her eyes, inside her ears, her nose, her mouth, her anus, and her vagina. It stings and scorches, splitting her open in agony, but then the road appears, and Savage's wings open new and black, spread full out and lift her into the sky above the City, flying the crow road into the past.

Savage swoops above the tarpaulin house, above the bridge. She lands on the pale yellow lozenge-topped lamppost, and waits, and watches. She feels the buzz of the light under her claws, the vertiginous afterglow of flight, the viscous heat of magic inside her, and she sees the woman hurrying over the grass, down towards the river. She looks younger, and she is heavy, too, but Savage knows it is the same woman who comes to the City, the one who watches.

Then the crow road speaks to Savage, with a voice that uncurls itself from her insides, that speaks inside her mind. *This is a crow story, too, the oldest one we have,* says the crow road.

Jenny is getting big, but she runs as best she can over the coarse grass down to the side of the river, where Mortimer Citytatters is waiting in the gloaming. She is coming for her letter. This is the last one, Jenny thinks. She is sure the war will be over soon, sure that Robin will be safe home again. She is glowing with the knowledge of her baby inside her, and imagining Robin's face when he sees, and making a family.

Mortimer Citytatters doesn't have a letter for Jenny today. Instead he shows Jenny his cruel beak, and she tries to run away, slipping up the river bank. Of course it is not hard to catch her, to hold her down on her back in the wet grass. Here is your bill, child, now we must always pay our bills, don't we? We got to keep these bargains nicely, see? *Jenny screams but it is not enough, it can never be enough, even if she screams the fish out of the water, the birds out of the trees. Mortimer Citytatters digs into her big warm belly with his razor beak, ripping the stretched flesh apart in jagged tears. He puts his hands inside and pulls out the tiny baby, and it is too soon for her to come out, but it doesn't matter because it is done.* I can see your insides, Jenny, all your secrets. *The crow bites into the umbilical cord, and then all three mouths are full of blood. Mortimer Citytatters tucks the baby under his wing and flies quickly away, leaving Jenny empty on the muddy grass bank.*

Savage Citytatters finds that she knows this story, too. *This is the hour of your birth.* She watches her mother spill her secrets onto the grass, her father ransacking her insides. The crow road speaks this to her, shows this to her, cracks her open like an egg, and Savage screams.

Mortimer Citytatters, triumphant father, looks up when he hears the crow cry, and sees the crow looking down on him. He shakes his head and hurries on, pushing the stolen baby deep into his feathers.

When her father glares up at her, Savage feels the magic in her turn to stone and pull her down. She cannot move her wings. Her claws skitter, she loses her grip and her balance, and she falls, hard, dropping out of the sky.

Savage falls off the crow road, and lands on the earth, in her own home, under the bridge. Her father is asleep in the nest. He has caught her stealing crow magic and when he wakes up he may punish her or praise her, she cannot guess.

Savage lies still for a long while, listening to the quiet earth, telling the crow road story over and over to herself. Sometime before dawn Savage at last sits up, crouches by the dying embers of the fire and reaches for a warm apple core. She is tired and thinks of crawling into the nest with her father. But her heart flutters wildly and longs to fly to her mother's side.

Night turns to morning, and Jenny wakes up next to her dead husband, but her tears are for her stolen child. She imagines the girl's hand warm inside her own. *Time to come home now, love,* Jenny whispers.

* * *

Mortimer Citytatters is awake. His beak is pushed under his black wing. One beady eye watches Savage crouching by the fire, chewing an apple core. There is crow in the girl already, he can see. So much. She has flown the crow road and seen the fact of her birth, and now, finally, Mortimer Citytatters can smell the human in her.

He watches her chewing her dirty fruit. Savage doesn't remember that she is any bit human at all, thinks she is full crow, but now she has flown the crow road she has woken up the secret of her human past. Now that Savage can find the human inside herself, now she can feel it and say where it is, in her belly or her eyes or her tongue or her womb or her heart, Mortimer Citytatters will pin her down and cut it out of her with his iron beak, and then she will be fully crow forever.

This is how the spells are passed, from daughter to father, from son to mother. And yes, Mortimer Citytatters was once a boy, though no one can remember, for a long time ago his mother cut out his heart for black crow magic. This is the crow way.

Mortimer Citytatters calls to his daughter. *Darkling vane, your wings grow so black.*

Savage does not have to decide. It is natural for her to creep under her father's wing, into his humid embrace. It is love.

Now tell me where it hurts, croaks her father, in his velvet voodoo song.

YOUR NAME IS EVE

Michael M. Jones

O n Monday, Clancy and Eve went out to dinner. They found the ideal place in the dreams of an exhausted Wisconsin woman, a young mother who'd fallen asleep on the couch while watching the Food Network late at night, after an exhausting day taking care of her toddler. She dreamed of cooking with today's secret ingredient, sweet potatoes, and a host of delicious, wonderful dishes were served up by handsome men with swimmers' bodies and the faces of famous network chefs. As part of the judging committee, Clancy and Eve tested a series of dishes, from delicate appetizers to a rich soup, from spiced chicken to a desert casserole, each using the secret ingredient to great result.

Quite satisfied with the results, they gave the young woman high marks, granting her the title of Chef Supreme. While the new champion received congratulations and accolades from everyone she'd ever known and respected, Clancy and Eve made a quiet exit from the arena. As "payment" for the experience, Clancy wove some dreamstuff together into a moment of pure joy, and gently blew it from his fingers. It drifted away, caught by a tiny cinnamon-scented wind until it wrapped around the young mother. She'd awake with a smile on her lips, the unspoken conviction that all was right with her world, and the renewed desire to cook for pleasure. Perhaps someday, it would take her further, to a cookbook, or a cooking show of her own.

As they lingered on the dream's outskirts, Clancy and Eve made quiet conversation, exchanging their opinions of the meal, their words dissipating rapidly in the way such things do in dreams. Clancy complimented the overall meal, though he admitted one dish had too much nutmeg. While he occasionally changed his appearance, tonight he wore his favorite guise: that of a tall, lean man with dark eyes and darker hair, with forgettable, yet familiar features. Were someone to describe him, they'd invariably compare him to one of those character actors, the one who played the friend in that movie, you know? He was impeccably dressed in a suit that had been fashionable in the early 1940s, and he carried the look as though it was made for him.

Eve agreed on the nutmeg issue, but felt it hadn't detracted from the overall experience, which was quite splendid, if a little unsophisticated. Then, wryly, she admitted that she didn't mind that sort of thing, as the fancier things always intimidated her a little. But, she reassured Clancy, his presence always made things easier, part of why she enjoyed their outings. Unlike Clancy, she remained constant, appearing as a young woman in her early twenties, daisy-blonde and blue-eyed, with soft features and an often perplexed expression, as though trying to remember something just out of reach. Tonight, she wore a cream-colored dress with blue accents, a simple affair that flashed hints of thigh every so often, catching Clancy's gaze more than once.

They wrapped up their after-dinner conversation by deciding when and where to meet next time. At first, they batted around the idea of dinner again, with Clancy claiming he knew a one-legged Mediterranean fisherman who would change the way Eve saw Greek food forever. Then Eve pointed out that they did dinner a lot, and she wouldn't mind a change of pace. Eventually, a decision was reached, and they parted ways. Clancy melted into the white clouds surrounding them, while Eve drifted away on the tides of the dreamwinds. Neither spoke of what they did or where they went when not together, for Eve did not remember and Clancy did not care to share. Such was the way of it all. They'd been doing this for as long as Eve could recall, the date of their first meeting lost somewhere in the past.

On Wednesday, Clancy took Eve dancing in the dreams of an old Southern woman who'd spent the past decade living in a nursing home and waiting for the slow, if inevitable, end. She dreamed of her youth, of wearing short skirts and bobbing her hair and acting entirely inappropriately for the time and place, and thus fashioned for herself an idealized Prohibition-era speakeasy, complete with jazz band. Clancy, in deference to the occasion, donned a knee-length raccoon coat he'd seen once upon a time, while Eve wore an archetypical flapper's dress, showing off generous portions of leg up to the knee whenever she moved too enthusiastically, which was frequently. Clancy and Eve danced the Charleston, the Shimmy, the Bunny Hug, and the Black Bottom, before breaking for drinks, where a dark-eyed bartender served them in solemn silence. Laughing with delight, exhausted from their efforts, they scored a small table off to the side, where they could listen to the music and watch faceless couples go through other, less defined dances of the era, while their dreamer fell in love all over again with a man who'd break her heart.

As usual, Eve was the one to initiate conversation. As she swirled her cocktail around in its glass, watching the contents spiral, she commented upon the quaintness of it all, how dull it was compared to modern culture, and how shocking it had been once upon a time.

Clancy, far more interested in watching Eve than in drinking, nodded slowly in agreement, though he wasn't inclined to elaborate on what he thought. This was nothing new; he was a man of few words even at the best of times, as though he'd heard it all and said it all and disliked repetition. As a result, their conversation was idle, conducted between drinks and dancing, with words fading like static in the background. Oddly content with this arrangement, Clancy was surprised when the dream came to an end and it was time for them to part ways.

This time, Clancy took Eve into his arms, giving in to the desire to hold her close for a long, tender moment. She nestled in against his chest, head fitting under his chin perfectly. He held her like that, allowing himself to feel something strange and warm inside, but released her before he could put a name to the feeling. It represented something, a subtle change in the way they'd interacted before, and he wasn't sure what to make of it.

When Eve vanished into the mists, Clancy remained behind, surrounded by the evaporating wisps of the dream, hands buried in his pockets. For several long moments, he stood still, lost in thought, and then he too faded. In the waking world, their host startled awake, and it took several minutes before the pangs of nostalgia and lost youth faded. Her memories of youth, normally hazy and fuddled, were crystal clear for the first time in years. This was Clancy's gift to her for time well spent.

On Saturday, Clancy and Eve went to a concert. Knowing that Eve was fond of a certain era of music, Clancy had gone to quite some trouble to have the perfect dream crafted for an aging hippie in Portland. Their host, who'd spent quite a few years stoned out of his mind before settling down to begrudging respectability as a music reviewer, embraced the dream fondly, made it his, and breathed life into it, conjuring up a Woodstock that almost certainly hadn't happened. The lineup in this dream included Janis Joplin, the Grateful Dead, The Who, Jimi Hendrix, the Beatles, the Doors, and Led Zeppelin, performing their greatest hits with a passion rarely found in the waking world.

Clancy, it must be confessed, cared little for the entertainment, and was uncomfortable in the outfit he wore to blend in, which he felt somehow offended his dignity, for all that he wore it well. Perhaps it was just that sense of having lived through it all before and finding it all terribly repetitious, or perhaps it was an underlying sense of chaos in the crowd that offended his propensity for control and order, but it was like an itch that wouldn't go away. He occupied part of his mind with ways to inspire new musicians, in order to bring about something new and interesting . . . or at least a variation on the old. Perhaps he could bring about a Neo-Pastoral resurgence, fused with the jazz from the other night . . .

Eve, however, was thrilled by the concert. Radiant in her flower child regalia, sunflowers decorating her unbound hair, she basked in her surroundings. As the music flowed through her, she was overcome by the urge to dance, tugging a protesting Clancy to his feet in a spontaneous display of appreciation. After a moment, Clancy allowed himself to give in to Eve's contagious enthusiasm. Though he'd never admit to enjoying himself, he did find the experience liberating. Perhaps he took things too solemnly, came a traitorous thought from deep within. He quickly buried it, lest it upset his carefully controlled existence.

When at last the final band had left the stage, the last notes of their most famous rock anthem still vibrating in the air, Clancy and Eve made their own farewells. Impulsively, Eve drew Clancy in for a kiss, a quick peck that refused to end, evolving into a long, lingering caress of the lips. She tasted of Spring, of fresh flowers and gentle rains and new life, and

Clancy was too startled by this to do anything other than
return the kiss in kind. The dream faded around them, its
essence returning to formless chaos. Eve finally pulled away,
cheeks flushed and blue eyes bright. She placed a palm on
Clancy's cheek, staring up into his own dark eyes for a long
moment. Evidently, she approved of whatever she found there,
for she smiled brilliantly before reclaiming her hand and
taking a step back. When they made the arrangements for
their next meeting, Clancy's voice was just a little raspy,
though he was quick to regain his sense of self and
equilibrium. He was sure that he wasn't supposed to let this
sort of thing get to him. They went their separate ways, even
as the hippie in Portland woke with a brilliant idea for a
murder mystery set at a rock festival.

On Tuesday, Clancy and Eve went to the zoo, an outing
suggested by Clancy as a way of reestablishing the control he'd
felt starting to slip. Theirs was a delightful, casual stroll
through a vast array of strange creatures, many mythological
and others long-extinct, all housed in exacting replicas of their
natural (or unnatural) habitats. Eve cooed over the unicorns,
fed the dodos, traded riddles with the sphinx, and cringed
when the kraken extended an impossibly large tentacle
towards her, even though she was well out of its reach. She
squealed with delight when a jet-black bat-winged horse
accepted sugar cubes from her hands, snorting little puffs of
fire in return. Only Clancy knew that this was no dream they
wandered through, but one of the few permanent structures to
be found in the dreamworld, a refuge for things that had no
place in the waking world any longer. He was a collector of
sorts, fond of these lost children and lingering remnants of
earlier ages. Eve, enchanted by the magnificent and bizarre
menagerie that continued to reveal itself around every new
turn in the path, never thought to ask where such a dream had
been found, and Clancy neglected to volunteer the information.
While he'd brought visitors here in the past, he'd never brought

a friend—a date?—here before, and he wasn't sure what this meant.

Instead, they spoke of quiet inconsequentials, though Eve looked more and more troubled as time passed. Finally, even Clancy couldn't miss the nervous pauses, the conversational stops and starts, and he asked what bothered her. Eve, tone distressed, blurted out that she'd been trying and trying, and couldn't seem to remember her past as anything more than a hazy series of loose, unconnected scenes, and she wasn't even sure they were *her* memories. Clancy was quick to soothe her, explaining patiently that such was the nature of the world of dreams, where most things were ephemeral, and very little remained constant for any length of time. For ones such as they, to live out a life in dreams, the past was an alien concept, old experiences fading away to make room for new ones. Eve, swayed by his knowing, caring tone, accepted this explanation, as one generally accepts dream logic. Clancy brushed the back of a hand against her cheek, comfortingly, and she smiled at him with such affection that it seeped into his very bones, warming him.

When the time came for them to go their separate ways, it was a reluctant moment on both sides, though neither voiced this sentiment. Instead, they came together, and spent a long time kissing, while the hippogryphs and thylacines watched from either side of the path. Eve's body was warm and soft against Clancy's, and he took an unaccustomed pleasure in holding her closely. Hands roamed and mouths explored, until finally one pushed away from the other. Clancy had his dignity to think about, Eve her propriety. It was hard to keep the flames of gentle passion fanned with extinct mammals watching in fascination, anyway. Awkwardly, they settled upon their next meeting, and Eve fled into the ether, leaving Clancy behind to glare at the residents of the zoo defiantly. Some of the creatures capable of speech speculated upon whether their lord and master was finally thawing, but Clancy exited the zoo without a response. He had no answers for anyone, least of all himself, as to what was going on here. Surely he'd spent time with other women in the past. Surely he'd felt something for them. But this was different. This was special. Eve was special. He waved the feelings aside, for he had work to do, work that wasn't being done while he mooned over a certain blue-eyed blonde.

On Friday, Clancy and Eve met in the faded memory of an old resort, a beachside property that had once hosted kings and emperors, millionaires and celebrities, back in a more glamorous era. In the mortal world, it was crumbling and decayed, ruined by years of neglect, thanks to economic downturns and the fickle ways of man. Here in the world of dreams, it lingered, a little ragged around the edges but still in its prime. The grounds were green and immaculate, the crystal chandeliers sparkled and the brass trim work shone, and even the air smelled of luxury and grandeur. Its halls and rooms were filled with dreamers yearning for a taste of that romantic era, and among them moved Clancy, dressed to the nines in a crisp tuxedo, with Eve, looking majestic in a soft blue gown, at his side.

This was a night of opulence and comfort, where they were treated like royalty, every wish coming true with but a murmur. They sampled a dozen different courses for dinner, each inspired by a different cuisine, a sublime medley of tastes that defied description. From a white, flaky citron-infused fish that seemed to burst with flavor, to churrasco-grilled sirloin sliced paper-thin, to a subtle vegetable soup, every new dish was an experience unto itself, crafted by the ghost of a once-famous chef who'd lingered for years, hoping for such a chance. For dessert, a silent server brought out a selection of delicate spun-sugar confections. He presented them with the precision of a sacred ceremony, eyes dark and inscrutable as he bowed once and withdrew. When at last it was over, the last morsel devoured, the chef came out from the kitchen, and stared at his guests hopefully. Eve smiled, and Clancy bowed his head in silent praise, and the chef finally allowed himself to move on to what lies beyond.

This led to dancing in the ballroom, where Clancy led Eve through a series of waltzes, both Viennese and regular, teaching her the moves when she seemed ready to falter. And if he ever felt frustration at her lack of experience, he never let it show, his expression ever patient and his hands gentle. As they grew more comfortable with the movements, and Eve's confidence strengthened, she dared to meet his eyes rather than watch her footsteps. Clancy was taken aback, albeit briefly, by the spark of connection between them, and it was his turn to stumble momentarily before catching himself. They'd been acquaintances, dining partners, friends— inasmuch as he had friends—and something more of late, and now he was certain that the fires burned brightly indeed for them both. When the next dance ended, they hesitated, there in the center of the ballroom. Eve leaned in to plant a feather-soft kiss on Clancy's lips, and through mutual, unspoken decision, they left the dance floor.

They progressed through the halls and up the stairs, Clancy leading the way to what was unquestionably the finest room in the entire resort. Unfortunately, its understated beauty and expensive décor went almost entirely unnoticed, as by now, the two had eyes only for one another. The second the door shut behind them, Clancy pulled a very willing Eve into his arms, and they resumed kissing, without restraint or hesitation. As they touched one another, clothes seemed to fall away with the merest tug; every time bare skin met bare skin, there was a fresh surge of electrifying desire. The room's light faded, until all that remained to illuminate the lovers was the not-quite-full moon hanging outside, reflecting off the ocean waters. Their bodies glowed, Clancy's a pale silver and Eve's a gentle golden, and they became one, making love in a way found only in fiction, movies, and dreams. Eventually, they curled up together, tired and satisfied, Eve tucked into Clancy's arms as though she might never leave. He ran his fingers through her hair, feeling that sense of completion, of perfection, and regretted that for all his power, he couldn't stop time. And even in the world of dreams, one can find sleep. It came easily for Eve, though Clancy remained awake, giving serious thought to his next move. He knew what he wanted, but the timing was not yet right. Not yet. Some things had to be done properly, or not at all.

In the morning, they prepared to go back to their separate lives, and it was the hardest separation yet. They exchanged words of affection and desire, regret and longing. Finally, Eve stole her hands from Clancy's, before she broke into tears. Clancy watched her go, satisfied that this would be the last time the day parted them. A smile tugged at his lips—he, who rarely smiled when alone—and he went to make his preparations.

On Saturday, Clancy arrived early at their designated meeting spot, a small Parisian outdoor café conjured up by a woman who dreamed of the places she knew she'd never visit. As he sipped at a drink he barely tasted, his hand frequently darted into a pocket, checking to make sure the small velvet box it contained was still safe. In that box was an elegantly subtle diamond ring, the gem carved from a tiny piece of the purest moment of perfection he could find. He went over the way he'd present it once more, determined to do it just right. After all, with an untold number of centuries lying ahead, he wanted this moment to be the one that shone brightly, unforgettable and eternal. And he waited.

And he waited.

And Eve did not come.

All nights end, and all dreamers awake sooner or later. With so sign of Eve, and the cafe fading into mist around him, Clancy reluctantly left the dream, a profound sense of unease tugging at his very soul. If Eve would not, or could not, come to him, then clearly he had to find her. As a dull ache throbbed deep within him, he accepted that the time for pretenses and playacting was over. Slowly, unwillingly, the Lord of Dreams raised his Aspect, shrugging off that fragile mask of humanity he'd adopted for dealing with mortals, and then he went for a walk.

For three days and nights, Clancy walked through dreams. On the first day, he explored the dreams of mortals, touching upon them as they slept, looking everywhere for the missing Eve. Steadily, methodically, he explored them all, young and old alike. In his wake, he left unsettled sleepers and crying babies, inexplicable bouts of insomnia and night terrors, far too intent on his quest to be gentle. Still, there was no sign of Eve, no trace of her passing. She was not to be found in any of the dreams they'd visited in the past.

On the second day, Clancy took his search into the dreams of the Mysteries, all of those strange and supernatural beings who chose to live unseen amongst an unknowing humanity, or in hidden pockets tucked away in strange corners of the world. Here, too, he had no luck, though he tore through protections and wards designed to protect their casters from nocturnal intrusions. Even those who feared nothing else were disturbed by the careless, uncaring way in which the Lord of Dreams bullied into their privacy and moved on. Mystics and psychics, shapeshifters and monsters, they all shared the same experience, and all they knew was that Clancy sought *something* without success. But Clancy did not care to explain himself, or even look back, since they could not lead him to Eve.

On the third day, Clancy stepped outside the world proper, into the restless dreams of the Earth itself. Here dwelt the Inverse Ones, unspeakable and alien, forever exiled from the mortal world and perpetually trying to force their way back in. Here he moved with care and grace, picking his way cautiously, for he and the Inverse Ones were of an equal power; they were older, but weakened by their long absence from the waking world. Only a thin truce kept things civil, so he did not overstay his welcome, remaining only long enough to ascertain that even in this place, there was no sign of Eve.

On the fourth and final day, Clancy grew desperate, the repeated failures of his search eating away at his patience. He journeyed to the farthest reaches of his realm, where the membranes between worlds are at their thinnest and sleep is forever intertwined with death. He raised his hand to tear down the walls and boldly invade the kingdom of no return, but was stopped, a mighty Presence blocking his way with a great shadow and a thunderous whisper. As Clancy protested, the voice spoke to him, the words quiet and implacable. It spoke of pacts and powers, boundaries and responsibilities. It murmured disapprovingly of souls kept past their time, of arrogance and trespasses, of prices and penalties. When Clancy disregarded this, powerful wings buffeted him back, dancing swords of fire making it quite clear he would not invade the realm eternal. Such was not for him, the Lord of Dreams.

The voice faded to nothing, leaving Clancy alone in the grey depths of his despair. Like one of the travelers through his realm, he woke to see what he'd missed before: a dark figure moving through dreams as his shadow. The presenter who'd unveiled a secret ingredient of sweet potatoes. The speakeasy's bartender. A hollow-eyed drummer at the concert. The flame-snorting, bat-winged equine in the zoo. That final waiter at the resort hotel. There, out of the corner of the eye at every turn, flitting past, immediately forgotten. Subtle and omnipresent. And Clancy *knew* as though the story unfolded before his eyes. A young woman, daisy-blonde and blue-eyed, with soft features, lying still and absent in a Des Moines hospital, her mind cut loose to drift on the winds of his realm. A friendship evolving into courtship, then into love affair. Their relationship allowed to progress under the shadow of dark wings. A figure visiting the young woman. Fingers brushing her eyelids, arms gathering her up, taking her away at last.

Clancy had been too late. Had he reached out to her, rendered her a thing of dreams, taken her into his world for good just one day sooner, and untouchable . . . no. Even he could not challenge this power, which ultimately claims all who dream.

Clancy's grief exploded across the world, millions of people startling awake with a palpable sense of loss and longing for something they couldn't identify. Parents rushed to comfort children, lovers clung to one another for reassurance, dogs howled, and for a night, the world mourned without knowing why. For those who'd known the young woman, he shared just a fraction of the joy he'd once felt with her, and they knew she'd been loved by something great and powerful.

He returned to his work. The waking world soon forgot about that night of grief and despair.

One day, Clancy grew lonely.

It was a Monday, for such things always happen on Mondays, it seems, when he had an idea. Long-legged and long-fingered, he stalked through a thousand dreams, gathering a wisp here and a wisp there. He wove them together with delicate, painstaking care, adding a cat's breath, a child's laugh, a raindrop's touch, a dandelion's puff. He gave his creation a mother's love and a father's protection, a sibling's tolerance and a friend's rivalry, a teacher's admiration and an enemy's respect. He shaped and molded according to his memories, stepping back when he was satisfied with the results. And yet, it was not what he had imagined. Like a dream, it had changed without rhyme or reason.

This one was in her late twenties, a dark-eyed brunette with long curls and lush curves, dressed in blue jeans and a green Tuesday University sweatshirt. Her eyes fluttered open with the spark of life as Clancy watched, and she looked ever so out of place, lost and bewildered. Wrapped in his mortal persona once again, Clancy slowly approached, exuding an air of comfort and reassurance. The woman looked to him, hope and confusion warring in her expression. She felt so strange, she admitted. She had no idea where she was, or how she'd come there. She didn't even remember who she was . . . but for some reason, she knew she could trust him. Were they friends?

A shadow swept over them, a cloud blocking the sun in a sky lacking both clouds and sun. Clancy, gaze intent upon the young woman, did not notice. He smiled gently at her, and in a manner suggesting easy familiarity, said, "Your name is Eve."

HELL FRIEND

Gemma Files

You could make paste for Hell stuff from flour in a pinch, but it didn't burn as well and customers didn't like the smell, which even incense wouldn't cover. Jin-li Song bought three unmixed boxes for five bucks at the Dollar Store—just add water—and negotiated her way back out, threading a narrow path between teetering wicker receptacles of every given size stuffed haphazardly in/on top of each other and piles of open boxes packed full of Fung's Gold Rosette soap, scented sandalwood, rose or jasmine.

Outside, the air reeked like smeared goose-shit, pressing down with a palpable weight. It almost hurt to breathe as Jin drifted back slowly, through Chinatown's sluggish, skipping heart. The smells of home were everywhere, thick enough to slice: Dhurrian and fire-works gunpowder, dried persimmon, pickled ginger, red bean jelly. The stiff stock and vinegary dyes of Hell Money. The sweet stink of joss-sticks. Kuan Yin and the Monkey King staring down, smiling and glaring. The Zodiac's animals, rat to pig and back again, contorted in red lacquer poses.

And since it was the last week of *Zhong Yuan Jie*, after all, *getai* were indeed everywhere, just as her Ah-Ma had warned her—blooming in every doorway, on every porch and corner: Little shrines, wilting plates of food, smoking joss-sticks. Passersby whose ages ranged from roughly eight to eighty swirled carelessly around them, wearing brightly colored clothes designed to insulate their *chi* against the streets' death-heavy atmosphere; everywhere Jin looked, people (maybe tourists, maybe not) could be seen laughing, dancing and singing to entertain whatever ghosts might be lurking—resentfully, implacably, invisibly—in their immediate vicinity.

Step lightly, Jin, Ah-Ma would say if she was here, and even if she wasn't. *This is a time of confusion, in which every decision—no matter how well-intentioned—may bring harm . . . less a celebration than an inconvenience, even to we who honor it. The doors of Hell stand open, letting the dead back up onto the earth. And so, though we may make money from Hungry Ghost Month, it is Hell Money only . . .*

Yeah: Hell cash, thick and crisp and useless; only fit to spend *in* Hell, by those who lived there—or rather, who didn't. And this was what Jin's Ma spent her days cobbling into commissions, stuff made expressly to burn, falling down through the fire to give some lucky ancestor's ghost a big surprise—Hell cars, Hell fridges, Hell air conditioners. Hell cellphones.

While up here above, there was no buying a new house, no renovating the old one, no going on vacation or hanging at the beach, for fear of ghosts luring you down into the water . . .

Jin stopped short in front of the Empress' Noodle Restaurant, between its flanking totem dragons, and bent over for a minute, rummaging for her inhaler. Inside, framed by the front window's fever-red rows of halved pigs and Peking duck-flesh, Mrs. Yau—the Empress' owner—sat alone at her usual table near the back, playing mah-jongg with herself. A cup of green tea steaming at one elbow.

Her name is Yau Yan-er, was all Ah-Ma had said the first time she'd caught Jin studying her, out of the corner of one eye. *You don't ever go in there,* wei? *Don't speak to her, don't look at her . . .*

Why not, Ah-Ma?

Ah-Ma had sighed. *Because. People like us—we don't want people like her to even know we're here. It's safer, that way.*

Sometimes, like now, Jin wondered exactly what Mrs. Yau must have done—what she must *be*—to have become "people like her," in Ah-Ma's eyes. From the outside-in, at least, she seemed perfection itself, a T'ang Dynasty screen-painting come to graceful life—regally slim, black hair tamed into an elaborate, chopstick-skewered crown, veins showing faintly green as milky jade beneath the pale skin of her long-fingered hands . . .

. . . and her eyes, black stones, raising suddenly from a cast-down fistful of Plum Blossom, Knot, the Centre, White . . . to meet with Jin's own, through the glass. Faint twitch at the temples, those high, nude arcs where her eye-brows ought to be; she raised one palm slightly, a subtle yet unmistakable gesture of beckoning. Jin coughed on the draw, tucked her inhaler away again, and stared: *You mean me? NOW?*

Apparently, yes.

But: *Don't look. Don't speak. NEVER go in.*

Waaah, Jin thought. *I'm thirteen, for God's sake. I'll do what I want, this one time. If not now, when?*

When indeed.

Jin straightened, touched her hair lightly, then gave up on getting it to look any better than it already did. Shrugged Ah-Ma's voice away, like a horse switching flies—

—and opened the door.

* * *

Though the summer job she'd lined up to start a week from now would officially be her "first," Jin'd been an unpaid worker in Ah-Ma's Gods Material Shop pretty much ever since she, Ba, and Ma had come over from Taiwan, when Jin was five. Which meant she could reckon Federal and Provincial tax in her head, make chit-chat in enough other dialects to deal with people who didn't speak Cantonese (or English), and locate back-stock items without checking the book (mostly).

But none of this impressed Ah-Ma enough to stop her from taking Jin—and Ma—off the floor whenever she could; though she often said it was because Jin's Ma was "so good!" in the workshop that she wanted Jin to pick up her skills, Jin suspected different.

"Ma," Jin had overheard her Ba saying that afternoon, quietly, as she let herself in by the delivery door, "you have to stop. Eun-Joo is Asian as you or me . . . "

"*Not* like you and I, and you know it. What good does it do to pretend?"

"That's just . . . *insanely* racist, even for you. Besides which, you do get that if my wife is unacceptable, that makes Jin at least *half*-unacceptable, right?"

"*Ai-yaaah!* You know I love Jin, but things will be hard enough for her, without drawing attention. How can she ever make a good marriage? So tall, with so much color in her skin? And her face, so long—like a melon!"

At this, Ba had huffed, and fell straight back into Cantonese: "*Wan jun, Ma! Dim gai lay gum saw?*" Which would surely have brought on an exchange too quick for Jin to completely follow, given how red Ah-Ma's face went, if they hadn't both suddenly spotted Jin where she stood, rooted to the spot by throat-roughening embarassment.

Ba coughed, looking down. "Uh . . . Ma's not back yet, *ah bee*. You could start setting up, I guess . . . "

Ah-Ma nodded. "Best, yes. Do you have enough paste?"

"I think I forgot," Jin said. "I could . . . go and get some." As Ba reached for his wallet: "No, I can . . . I've got it. No problem."

And: "Watch out for *getai*," Ah-Ma told her, as she turned. "Remember, mind where you step. Don't get in any ghosts' way. It's their time—they expect politeness."

Jin's mind raced, a thousand replies suggesting themselves: *Wish I was a ghost,* uppermost. But it wasn't even vaguely worth the trouble, considering that come tomorrow, they'd all still have to live together.

So she nodded instead, avoiding Ba's sad eyes: "*Wei,* Ah-Ma." Bowing her too-long melon head, pulling in her too-long limbs, crushing down her too-tall half-Korean self in general —almost to "normal" height, or close as she could get—as she went.

Inside the Empress' Noodle, meanwhile, everything was cool and dim. Mrs. Yau flicked shut once more the same hand she'd used to entice Jin closer, a five-fingered fan, and nodded to the chair at her left elbow; as she did, red-shaded lantern-light glinted off nails grown just a half-inch longer than anyone Jin had ever seen before wore theirs. Jin nodded back without thinking twice, and found herself already sitting.

"*Ni hao, mei mei,*" Mrs. Yau said, her Cantonese softened by a wind-through-willows shading of Mandarin. "What is your name, please?"

"Jin-Li Song."

Mrs. Yau pursed her soft lips, disapprovingly. "Song Jin-Li-ah, *ai-yaaah*. Don't your parents know enough to teach you how to properly say your own name?"

"Well, uh . . . that's how we say it at school, so . . . "

Another nod. "So. How *they* say it, the long-noses. But *mei shi,* never mind. Perhaps this is only proper, given the age we live in: Two names for two different worlds—one for use amongst the *gweilo,* the barbarians, and one to use here, amongst ourselves. Still, one cannot live in two places at the same time, *wei?*"

" . . . no?"

"No." She peered closer at Jin then, eyes narrowing further. "You must be Song Pei-Pei's granddaughter, I think."

At the sound of Ah-Ma's "real" name, Jin lowered her head, blushing once more. "*Wei,* Mrs. Yau."

"And how does her business flourish? Very well, I'm sure, this time of year."

Jin didn't know what to say, so she said nothing. It was true that Gods Material Shops often stayed open around the clock during Hungry Ghost Month; only a year ago, when Ah-Ba was still alive, they'd probably have set money aside to hire extra help. Now it was just them—Ba and Ah-Ma out front, Ma and Jin in the back. And she was wasting time dawdling here, under Mrs. Yau's unreflective gaze—her eyes that took everything in, gave back nothing . . .

A small nod, as though Jin's silence constituted a valid answer. Mrs. Yau tapped the tablecloth between them, just once. Asking—

"Do you know this design, Song Jin-Li-ah?"

"Sure: *Yin-yang.* Right?"

"Yes. See how it is: One here, one there. They twine around each other, mix together—a little spot of *yin* in *yang*, a little spot of *yang* in *yin. Yin* is female, dark, cool; *yang* is light, hot, male. *Yang* acts. *Yin* is. Both are necessary. The building blocks of the world—without both working at once, in harmony, the mechanism no longer functions cleanly. But there is another thing too, something you don't see here . . . it may be inside, or outside, or invisible. *Yomi.* Hell. Ten thousand kinds of Hell. Another thing to thank the long-noses for. *Yomi* is what's hidden, what lies beneath. It is not for you. Not for anyone, unless . . . what time is it now, Jin-ah?"

"5:45 . . . oh, I'm sorry. Hungry Ghost Month."

"Yes. So be careful, *mei mei*—little sister. Careful of what you see, and what you don't. Because this month, what is hidden becomes revealed; what was obscure becomes obvious, without warning. Consider this my gift to you, and come back later on, perhaps, once my advice has been of some use. You may even call me Grandmother, if you wish."

Jin frowned, studying the odd curl of Mrs. Yau's tiny pink smile across her pale, pale face, and feeling as though the dim red world around her had somehow begun—almost imperceptibly—to swim.

With effort: "But—you're not old enough to be anybody's grandmother."

The smile widened, pink deepening. And: "Oh, I am old enough to be your grandmother's grandmother, child," said Mrs. Yau, without much emphasis. "Old enough to be *everyone's* grandmother."

"You're not a ghost, are you?"

"Ah, no." But here Mrs. Yau bent her beautiful head, and took a single sip of tea from her thumbnail bone-china cup, adding—

"I am *far* worse than that."

*R*ead the Ullambana Sutra, was all Ah-Ma said, when Jin first asked her where the idea for Hungry Ghost Month came from, exactly. But Ba, knowing she never would, had been the one to paraphrase: How one time, long ago, there was a guy who ran away from home to hang with Buddha and become a monk—Maudgalyayana, that was his name. After he attained enlightenment, he looked around to see what his parents had been doing in the meantime, and found his father in heaven. His mother, though . . .

She didn't approve of Maudgalyayana's choices, Ba said, his eyes on Ah-Ma's scrupulously turned back, where she stood at the till sorting money. *So because she was stingy and unforgiving, the gods condemned her to Hell, where she turned into a hungry ghost.*

The sutra says her skin was like that of a golden pheasant when its feathers have been plucked, Ah-Ma seemed unable to resist adding, without turning around. *Her bones like round stones, placed one beside the other. Her head was big as a ball, her neck thin as a thread, and because her throat was too narrow to eat or drink, her belly swelled out in front of her as though she was pregnant. So she went terribly hungry, but when her son tried to feed her, the rice and water he gave her caught fire inside her, and choked her throat with smoke . . .*

That's the story, anyways, ah bee, Ba put in, quickly. *And that's why we spend Hungry Ghost Month being nice not just to our ancestors—we're nice to* THEM *all year 'round—but to* HUNGRY *ghosts, ghosts of people we maybe don't even know, they're the ones with no one left to take care of them, wandering between earth and heaven. So we pray for them and leave them food, put on shows for them, burn Hell Money to help them buy a happier life in the afterworld—*

So they won't stay up here, and make trouble, Ah-Ma said. *So they won't scare us, and feed off our fear.*

So they'll be at peace, Ba corrected. *So they can—*

Ah-Ma snapped the drawer back in, with a sharp rattle of change. Saying, as she did—

So they'll leave us alone. Everything else is—

(A quick glance at the shop's front display, here—two whole tiers of magical feng-shui items arranged to best advantage, under hot lights and gaily-painted banners. Male and female Fu dog pairs, Seven Stars Swords and Elliptical Coins, the Universal Cosmic Tortoise with a Buddhist mandala stencilled on its back, a whole dish full of Hum pendants strung on neon "silk" thread. Images of Kwan Kung standing at fierce attention, pointed towards the front door—once a mere human general, now simultaneous Taoist God of War and Wealth. At his side, more deities: La Zha, most potent of all the gods. Chung Kwei, the "ghost catcher," festooned with bats, as symbols of abundant good luck and great continued happiness . . .)

—"*window dressing,*" Ah-Ma concluded, finally. *Nothing more. Or less.*

Whatever *that* was supposed to mean.

But maybe, Jin mused, as she paused to wait for the crosswalk to change—maybe what it meant was that ghosts (hungry or otherwise) didn't *have* to look like that guy's mom in the story, after all. Maybe it meant they could look like whatever they wanted to . . . like anything. Anyone.

Which meant, in turn, that half the "people" she saw every day could not be people at all, and she wouldn't even know: That crazy dude on the other side, crab-walking along, arguing out loud with himself. That little girl with the massive Hello Kitty plushie, trailing along behind a couple who might be her parents, but pointedly not holding either of their hands. Jin's own wavery reflection in the Bank of Macau's frosted window, rendered suddenly sketchy enough to seem eyeless, alien.

(Ah, no. I am FAR *worse than that.)*

(mei mei)

"Ma. What's worse than a ghost?"

"What?" Ma looked up from her last few finishing touches on the Po family's Hell House, blinking short-sightedly; as ever, she'd taken her glasses off for the close work. Claimed they made her eyes cross. "Did you get the paste Ah-Ma sent you out for?"

"Right here." Jin sat down next to Ma. "What I meant was . . . if somebody said something was *worse* than being a ghost, what would they be talking about?"

Ma's voice dropped, conspiratorially. "You know I don't believe in ghosts, *ah bee.*"

"You better not say that where Ah-Ma can hear you."

"I know. She thinks we'd lose half our customers." Ma smiled, wearily. "It's good to see you, Jin. Ah-Ma gives you long hours, doesn't she?"

Jin shrugged. "I don't mind. Want me to paint anything?"

"Hmm . . . no, I think everything's done, actually. Just in time, too."

"In time for what?"

Ah-Ma gave a disapproving sniff, from somewhere near the workshop door—how long had she been there, anyways? "Don't you listen, Jin-ah? Po family *getai* is tonight—they need this Hell House for their daughter, dry and ready to burn." She stepped in, wiping her hands on her skirt, eyes skipping over Ma like she was something hot. "Why are you so late back, huh?"

"I, uh, got held up." Adding, reluctantly, as Ah-Ma's raised eyebrows made it clear she wouldn't take vague for an answer: "Talking . . . at the Empress' Noodle. To Mrs. Yau."

"You *spoke* to Yau Yan-er? *Ai-yaaah!* What did I *tell* you, girl?"

Jin flushed resentfully, thinking: *Uh, get good grades . . . don't talk to boys . . .* gweilo *may run the world right now, but that won't last, and they don't know everything, either. They're all just long-nosed barbarians, at heart . . .*

"Always be polite to older people if you can, because they're closer to the ancestors?" she ventured, at last.

"Don't be smart!" And then—wow, this really *must* be bad, because Ah-Ma actually turned to Ma directly, barking: "Eun-Joo, I need to talk with you. Come with me, please."

"Oh, Ah-Ma, I don't think—"

"Right now. *Alone.*"

Ah-Ma cast a single, significant glance back Jin's way; Ma sighed and bowed her head. "Yes, all right," she said. To Jin: "We'll be back in a minute, *ah bee*. Don't touch the Po house, all right? I think it might still be a little tacky."

The door closed behind them, with a definitive click. But Jin could hear the thrum of their voices anyhow—Ah-Ma's rising, thinning, dumping tense and conjunctions as annoyance sent her grammar sliding back towards Cantonese. While Ma's stayed carefully quiet, deferential, respectful—not rising to the bait no matter how vigorously Ah-Ma might fish for a penultimate blow-up, the argument which would finally force Ba to choose sides (badly-selected *farang* wife vs. good Chinese mother, mother of his melon-faced halfbreed child vs. wife of his own dead, much-beloved father), forever.

And if, maybe, at the beginning, there had been some note other than anger in Ah-ma's voice—something like fear, a shadow of genuine dread, at the name of Yau Yan-er—it was forgotten now, like Jin herself, in that endless, pointless hostility, that grudge-match negative feedback loop.

Jin shut her eyes, wishing it all away—*them* all, even Ba and Ma, in this one painful moment.

And heard Wu Mingshi speak up from behind her at the exact same moment, as though in answer to her pain—his light voice soothing-soft, liquid as a Cantopop ballad, welcome beyond all words—

"Are they both gone, flower?"

Jin's heart shivered inside her at the mere smell of him, flopping like a fish. "Yes," she whispered.

"Good. Then it can be just you and I."

So she turned, and there he was: Right *there,* like always, wrapping her in his arms. Enfolding her completely. Mingshi, with his perfect almond-flesh skin, his liquorice eyes as smoothly shaped as pumpkin-seeds, his whole face symmetrically stunning: Shiny, shining, lambent and airbrushed, like any given Disney Studios' multiracial hunk-of-the-month.

"I die so much when you're not here with me," he murmured, with perfect sincerity. "Me too," she whispered back, thinking: *It's like a soap opera, isn't it? So corny. So glorious. Oh God, it's like a dream . . .*

Could it really only be two weeks since she'd met him?
When he'd told her he lived inside the Po family Hell House,
she'd just laughed—until he'd shown her. *Taken* her. In
through the same door she saw her Ma paint on, to a room
whose nude grey cardboard walls were hung with bright red
marriage-bed silk. And under those billowing curtains, on a
genie-in-the-bottle nest made from folded Hell Bank-Notes
and crumpled paper wads of Hell Cash, he'd laid her down
and climbed on top of her, fitting himself to her like a velvet-
lined glove. Gave her her very first kiss, in super-slow step-
print stop-motion—and now just looking at him made her
delirious, hot-and-cold shaky, like malaria. Like love.

But: How could he possibly fit in there? Let alone make
her fit in there?

(Didn't matter.)

Of course not, no. But . . . how did he even know English?
Or was that Cantonese—Mandarin?—they were both speaking?

(Didn't matter.)

Yes, but how—

Didn't *matter*, any of it: It was like *Twilight*, like
Titanic, like *High School Musical 1, 2* and *3*. He was Edward,
she was Bella; she was Claire Danes and he was Leonardo
DiCaprio, before he grew that grody beard. It was *Romeo +
Juliet*, but without the dying part. Fate.

Say it Jin-Li Song or Song Jin-Li, the facts stay
the same either way: She was so ugly, so insignificant,
belonging nowhere, to no one. But Mingshi, her Hell Friend,
he chose *her*—

(*This month, you should be careful of what you see . . .
and of what you don't.*)

And: "Come with me," he said, tugging her back towards
the House; Jin came, of course. Willingly. Without question.
Stammering, as she did—

"I brought you some food, Mingshi—stole it from the
corner. Ghost-food . . . my Ah-Ma'd have a cow, if she knew . . . "

"Oh, I don't care about that. Kiss me, Jin. I'm cold; just lie with me a bit, will you? Kiss me. Keep me warm."

Into the Hell House again, wrapped tight in Mingshi's arms—and vaguely, as if seeping down through slow fathoms, she thought she could hear her Ba calling from outside, her Ma, her Ah-Ma: *Jin—where is that girl? Jin? Jin, we have to go . . . just load it up, the Po family won't wait, the* getai *for their daughter is tonight . . . she'll be fine, she has keys . . .*

After which came a rocking, a heave and a lifting, a slam followed by rumbling, a pulling away. And throughout it, Mingshi just kept on holding her—close, closer, closest; tighter than she'd ever been held before, by anybody. So tight, she never wanted him to stop.

Yet Jin could still hear Mrs. Yau's voice as well, buzzing always in one ear, dragonfly-insistent—the voice which never quite dimmed enough to become unintelligible, never *quite* went away. Mrs. Yau's sussurant murmur, *yin*-tinged like every other Mandarin accent, even Mingshi's own. Saying, over and over:

Remember, what's hidden, what lies beneath . . . is not for you, little sister. Not for anyone. Unless . . .

Snatches glimpsed through the Hell House's windows, fragments of sorrowful revelry: The Po family's *getai*, already at its halfway point. Jin caught flashes of light and moving color, a community centre banquet hall full of neighbours, relatives, tourists all clustered around tables set with lazy Susans, stuffing themselves with Taoist Association food offerings the ghosts have supposedly already "fed" on. Earlier in the evening, there would have been an auction of auspicious items—more *feng shui* stuff, some donated by Ah-Ma, some by other Gods Material shopkeepers—with all the proceeds collected in one common public purse, to cover next Hungry Ghost Month's expenses.

Ghosts like a party, Ah-Ma told Jin, this time last year. *So we use that, to bribe them to stay out of our affairs—we get to eat and dance, they get to watch. Not such a good bargain, on their part. But—*

(better than Hell)

The red silk hangings flapped, as Mingshi pulled her ever-further into his warm, strong, inescapable embrace: Apparently, it was opera time now, the classic aria from *Bawang Bie Ji* rising and falling in mournful ecstasy, as Yuji expressed her fatal loyalty to the King of the state of Chu . . . and yet this too was already dying away, time skipping a beat to admit a steady stream of ringing gongs, droning scripture, Mrs. Po's weeping. Even clutched to Mingshi's chest, his heart pounding quick in her ear, Jin could hear the Taoist master praying out loud as he waved a fistful of lit joss, his other hand simultaneously touching an open flame to the sheaves of Hell Money which fringed the Hell House's roof and walls: *May this house be a home for Po Ching-hsia, her life continue uninterrupted, may she live there happily, with her new friend, and never again be lonely . . .*

(She took her own life, that girl, you know, Ah-Ma whispered in Jin's brain. *Ai-yaaah, the shame—such a pity, for one so young, so rich, so full of promise. Her poor family! She was only just your own age, Jin-ah . . .)*

But: "Don't listen, Jin-ah," Mingshi said, at the same time—a sudden catch in his too-beautiful voice, like he'd been crying. "Don't look, not at them. They don't have anything you need. Look only at me, at *me* . . . "

The smoke filled her nose, her throat, her eyes, making her cough and weep. Had the Hell House always been so *small?* She couldn't remember. Couldn't think.

Look away, mei mei, Mrs. Yau's tiny buzzing voice said then, quiet, yet loud enough to drown out everything else. *Look back outside, no matter how he begs you. See how things really are.*

Jin listened; she couldn't help it. She looked—

(*only at* ME, *oh no*)

—and saw the whole first row of chairs, seating strictly reserved for ghosts, occupied by the same people her eyes had scudded over all day, along with many more she'd never seen before: The little girl with her plushie, the crazy man—a woman her Ah-Ma's age, in a flowered dress with yellow sweat-stains down both sides from armpit to waist, who scowled hatefully at Jin as she hugged a double load of tattered plastic shopping bags crammed with rags to her breasts, balancing them on her ample lap. A perfect *anime*-character teenager in private school uniform and Japanese loose socks, violet-streaked hair in two bouncy pigtails, who held up her spectral cellphone to snap a photo of the Hell House as it brightened, blackened, began to crisp and fold. All sat there staring, rapt and ravenous, waiting to see her burn.

They want me dead, like them, Jin thought, horrified. Then looked Mingshi straight in the eyes, equally appalled by what she'd finally caught looking back at her, and blurted, out loud—

"*You* want me dead, too. Don't you?"

Mingshi shook his head. "No, never. I love you, flower."

"But . . . you're not even real. You're . . . "

(His perfect teeth shifting askew in that kissable mouth, even as she watched; perfect hair already fire-touched, sending up sparks. His face, far too gorgeous to be true, a mere compilation of every Clearasil ad, every music video, every doll Jin'd ever owned, or coveted.)

" . . . made of paper."

His face crumpled, literally. He knew she knew, and she knew it. Pleading with her shamelessly, in that dreadful, broken voice—

"Oh no, oh please . . . stay with me, Jin . . . *come* with me. I don't know that girl, Po Ching-hsia. She's nothing to me; we're nothing to each other. Hell is such a dreadful place—I don't want to go there alone, not after having met you. I'm afraid . . . "

Which was good to hear, Jin supposed, given everything he'd put her through, but not quite good enough. Not nearly.

So: "I'm sorry," was all Jin could find to say, as she stood up—

—only to find herself abruptly full-size again, bigger than the Hell House itself, ripping back out of it in one not-so-smooth move: A shattered plaster cast, a husk, a shell—a burning birthday cake, and her some soot-covered stripper. The pain was immediate, all over, fifty torn Band-Aids at once; she could see half of her own hair already hanging chunk-charred, one arm of her shirt still smoldering, as she stumbled off the stage, cleared the front row (ghosts melting back from her on every side in a wave of angry regret, hissing like rainy night arson) and ran straight into her shell-shocked parents' open arms.

Weirdly, Ah-Ma was the only one who thought to grab a pitcher from the nearest table, and soak her with it. Ma just hugged Jin tight, holding on for dear life, while Ba just stood there, mouth open.

"*Wo cao!*" he blurted, finally. Ah-Ma immediately rapped him hard on the side of the head, snapping—

"*Waaah, on gau*, filthy-mouth man! Look at the House, ruined, totally useless—the Po family will run us out of town." She turned to Jin, voice full of a mixture of worry and anger. "And *you*, what were you *doing* in there? Playing a silly trick in the middle of Ghost Month? *Mahn chun yoh yeuk yee!* You think we're made of money? Who's going to pay for all this?"

"I think we should probably go, while they're still distracted," said Ma. Adding, pointedly, to Ah-Ma: "Unless you want it to be *you*."

Ah-Ma looked at Ba, who nodded; Ah-Ma snorted, and rolled her eyes.

"You are all against me," she said, with great, despairing dignity. And suddenly hugged Jin as well, without any warning—so hard, so fiercely, Jin almost thought both their arms were going to break.

A fterward, once the entire strange tale had been told and—wonder of wonders—digested, Ma apologized to Jin for not telling her Mrs. Po had commissioned her to make Po Ching-hsia a Hell Friend to go with her Hell House, because she'd thought Jin would think it was creepy. "*I* thought it was creepy," Ma admitted.

"I . . . don't know how we could have possibly known . . ." Jin began to say, then trailed away. Everyone nodded; exactly.

"You said his name was Wu Mingshi?" Ba asked, a few minutes later. When Jin nodded: "*Ai-yaaah, ah bee,* that's like calling somebody mister—Nobody No-Name, or something. John Doe."

"Huh. Weird."

But no weirder than anything else, really.

T he next week, Ah-Ma announced she and Ba were selling the shop to the Po family, for a hefty price. Now Ah-Ma would be able to retire the way she'd always wanted—perhaps to Australia, where there were many other "good Chinese" —while Jin, Ba, and Ma could move to Vancouver, where Ma's family ran a computer store.

That Friday, however, Jin found herself once more inside the Empress' Noodle, sitting across from its owner as the lanterns shone overhead like dim red moons, casting barely enough light to see how little there was to see by.

"*Ni hao,* Song Jin-Li."

"*Ni hao,* Mrs. Yau."

Mrs. Yau laughed, a throat-sung trill of touched-glass music. "I said you might feel free to call me Grandmother, child," she reminded Jin, softly.

"*Wei,* I remember, and thank you, very much. But . . . I don't. Feel free."

Again, that one-eyebrow/no-eyebrow twitch, twinned with a delicate quirk of lip. "Ah. So you are finally becoming wise, *mei mei*—or wiser, at the very least. How it gladdens my heart to see this."

Jin swallowed. "Did you know? About . . . him?"

"Your little paper husband? Not directly, no. Though I did see some sort of influence trailing behind you when you first passed my window—something foul with too much *yin,* like a snail's track, leaving a stain. And seeing how you shone with *yang,* I thought that if that stain were to be removed from you, you might be better off."

"That stain." Jin's first love. A cold and lonely thing, made only to be burnt, which had reached out blindly, grabbing at the first warm hand it found; a liar and a thief, perfectly happy to get Jin killed as long as he got something out of it. Mister Nobody No-Name Nothing . . .

But beautiful, nevertheless. More so, Jin feared—late at night, when she had nothing else left to think about—than anyone else she was ever likely to meet for the rest of her boringly normal life.

"Well, anyways," she said, at last. "Looks like you saved me."

Mrs. Yau shook her head. "No. Because you trusted in everything you saw, I simply showed you what it really was you trusted—after which you saved yourself, as I'd hoped you might. Very impressive, Song Jin-Li-ah."

"If you say so." Jin cracked a small smile. "Definitely lost me my summer job, though."

"Then for that I am sorry. Would you like another, perhaps?"

"What, work here? For you? I . . . can't cook, or anything."

"Ah. *Mei shi,* little sister—never mind, no matter, not to worry. A restaurant holds many different jobs. Beside which, this is hardly the only business I own."

Jin nodded. "Uh, um—no offense, but—I don't know you very well."

"True enough." A beat. "Would you like to?"

" . . . what do you mean?"

Another beat, held longer, like a drawn breath. And: "Hmm," Mrs. Yau asked, musingly, of no one in particular. "What *do* I?"

Jin felt herself trembling on some kind of precipice, with no real idea of how she might have gotten up there, in the first place—so high, so exposed. So very much in danger.

"Look closer, *mei mei,*" said Mrs. Yau, her lips barely seeming to move. "*Look,* and see. *See me,* now . . . "

 . . . fully revealed, reigning Empress of all the New World's *hsi-hsue-kuei*—suck-blood devils, half-soulled Chinese vampires, worse indeed than any ghost who ever lived once (but doesn't anymore). Enthroned in her antipathic Dragon-boned Lady glory, and terrible as an army with banners: Her unbound mass of hair floating up and away like drowning weed, tendrils seeking delicately in every direction for any scent of blood on the air, with her porcelain mask-face the one seed of light still left in this whole black velvet poison-flower. Lotus feet in tiny jade-green slippers, curled and atrophied like mushrooms; nine-inch nails girt with golden sheaths so long, so sharp they scratched the tablecloth beneath as she gestured, cut the air around her, made it bleed. And worst of all, what might be a train or even a tail switching drily under the table, its jewel-scales rustling along the floor like toxic leaves . . .

Best to leave Yau Yan-er alone, Jin-ah—it's safer. She's NOT *like us. Not like—*

(anyone)

My Hell Friend, Jin thought, unable to stop herself. *My* REAL *Hell Friend.*

"And now, as the old tale goes, you have seen the witch in her true ornament," Grandmother Yau Yan-er said, softly. "For we are seldom any of us what we seem, Song Jin-Li-ah, as you will always do well to remember. Perhaps you too will be something other than you seem, in time."

A ghost; the idea came to her, numbly—maybe that, yes. Everyone would be a ghost, eventually, after all.

Everyone but Mrs. Yau.

"Thank you," Jin said, again, bowing her head. As was only polite.

"You are most welcome. And remember this, too: You *may* still return to see me yet—when you are older, perhaps, and have come into your full power. Whenever—*if* ever—you feel most . . . comfortable."

"And how will you be then, Grandmother, if I do?" Jin-Li Song was unable to stop herself from asking, no matter how she tried—lips tight around the question, mouth dry and strained, as though the words themselves were carved from salt.

But Grandmother Yau Yan-er just inclined her beautiful head further, obviously seeing no insult was intended. And murmured, so softly it might only have been to herself—

"Oh, me? As to that, I will probably be . . . "

. . . much the same.

BRAIDING THE GHOSTS

C.S.E. Cooney

That first year, when Nin was eight, she wanted her mother so desperately. But Noir was dead, she was dead, and *would always be dead*, thanks to Reshka.

Reshka liked to say, "I'm not above keeping ghosts in the house for handmaids and men-of-all-work. There must be ghosts for sweeping, for scrubbing, ghosts for plunging the toilets or repairing the roof, ghosts to fix the swamp cooler and to wash and dry the dishes. But," said Reshka, "but *I will be damned*—I will be damned and in hell and dancing for the Devil—before I summon any daughter of mine from the grave."

So Reshka had Noir cremated three days after her death. Afterward, she prepared the funeral feast in Noir and Nin's small apartment kitchen.

"This is a family affair," she told Nin, who sat numb at the table, feet dangling above the floor. "*This* is a meal no ghost may touch."

Instead of salt or herbs, Reshka scattered ashes over the meat. The buttered bread and the broccoli she dusted with

Noir's remains. Ash in Reshka's wineglass, and in Nin's chocolate milk.

The taste never left Nin's mouth. Everything she ate or drank after that was death and dust—but it was also Noir. So Nin ate and drank and did not complain.

When they drove away from the apartment where Noir had quietly died, Nin did not cry. She sat with the black cat Behemoth purring on her lap, and she looked out the window, her thoughts a great buzzing silence.

Behemoth was warm and indolent, matted at the back, soft at the belly. A large cat at full stretch, he possessed the ability to curl up into improbably kittenish proportions. Now, though he seemed asleep, his tail danced. Like most cats, Behemoth was a very good liar.

Nin stroked her mother's cat, playing catch with his clever tail. She had nothing else of Noir's. Reshka had sold it all, or given it to Goodwill.

The sunlight glinted off a crack in the windshield, lancing her dry, dry eyes. Ahead, the road sign read, *Lake Argentine, 2 miles.*

Nin was pretty sure they had hundreds of miles to drive. Reshka said at the outset that they wouldn't arrive at Stix Haunt 'til midnight. But at the Lake Argentine exit, they swerved off the freeway and jounced down the narrow lake road. Reshka offered no explanations. Nin did not ask. Something in her grandmother's tight, pink, unpleasant smile put a padlock to Nin's curiosity.

Noir used to tease her daughter about her constant . questioning, saying, "Nin, my love, you live in the Age of Information—just Google it!" This, even if all Nin asked was, "What's for dinner?"

But Reshka was not Noir. Noir who had died with wrinkles on her brow and bruises under her eyes. Reshka's face was perfectly made up, in peaches and corals and cream. Her complexion had neither the flush nor pliancy of flesh, but seemed to ring like pure hard porcelain. Her hair, plaited into two dozen tiny braids, was golden in color, but of a bright and brittle gold, like autumn oak leaves that rattle juicelessly from jaded stems. Nin could not understand how a woman with no wrinkles or gray hairs could be the mother of Noir.

Noir's last words?

"Nin—my love. Have I. Told you. About your . . . grandmother?"

If tissue paper had a heartbeat, that was Noir's heartbeat. When cobwebs breathed, they exhaled more vigorously than she. Nin touched the hem of Noir's nightgown. Contact with any part of Noir's skin made her cry out.

"Her name is Reshka." For comic effect, to make her mother's eyes smile, Nin rolled her own, the way Noir did whenever mentioning Reshka's name. *"She lives in a place called Haunt and you two do not get on."*

"No—we never . . . did." Noir's voice was shy of a whisper. Still it laughed. *"Nin. Come. Close. Hand . . . shears?"*

Nin brought the shears. Noir could not close her fingers over the handle.

"I'll do it," Nin said. *"What do you want cut?"*

Noir told her, and Nin performed the small, bloodless surgery.

"Keep," Noir said. *"Hide it. Don't . . . Reshka."*

"I won't tell her."

Nin did not ask why Reshka must come; of course she must. Under her mother's bright, fading gaze, she put the curl of gray hair away, in an envelope, in a plastic bag, in a metal box. Which rode in the truck with Nin now, in her ratty old Superman backpack.

Reshka's truck humped along the lumpy lake road. The sun shone on gentle hills and flashed on the rumps of small wild things running. Reshka drove her truck right up to the gravelly shore, her tires rolling over the bravest waves. Then she turned off the ignition.

Without looking at Nin, Reshka said, "Give me the cat."

Bemused, a little sleepy, Nin did so. Reshka opened the driver's side door. "Stay here."

Nin stayed. She watched her grandmother walk, straight-legged in her high heels and stockings, into Lake Argentine. Reshka walked into the lake as if she did not see it, stopping only when the hem of her tea-length linen skirt began to drag the waters. Nin stayed, watching, as Reshka squatted suddenly, and with one violent thrust slammed the black cat Behemoth into the lake water and held him under.

The world whited out. Nin clawed her seat belt. She heard herself breathing in ragged gasps. Her thoughts raced ahead of her body, already diving down beneath the lake.

"No!" she shouted. But she was sealed in the truck, and Reshka did not hear. "No!" she shouted anyway, scrabbling for the lock on her door. Finding it, she flicked it up and spilled out onto the shore. The stony ground cut her bare feet. Nin ignored the stones, her feet, the blood, everything but running, dashing into the water.

"No!" she screamed, dividing air and water in a breast-stroke. "No, you *can't!*"

Reshka was not a large woman and Nin was tall for her age. She leapt onto her grandmother's back, pummeling and kicking and scratching and shrieking.

"Stop it! Stop! Please! Give him back! Give him back!"

But her grandmother remained solid in her squat, both arms straight down and rigid, showing no strain though surely the black cat Behemoth struggled. No sign of the writhing thing in her hands or on her back fretted Reshka's artful and implacable face.

When the deed was done—Nin still screaming—Reshka stood up, abrupt and smooth, the way she had gone down. This overset Nin, who fell backwards into the lake. Green water closed over her, cool and silent.

Nin thought, Just let me stay.

One-armed, Reshka hauled her out. One-armed, Reshka forced Nin upright, her polished yellow claws sunk into her shoulder.

"Hey, you!" Reshka said, shaking her. "You!"

She slapped Nin on one cheek, then the other.

"None of that from you!" she said, slapping her mouth. Until the blow fell, Nin had not realized she was still screaming. Had been, even underwater. Even choking.

"Listen!" ordered Reshka, sounding more exasperated than angry. "Listen to me, you." Her voice, like her fingernails, was older than her face and hair. It was old and dry and it shook.

"Cats can't abide ghosts," she said. "Nor do ghosts bide well with cats. I'd keep a crazy household if I kept a live cat at Stix Haunt. Here." And Reshka thrust something soggy and awful and dead into Nin's arms. "Put it in the truck bed. If it bothers you so much, I'll give it a raising up when we get home. It'll be just the same, only you won't have to feed it."

Nin clutched the sodden black drowned dead thing close to her chest.

"He won't be just the same!" Her raw voice carried weirdly across the water. "He'll be dead! He's dead! And you killed him! I won't let you touch him! I'll burn him first! I'll burn him myself!"

"Suit yourself, Little Miss Nin It's My Whim," said Reshka coolly.

Nin turned her head and spat.

Later, she came to wonder if burning was what her grandmother had intended all along. She was to discover that Reshka considered it beneath her dignity to bind and braid the ghosts of dumb animals.

* * *

L ife before Reshka had been quiet. Life after Noir was silent.
Noir used to say, "Let's have an hour of quiet time, Nin,
my love. Read if you want, or draw. Mama's just going to lie
down and shut her eyes."

But at Stix Haunt, all hours were quiet. The house was
a sprawling shamble of gray stone and stucco, with peeling
columns, peaked roof and dark cupola, its rotten porches and
balconies webbed all about with decrepit scrollwork. It could
not have been more different from that cozy, shabby apartment
in the city. Woodland and wetland bordered the property on all
sides. Only one dark road under dark trees led to a small town
that did not like to remember it had a Haunt at all.

Nin never saw Reshka sleep, never caught her still or
off her guard. Reshka prowled the house and grounds day and
night. Making her rounds. Check the saltshakers for sugar and
the shampoo bottles for honey. Was there superglue in the
conditioner? Was there sawdust in the Quaker Oats?
Sometimes the ice cube trays were full of flies. Sometimes the
meat crawled with maggots.

Because sometimes the ghosts got things wrong.

"Death doesn't cure stupidity," Reshka was fond of
saying. She did not talk to Nin much, and tended to repeat
herself when she did. "Death makes a dumbie dumber. So keep
your eyes open!"

Nin did not think the ghosts were stupid. She thought
maybe they were angry. Or, scarier still, that they had a sly,
prankish sense of humor. Or both.

Many nights Nin went to bed short-sheeted or with
crickets in her pillowcase. She was careful not to gasp or laugh
or do anything to draw attention. She did not want the ghosts
to notice her at all.

Reshka depended on them for everything. They drew
her bath and chose her clothes, groomed her, perfumed her,
prepared her meals. They did what they were told, silent and
unseen, slight freezing breezes in Reshka's great grey house.

The first year was the hardest. Nin was always cold, and her skin—especially her face—was chapped. Asleep or awake, she wept. And she was not awake often.

The second year, she started reading again. The few books she owned palled quickly, so Nin stole Reshka's, who had hundreds but never touched them. Reshka did not own a TV. She had a dinosaur of a computer that she kept unplugged most of the time. It had a dial-up connection that she used when ordering food or clothes online. Delivery vans dropped the boxes at the gate and never ventured an inch beyond it.

The mistress of Stix Haunt had little contact with the outside world. Nin had none.

When Nin was not reading, she wrote letters to Noir. She drew pictures of live cats and dead grandmothers. She never spoke. Most days she slept. Not in her bed, which, due to the ghosts, was not to be trusted, but out under the willow tree. This was where Nin had buried the little curl of Noir's hair, safe in its white envelope, the envelope sealed in a plastic bag, and the plastic bag placed in a metal box. A small grave. Nin's special place.

The willow tree marked the boundary between Reshka's ghost-kept gardens and the wild Heron Marsh that ruffled and rippled and sprawled beyond. It was not quiet beneath that green umbrella. There were flies and mosquitoes and curious bees. Bird chatter and squirrel quarrels drifted down like leaves, and the marsh grass hissed under a constant low wind.

This was where Nin slept, dreaming through those first sad years. She dreamed of Noir.

"Nin, my love," said her mother, the day after Nin's birthday.

"Yes, Noir, my love?" Nin replied.

Noir sighed. Immediately, Nin crawled straight onto her mother's lap, even though she was thirteen now and tall for her age.

"Nin," said Noir, "Reshka's going to begin teaching you soon."

Nin grimaced. "Teach me what? She can barely stand to hear me breathe." She paused. "But she doesn't have much practice with people who can breathe, does she?"

"No!" Noir laughed. "She's useless with the living. Always was."

When Noir laughed, she threw back her head, giving her full throat to the sky. They sat on a large boulder in the middle of Lake Argentine, the waters flat as ink and cobalt blue, the sky glowing like a dome of jade above them. There was never any sun that Nin could see—only her mother, who sometimes seemed to glow.

"Listen." Noir stroked the nape of Nin's neck. "Reshka will teach you the four winds. Piccolo, flute, oboe, bass recorder. She will teach you songs of luring, of binding and braiding. She will teach you how to break a gravestone and make a grave-ring. She will teach you about silver, about lilies and bitter red myrrh, for you are the last of her line, now that I am gone."

"You're not gone," replied Nin in a soft voice, hugging her mother. "You're right here."

She bent her head and took a deep whiff of Noir's hair. Noir wore it short and dark and curly, never long enough to braid. Her mother smelled sweet and slightly messy, like baby oil.

"My darling," murmured Noir, tightening her arms around Nin. "How's school?"

Nin's laughter was rusty, like a lawnmower left out in the rain.

"I don't go," she said. "Reshka says school is for morons, and the bus won't stop at the Haunt, and she won't drive me. Everyone's afraid of her. Reshka says sorcerers like her are revered as gods among men."

Noir snorted.

"Sorcerers!" she said scornfully. "Reshka talks of sorcerers as if there were others like her. There aren't, Nin. There *aren't!* Before I had you, I traveled—well—I traveled everywhere, wherever I could, searching for others. Reshka was always whispering warnings about them: to beware, to guard my tongue, to learn everything and grow strong. A day will come, she said, when my powers would be pitted against another like me, only far more puissant and merciless. There were nights I couldn't sleep for terror."

"I'm sorry, Mama."

But Noir merely patted her head. "There are no sorcerers in the real world, Nin. There are used car salesmen. And lawyers. Boys in black overcoats who pretend to be wizards. Pregnant teenagers working at McDonalds who call themselves High Priestesses of Discord. Peyote-swallowers and acid-tasters—even true shamans. But there is no one like Reshka Stix of Stix Haunt, or like her mother before her. There was no one like me, born of a sorcerer and a ghost on Dark Eve. And no one like you, my Nin, although I chose for you a living father, that you might be more alive than dead when you came into this world."

By now both Noir and Nin were sitting upright, arms locked wrist to forearm. Two pairs of gray eyes gazed at each other.

"Noir?" Nin's voice was very small.

Noir's grip on her daughter relaxed.

"Reshka has no equal," she said. "She has no living friends and her enemies are not alive. The house she lives in was built by the dead. That's why people are afraid. Reshka is unnatural."

"Are you unnatural?" Nin asked. She wanted to ask, "Am I?" but knew better, even dreaming.

Her mother pinched Nin's chin and smiled, and her smile was like a lilac blooming in the snow. All she said was, "Reshka will start teaching you soon."

Nin cocked her head to one side. "And should I learn?"

"Oh, yes," breathed Noir. "Learn everything. Grow bold and strong. And stay awake!"

Nin woke.

Learning the instruments took the better part of the next two years. There were only four songs, one for each wind, but Nin had to learn them pitch perfect, note perfect. She had to be able to play them dancing, or lying down, or walking barefoot on the ridge of the roof. Four songs for the four winds: lure with the piccolo, bind with the flute, braid with the oboe, and with the bass recorder break the stone.

But songs were not all she learned. When Nin turned fourteen, Reshka taught her how to make grave-rings out of silver clay, a substance made of fine silver powder, water, and organic binder. Nin learned to etch the entire alphabet on the inner band of a ring, in tiny, precise letters so small they could only be read by magnifying glass. She learned how to fire the rings in a kiln until they were hard, how to tumble them and finish them until they shone like mirrors, smooth as satin.

"Why silver?" Nin asked her grandmother. "Why not gold?"

"Silver's a repellent," Reshka said. "Like salt. Some say running water—but they lie."

They worked in the Ring Room, as Nin called the small chamber off Reshka's bedroom. Illuminated by dazzling electric lights, it was the brightest, harshest room in the house. Reshka had installed salt trenches along threshold and windowsills. Silver wire ran all around the room at the baseboards so that no ghosts could enter. An enormous worktable and two long wooden benches took up most of the space. Supply shelves crowded the walls.

In that room, Nin fashioned hundreds of silver rings, and Reshka destroyed them all. The work of hours, weeks, months gone in an instant, slapped to the floor, and the worker slapped too, for good measure. Nothing satisfied her grandmother.

"No!" she would croak. "Another! Again! They must be beautiful. They must be perfect."

"Why?" asked Nin.

"Because, Nin the Dim—" dry, dry, Reshka was dry as an old well with bones at the bottom "—they are each to become a tombstone."

As Nin's fifteenth birthday neared, the new difficulty became choosing her first ghost.

Pieta Cemetery lay between the town and its woodland like a farm that grew only corpses. Nin sat beside her grandmother in the parked truck, staring out over the desolate miscellany. Mausoleums and monuments, tablets and tombs, vaults, angels, cherubs, reapers, veiled Madonnas, all spread out before them in orderly serenity. Like a country girl come to the big city for the first time, Nin felt flushed and giddy. She was used to the dead outnumbering the living—but not on this scale!

Smiling to herself, she muttered, "Pick a gravestone, any gravestone."

"Not *any* gravestone!" Reshka shouted. "Stupid girl!"

Nin smoothed out her smile.

"You must choose your ghost with care," Reshka explained in her raspy, exasperated way. "It must not be an infant. Infants are fractious, unformed. Nothing appeases them. They teethe on the furniture. They break things. They're always underfoot. Nor do you want an old ghost—imagine!" And here Reshka laughed, a skeletal sound. "Imagine! Raising *me* as your ghost! You couldn't boss her around. *She'd* boss *you!* She'd own you! Never let a ghost own you, Little Miss Nin the Grim. *You* own *it.* You got that? *You* own your ghost! Or she'll eat you up, all but your teeth."

Nin nodded. The cab of the truck, she decided, smelled like mildew. She was surprised the engine had coughed to life in the first place. Probably Reshka kept a ghost as a mechanic.

"No," concluded Reshka, "you do not want the very old, or the very young. You do not want a teenager—don't I know? How tiresome they are, moping around and popping pimples. Choose a ghost in the full strength of its youth, a beautiful ghost in its prime, who will do as you bid or be whipped for it. Go."

Nin slipped out of the truck and entered the deserted cemetery. The grass underfoot was warm and wet. Nin, who never went shod at Stix Haunt, had gotten out of the habit of shoes. The grass tickled her ankles and the sun pounded on her scalp. She began perusing the stones.

1896-1909. A boy. An adolescent. Timothy Hearn. No.

1890-1915. A soldier. Robert John Henehan. Nin did not want a soldier.

1856-1934. Mary Pritchett had outlived all of her children and her husband. Too sad. Too sad and too old.

At Reshka's step behind her, Nin asked carefully, "How do you whip a ghost?"

"Ah!" cried Reshka. "Ha! Why, you have his name! With the song of breaking, you destroy his gravestone. He can't remember who he is. Nobody alive knows or cares. This site," she gestured around with her manicured claws, "is a historical landmark. No one uses it anymore. But you—you've got his name, his birth and death, etched in silver on a ring. You wear it against your flesh, and he must return to you. You're his gravestone. You're his home. Your power over him is complete. With the songs of binding and braiding, you've trapped his soul; you've twisted his spirit into your hair, until he's so tangled in the strands, he'll never come loose. Say he misbehaves. All you have to do is this."

She pinched one of her skinny blonde braids between her fingers. From the very tip of it, she plucked a single hair.

Then she dug around awhile in her large suede purse, at last drawing out a lighter.

Flick of the wheel—flame. It made nothing of that little hair in an acrid instant.

Howling filled the steamy August afternoon. A great coldness rushed over Nin, followed by sobbing. One of her grandmother's ghosts was near, she knew. Must have followed them from Stix Haunt.

Even with her hands clapped over her ears, Nin could hear the ghost crying.

Reshka held out one hand to the air, like a queen to her vassal. The silver rings she wore, two for each finger and three on her thumbs, glinted smugly. The sobbing quieted, replaced by a whispering unwet suction, like fervent kisses.

If she squinted at the air around Reshka's hand, Nin could almost make out the ghost. It was more difficult in daylight. But, yes, there was a haze—a disturbance, colorless, like a mirage, not of heat but of deep and biting cold.

Reshka waved the ghost away.

"Do you see?" she asked.

Nin nodded.

"They must be disciplined." Reshka's pursed pink mouth smiled. "When you have a ghost of your own," her outthrust fingernail caught Nin squarely on the nose, "I expect your bed to be made every morning. I don't understand why you've salted my ghosts from your room, but your slovenliness is intolerable. Of course, what else is to be expected of Noir's daughter? She was a slob too, and ungrateful. But come your first raising, you'll have no excuse for your messes. Either in your room or on your person. Do you hear me?"

"Yes, Reshka."

But Nin was no longer paying attention. She had found what she was looking for.

The gravestone read:

Mason Ezekiel Gont
1901-1924
Son, Brother, Friend
Mason Ezekiel Gont.

The words rang like bells. The sweetest, most clangorous, most dangerous clamor. Mason. Ezekiel. Gont. Mason Ezekiel Gont.

Son. Brother. *Friend.*

The night of the raising, Nin dressed with care.

She had grown up wearing Reshka's castoffs, or ancient garments rifled from attic and cupola. But for this special occasion, which marked her fifteenth birthday and her very first ghost, Nin ordered a new wardrobe from online catalogues like Gypsy Moon and the Tudor Shoppe. She used Reshka's credit card.

Most of what Nin bought came in some shade of red.

Her poppy-petal skirt fell to her ankles, embroidered and deeply flounced. Her shirt was dyed a vibrant arterial red, with scarlet ribbons running through the collar and cuffs. Around her waist she tied a golden scarf with firebird patterns and a beaded fringe. She wore bells on her ankles. Her hair, black and rough and loose, covered her bare arms. Her skin, scrubbed with salted water, shone pink as hope.

She did not want her ghost to mistake her for a mere shade. She wanted to be seen.

Reshka had commissioned Nin a carrying case for the four winds. It was ebony, lined in blue velvet, with separate compartments for the instruments. Flute, piccolo, oboe, bass recorder, each fit cunningly in its own place.

"It's better than you deserve," Reshka said.

Nin did not argue. Neither did she say thank you.

They accomplished the drive to Pieta Cemetery in their customary silence, arriving at an hour so late it was technically morning. There was no telling sky from tomb, everything was so black and still. Pulling up outside the gates, Reshka let the truck idle. Old Stix and young Stix stared straight ahead, neither looking at the other.

"Tonight," said Reshka, "we'll see if the sorcery runs true in you. I'll never know why Noir insisted on diluting your bloodline with a living sire. You favor your bag boy father in everything but the eyes."

Nin sprang out of the truck. Before slamming the door, she leaned in and stared Reshka dead in the eye.

"I look like Noir, except I'm taller and my hair is black. I look like Noir Stix, you old bitch. Don't wait up."

And she turned and stalked away.

But no sooner did Nin step through the gates than she felt the ire slipping from her shoulders. To be alone at last, and a year older, and dressed to tryst! All around the graveyard sang, in cricket song, frog-throb, and the call of night birds from hundred-year-old trees. Moss fell from low branches like silver veils.

The dead are close, Nin thought, but not awake. The dead are underfoot.

She knew the way to his grave by heart. Since discovering him, Nin had visited often, sneaking off early from Stix Haunt to tramp those five miles down the dark road on foot, just to bring him wildflowers. Wooing him, she hoped.

Mason Ezekiel Gont. 1901-1924. She wished there had been room to etch, "Son, Brother, Friend," on the inner band of the grave-ring, but she carried the words hard in her heart, that they would not be destroyed when his headstone fell.

And there it was, his quiet resting place.

Nin laid a shallow bowl of alabaster before his headstone, lighting the coals inside it. Then, sifting resin of red myrrh over the smolder, she knelt and placed a circle of white lilies in her hair. Bitter smoke snaked skyward, leaving a pale echo of vanilla in the air. She opened the ebony carrying case.

First, the luring song.

Pipe it on the piccolo, high and sweet and blithe. Pipe it playful on your tiptoes, and dance you 'round his grave. Three times three, you dance—and trill and tease and coax:

Come out to me!
Come dance and leap!
Rise up, rise out!
Come play!

Nin played the lure perfectly. But it was very, very hard.

Reshka never told her that it would hurt. Or of the horrors.

Her lips burned. Her tongue burst into blisters, which burst into vile juices that ran down her throat. The sky ripped open and a bleak wind dove down from the stars, beating black wings and shrieking. Reshka never said how a greater darkness would fall over the night like a hand smothering heaven, how every note she played would cost her a heartbeat, how the earth shuddered away from her naked, dancing feet as though it could not bear her touch.

And then Mason Ezekiel Gont appeared in the smoke of the burning myrrh.

"Ghosts can't take flesh," Reshka had said. "But they can take form. In water, in windows, in smoke and mirror, in steam and flame. If you are lucky and if they're strong, they can shape a shadow you can almost touch."

He was there. The lure was over. Nin stopped playing and stood still and looked her fill.

The ghost rose uncertainly from the burning coals, upright and blinking, but not quite awake. His hands, which were vague, which were vapor, moved to touch his face, before falling to his sides again, in fists. A look of terrible confusion made his whole body waver, shred apart, form again. He could not feel himself.

Remembering just in time, Nin snatched the crown of lilies from her hair and tossed it over his head. The flowers fell through him, landing in a perfect circle around the alabaster bowl. She had practiced that toss a hundred thousand times.

The ghost glanced down at the lilies, then back up at Nin. She was not supposed to speak until he was hers for sure, but she smiled, hoping to reassure him.

Don't worry, she wanted to say. *They're to keep you safe. Keep you from straying.*

She put the piccolo away and picked up the flute.

The binding song was a lightning series of notes, arpeggios and scales both wild and shrill (Nin had never really mastered the flute; Reshka kept telling her she played like a flock of slaughtered turkeys), and even the ghost winced to hear them.

The flute screamed, and then it seemed the ghost screamed, and frost settled over Pieta Cemetery. It came from nowhere and everywhere. The graves began to glisten. The trees were draped in diamonds. Nin's lips froze to the lip of the flute. Her fingers slowed on the notes, turned blue, stiffened and stuck. It was like she played an instrument made of angry ice.

It was not music anymore. Nothing like music. Only one long, sustained, horrible noise, like a stake hammered into frozen ground, making a claim.

You are mine
You will stay with me
For all eternity

And then the binding was over. The flute fell from Nin's nerveless hands.

The ghost stared at her. His eyes were the color of burning myrrh. The trees were white and still beneath a sheen of frost, and he was still too, trapped within the chain of lilies.

Nin began to braid a single lock of her hair. It was no simple braid, but a sturdy rope of many strands, with a series of intricate knots at the end. She had spent a year practicing this braid, first with embroidery thread, then with spiderwebs, then on a doll with human hair that had been from the head of her great-grandmother's grandmother.

"The hair of a madwoman," Reshka had said. "So you know what lunacy feels like."

Nin had practiced the braid in her own hair too, but it had not been like this. There was a song of braiding. She hummed it now, and would later seal the braid with the same tune on the oboe, after the last knot was tied.

The song filled her mouth with wasps. She kept humming, though the wasps stung her tongue and crawled over her teeth. She hummed and braided, even though her hair was suddenly tough as steel, sharp as needles, poisonous as nettles. Already burnt and frozen, now her hands stung, now they trembled and bled, until her hair was wet with her own blood.

And still she braided and hummed, and the ghost watched.

> *Bind and wind and knot and weave*
> *A labyrinth of grief and need*
> *Way and wall and maze and path*
> *A labyrinth of want and wrath*
> Mason Ezekiel Gont—*I braid thee, my ghost*
> *I braid thee in my hair*

She tied the end of the braid with silver thread, coughing out a mouthful of crawling white wasps as she did so, and took up the oboe, and sealed the braid with a song. When it was over, Nin wept.

The ghost looked on her tears with curiosity, maybe even pity, but his fists did not relax.

The bass recorder was a lean length of polished ivory, ending in a gentle bell. It shook in her hands.

> *Break,* she played
> *Break, stone, and be forgotten*
> *Nothing but bones beneath, and those are dust*
> *Break stone, break name, break birth and death*

Break old, forgotten words and go to dust
I will keep him, I will hold him
My flesh shall be his gravestone
I alone shall name him
Break, break, stone—and be forgotten . . .

Nin did not know how long she played. She played until "Son, Brother, Friend," collapsed to pebbly rubble. Until the day her ghost was born and the day he died turned to gravel, and his name, his beautiful name, decayed to dirt and fell to dirt, indistinguishable from the rest of the earth.

When the song was done, she packed up the lilies and the alabaster bowl so that nothing would mark the place. She slung the strap of her carrying case over her shoulder.

From her pocket, she drew the silver grave-ring and slipped it over her finger.

"Mason Ezekiel Gont," said Nin Stix. "Follow me home."

Even the silence changed after that. Everything was music. When the last of her wounds healed, the frostbite and heat blisters and wasp stings leaving numb spots and small scars, Nin started reading to her ghost. All her old favorites, Pushkin to Pratchett, Yourcenar to Yolen, J.M. Barrie to Gene Wolfe: dog-eared and thumbed-through as these books were, she took them out and began them again, this time out loud. She read the ghost her old letters to Noir, showed him her sketchbooks, and led him to her secret place beneath the willow tree. She even vacuumed the salt from her threshold and windowsill that the ghost might come and go as he pleased.

Because he shared it with her, Nin straightened her room every day. She made her bed with what Noir had called "Marine Corps precision"—hoping that Reshka would never suspect it was Nin's work and none of the ghost's. She began to wear perfume and dressed in her new clothes every day. For the first time in seven years, Nin was happy.

And she was beginning to see the ghost more clearly.

* * *

One night, several weeks after the raising, Nin sat at the edge of her bed and lit a candle. Like magic, the ghost's shadow sprang to the wall, man-sized, as though he were standing right in front of her, with her flame shining bright upon him. Nin smiled. The shadow stepped off the wall and sat down at the foot of the bed.

"Mason," she whispered.

He turned towards her, rayless, faceless, dense. She could not see through him.

"I'm sorry you can't sleep," she said. "You must miss dreaming."

The ghost gave a small shrug, out of courtesy or despair. It might have meant a thousand things.

"Rest, please, you must rest—if you can," said Nin. "On the bed, if you want. I'll sleep on the floor. If you want."

In answer, the ghost drew back her covers, his shadow hands deliberate and careful, and then gestured Nin beneath the sheets. The moment her bare feet brushed the footboard, he pulled the blankets up to her chin, smoothed them, and lay down beside her, on top of the white eyelet lace. Nin turned onto her side, facing away from him, barely breathing. The ghost gathered her against him, one arm tucked snug against her stomach. For a long time, wrapped in his shadow, Nin stared at the candle and did not sleep.

She awoke with dark blue bruises on the places he had pressed against all night. Her stomach, the back of her neck, all along her spine. Frost hung in her black hair where he had breathed on her, a mist of crystals everywhere but on a single braid.

Soon after this, she took him to meet her mother.

* * *

Beneath the willow tree, Nin dreamed her willow dreams. It was September, and the Heron Marsh was restless. Greens bled to gold, gold grew dense and dry. Insects chafed. Long-legged birds took wing. The ghost followed Nin into dreaming.

"Oh, my," said Noir the first time she saw him.

They were curled on the boulder, out in the middle of Lake Argentine. A warm green breeze moved down from the languid sky.

Mother and daughter regarded the ghost as he treaded the too-blue water, splashing about, sometimes diving under to swim with the black fish-cat who lived beneath, a sleekly furred beast with the head of a panther and the body of an eel.

Once or twice, it twined with the ghost's feet as he swam, trying to pull him under.

Mason dodged the fish-cat and swam up to rest against Nin's legs where they dangled in the water. His dark, wet head nudged her knobbly knees. Nin stroked his hair.

"I can see him so clearly here," Nin said. "He's like a silhouette that grew dimensions. And he's not cold at all!"

Her mother ran her fingers through her own short curls, her smile rueful, and glanced from Nin's face to the ghost.

"Well," said Noir. "Nice to meet you finally. What's your name?"

The ghost glanced at Nin, radiating inquiry.

"Mason Ezekiel Gont," Nin replied with a proud smile. She could never say his name without smiling. She said it whenever she could. "Mason Gont. The Gont of Haunt. Mason. His name is Mason."

"Mason," Noir repeated, never taking her eyes from the ghost's face. "Mason."

"Mason," said the ghost. Then, "I won't remember it."

Nin clapped a hand to her mouth in shock. Her ghost had never spoken before. Her mother did not look surprised, only compassionate. And a little angry.

"I know you won't remember, Mason. But while you're here, we'll do what we can."

The ghost spread his hands, palms up, treading water. Noir leaned down to touch his shoulder.

"Is my daughter kind to you?"

"Is she kind?" He lifted his head from Nin's knees to stare at her. His eyes were darker than the rest of him, a deep and glossy black beaming like volcano glass from the chiseled planes and contours of his face. Every eyelash showed in spiky, sharp relief.

Nin and her ghost watched each other, forgetting to breathe. Both remembered the shower they had shared that morning. How he had spilled into shape, hot spray and viscid steam, touching her with hands that were rivulets, that were waterfalls, soaping her body and washing the suds from her hair. Nin had not asked him into the bathroom with her. But he had entered anyway, uninvited, and she did not order him away.

After the shower, when she was clean and sweet smelling, when his icy and invisible arms wrapped the towel around her flushed body, she had wiped the steam from the mirror with the heel of her hand and saw them both inside it. The ghost stood behind her, vivid as any man.

Mason's nose was too large for his face. His eyebrows grew straight and ferocious, very dark. Most of his skin was luminous with spectral pallor, wet and bare, steaming from the shower, but his cheekbones were hectic, as though fever-eaten. His hair was shaggy, almost as curly as Noir's, almost as black as Nin's—a warm black, with hints of brown and glints of red. His lips were thin and seemed naturally pensive.

Nin wondered if she could ever make him laugh.

Even as she thought this, he began to smile, matching the thoroughness of her inspection with the intensity of his own.

And then he bent his head. And placed his mouth on her neck.

Soft as lilies, sore as stinging nettles. The shock went through her like a bitter wind. And when he lifted his head again, they stared at each other in the glass, stunned, and she knew that he had felt what she had felt, on his side of the mirror.

"Yes," Mason Ezekiel Gont told her mother, in the water of Nin's willow dream. "Nin has been very kind."

"My name is Noir," said Noir, with a terrible pity in her eyes. "You are welcome beneath my tree any time."

In the second week of October, Reshka summoned Nin to the Ring Room. The ghost accompanied Nin up to the door but no further; the salt trenches on the threshold stopped him.

When she stepped through the doorway, Nin could no longer see him, or even sense his presence. The braid in her hair hung listless, but the silver grave-ring burned against her finger. By this alone she knew the ghost was disturbed. He could not find her. He could not follow her. He could not even know the room existed.

"What do you want?" Nin asked, not patiently.

Reshka hunched like a harpy on one of the benches. Mockery whetted her round blue eyes.

"All Souls' soon," she said.

Nin never paid attention to the holidays. Mostly, she slept through them.

"So?"

"So?" Reshka sneered. Her voice was like taking ice cubes to a cheese grater, always at odds with her varnished face. "So? You've not lived through a Souls' Day yet, girl. Or the Eve of it, either."

Nin sighed.

"Every Dark Eve," Reshka went on, "I've drugged your food and drink to make you sleep. I've circled your bed with salt and locked your door with a silver key. I've kept you safe from the ghosts of Stix Haunt—and *so*, you ask? So! You have no idea, do you, girl, what happens when the dead walk? *When the dead take flesh and come walking!*"

That parched old voice, never less than awful, now cracked under the strain of something more. Nin had never seen Reshka's fear. She did not know how to respond to it.

"They come walking?" she asked. "In the flesh? But you said . . . "

Reshka ignored her. "I won't drug you this year. You're grown—got a ghost of your own now, don't you, girl? I've seen. You're careless, treat him like a pet, let him walk all over you. Let him take liberties. You'll deserve what happens when he walks. He'll destroy everything you own, searching for that little ring you wear. Might be he'll gobble you in your bed. But I don't know." Reshka's pink lips curled. "Might be you want that, to die as ghoul food? Noir's daughter is fool enough for such, I guess."

Nin clenched her hands. "Leave Noir out of this, Reshka! If you have something to teach me, teach me!"

Her grandmother's immaculate claws shot out, quick and callous as they had been seven years ago at Lake Argentine, when they drowned the black cat Behemoth. Now they closed around Nin's wrist and sunk deep, drawing blood.

Nin's grave-ring flared—agony! agony!—and her knees gave out. She fell hard at Reshka's feet, her arm twisted in her grandmother's grip, seized fast.

"The dead will come walking." Reshka's voice shook, but her talons never faltered. "They come looking for their names. You stay in your salt circle, with a silver veil cast over your braid, and you keep still. You don't move. You barely breathe. They'll take the house apart searching. That's of no matter—I make them put it to rights again the next day. They'll do it, or I'll hurt them as only the dead can be hurt, I'll burn little bits of them to dust.

"But that's for morning. At night, on Dark Eve, so long as they walk, you stay still, you never leave the circle. And you never, *ever* remove your silver veil. Or else they'll *see*. The salt might stop them—maybe, maybe not—but best not test it. Do this and don't stray, Noir's daughter, or I'll hang you from that willow tree you love. Then I'll raise you up again by the four winds, and you'll be scrubbing my back and brushing my teeth for all eternity. You got that, Nin the Necrophilian? Am I clear enough, Miss Nin?"

"Clear!" Nin gasped, hating herself. She might as well have cried mercy. Reshka flung her wrist away with a disgusted hiss.

"Then get out," said her grandmother. "And prepare while you still can."

It rained all day on the Dark Eve.

No trick-or-treaters came skipping down the road from town, plastic pumpkin heads in hand. No teens dressed in black T-shirts and glow-in-the-dark bones came to teepee the lawns and throw stones at the windows of Stix Haunt.

Nin stayed at her window all day, pretending to watch the rain. But it was Mason she watched, following his restlessness as he paced wall to wall in the reflection of her room.

"It's all right," she told him. "You'll walk tonight."

He paused long enough to give her a single, unfathomable look.

"I wish I could go to the willow tree," Nin said. "But on a day like this I'd drown."

The ghost drifted towards her in the window. Nin felt him at her back. But before he touched her, before his arctic breath sent chills down her neck, he turned away. He walked through one of her walls, and he did not return.

Nin tried not to cry. She'd wanted him out anyway. Now she could begin her preparations. The first part was easy. All she needed was scissors.

* * *

The hour before midnight, Nin lit a line of red pillar candles. Hot cinnamon wax scented the air. She had covered her windows with shawls and scarves, so that no one outside—alive or dead—could look in.

By candlelight, Nin laid her circle of salt, three thick lines of it. Sea salt, then road salt, then perfumed bath salts that smelled like lavender. When the circle met itself, when even Nin forgot where it began and ended, she stepped out of her clothes and shoes, folded them neatly and put them away, and flung a dark gray veil, heavy with silver embroidery and longer than she was tall, over her head. Then she moved over the lines of salt into the heart of the circle, and sat on the floor to wait.

Reshka's grandfather clock struck midnight. Dark Eve was over, and All Souls' began. So did the noises.

Downstairs, down the hall, starting in the kitchen, a great clashing started up. Glass broke. Drawers pulled out and upended. Knives hurled at the walls. A huge, frightening crash—perhaps the refrigerator tipping over. Bookcases toppled. Books ripped apart. Curtain rods torn down. Someone singing an awful song. Someone flushing and flushing the toilet. (Nin wondered what they were flushing.) Cabinet doors ripped off. Doors slamming. Outside, shrubs uprooted, banged against the house, tossed through the windows. Someone pounding holes in the porch with something blunt. A furious gibbering. People who had forgotten how to speak. Whistlings and whispers and wet slobbering sobs sliding through the cracks in the plaster.

The ghosts walked in flesh. The search was on.

Below, Nin knew, Reshka was in hiding, sealed in the Ring Room behind salt and silver. The ghosts could not harrow her from that secret place, to reclaim what she wore on her fingers, in her hair. Thwarted, they grew restless. Further and further out they ranged, into the woods and the marshes, maybe as far as the town, knocking on doors, rapping on windows, searching for their names. The calamity of their passing faded to a distant wailing.

Nin's door opened and Mason Ezekiel Gont stepped inside.

He did not see Nin, invisible behind her barrier of salt, with the gray veil over her. He walked to her bed and stared at it for some time, then stroked the white eyelet lace. He could feel what he touched. He did not, precisely, smile.

Mason moved through the candlelight, a ghost in the flesh, casting no shadow. He ran his fingers over everything, the fringes of her scarves, the beads hanging from her ceiling fan, the cotton underwear in her drawer. Always with that expression that was not entirely sweet or bitter, but concentrated. Perhaps hungry.

Three times he passed the mirror before he dared look at himself. When he did, he stepped right up to the glass, pressed his nose to it. Forehead to reflected forehead, he studied himself. His left palm flattened to his breastbone, where no heart beat. Mason and Mason-in-the-mirror stayed that way for a long time.

While he stared, Nin stood up in her circle. Almost carelessly, almost by accident, she stretched one bare big toe towards him. The toe smudged a few grains of salt out of place. It took only that, and Mason Ezekiel Gont turned to look at her.

Two strides, and he reached through the circle, pulling the veil from her face.

He said, "Your hair."

"Yes," said Nin. "Now I know why Noir kept it so short."

He shook his head, wordlessly reaching out again. But Nin sidestepped his grasp and backed away, until the back of her knees met the edge of her bed and she sank down. She rubbed the stubble on her head, more acutely aware of its unpredictable tufts than of her nakedness.

Frowning down at her feet, Nin could not see him coming, but she heard his tread. And then he was there, standing knee to knee with her.

"Will you sit?" she invited him.

"Do you command it?"

"No."

"I will not sit."

Nin glanced up. For the first time since he had entered her room, she recognized the expression on his face as anger. He was so angry, heat simmered off his skin. He looked not into her eyes, but at her skull, her scalp, the absence of her hair—the absence of the braid where his soul was bound. Once she saw his gaze flicker to her ring finger, which was bare.

"It—it—was never right to call you," she stammered. "Or, having called you, to keep you. But I was so . . . " She shrugged. She could not say the words she had practiced a hundred times.

"Where is it?" asked Mason in his soft way. "You still have it somewhere. You have not released me. It's here. Very near. My soul, braided and bound in you. Do you think I can't feel it? Is this a trick? What did you do with your hair?"

"I was going to give it to you . . . "

"Do it now," he said. "Do it, please, before the others come back and pull me into their madness. I am that close to going over . . . I am so close, Nin."

Nin, he said, and his rage broke a little.

Nin began to weep. The ghost placed his hands on her naked shoulders. His hands, heavy with borrowed life, were smooth and lineless, without fingerprints or scars or calluses. They bore her against the mattress, and she did not fight, knowing that he was no more relentless than she had been.

"Nin," he said, "I need my name. I need it. I need it back. Where did you put it? Where is your hair?"

Her nose was clogged from crying. "You are my only friend."

"And I'm here, Nin," he whispered. His breath was white waste and winter night. "I'm right here. And I am your friend. But I have neither eaten nor drunk for one hundred years. I have not felt flesh beneath my fingers in one hundred years. Nin, I am hungry—and I have no name to recall me to myself, or the honor I once believed in!"

His hands were warm, and his breath was cold, and her own breath was coming too fast.

"Please," said Nin.

"Stop me," begged the ghost. "Nin, stop me."

"I can't."

"Please." His voice grew ragged. His hands moved down her body, fingers hard on her thighs. His mouth suckled at her skin, not so much kissing as tasting raised flesh, heartbeat, the pulse of the artery running through her belly. She grasped his curls and his head slid lower. Even his hair was alive, twining around her fingers like damp, sleepy ferns.

Nin reached one hand beneath her pillow to draw out a silver-embroidered sack ungainly with salt. The knot that bound it was simple, but Mason's mouth complicated everything. When her trembling fingers finally undid the knot, salt spilled everywhere, along with a single black braid, which she had bound on both ends in silver, and looped through a little silver ring. The inner band of the ring was engraved with a name and two dates.

Mason raised his head and saw the braid.

"It's for you," Nin said. "It's yours."

His hand shot out so fast she did not see it move. The braid and the silver ring disappeared into his clenched fist.

"I am Nin Stix," Nin said. "What's your name?"

"I am Mason Ezekiel Gont," said the ghost, and then he laughed. The sound seemed to surprise him. Then, surprising Nin, he dipped his head and brushed her belly with a kiss.

"And I am pleased," he said, "I am most pleased to meet you, Nin Stix." He kissed her belly again, the spot between her breasts, the side of her throat.

Then, in a whisper she almost missed: "Stop me, Nin."

"No," she said. "You're free. You're my friend. You're the only one I want."

His tongue licked a few grains of salt from the spill across her belly. His exhale moved, frozen, across her skin. Nin felt a thin ice crust her stomach.

"Mason," she began.

"Nin Stix."

"Mason Ezekiel Gont."

"Nin Stix, sorceress." His tongue worked on her, his lips, his teeth. The hunger of a hundred years. "Nin, gentle mistress. Nin of the Four Winds . . . "

"Mason . . . "

"Nin, do not stop me now . . . "

"Mason—finish it!"

And he did.

All Souls' day passed in a dream, and then night came. Nin and Mason lay together, foreheads touching, and Nin wept to realize that Mason's kiss had driven the taste of ash from her mouth. She burrowed against him, driving her flesh to his, knowing she would not be able to touch him again after midnight.

"Nin." His breath was warm now, warm on her scalp, and it smelled of lily and of myrrh. "Nin, my Nin, what will you do now?"

She knew what he was asking. He was asking, "What are you going to do without me?" He was asking, "How will you live, when I leave you alone—more alone than anyone has ever been alone?"

Nin shook her head. "It doesn't matter."

"It does," he insisted. "I know it does. What will you do?"

The answer came to her then, like a bruise behind the eyes, or a freezer-burn of the marrow bone, and she put both her hands over her face and stayed that way for some time.

"Nin?"

"This can't continue."

"What can't?" the ghost asked carefully.

Nin rolled onto her back, her neck cradled in the crook of his arm. "Any of it."

Reshka Stix waited out the day in her Ring Room.

She had lived through one hundred eight All Souls', midnight to midnight; she knew what to do. For twenty-three hours, she had been supine upon her worktable, covered in a net of silver that glittered under the bright electric lights. She barely breathed, keeping a light trance that let her listen for the ghosts. Even when they left the Haunt, she could hear them. Reshka Stix could always hear them, screaming through the marshes, baying in the woods, frightening the water moccasins and the foxes and the owls to stony deaths. Searching for their names.

She could name them all.

No one in the house now but Noir's mouse, mooning for her ghost boy. That girl would end up gobbled. Or she'd end up too weepy and weak for the sorcery, and abandon the Haunt as Noir had done, salting her footsteps so the ghosts could not bring her back . . .

Shimmering under silver and memory, Reshka did not hear her granddaughter creep up to the Ring Room door. Reshka never heard the living so well as the dead. So when Nin poured water into the salt trenches at the Ring Room's threshold, Reshka did not know it.

Only when the ghosts came back did she know. She knew, and they knew, and they poured back into the Haunt so fast they blew the front door off its hinges and left it for splinters on the floor. A horde of ghosts descended upon her, twenty-two shrieking things, crowding the bright-lit chamber where silver rings were made. Reshka Stix could name them all.

The oldest saw her first. Perhaps her foot twitched beneath the net of silver. Or her breathing gave her away. In a flash, in a blink, moving as only a ghost could move—he was upon her, ripping off the silver veil with one hand, while the other lunged for her braided hair.

Each ghost who could reach one seized a braid, and those who could not started chewing, chomping, gnawing the rings off her fingers with their teeth, gnawing off her fingers one by one.

Reshka Stix did not scream. Even when they tore the braids out of her scalp, taking chunks of skin and clots of blood, she kept her tight pink lips compressed. And when they sucked the flesh from her severed fingers to get to the grave-rings, even then, proud Reshka made no sound. Of course, by that time, she was dead.

So there was no one alive at Stix Haunt that night to stop the ghosts from setting it ablaze.

"Nin, my love?"

"Yes, Noir, my love?"

"Is it over?"

"Yes. It's over and he is gone."

"It's morning, Nin. It's very late, in fact. I think you should wake."

"Did I really . . . Is Reshka . . . ?"

"*Wake . . .* "

The morning smelled like a funeral feast. Ashy air filled Nin's mouth, and she coughed, then turned onto her side and retched.

She had no recollection of leaving Stix Haunt after Reshka's ghosts came ravening back through. Mason must have done something, put her to sleep somehow and carried her to the willow tree—but she remembered nothing of that. Nin rubbed her head. She missed her hair, but not as much as she missed the braid and what it had bound. On hands and knees, she crawled from her damp shelter. It was in this genuflection that she had her first sight of the Haunt—what it had become.

Smoke filtered the sweet colors from the air. Reshka's house was a charred shell, clung about with trembling curtains of heat. A few piles of rubble smoldered yet. Nin made a sound between a cough and a cry.

"Oh, Noir! Oh, Mason—what have I done?"

The distance from willow to ruin might have been the distance between stars. She could not bear to go any closer. Palms pressed to eyes, she dropped until her forehead rested on the ground. Something cold kissed her forehead.

Nin did not have to see the ring to recognize it. His ring, his name, his birth and death—his broken and stolen tombstone—the ring she had returned to him, encircled her finger once again. Mason had put it there, he must have done, had bequeathed it to her, making her his resting place.

"Nin, my Nin," the ghost had asked, "what will you do now?"

Nin pushed to her knees and wiped her face.

SURROGATES

Cat Rambo

Floor 13: Government Offices

They were married on a Monday in the Matrimony office. A poster on the wall said, "Welcome to your new life!" Belinda signed the forms in her careful penmanship, but Bingo simply spit-signed, letting his DNA testify to his presence. There were three rooms processing couples and triads—larger family structure required even more complicated licenses than the one they had secured. This room was painted blue, and one wall was an enormous fish tank.

Three fish spoke to Belinda, but she ignored them. She wished she'd remembered to have the Insanity Chip nullified for the ceremony, but it had been a busy week. The fish pressed their mouths to the plastic separating them from her world. Word pearls rose from their lips, seeped upward, through the barrier, and whispered in the room.

After the computer had pronounced them spouses, Belinda and Bingo stood there grinning at each other while behind them silver fish swam back and forth, back and forth, as though imitating the waves they'd never known. A wall camera took their picture.

In a few moments, a wall slot spat out a plastic bag containing two chipkeys, a silver-colored frame around their wedding picture, and a checklist of Entitlements on a slip of dissolvable paper, already graying around the edges.

The clerk handed over the items. "This is where I tell you that you should treat everything as though it's new," she said. "Studies have shown that the marriages which survive the longest are the ones where the newlyweds begin to build their new life together."

"Thanks!" Bingo said with a bright smile. Belinda could tell how happy he was, like he couldn't stop smiling. He looked at her, and the fish tried even more frantically to say something, battering themselves against the plastic until they were just blood and silver scraps drifting in the water, but she ignored them and focused on Bingo and thoughts of butterflies.

Floor 22: Surrogates

"Preferences haven't changed?" the technician asked as he strapped Belinda into the configuring bed. The straps turned into flowers, tiny lilac-colored bells that smelled like uncertainty.

"No," Belinda said. The question surprised her. They had filled out the forms for marriage only two weeks ago, including the list of preferences for her latest surrogate. It was something she'd thought about for a long time. Her old surrogate had been given to her when she first started having sexual feelings, and she had put it away for good a few years ago, when she'd met Bingo.

"Do people really change their preferences at the last minute?" she asked.

"It's not that their preferences really change, so much," the tech said. "But sometimes after they've spent a little time thinking about it, they realize things that they didn't realize they want."

He checked his data pad. "Blue eyes, blonde hair, skin pigment pale brown, no scars, no disfigurements, face model Adam?"

"That's it," Belinda said. She'd picked a generic face. She didn't believe in getting attached to surrogates. Her father had chosen to keep the one she'd used all through her teenage years rather than recycle it. The choice was vaguely illegal by virtue of a statute that was rarely enforced. A person was entitled to one surrogate, which could be replaced whenever you changed status levels, as she and Bingo had done by marrying. But her father was a sentimental sort. She wondered how he would cope now that she was out of the apartment and he was living by himself.

The flower straps tickled her wrists. Perfume netted her, dragged her into sleep, content and dreamy as the machine went about its work, measuring her and calibrating the surrogate to her dimensions.

Afterwards they looked at the visuals of their surrogates. She was surprised by Bingo's choices: he had gone into much more detail than she had, as though designing a flower or piece of jewelry. Her face model was Maria and she wore elaborate blue tattoos like webbing over her arms and spreading across her nipples, half obscured by her long red hair.

Belinda liked the simpler look of her surrogate and she liked knowing that it was specifically designed for her, that it would smell and feel right, that it was *hers* in a way nothing else would ever be.

"They'll be delivered tomorrow, after we've done the final calibration," the clerk said. They signed data pads. "Congratulations," she said in a perfunctory tone and checked to make sure their names were spelled correctly.

* * *

Floor 77: Mental Services

On Floor 77, Belinda had her Insanity Chip reset so it would factor in her marriage. The Chips were subtle, she knew. They altered your perceptions, they showed the world in the way you wanted to see it. When she'd had a fight with her best friend Angie, she'd had the Chip set so she couldn't see Angie for a week, even when the other girl was standing, shouting in her face. When she'd finally relented, missing Angie, though, she'd found the other had gone, moved away.

"I don't want the Chip to change Bingo," she told the doctor. "Let him stay constant."

The doctor fiddled with the machine, her stubby fingers recalibrating the keys. "Do you want hallucinations amped up or down?"

"What I want," Belinda said, "is for everything to seem more significant somehow. Can you do that?"

"Of course," the doctor said. She pressed a few more buttons and turned into a giant jellyfish that hung in the air, glistening greasily. "How is that?" Her voice was muffled, as though coming through water.

"Perfect," Belinda said.

Bingo was in the waiting room. He had worn his best for the wedding: gleaming black pants, a silver hoop in one ear, goatee trimmed to a point. His feet were bare. He was talking to the child beside him but he broke off when Belinda came in. He smiled at her, rising.

"Ready to go home?" he asked.

Behind him the child wavered into a frog, a puddle, a big-eyed kitten.

"Perfect," Belinda said again.

* * *

Elevator 17-3

In the elevator between floors 45-75, Belinda said, "You never thought about having an Insanity Chip? Life is more interesting that way."

He kissed her despite the two other women in the elevator. "Life is already interesting."

The younger woman sniffed and stared at the wall; the older woman smiled at them before she got off on floor 82. Belinda saw stars in her eyes, promise in her smile, omens spilling out of the net bag she carried.

In the shop, they bought a new bedspread, dishes, cleaning liquids. They ordered an assortment of food and chose the color of their walls. Belinda liked a yellow and white diamond pattern because it seemed to her, when she stared at it long enough, figures danced across it, harlequins in shoes with long pointed toes, kicking them up and down as they capered. She heard it in her head like a complicated marching tune.

Bingo gave her a dubious look. He liked a plain blue. But he let her pick the wall pattern and in return she let him pick a muted grey rug flecked with earth tones, like walking across fabric pebbles, a gentle hum underfoot in the key of C.

Floor 689: Green Leaf Living Quarters

Floors 650-700 were Green Leaf Living Quarters. They would live on 689, in a studio that overlooked one of the four great hollow spaces contained inside the sector.

They kissed as they entered, dropping their bags in a cloud of butterflies beside the door. The curtains matched the walls, which had been prepared in the time they'd spent travelling on the elevator. It was as far in the Building as Belinda had ever travelled in one day. Bingo had been outside it to two other Buildings, but travel like that had never interested her. From what she'd seen on the holovids, every place looked much the same. Belinda kissed the tip of Bingo's nose before she went to the window and looked out.

Portals marked the sides of the living unit walls, and zip lines led from one to another, letting people circumvent the space on handheld lines. Down below was a great green park, filled with grass carpets and plants in pots. Over it stretched the mesh that would catch those who missed the safety straps, or the multitudes of young who delighted in falling, landing on the stretchy softness of the field.

Bingo started supper and she rearranged the pillows on the sofa, then unpacked her clothes into the wall drawers and shelves. Bingo came in smelling of spices and steam and kissed her again.

Bingo worked in advertising and Belinda was an assistant textile designer. That was how they had met. Belinda didn't think it very romantic, but Bingo always told the story as though he was writing an advertisement for it: I Saw Her And Then Wham Be Still My Heart. It made Belinda smile when Bingo talked like that.

After dinner they fucked, and fucked again. Bingo nibbled her ears and she tickled his nipples and they gave themselves to each other and murmured sweet things until they fell asleep.

Before breakfast, they uncrated the surrogates and turned them on, flipping the knob on the back of their necks. The surrogates clicked to life, their wide eyes fastening on Bingo and Belinda's faces. After orders, both went to the kitchen and started breakfast, then Maria emerged and began putting their belongings away. While they ate breakfast, the surrogates worked.

An animal came out of the crate that Adam had been in, which lay dissolving on the floor with the other one. Belinda didn't know what it was. It had the usual animal shape. It turned cartwheels on the floor and made Belinda laugh.

"What?" Bingo said. He was watching her face, the movement of her eyes tracking the back and forth of the animal, which had purple fur and hair made out of noodles.

"The Chip makes me see funny things sometimes," she said. He reached out and took her hand in his. "Funnier than me?" he said. The animal was behind him, hanging from the ceiling. Its noodles hung down, limp and shiny. The surrogates came in; they were done, so they went into their closet, ignoring Belinda and Bingo. "I don't think of you as funny," she said.

They fucked on the kitchen table. The cupboards talked to Belinda while she jolted back and forth, flapping plywood tongues. They sang folksongs, oh my darling Clementine and green hills hop to my Lou and sweet sweet summer enviro-clime.

On Sundays they went to her father's for dinner with his parents, who were still married and her other father, who was not. This father, Father Bob, worked as a restaurant manager, and they ate well on last night's restaurant leftovers, fungus shaped into simulacrums of more expensive creatures, scallops and firm-fleshed shrimp and exquisite orange roe.

Father Anton worked in a news studio and would tell them about the Anchors, what they liked, what they said. He had a fervid adoration for one Morning Host, a perky blonde woman a quarter his age, and when he told stories about her, he did so in hushed tones, like a primitive talking about God.

They drank liters of homemade beer, which Bingo's mother distilled in her kitchen and always brought, and afterwards they played cards around the table while the holovision blared news of the Building.

Father Bob kept the surrogates, his and Belinda's, out for company much of the time. She went over a couple of times to pick up belongings she'd left behind and found the three sitting watching holovid. Hers was the size of a fourteen- or fifteen-year-old boy; it was propped in an easy chair while the other surrogate leaned on the sofa beside Bob.

She had decorated this place herself, but since her departure, Bob had been pulling it slowly but inexorably into his own style. Restaurant containers filled the cooler. He had hung up several old pictures scavenged from the last remodel, which Belinda had designed the fabric for. The pictures showed leaves and golden light and flowers like great white cups drowning in blue water. They did not match the pink and orange carpet underfoot; they made it look old and shoddy. She did not like pictures of water. The tank in the Matrimony office had creeped her out.

She realized Father Bob was talking to her.

She said, "What?"

"Are you okay?" He got up from the sofa and peered at her. Behind him on the wall, the pictures undulated and swayed as though they were windows to some vast, tide-drawn lake.

"Sure," she said. "I was just thinking about what it was like, growing up with you and Father Anton." She liked the new place better; she liked the tiny balcony, the view out onto the park. Here was quieter, certainly, a bit more privileged, but there was something to be said for the hubbub that surrounded them, the people swinging past on the zip lines, taking a shortcut across the space rather than circle around the living area.

"You had a better childhood than I did," he said. It was a familiar refrain and she tuned out the details of how his family had worked maintenance for years and finally been given the chance to emigrate to this Building, far above the ruined, rotting planet. The food riots. The cold.

She knew Bob had begged on the street and he'd been rather good at it. The same charm and glibness that served him well running the restaurant had allowed him to cajole money, food, a couch to sleep on from people. He had lived a nomadic, room-to-curb existence for several years before becoming more established. He had moved in with Anton two years before they had decided to have Belinda. And life was good now for him. They could afford surrogates to do their daily work, let them concentrate on important things.

Belinda was a Creative type, always had been, and she did appreciate the chance at that which Anton and Bob's bloodlines had bought her, not having had to fight her way out of a less interesting job. She liked what she did and she was good at it.

Buzzing bees, colored violet and licorice and steel, swarmed through the air and she almost flinched.

"Why do you keep that Chip?" Bob said. "You're not a child anymore, Belinda. You don't need constant entertainment."

"It makes me think of things differently," she said. "It keeps me on my toes."

She liked her unexpected world, hidden from most. She liked to know that she, and she alone, could see the faces in the wall work, the swords in the grass, the walking trees that paraded across the park every dark, late, when almost everyone was sleeping, the surrogates in the closet unless Bingo had taken his to bed already.

Sometimes Belinda wondered what life would be like without the surrogates. Most of the time she didn't. The surrogates were there to do their work, but also in case one of them wanted sex when the other didn't. Two weeks after the marriage, Belinda didn't feel like it, so Bingo brought his surrogate in and fucked it there in the bed beside her.

After that she felt aroused. When Bingo just turned over, she went and got her own surrogate. Its rubbery cock stood up like a dildo, caramel colored. It went down on her, lips vibrating as she writhed, then fucked her. She thought that maybe Bingo would rouse again, that they'd fall into an endless sexual loop, but he kept snoring.

It surprised her how much she thought about that act afterwards. The surrogates were engineered deliberately so they didn't look like real people. Their eyes didn't track right and there was an odd translucency to their flesh. So it hadn't been as though it was another person Bingo had been focusing on, his eyes half-closed, looking somewhere inside himself. Had he been thinking about her? She felt oddly reluctant to ask, even though they were always frank with each other about what they liked and didn't like in bed.

On Bingo's birthday, Belinda made a cake by mixing the contents of one packet with another and letting it set inside a plastic shaping ring. She did it herself and frosted it, painting the white surface with green fish, punk flowers, yellow guitars. The cake sang to her as she painted it and later as she woke Bingo in the morning, singing his favorite song with the cake, "Baby baby flower baby."

She got home earlier than Bingo and she took to using the surrogate when she first did, then showering so she met him, freshly washed and ready, in the hallway, on the kitchen table, on the balcony. Today she fucked it and then showered while it and the other surrogate put up green and pink streamers that she'd pocketed from work.

Several of his friends and hers came over for dinner. She privately considered his friends brittle, and she'd heard him call hers vapid. Alfa and Veronika wrote musicals; Jonny and Leeza were clothing buyers. Veronika had an Insanity Chip too, but she made a point of saying that she did it for the sake of Creativity.

"It lets you drill down into the psyche of the really great artists," she enthused. "Van Gogh. Pound. Bacon. Doesn't it help you think up some really great designs, Belinda-baby?"

"Sure," Belinda said. She looked around. She had printed up some of the fabric swatches from work. They hung on the walls in odd trapezoidal shapes, angled in and out like blueprints of rocks. She wished she hadn't picked yellow for the curtains but she changed her mind when daffodil butterflies flew out of the fabric and spelled out words in the air: *Go Belinda you're great.*

Bingo flirted with Veronika; he asked her what her Chip made her see and gave her wide-eyed looks that were almost, but not quite mocking. Veronika bit into it and wouldn't stop talking. Over her head, Bingo gave Belinda ironic glances until she got the hiccups from suppressing giggles.

They drank wine and ate and played cards. Belinda had a hard time focusing on the hands, and Bingo said, a little irritably, "Can't you manage to keep track of the simplest thing?"

It made her want to cry, and that made the cards even blurrier.

"Oh, baby," Bingo said, instantly contrite. He took her cards and put them face down on the table; he brought her hand to his lips, kissing at them. "Baby, I'm sorry, what's wrong?"

She lied. "It was something I saw. Something the Chip showed me."

He frowned. Much later, after they'd gone to bed, he said, "Why do you keep the Chip? You have me now."

"It makes the world less boring," she said.

"Don't I do enough of that for you?"

She faltered, not sure what to say. "But there are times when I'm not with you," she said.

He didn't say anything, there in the darkness, and after a while, she said, "I could get the Chip modified so it doesn't go off when you're around." The words came out of her mouth and swelled like glowing balloons, colored coral and amber and pumpkin and gold.

"All right," he said quickly.

The next day she had the modification made. It was easy She rode home on the elevator on waves of blue, and her feet turned into fish, into birds, into kittens, and then Bingo was walking down the corridor towards her and everything was gone.

It was odd that evening, sitting across the table from him to eat food that stayed still and silent on the plate. She curled up next to him on the sofa and they held each other in the grey quiet, while the purple diamonds stood statue-still on the wall.

When Bingo wasn't around, she could fuck the surrogate and ride silver rails of scent, could press her hands on his skin and feel centipedes coiling underneath, could see his eyes full of daffodils and roses.

Sometimes she hid from Bingo, stepped into the closet and closed her eyes. The clothing wrapped its arms around her and she sailed away into stars and fireworks. She could feel him outside the doorway like a leaden eye, a cloud of smoke. She wanted Adam to sneak up behind him and then . . . she wasn't sure what. She wasn't sure what at all. And so she squeezed her eyes tighter and thought of light and its equations, like numbers on the inside of her head, and tried to dream even though she'd been forced awake.

It wasn't enough. She began to think she had agreed to things too quickly. She said to Bingo, "What if I had the Chip gimmicked so it was just a little bleed-through when you're around?"

His face darkened. "Why?"

"It helps me think," she said. She fussed with the food on the counter in front of her, making dinner. She laid a slice of bread on each plate, then a slice of cheese at an angle, so the food formed an eight-pointed star.

"Are you having trouble thinking?"

"Sometimes," she said.

"But only when you're with me."

"Never mind," she said. She poured white sauce over the cheese in a spiral and sprinkled it with green flakes. She could feel him watching her.

"I want you to be happy, Belinda, you know that," he said.

Then why do you want me to be something different than
I am, she wondered. But she didn't speak the words aloud. It
was the first time she'd ever censored herself for Bingo's sake
and that night she lay awake, wondering what it meant. Bingo
breathed beside her, the long slow sounds of sleep, and didn't
stir when she got up and went into the other room.

There, without Bingo, an enormous golden figure eight
hung in the air, blazing with a meaning she couldn't guess at.
She sat down on the sofa. Her surrogate stirred in its closet,
emerged, sat down beside her. It was ready to do whatever she
liked, but all she did was take its hand, flesh and plastic
intertwining.

The next day Bingo said, "You could get rid of the Chip.
It's silly. People laugh at you for having it."

That struck her to the quick. "Who's laughing at me?"

"Everyone," Bingo said. "Your friends and mine. Even
Bob and Anton think it's funny."

She thought that might not be true. She thought of Bob,
sitting with his own surrogate, her discarded one, a plastic
family. She knew that it was wrong to think of them like that,
she knew it was like befriending a toaster or a clock. But then
Bingo left the room and their toaster smiled at her, chirped hello,
and slid out two pieces of toast, perfect and brown, just the way
she liked them, even though she hadn't planned on breakfast.

When she came home from work, Veronika was sitting
on the couch.

"Bingo let me in," she said. "But he went to get some
groceries. Belinda, darling, I've got to talk to you about
something."

"The Chip," Belinda said. She looked at Veronika, at the
glossy red hair, the wide eyes.

"Bingo thinks you want something else, that's why you
won't give up the Chip."

Veronika's face was too solicitous. Belinda thought
about the two of them discussing her, discussing the Chip.

Discussing Bingo's dissatisfaction. It felt like a terrible betrayal.

"Get out," she said.

She expected Bingo to bring it up again that night, but instead he said, "Have you ever thought we might change our marriage, make it a triad?"

"I don't want to marry Veronika," she said without preamble. He flushed at the accuracy of the guess. She said, "Isn't your surrogate enough?"

"I have a surrogate," he said. "I don't have you."

It made her sound like a possession, like a thing, like a toaster. She didn't know what to say, how to reassure him that he didn't *need* her.

His voice was tired. "Let's go to bed. Think about it. We'll talk more in the morning."

She left in the middle of the night as he slept. She travelled to Floor 77, to one of the many building offices that never closed. Riding in the elevator, the buttons sang to her, the carpet advised, the lights shed waves of warmth that settled on her like a feather cloak.

In the morning, he said, "Have you thought of it?" But she went on talking to the cabinets.

He said, "I thought you made it so the Chip doesn't work when I'm around!"

"It's a fine morning," Belinda said to the table, watching the wood grain melt and puddle. And then she turned and left without looking at him, because she didn't see him anymore and only a tickle of memory remained.

LUCYNA'S GAZE

Gregory Frost

She's not very far away from me. Her head is canted a little.
Her eyes don't meet mine. So shy. It's been like that always
with her—that demure pose, those eyelids half-lowered, which
I've always taken as an invitation to move nearer, move to the
side, make her look up. I've almost done that more than once.
In the bakery, more than once.

She has what they call a heart-shaped face, with the
wide cheeks and a tiny cleft in her sharp chin. A valentine
heart.

From here, also I can see her foot, just the one, extended
toward me as if she thinks she is Cinderella and I'm to be the
prince, fitting the slipper onto her foot. The two of us. Happily
ever after—now, there is a dream.

Her name is Lucyna.

The first time I saw her was back when I drove the
delivery van for Ryszard. I was twenty-three then, a medical
student who had run out of money for school. Who knows what
we were delivering—probably furniture. Furniture constituted

most of what we delivered then. Mind you, this was before "furniture" became a euphemism for guns.

That hybrid-fuel van of his, it barely could make the mountains, the engine always backfiring and rattling and threatening to strand us.

Ryszard went off someplace. Maybe he was lunching with a customer. He liked to do that, pretend to be comfortably well off, a playboy of the world who could buy your meal while he steered the conversation to reveal that he was educated, could have been anything he wanted—doctor, advocate, priest even—but who preferred the vagabond life of taking orders and delivering the goods. He would even sometimes get me to call him on my cell so that he could pretend to be receiving an important conference call. It was a pathetic act really. Even I knew it, and if I knew it, everyone did. Nevertheless, I owe him for his pathetic act, because his leaving me alone is how I met Lucyna.

Her village wasn't much of a place. Built on a hillside, with one street of worn and broken paving stones surely as old as Napoleon's army. The street snaked down between the buildings, out the lower end and down a perilous slope to run flat along the river. We must have delivered to a dozen such places, all of them tiny, mountainous, distrustful of the modern world despite their cell phones, computers, and little satellite dishes. The more the world got in through the cracks of their lives, the more they distrusted it. And they were hardly wrong, were they? (I am quite sure I'm taking forever to get to the point, as they say, but it isn't as if we're going anywhere, is it?)

I parked the van and walked into the bakery to get something of my own to eat, and there she was. She would have been seventeen or eighteen then. She stood behind the varnished wooden counter. I remember that she was handing a round loaf of bread half-wrapped in brown paper to a customer. I don't recall the customer at all. Lucyna, though—she had a bandana upon her head that gathered up her hair, very gypsy-like. With her arm outstretched a small tuft of dark hair showed in her armpit. Her arm itself was the golden color of gingerbread and her face was dusted with flour. She must surely have been there since four or five in the morning, probably she'd arrived at about the time I climbed into the truck with Ryszard. At least, I was quite willing to pretend this, even to believe it and so forge an illusory link to her in this way. Bread loaves filled the angled shelves behind her, making her seem to be surrounded by gold like one of those Byzantine icons scarved in foil haloes.

For a moment as I approached she glanced my way, looking straight at me, bold in her assessment, but as quickly she cut me loose, her gaze rolled away, her eyelids descended, exactly like now, exactly like every time I saw her after that, as if something more interesting just a little to the side of me had captured her attention, a pleasant memory of laughing children or of carrying laundry down to the river in the company of other women, and which caused her to smile the slightest bit as she blushed at her own forwardness.

I recall that I ordered a pastry, a crème-filled confection, and she placed it on the tiny piece of parchment paper and handed it across to me, and our fingers touched. She abandoned her shyness then and looked me in the eyes and I, with what self-assurance I do not know, asked her what her name was, and she answered me in a voice that sounded surprised to be speaking her name. As quickly her eyes shifted away and focused elsewhere, and I had the odd sensation of watching someone look into the future, seeing what fate might await the two of us if she dared to say more. It was a foolish idea, I suppose, but now I've seen this future, I understand how one would want to know.

Then we parted. I took my pastry out of the shop and out of her world. I hoped that she watched me leave, but I didn't turn back and look, didn't want to be so obvious. It was enough of a triumph that I had her name in my keeping.

Of course it was months and months before Ryszard and
I returned to that village, and time moved along there as it did
wherever I drove. When I saw her again, it was like the very
first, save that I think her little teasing smile grew somewhat,
the amusement of my reappearance become larger for her, but
not so that her eyes would hold mine. Her shyness like a veil
never fell away.

And so over the next two years I must have returned
perhaps seven or eight times. I always went into the bakery,
whether Ryszard had anything to do there or not. In that space
of time she married someone and became pregnant with a
child. I'm sure I burned with jealousy when I discovered this,
cursing myself for having not spoken up. A ludicrous notion,
given our circumstances. Besides, nothing between us had
changed, and she glowed with happiness that time, and the
next, when the baby had come. I was happy for her but I
regretted not being its cause. By then Ryszard and I were
moving things other than furniture, and being paid more
money for the risk. The world, too, was moving in a certain
direction that was in keeping with our new cargo. I had enough
set aside now to return to medical school, but I'd fallen in love
with the danger of what we were doing just as I had fallen in
love with my fantastical notion of Lucyna. It comes as no
surprise to you that the world does not concern itself with such
private dreams.

Thus it was the last time I entered the shop, standing
there with my hand on a sticky sweet sekerpare I had just
purchased from her, that the world which had remained in
the background, only a vague insinuation of a threat, broke
loose.

The door to the shop opened and three soldiers entered.
All were armed and all held their weapons out. At us. They
were the new breed of soldiers coming out of the west, with
cybernetic interfaces in their helmets and cell receivers under
the skin of their heads, in constant contact with each other and

their superiors. I recognized the helmets they wore. I doubt anyone else in that shop would have seen one before, but Ryszard and I, we had carried such things as cargo and talked with a few people about such things. At that point, nobody yet understood what was happening. You would think I ought to have, but I had been safe for so long, for years, that it never occurred to me I might finally be snared. The soldiers asked the crowd who owned the van that had arrived in town, and who had taken delivery of its contents. Then I understood.

Lucyna looked at me that once—straight at me without shyness. This was, I thought, the thing she had seen before, that first time as she stared into the future. To the soldiers she said, "Everyone here is of the village." They seemed to believe her, but in the end it made little difference. Before the sun had set, two large cargo transports floated down out of the sky and everyone—every single man, woman, and child in that village—was herded into them. Houses stood with open doors, lights on, meals served or cooking. Probably fires would break out in some of the houses before morning, but we would never see them. I rode in the same transporter as Lucyna but half the village separated us, just like now. Ryszard hadn't escaped either, but he was in the second one. I didn't see him again until after we'd been released into the camps.

The enemy had come at last. The mountains, breeding ground for resistance, as Ryszard and I knew too well, were being systematically stripped of inhabitants. The presence of our van had been an excuse. The enemy would have rounded up everyone regardless, pulling the fangs of the resistance by eliminating any hope of a sustained network. "They won't get all of us," Ryszard whispered to me our first night in the camp. "There will be pockets of rebels they don't find—after all, they didn't find the guns we delivered, did they?" I didn't know if they had or not, but I wanted to believe him when he said that. The guns had gotten out of the village before the enemy had arrived. But mountains are like walls, and from those heights you cannot defend the cities in the valleys, on the plains. You can only remain in the mountains and hope the occupiers withdraw. Ryszard was no revolutionary. He was a man making money off them, and it was no different in the camps. He knew how to barter with the other prisoners, even with the soldiers, not all of whom were cruel, were villains. Some—the lowly ones who weren't considered worthy of the more advanced, expensive technology—understood that there was little separating us from them, that we could easily have traded uniforms and circumstances. They operated from fear. Those were the ones Ryszard approached. He had an unerring sense of who could be bought, and I, by association, benefited from his skill. Nevertheless, there was only one thing I wanted, one piece of information I needed to know, and that proved challenging. Ryszard told me, "You must assume she is alive in the women's camp. But we have to tread carefully in inquiring, because it requires ripples of influence well beyond our control. A lot of trust. That is going to take some time."

As it happened, I didn't have to wait. I saw her in the yard across the razor wire. She and three other prisoners were being led somewhere. They'd all been shorn the same as us, but that didn't matter, I could not help recognizing the shape of that face I adored, that I had closed my eyes and imagined on so many nights, alone, in an act of furious frenzy that accompanied something I meant to be tender. We are, all of us, animals lusting after grace.

She was too far away that time. If I'd called out her name she might have heard but I would have been taken away and beaten. For every guard who was decent to us, there were five more who came to torture like wolves to a feeding ground. Ryszard was the one who told me about the stories—the stories of what happened on the women's side of the wire. Some of it was happening on our side as well. There were guards who preferred men or boys. Most of them found their pleasure on the other side. Since he'd protected me, I asked if there was

anything Ryszard could do to protect Lucyna. "Impossible," he
said. "We don't know where she is there. All you would do is
draw attention to her, and the rutting jackals would wonder
why, and they would notice her. And fucking's not a thing you
can influence that way. They'll take your contraband and then
go ahead and have their sport. What would you do about it?
Not a thing."

It was six months then before I saw her close up.
Christmas. We had spent the cold and rainy fall and winter
building housing for more prisoners, for more guards and
administrators. Word of the larger war leaked to us, of course.
We heard that a coalition of enemy nations had turned on us,
and while others had condemned the annexation of our
country, a slaughter that was being called genocide was taking
place and nobody was attempting to stop it. We heard that
there was resistance in the mountains that had swept down
into the cities, but could not hope to do more without outside
aid, and the world was holding its breath, as if hoping the
slaughter would simply stop, the enemy come to their senses
and withdraw. "The world," Ryszard said to me, "is collectively
an organization of cowards who speak in lofty phrases until
action is required, and then who withdraw into the shadows,
pretending that statements of condemnation should be enough.
The cowards never act unless there's a profit to be made in
intervention; then they are more than willing to send others to
their deaths while they and their friends grow rich. Look at
me, after all. I profited. So did you. Did you care for causes?
No, you wished to make enough money for you. It's the same
the world over. Whoever says otherwise, he's a liar and
probably already profiting handsomely."

A few months after we'd been brought here, there was
an attempted escape. We in our building—one of eight on our
side of the wire—knew nothing about it. The escapees had
wisely concluded that they should tell no one, and even so they
were, most of them, captured. Rumors claimed that three men

had succeeded in escaping. If so, their freedom came at a very high price, because the dozen who'd been caught were summarily executed the following day. We were herded out and ordered to watch, but we were segregated so that we could not speak with their comrades, the ones from their building. I happened to look back and saw that the women had been marched up to the wire to see, too. I scanned them for Lucyna but couldn't find her. The line of women stretched the length of the wire, though, and I couldn't see most of them. There were screams of protest and despair from some of them as they recognized the naked men who were to be shot. One woman leapt onto the wire, which only sliced her savagely before others dragged her off, but it wasn't Lucyna.

Other men from that building were assigned the task of carrying their friends' corpses out of the compound to the pits. The rest of us were led back to whatever jobs we were supposed to be doing, and life went on as if nothing unusual had occurred. We continued building new prefabricated facilities for our captors. It was a walled palace we were erecting. They were planning to stay a good long time.

Fall rotted into winter. More of us died from cold and hunger. Some took their own lives. So far as I knew, nobody else attempted to escape.

For Christmas our captors rewarded us by opening the gates between our side and the women. After half a year of isolation from them, we were allowed to mingle for a few hours. Husbands sought their wives, sons their mothers, daughters their fathers. I looked for Lucyna. I had no illusions. I knew she had a husband, a child. I wouldn't be the party she sought and more than likely I would be forced to observe the affection I wanted and couldn't have. Instead, when I found her, she was alone. No husband, no child. She was thin, her eyes darkly ringed. Cautiously, I approached. She didn't look up from that same distant gaze. Now it looked farther into the future than ever, to the end of her life and beyond.

Another woman saw me standing there, unable to make myself approach but unable to back away, and she came up. "Do you know her?" she asked me. I told her that I did, that I knew her from the bakery in her village. The woman asked my name and I gave it. She walked up to Lucyna and said that I was here to see her. The fog seemed to clear a bit from her eyes then. She looked my way but there was little recognition. Maybe none at all. It might have been nothing but my hope of recognition. And so I stepped forward and said, "I wished to buy a loaf of bread from you." Her eyes welled with tears then, and her chin quivered, and she threw her arms around me. I held her. For minutes, hours, it could have been forever. We all stank like rotting meat, even though we had been allowed showers earlier, but not our clothes of course. I reveled in her closeness, my face to her neck, seeking the smell of her underneath that stink. She cried and cried. She muttered names—again and again she said, "Janek." She never said mine, not knowing it, nor asked it of me. She started to kiss me, kissed my mouth, my face, all the while saying, "Janek, my darling, my love, Janek." While she clung to me, the other woman said, "He was executed that day—you remember that escape attempt. Did you know him?"

I said, no, we were housed separately. Different parts of the camp.

Her baby hadn't lived through the first month. Likely, her husband didn't know. He also didn't know how she had been used by the guards, either. They liked her looks, her breasts swollen with milk. She'd gone mad long ago. She was kissing her husband, not me. I wasn't even there. Yet I accepted my role, because she was looking steadily in my eyes with all the love, the passion I had only imagined.

Finally we were ordered back to our separate sides. Lucyna began to wail, and I held her face in my hands and said, "No, no, stop now. We'll be together again. I'll come back. Live for me, please, and I'll live for you. I promise I'll come back."

She did then. She swore, promised. If she had any inkling I was not Janek, she gave not a single outward sign, and I suspect she didn't know. She had seen a familiar face and it had replaced his in her shattered mind.

I walked away backwards, watching her as long as I could. Ryszard caught up with me. "So, did you find your woman? Did she remember you?"

"I found her," I answered.

He patted me on the shoulder. "I found out that we're going to leave here," he said.

"What?"

"After the New Year. Their palatial embassy is almost complete and we're going to leave. I had to bribe a few guards to get the information."

"What about them? The women?"

"I would think they'll be going, too. All of us together."

All of us together. Such a hopeful phrase.

It was all of us together two weeks later as we filthy men marched across the yard to the communal shower once more. We saw three bulbous transports settling onto the field outside the wire as we walked. Come to take us away, I recall thinking. They're going to let us leave after all. Inside again, we stripped down and waited for the water that never came. A moment of panic, terror, the realization that you're in a sealed room, a vault. And then it was over, so quickly that I don't know what it was. Electricity, gas, something we had never heard of. There was no smell, no warning. Dead in an instant. All of us together.

The transports brought new workers, their people this time rather than ours. We had built their massive embassy complex and now the workers had come to inhabit the complex. Like those who had built the pyramids for the Egyptians long ago, we'd finished our task.

One small cadre of prisoners remained, who would act as servants to their new masters as soon as they had completed just one distasteful act. They carried us naked from the sealed

room and tossed us in the dirt. Then earth moving equipment
with scoops pushed the piles of us into the pits. The women . . .
the same thing had happened to them. Ryszard vanished in the
tumble, crushed far below me. I fell near the top, as did
Lucyna. She's there, canted on her side across from me now,
with that one naked foot of hers protruding from between the
other bodies, as if she's Cinderella and I'm about to fit the
slipper upon her. Of course it will fit. Her golden skin is dusted
with the first sprinkle of lime. Any second now she's going to
turn those beautiful, distant, half-lidded eyes my way, and I'll
hold her gaze as darkness rains upon us, and I'll calm her,
saying "See, my darling, I lived for you."

EYES OF CARVEN EMERALD

Shweta Narayan

S unrise glinted bloody on giant tumbles of statue; it edged
the palace beyond with blood.

A limestone arm, severed elbow to thumb, came almost
up to Alexandros' waist. Fingers thick as logs lay scattered
behind it. Sunrise glimmered in the statue's blank, rain-filled
eyes and trickled down the pitted stone cheek. So too would
Dareios of Persia have fallen, had the coward not fled.

But the statue had been a symbol of Persia's might; it
could serve Alexandros' purpose well enough. "Leave it," he
said, turning away. To his general Kleitos' raised eyebrows he
added, "They will see our victory in it."

"But . . . " Kleitos shook his head. "Basileu, it had
nothing to do with our victory. We simply outnumbered—"

"It trembled in fear of our coming, and fell at the taste
of defeat."

"It did?"

"They will see it so." As they saw him, more clearly with
every city he took, as unstoppable. With Egypt, with all the

length of Persia's royal road, and now even Persepolis in
Alexandros' power, Dareios knew he fought a losing war, and
his knowing made it so.

Which was as it should be. And yet . . .

"As you say." Kleitos' voice held little understanding
and less curiosity; like most of the men, he fought only for land.
Alexandros bit back irritation and wished once more that he
had Hephaistion at his side. At his side, on the field, in his bed;
but his reasons were the same ones that had sent Hephaistion,
not Kleitos, back to Babylon to quell an uprising.

He said, "Call it a reminder."

"And of course they will need that reminder, Basileu,"
said a woman's voice, "because you and your restless army will
move on."

He spun, hand going to his sword; felt Kleitos brush by.
A piece of the statue's crown shifted. It spread wings and
hopped with a whirr of gears onto the nose. Its feathers were
tarnished bronze, blurred with age, and it had human hands
instead of claws. Not sharp. Little chance they would be
poisoned. Keeping an eye on the beak for darts, Alexandros
said, "Of course. Persepolis could not hold me, not with half the
world yet to see."

"And conquer."

He lifted a shoulder, not bothering to respond to the
obvious. "Do Persian automata generally speak to kings
without offering so much as a name?"

"I wouldn't know," said the bird. "Those creaking
parodies aren't worth my words."

Alexandros' eyes narrowed with the first glimmerings
of interest. What might this mechanism be, if not Persian?
Surely not Northern barbarian work; it was too fine, though
it wore around its neck a ring of shining gold, as they did. It
looked old, but shifted without noise or stiffness. And it spoke
Greek like a Persian; badly, but with meaning beneath the
words.

And that last mystery implied a challenge worth taking. Alexandros said, "To whom do you belong? A king who is long dead, it would seem, or else one who neglects you."

The bird rustled its feathers. "The last king who tried to own me died of slow poison while his city burned."

"A queen, then."

A rapid, ratcheting click, and the wings rose. Kleitos stepped in front of Alexandros, arm up. Alexandros put his own hand on the arm and said, "Do you mean me harm, bird?"

"Not yet, King of Asia." The wings came slowly down. "But keep trying to weight me down with an owner, and I might. I had heard the Greeks were barely civilized, but I had expected better from a student of Aristoteles."

"And not from a son of Zeus-Amun?" said Alexandros around a surge of anger. To dismiss one the Oracle had named half-divine as a mere student—

The bird laughed, a strangely human sound. Womanly.

Well, and if she wanted Alexandros rash in anger, he would not be. He nudged Kleitos aside and drifted close enough to inspect her, his hand a deliberate three fingers from his sword. At Kleitos' wordless protest he said, "She said she meant me no harm, old friend, and telling a lie in Persepolis is suicide." The sun warmed the back of his neck. If the bird was indeed reckless enough to have lied, it would glare in her eyes.

She met his gaze without fear, though there was not a weapon to be seen on her. Nor was she a bribe, with so sour a tongue, and she had yet to convey a message or say who sent her. A scout, then, albeit an ill-mannered one. "Now where," Alexandros said soft-voiced, "do they say Macedon lacks civilization? I have conquered half the world and never heard of such a people."

Kleitos' breath caught at his tone. Alexandros started to smile.

"Were you to follow the sun," said the bird, "you might find them. But I would not advise you to try."

East. The edge of the known world. And—"East. Where your cur of a king ran, leaving his womenfolk behind."

Though in that, Dareios could hardly have been more useful to Alexandros. His mother Sisygambis had met abandonment with cold fury; her nature was not forgiving. She had allied with Alexandros against her traitor son, and the information she now sent him was timely and precise.

With a click of gears, the bird tilted her head arrogantly up. "No king of *mine,*" she said.

"A wise choice." She was a pretty thing, even tarnished. On what board might so valuable a piece be placed so deep in enemy territory? How large a game was Alexandros being challenged to—and how far into lands half-imagined did it stretch? He took a breath, tasted for the first time the new-washed air, the honey hint of something more than tedious, played-out endings. "What are you called, bird who belongs to nobody and claims nobody?"

She tilted her head. Sunlight ran liquid down her neck. "I have borne different names," she said, "in different lands and times. Most recently I am called *Vaacha Devi.* The voice."

"What is it you give voice to?"

"Tales, Basileu. I weave stories."

Once, long ago, before the time of the first Darayu, before even the time of Kurush, before empire claimed these lands, there lived a prince not so much younger than yourself.

This prince's father had conquered vast territories, and in his endless war he won a city in the hills made of alabaster filigree and blown glass, of gemstones and spinning gears, a city of artisans and merchants and artificers. And the people of this city were made of beaten bronze and copper springs, as I myself am made.

Now the prince's father did not stay in his alabaster city, for he was too busy fighting over new lands to enjoy the ones he had, but the prince lived there with his mother. He befriended the only son of the city's richest jeweller. They were tutored together; they fell together into mischief; and when they were older they travelled together, bronze boy and flesh.

They snuck out one summer day to ride across the land. But they were very young men, and raised with servants; they did not think to check how tightly their horses had been wound. So it was that they ground to a wobbly stop in the middle of an arid plain, forced to wind springs under the glaring sun. The horses stood with legs splayed and heads down, skin pinging with the heat that poured from them. The prince had to wrap his key in saddlecloth not to be burned. And by the time the horses were well again his friend had run down, heartspring nearly undone, and the prince had to wind him up too.

All this left the young prince hotter and thirstier than he ever had been in his life, and when he saw the smoke of a village, he whistled his horse to a gallop and left his friend far behind.

At the village well, he found a mechanical girl of surpassing beauty. She wore a frock of sackcloth and went barefoot, but her legs were shapely, her movement graceful, her body adorned with a winding, green-enamelled snake. Her eyes when she turned to look at him were blown glass clear as the desert air.

"Water," croaked the prince. The girl tossed a bucket into the well and drew it up with ease. Then she looked thoughtfully at him, smiled, and poured water from the bucket into an amphora.

But when the prince reached for the amphora, the girl pulled it away, laughed, and poured the water back into the bucket. Again the prince reached. Again the girl poured water from one vessel into another, and again, making him watch its crystal stream and listen to its cool music. Only when his friend drew near did she hold the amphora up. "Now," she said, "you may have it."

"Why now?" the prince demanded, though it was a whisper through his parched throat. "When I have been thirsty all this time?"

"You were overheated," said the girl, "and the water icy. Such opposites make humans ill."

He drank. It was sweet and fresh and still so cold it sent jolts of stabbing pain into his forehead. And in the girl's beauty and her cleverness, and the rushing joy of water after too great a thirst, he fell in love. "Tell me your name," he begged. "Tell me why you live here, when you would bring grace and beauty even to the city of golden clockwork and alabaster light."

"My name is Anaeet," she said, returning to the well to draw more water. "As for why I am here, I am enslaved to the headman of this village."

The prince slid down from his horse. "I will free you," he said. He took her hands in his, but she would not let go of the bucket's rope. "I will marry you."

She said, "What is your trade?"

For a moment he stood stunned. Then he laughed. "Am I so covered in dust as to seem a tradesman? I am the prince of this land. My father is lord over everything you see, from the greatest house to the lightest feather. Why should I have a trade?"

He laughed again, but she only shook her head. "When your father's men came through these lands, prince," she said, "they kept only the tradesmen and dismantled everybody else. I remember it still. I shall not wed a man without a trade."

Persepolis sat quiet, its daily work muted. Behind the fallen statue, palace walls glowed bright as alabaster in the red-gold light. Alexandros cleared his throat. "Hardly a prince worth the name," he said, "if he thought he loved a village automaton."

"Nevertheless," the bird replied, "he did. But if the story is not to your taste, Basileu, I do not need to tell it."

So lightly did she shrink the world to dullness. And no hint yet of who she came from, or why. Alexandros hesitated, glanced back toward his camp. He turned back. "Tell it quickly," he said. "There is work waiting. A true king hasn't time to learn a common trade."

She flitted from the dead king's nose to his sheared-off knee, above their heads. "As the statue fell without you, King of Asia," she said, "so too does a story go at its own pace and not yours. If you haven't the patience to hear it, someone else will."

"Are you *asking* to be caged?"

She looked down her beak at him, wordless, then took to the air. Kleitos pulled a knife and aimed in one smooth motion; and indeed she was an easy target, bright-edged in the sun. Too easy. Alexandros put out a hand again to stop the throw. "No," he said. "I would not simply destroy a wonder."

"It's an automaton."

"There's a mind there." That itself was a marvel. Whose? "And one behind that, guiding her moves. I made one bad throw, yes; I shall not make another."

"Another?"

"She'll be back." His hand still lay on Kleitos' arm; he turned the gesture into a caress, eyes on the bird as she shrank to a gleam. "I wonder how she works," he said.

He had darker questions that night, when fire broke out in the palace and grew to paint half Persepolis in deadly light. *The last king who tried to own me . . .* He pushed through men scurrying like ants with buckets and blankets, reached the statue, and climbed onto its arm. Tilting his head up to watch smoke eat the stars, he said, "Your point is made, bird." He fingered the charm at the nape of his neck. "But poison will not touch *me,* and the stories that spread from this night will not hurt my name."

Scant days later, he marched on.

* * *

The Phoinikes dare any siege to break the island of Tura, whose walls rise, impregnable, from the ocean itself. No ship can break down those walls, and no men can land. The island's men mock Macedon.

"They say we cannot take them by sea?" asks Alexandros, soft-voiced. "Well enough; I say we have no need to." He gestures around at the smoking ruins of Tura's mainland sister. "We have stone, do we not? Build me a causeway."

Remembering, he smiles. His challenger may seek mystery, may not choose to reveal himself, but he has already revealed arrogance. He will have blind spots, as they all do, and blind spots stand unprotected.

He next saw her in the middle of a dusty road, perched over a body in a broken ox cart. She was a point of brightness in the grey day, her tarnished wings replaced with feathers of polished and graven copper.

The body was that of Dareios.

Alexandros said sharply, "Did you kill him?"

"No," said the bird. "Did you want me to?"

"I might have taken his surrender." A meager victory, this, and ashen. Dareios. Dead. By another's hand. "His mother—" he had another missive from Sisygambis, received just the previous day— "His mother was owed, is owed, an explanation. His daughters will want to know."

Stateira would want to know. He raised a hand to the base of his scalp, to the spell woven of her hair and braided into his, waiting to quench poison and turn away the sword. More a sign of Sisygambis' ambition than of the girl's fondness for Alexandros, surely, but the token reassured. And he could not deny that Dareios' daughter might make a useful wife for Dareios' successor.

If that was all he meant to be.

The bird said, "For his mother, then—his kinsman killed him, and now lays claim to the name of Artaxerxes. Will she mourn, do you think?"

Ha. *The only son I have is Alexandros,* she had written. *Persia misses him, and I will find joy only when he comes home.* He said merely, "I will tell her."

"And will you turn back now, with Darayu dead and your vengeance fulfilled?"

Alexandros smiled grimly. "This Artaxerxes displeases me. And there are lands yet to claim."

"But how much more will you take, whose empire borders five oceans?"

"A sixth." His smile grew a touch. "To the east and the south, past the river called Indos." It lay as far from Persepolis as Persepolis did from Macedon, but he had come that distance once and could cover it once more. "The land bordering that sea is a rich one; they trade gemstones and silk and cinnamon. Their warriors ride elephants, and their defeat could bring glory even to the king of Asia." Such a land, unknown, unseen, might hold even a city of alabaster and blown glass . . . "I will own it, and I will ride it down to fabled Khaberis itself."

When the bird did not reply, Alexandros said, "I hear the Eastern mountains are home to children of Typhon who live in lakes and bring storms, who fly without wings, whose wisdom challenges the gods."

"Oh yes," said the bird. "They are called *Zhug*. But an army would never see one, only the ice storm sweeping down to blot out their final sunset." She raised wings of molten fire, hesitated. "But I had been telling you a story," she added slowly, lowering her wings. "Would you hear the rest?"

"I could listen for a time," said Alexandros, "if you will ride with me."

* * *

The prince returned home that day thinking so hard that
he barely noticed frightened servants scolding over
stolen horses. The next morning, when sunlight spilled over
the alabaster city and its clocktower cockerels crowed
harmonies, he went with but one slave to his friend's father,
the jeweller. And he said, "I would learn to cut gems so that
stars wake inside them, and set them in beaten gold to dazzle
every eye."

He was a diligent student, at his studies by dawn so he
might return to his duties by noon. And so he came quietly into
a trade. He made rings and armbands and jewel-studded shoes,
and discovered a genius for fine detail. He made glittering
planets the size of pomegranate seeds, their metal entirely
covered in a dusting of stones. He engraved a golden sun no
bigger than the tip of his thumb, and he helped his master set
them all into a miniature orrery. And he watched, amazed, as
it turned with astrological precision.

For his masterwork he made a bracelet set with a tiny
clock. A green snake circled the face; its head, marking noon,
was a diamond clear as Anaeet's eyes.

Oh, I remember your complaint. She was a mere
automaton. But he wanted to impress her, so back he went to
the little village across a barren plain. "I have a trade now," he
told her proudly.

She took the bracelet from him and turned it over and
over. She examined its hinge and clasp, and checked the clock
against the sun. Slowly, she wound it up. "Yes," she said to its
regular tick. "It seems you have a trade."

He said, "So when next the stars bring fortune, we shall
be wed."

The ceremony was grand, for she was his first wife, and
a sign moreover of the new peace between human and
mechanical. And she was lovely. When she rode into the city
over flower-strewn streets on a silver-plated horse, her prince
was not the only young man to stare.

Now, Anaeet had been a scholar of law before her slavery, so the prince started giving her documents of taxes and properties and inheritance. He sat nearby while she studied them, sketching, or sorting gems, or twisting wires of gold into filigree, and later she would tell him what he needed to know. Soon she was ruling beside him. The mechanicals adored her, for they now could gain fair trials without bribing the jeweller or his son; and for her reason and forethought the humans came to respect her word. And every night, with loving hands, the prince wound her heartspring tight.

When they had been married a year he added a sun-room to his palace, and set thin slices of mica into the cross-hatched roof. They took to holding court there, hearing their people's quarrels and complaints amidst slanting diamonds of light—and so they could have lived for many years. But the army returned, bearing news. The king had died in a distant land.

The general who brought these tidings was loyal to the old king, but he hated the thought that his men should fall into the hands of an unblooded boy. It mattered little to him that the new king was an able administrator who would bring justice to the land and care for the ragged, exhausted troops; the general's only trade was war, and the young king was no warrior. Worse —he had married one of the conquered, foreign mechanicals.

So when the new king and queen came out from the city to greet the troops, the general drew his sword on them.

And although the king had been raised among mechanicals, travelled with one, learned from one, and taken one to wife, he learned something new about them then. There was a whirr, a clang, a snap. Before the king could so much as flinch, the general was dead at Anaeet's feet. She bent over him, clutching her left arm; it bore a deep groove, seeping oil where the sword had split skin. And shards of glass from her shattered left eye glinted on the road like tiny diamonds.

The general's second fell to his knees. He offered his life for this treason, asking only that the men might be spared; in

response, the king set him in command. Then he ordered the
people of the city to care for the soldiers, and he took his queen
home to mend.

They called in a master smith to hammer the dent from
her arm and a master artificer to check her gears and springs
and make sure all was still in order. The king made new eyes for
her himself, grinding the lenses from two flawless emeralds,
perfectly matched to the snake coiled across her skin.

New-burnished, with eyes of polished stone, Anaeet was
more beautiful than ever. The court whispered about how lucky
she was to be so loved.

But have you ever looked through green lenses at
everything, King of Asia? They were fine, surely, but she might
have preferred glass; and the king never thought to ask.

A lexandros next saw the automaton a year and more later,
in a tower in Marakanda. He climbed while the world
slept, wrapped against the wind in a chlamys cloak and the
warm haze of wine, to find a bird-shaped hole cut into the
star-spattered night. She sat on a parapet, and the sliver of
moon behind her served only to darken her shadow.

He said, "I thought your cursed story was done."

She clicked her beak. "You of all people," she said,
"should know that stories do not end when a prince becomes
king."

"They merely go badly."

"So do they go badly for any of us if we choose to kill our
friends." A pause. "You're drunk beyond reason."

He put fists to his eyes. "I am drunk." Which made it
easier not to think. But harder not to talk. "I am never beyond
reason, though I grant the wine loosened my hand."

Silence.

"It was the wine loosed his tongue, too, but—how could
he think—he said I plotted to send him to an honorless death,
to lead all my Greek soldiers into a trap, to better be Persian

myself. Where did he hear such tales? Who did he tell them to in turn? If I wear Persian tunics under my cloak, do I not still speak Greek?" And why, after all, should Alexandros be merely one or the other?

"Hard to say what he thought," said the bird, "since you killed him."

"And not even the son of Zeus-Amun can bring him back to life." The words shredded his throat. Kleitos had been a loyal general till that quarrel, and almost as fine a lover as Hephaistion. If only Alexandros had more wine.

She said, "I am sorry for your—pain—but he is not the last of Greece that you stand to lose. Why will you not go home, Basileu?"

"Because I have not finished, bird." An echo of the words he had written to Sisygambis.

Feathers rattled irritably. "I am called Vaacha Devi."

"Yes, yes. I am so close to claiming that sixth ocean. It has jungles, they say, where you could walk from one tree to the next for ten days without ever catching sight of the ground."

"They say true."

"Then it will be worth it." To have a world larger than the limits of Kleitos' mind.

"But do they also say," the bird continued, "that the jungle goddess' tigers will hunt men who desecrate her land, and her swamp demons swarm up from the fetid water, so that days before you might see ground your army will be shrunk to a sad handful of men puking their stomachs out? For that too is true."

Alexandros turned away. "I prefer your story of the king and his mechanical queen."

Gears whirred. "They ruled for many years," said the bird. "From home." And she would say no more.

He saw her next in a town newly named Alexandria, in pouring rain that churned the streets to mud, perched on a huge statue of the long-eared sage the locals called Gautama. "In your story," he said, "did they kiss the king's hand?"

Her new-made, enameled tail shivered in distaste; the sound blended with the ping of raindrops off her skin. She said, "Such things humans do. Yes, it has been the tradition in Persia for a very long time."

"My generals don't like it either." Nor the men, whose eyes still reflected Kleitos' death. Alexandros glared over his shoulder at her, chin up. "But why should I not take Persian traditions? I am King of Persia."

"And Persia misses you."

He stilled, eyes narrowing, while rain stuck hair to his face and trickled down his back. That choice of words. Only one other had used them. He said, "And in all of Persia, did I ever find your home?"

"You did not."

"No. I would have known it." He looked into Gautama's calm smile. "Your king with the mechanical—he is not the only one whose own men tried to kill him."

"And it would be a pity if they succeeded," she said. "So take them home."

"Yes," he said slowly. Even the more loyal men looked to him with more appeal than ambition now. They were weary, cold, and ragged. "Yes, Vaacha Devi. Tell Sisygambis that I might."

He smiled a little, bitterly, at her surprise. The challenge had been petty after all; the win was worthless, and the wonders merely tales. And he was held back, yet again, by the limitations of those smaller than him.

Everyone knows of the ox cart that stands in Gordion's old palace. Everyone knows that the knot fastening it to its post cannot be undone.

Alexandros proves them wrong.

He has cause to pride himself on seeing what is there, not merely what is wanted. Wishing the world to be vast does not make it so. Wanting men to be brave and mothers to be patient does not make them so.

Perhaps Arabia will have marvels, if the East does not.

But a year later, over a smoky campfire, Alexandros had a new wife, a new battle, and a new will to press on. He might lack fond dreams of marvels, but Raja Porus was a foe worth meeting—and Rokhshna, who traveled with him as fearless as any warrior—a bride worth impressing. And every new day told Sisygambis who decided Alexandros' course—and who did not. Her missives were growing satisfyingly plaintive.

"Did you not suggest," Alexandros asked the bird, "that a king might like a clever wife?" He smiled like a petted cat. "You were right. I do. But you, of course, were thinking of Sisygambis' granddaughter when you said it."

The bird stammered in dismay, feathers clattering. She looked at Rokhshna through one eye, then another. And Rokhshna looked back with cool enmity.

Now, the young king found himself to be protector of vast lands. Many of them remembered a time before his father, and none welcomed a mechanical queen. In the first few years of his reign he put down rebellion in a land of ice and granite, rooted out banditry in a fever-ridden swamp, and fought a hard, heartbreaking battle with his own mutinous navy. But he married a girl from the land of ice and a girl from the swamps, and after some time and some children the lands quieted. And Anaeet still ruled at his side.

But one crystalline winter's day when the sun peeped pale and hesitant as a new bride over the alabaster roofs, he received word that one of his satraps, the ice girl's father, had gone missing in the mountains. And though his whole city searched, nobody found so much as a footprint.

Being young, with a thirst for adventure still un-
quenched, the king decided to find his vassal himself. He left
Anaeet to rule in his stead and his other wives in her care, and
took only his mechanical friend the gemcutter with him. This
time they rode horses of flesh and carried feed enough to last
them. They disguised themselves as wealthy tradesmen, with
tasseled blankets on the horses and fine jewelry in a box of
carven sandalwood.

Towards the sun they rode, over the desert and past
Anaeet's village, into mountains that rose like black talons
scratching at the snow-stuffed sky. And in every village they
came to, huddled between rock face and cliff, the friends
offered bracelets and jeweled pins for sale. The villagers could
not buy such wares, of course, but the king intended only for
word of them to spread. He reasoned that no ruler disappeared
by accident; greed and lust for power must be behind it. So he
called out to greed. And while he called, he listened for tidings
of his satrap.

The friends came finally to a town whose people spoke
of a noble hunting party, all grand in bronze and bearhide, that
had passed through one day and never returned. The king
chose to stay and learn more. And while he stayed two nobles
approached him and said, "We hear that you and your
mechanical are gemcutters."

"We are," the king agreed.

"We have found a cave full of gold and jewels," said one
noble, "and have hired a dozen village boys to help us transport
them, six human and six mechanical. But we would pay you well
to come with us and tell us which pieces are worth the most."

"We shall join you gladly," said the king, though joy was
far from his heart.

He followed the nobles quietly, with his friend and a
dozen villagers, to a cave set far into the mountains. Its mouth
glittered with icicle teeth, and ice rimed the walls. The path
was wide, but it sloped steeply downwards, and the ground

underfoot was slick and studded with gravel that broke free and rolled, echoing, into the black distance. The king had to walk with his head bowed, as he never had before, to keep it safe from low-hanging rocks.

So he did not see the two nobles step each one to a side into alcoves, and he took a step further. His feet met empty air. He fell, how far he did not know, and the other men tumbled after him. He came quickly to his feet; but the walls were sheer and icy, and the hole too far above.

Some men had been carrying torches, and in their fallen light he could make out huge cauldrons bubbling to each side. He peered into one; in it, gears and rods and mysterious pieces of shaped bronze bubbled in acid that scoured them clean.

He crossed over to the other side, and a wet carrion stench hit him. He gagged, but looked closer.

A hand rose to the bloody, bubbling surface, and seemed to reach for the king before sinking again into a mess of cooking guts. Then, in the slow churning of the cauldron, came the severed, staring head of the king's missing satrap.

"Enough," Rokhshna said. "This tale disgusts. Have done." Her face held no fear, but her voice was high and the words too fast.

Alexandros draped the corner of his chlamys over her shoulder. It offered scant warmth, though its embroidered hem glowed in the firelight, but she calmed under it. He said, "You have changed its nature greatly. To upset us? We march on no matter what you say."

"The story goes as it goes," the bird replied. "I merely tell it."

"Oh, surely," said Rokhshna. "And of course I am not meant to be the princess of ice, and the dead man not my father?"

Alexandros said, "If this is Sisygambis' way to lure me back, tell her I find it clumsy."

"I told you once that I serve nobody." The fickle light turned the bird into a gaudy toy, showed her indignation faintly ridiculous. "I will own that she and I share a goal, but—"

"Then in kindness to her I tell you only this: Begone."

"If you will not hear this voice, she is already gone." The bird spread her wings. An eye of new enamel stared at Alexandros from every feather's tip, liquid black against the copper. In each one danced a miniature fire. "But . . . " Her voice spoke regret. "You will not turn back from your folly, Basileu, though you sully the holy river Ganga herself?"

Alexandros' smile was cold as ice and dark as the belly of a cave. "A river," he said, "is only a river."

He founded a new town on the Hypasis, another Alexandria. But by the third day of its building he started to hear mutters and see the sidelong looks.

He called Hephaistion to his side. It was Koinos who came. Hephaistion was away again, as he was too often since Alexandros had married. "Tell me," Alexandros said, more abruptly than he meant to. "What is it they say to one another?"

"They say you want them to ford the Ganges next," said Koinos.

"So I do." He glowered at the rising sun. "What of it?"

"They say the Ganges is wider than even the Nile," Koinos said. "They say it runs so deep that a hundred men can drown, one on top of another, and never be found. They say it runs frothy brown at strange times, churned by the hooves of river horses that will strike us down with their hooves."

"Where do they hear such tales?" Alexandros demanded, turning on the older man. "It is a river. No more. And beyond these hills, over that river, the lands are ripe with game and fruit." And, rumor said, mechanical creatures as clever as the bird.

"Perhaps," said Koinos. "But those lands are ruled by the Gangaritai and the Praisioi. And the men have heard that their forces are allied against you, that the far side of the great river is lined with waiting horsemen and catapults and thousands of elephants, an army so large that an eagle in flight could not see both ends of it at once. They say one elephant in ten is an automaton, and that their trunks spew acid. They say there are pneumatic bows that fire a dozen dozen arrows at a time, their strings pulled so tight that they shoot right across the river. They say—"

"Where," Alexandros said again, "do they get these tales?" But even as he spoke, he knew.

Koinos reached out, appealing. "They believe them, Basileu. They are tired, and ill, and that breeds fear. They left so many brothers on the field when we fought Porus, and even Porus fears the Gangaritai. You may order them to march on, but you would be wiser not to, for the Greeks remember Kleitos and they will not go."

Alexandros said, "They will do as I tell them."

They did not. Mutters rose instead to shouts, and shouts to the clash of bronze on bronze. By the day's end, a hundred men lay dead and twice that many dying. With them lay three of the Macedon generals. Only two had fought for Alexandros.

Sisygambis had not played this move. She wanted him back. She did not want his vengeance, and she was not one to lose by winning.

If she was not the player now, had she ever been?

When Koinos came again to beg Alexandros to turn back, he paid more heed.

He walked alone again that night. The muddy streets had iced over. They crunched as he walked, and the stars shone bright as little suns, distant as the far side of the Ganges. Though he shivered, he let his chlamys cloak stream proudly out to show the embroidered tunic underneath. Faint on the wind came the moan of injured men.

At the end of town he called, softly. "Come out, bird. I know that you are here."

Silence. After a time, he added, "Vaacha Devi. My wife is safe abed. Come out."

Her voice came from shadow. "How did you know to find me?"

"Rokhshna is wary. You always appear in the wake of Sisygambis' missives. And your stories sent men of mine to their deaths today."

Silence again. Alexandros sighed and sat on a low wall. He grew tired sometimes, these days. Finally, finally he saw the picture correctly, and he could not even summon rage. "So," he said. "My men will go no further. Which is what you have worked for all along, isn't it."

Why hate her for his mistake? He had misread a player for a piece. Seen a smaller board than was offered after all. And been bested. "Though by the gods," he said bitterly, "I would know why."

Gears played a complex rhythm of quiet clicks. A wingbeat, two, and the bird landed delicately next to him. "No secret now," she said. "Sisygambis wants you back; I merely wanted . . . *want* you gone. The land beyond the Ganga, which you think of as a jewel to snatch, which you would paint bloody, and trample the rice and silence the smithies and taint the art with your notion of culture, that land is my home. And some of the Magadha mechanicals, your Gangaritai, are my kin."

Ah. Was there even a real army awaiting them? Bile rose at the thought that he would never know. He said, "Why not tell my men your tales earlier?"

"And risk an uprising that killed you?" The bird preened and spread her starlit feathers. "A ruby glittering in the pile of gravel that is humanity? I would not simply destroy a wonder."

"You might have."

"You came too close to my land."

Her land it might be, but her new feathers, the enamel work—their elegance was that of Persia. He said, "Though Sisygambis *was* your patron, and she wants me alive. Were you trying to marry me to the granddaughter, too? Will you tell me she is cleverer than Rokhshna?"

"Human marriages mean little to my kind," she said, "though tales of them intrigue. They sound messy."

Anger flared. He would have truth, at least, if it could be wrung from a mechanical. He grabbed for the bird's neck.

There was a whirr, a blur, a snap; then she was out of reach, and blood welled between his thumb and fingers, black in the starlight. "A ruby indeed," she said, a tremor in her voice. "I cannot fault you for trying."

Alexandros wrapped his throbbing hand in a corner of his chlamys cloak.

After a moment the bird said, "As to the girl—Rokhshna is the politician of the two, but you know Stateira's cleverness. And I wonder which you trust, when you talk behind the back of one and wear the charm the other made you."

His hurt hand twitched toward the charm. How did she know of that? She saw more clearly than even Hephaistion had. "*Is* she a wise woman?" he said. "Does it work?" Certainly poison had not touched him yet, and his wounds had never festered.

"Do I look like a magician? If it doesn't, you will doubtless find out."

Wind rustled in a pine tree, brought the scent of coming snow. A smell that was the same the world over. But the drooping, dancing branches of this Eastern pine were like nothing in Macedon, and under them gleamed rows of round puddles: elephants' footprints full of ice. Alexandros said, "Then we have nothing left to speak of." Odd, how that made it a little harder to breathe.

In denying him the rest of the world, she had shown him that it had been worth the attempt.

She looked at him through one eye, then the other, then said softly, "Unless . . . you wish to know what happened to that young king we left trapped inside a cave."

Ice was melting under Alexandros, biting into his fingers and seeping through the chlamys to chill his legs. He needed to plan his return—surely it would not be a retreat—home. And Rokhshna hated waking to find him gone.

Watching the foreign pine, he started to smile. "Yes," he said. "Yes, I would hear that, if you will tell it."

The king called up, "What place is this?"

"Your new home," one of the nobles said, "where you will make us jewelry enough to buy this satrapy. If you walk a little way down this tunnel you will find a workshop with a fire pit, and gold and gems enough to start your work."

The king glanced once more at his wife's dead father. "And the cauldrons?"

"You and your mechanical have nothing to fear in them, gemcutter," the other noble said. "They were men without a trade, worth only their parts and the tallow from their fat, which will light your work."

At this some of the villagers drew together and looked fearfully up. But the king said, "You must know a great deal about gemcutting, honored sirs. Most men of your class would have no idea that my mechanical and I have need of six helpers each."

Now in fact the nobles did not know any such thing, since the king had only just made it up, but they smiled knowingly down into the pit and left all twelve villagers their lives. The king made bracelets and bowls and statuettes; and slowly, invisibly, he began with fine work and flattery to gain the nobles' trust.

And so he spent years far from home, while Anaeet ruled so wisely that most people forgot they had or even needed a king.

One day he told the nobles, "Bring me gems of every type and gold enough to plate my arm, and I shall make a jewelled rhyton cup in the shape of a winged lion. It shall be fine enough for Queen Anaeet herself; she alone has the power to grant you your satrapy. In return I ask only that you set me up as your jeweler, for it pleases me to serve gentlemen of such exquisite taste."

The nobles brought him these things with glee and good wishes, and in time he fashioned a cup as long as his arm. As he had promised, its base was a lion. Its sides were wings set with diamonds and emeralds and rubies, and sapphires yellow and blue, so closely nestled together that no hint of gold showed through their glimmering, mottled pattern. The other prisoners gathered around while he worked, caught between interest and awe; and when the cup was finished the king gave it to his captors with unfeigned pride.

And they took it to the queen.

But the queen, through eyes of ground emerald, saw diamonds and yellow sapphires as green. And to her eyes, rubies and blue sapphires both were black as nighttime blood, and those black stones picked out writing across the green wings. And the words read, "Help me, Anaeet."

Finally, finally, Alexandros' face lit in simple gladness. "Ah," he said. "So having a clever wife did help him in the end."

The sky had grown lighter, stars fading into grey, as the tale wound to its close. Now the night silence fractured into the cries and clangs of the waking camp. Vaacha Devi spread her wings to catch the the sun's first rays; they lit her like a phoenix, turned enameled feathertips to blood. "It depends, young Alexandros," she said regretfully, "on what Anaeet did with that knowledge."

And with a musical shiver of wings, she was gone.

DRAGONS OF AMERICA

S.J. Hirons

I

All through winter and spring the dragons of America had flown in Anselm Einarsson's dreams. When summer finally came, and the first flight of them passed over the city heading for the eastern desert, he was so used to the idea of them that he almost slept through the crossing of that flock, mistaking the sound for low thunder. But they brought with them the odours of the semi-mythical land they came from: hamburgers, hot dogs, buttered popcorn, and beer. Green as dollar bills they would be and just as crinkly. So big they blocked out stars. Swift enough to turn on a dime, and change direction fleetly with the winds.

Anselm had been sleeping on the flat rooftop of the family home for the last two weeks in anticipation of their coming. Now he stirred, his pallid dreams turning Technicolor, full of chances that had not been there moments before; bright dreams clamouring for attention as the thunderous sounds above doubled in intensity, finally waking him. He rolled out from under the canvas he'd stretched on four poles above his bedding and stood, looking up.

He saw only one dragon—the others in the flock were far to the east already—but that one was worth waking for. Its wings ravished the darkness, sending a gust down that made him blink. The fragrance of magic wafted down, too, and he clapped his hands impulsively.

From neighbouring rooftops he heard the restless awe of local children and the laughter of their woken parents; the sighs of young women and the speculative chatter of men. A first camera flashed somewhere and then, as though it had been a signal, there came a paparazzo's worth of lightning tracing the route the dragons were flying over Arrowstorm. Down on Anselm's street he saw dusty white vans being driven east, doggedly following the flock as well as the ragged city roads and checkpoints allowed: their drivers would be stopped at the city wall by American soldiers, though.

Anselm Einarsson stilled his applause, shoving his hands into his armpits, and watched the huge form as it flew on, over the squat and square houses of the suburb. Its shadow fell through the air onto the white buildings and swept along dusty avenues lit by sodium streetlights, a drop of ink on the lit canvas of the city. Delight as sweet as soda from the fridge fizzed through him.

Then he remembered what he had to do next.

He went and sat back down on his bedroll. Car horns bleated across the city. Someone south of Linden Avenue was setting off fireworks. From downstairs Anselm could hear his sister, Dowsabel Einarsdottir, complaining volubly to their mother about the racket. They both had work in the morning and he had an early meeting with his tutor at the academy to attend: concerns had been raised that he was about to fail his course again. He was already repeating a year.

Even with that on his mind he had to sit for a long time looking east, through the TV antennas that shot up like corn on the rooftops, and beyond the city's eastern watchtowers, before he could stretch back out on the thin bedroll, cover himself with his sheet and sleep again.

When he did the dragons of America flew in his dreams.

For a month the dragons will fly over the city of Arrowstorm, heading for the hottest hells of the desert to mate. Great columns of black will rise on the horizon daily. At night that edge of the world will glow like the sides of a furnace door. The breeding grounds the dragons fly to are places of packed sand, as dry as stale biscuit, where ravines form crucibles of the sun. The Americans annexed this territory as soon as the dragons began using them over a century ago, the desert now forbidden land for the people of Arrowstorm.

Dragons mate quickly, lay their eggs within a day of copulation, and wait but a week while those eggs, buried in caves clawed into the rock-face, throb and mature. It's said in the oldest textbooks that the newborns learn quickly what they are, that they are tested in the desert fastnesses by their elders; that their nursery is a place where the sky governs the visible world from a searing archway and the far mountains punch out of the earth like fists.

Did he really have to go out there and steal an egg?

II

There had been only one boy in the library when Anselm walked in. Sat behind the set of books—*Essentiale Skilles, A Guide to Alchemical Workshops*, and *The Apprentice Book*—that the first-year students at the Vindaga Academy of Alchemy had already been instructed to absorb thoroughly if they wished to secure a place as second-year students, the other boy was obviously intent on forging ahead with due diligence.

Anselm had tried to plough through the same pile himself in much the same fashion. Failure, however, had taught him that he was a plodder; that it was better for him to separate one book from the pack and slowly devour it as best he could. Outside a September sky, pink with the end of the day, filled the windows. It had been a Friday afternoon, close to the beginning of the school year. On the other side of those windows Anselm's fellow students had been spilling out onto the quad, heading to the buses. As he'd glanced out he'd seen both his peers from last year and his new classmates in the year below, and envied them their ease.

The other boy looked up, his glance sliding off Anselm in a second, his thoughts maybe on some fiendish calculation or theorem, and Anselm recognised him: Renfred Rolandsson—he had heard the boy's name in the welcoming assembly for new students at the beginning of the week, dimly noting that Renfred had been assigned a place in the class for gifted and talented first-years.

Once upon a time Renfred and Anselm had been neighbours. Their fathers had done their National Service in Arrowstorm's civic militia together, those duties earning them basic city housing vouchers. But whereas Anselm's dad had been glad to accept his discharge at the end of his mandatory service, Renfred's father had pursued a career with the militia. As he ascended the ranks Roland's status allowed for better housing and he moved the family to a fine house in the north of the city as soon as he could. Anselm's earliest memories were of summery days playing with Renfred's older sister Tamasine Rolandsdottir in the family gardens: happier times in a happier world.

As he looked over at Renfred Rolandsson he recalled that the boy had once caught him and Tamasine sharing an exploratory kiss at the bottom of one of the gardens. Renfred had worn the same look then, as he observed his sister withdrawing her small mouth and wet lips from Anselm's surprised face; a look that combined the contemplation of something alien and off-putting with the close-up and clinical interest of an enraptured entomologist.

Was that about the last time Anselm had seen Renfred or Tamasine? Anselm rather thought it was. Around that time they'd moved away. Anselm dimly remembered his mother telling him recently that Renfred's father Roland, incapacitated during a raid on an insurgent safe house, lingered near death's door in the hospital where she worked. But when she spoke sorrowfully of Roland as a great hero and champion of the modernising city her words had somehow blurred, becoming empty speech balloons that bumped into the painful thought of his own poor father's demise: found dead on the north road outside of Arrowstorm, the victim of an apparent traffic collision five years ago, when Anselm was thirteen.

Anselm sidled over to the reading table and put down his copy of *The Life of Sacheverell*, spreading out his exercise book in front of him. He had an essay on the innovations of the legendary philtrist due in after the weekend for Master Hunfrith. Five minutes passed as he sat and stared at a single page, trying to corral the words into absorbable sense. He looked over at Renfred. A year younger and already a set above him, Anselm imagined Renfred Rolandsson probably knew Master Sacheverell's biography backwards. Maybe he could crib some quick notes and be done for the day. But when he opened his mouth to inquire if Renfred could aid him all that came out was a croak:

"Renfred . . ."

Renfred did not stir.

Anselm began again: "Renfred . . . I wonder . . ."

Renfred turned the page of the book he was so intent upon, his lips pursing.

Anselm Einarsson felt his cheeks burning. So, he was to be ignored—was that it? Wasn't good enough to be acknowledged, let alone assisted, now everyone knew he was repeating a year? A prick of slender anger pierced the back of his throat. He said:

"Your, ah . . . Your sister must be a very beautiful young woman by now."

Ha! Anselm thought. Let him hear *that*!

Renfred put down his pen and looked up. Behind the clear lenses of his thin, gold-rimmed glasses his eyes were stony.

"Anselm Einarsson," he said, in toneless recognition. His eyes flicked to the windows, narrowing as they encountered light, before levelling again on his former neighbour. "Tamasine takes many prizes at the girls' academy. She makes the family proud. A bright future lies ahead of her. What could you offer such a girl? I have heard you are a mediocre student of alchemy at best." As he spoke in this staccato fashion he spread his hands judiciously, eyeing his pile of books and Anselm's sole tome. "Already *I* am ahead of you. I mean no offence." Renfred's eyes flatly pronounced a different sentence, however, and Anselm flushed yet more. He gathered his things and stood, too stifled by mortification to even croak out a response. He was halfway across the library when Renfred spoke up again:

"Einarsson. Wait."

Anselm turned. Renfred had set aside his pen and now leant back in his chair, his hands behind his head. With his shirt unbuttoned at the neck and his school tie pulled aside he looked every inch the officious head-alchemist he would probably one day become in one of the nation's few remaining foundries or factories. His hair was the same white-gold as Anselm remembered Tamasine's was, but short and neat where hers had been beguilingly wild. Renfred nodded in the direction of the chair Anselm had just vacated: "Come, sit again."

Puzzled at this change of tack, Anselm ambled back over, aware now that his anger and humiliation had dappled him with sweat.

"I was a little harsh just then," Renfred admitted. "I apologise. One should not use old friends so." He nodded at the work before him. "But you truly know how demanding our studies are."

Anselm nodded. What he knew truly was that alchemy was an impenetrable mystery to *him*. It hadn't even been Anselm's choice to study the science of stones and sands: his mother had decided it was his best career option for him the year his father had been found dead and she'd steered him on this course ever since, averring that alchemy was the future. He doubted Renfred struggled much with the subject: he had been studious even as a little boy.

Renfred sat forward, pushing aside his work, and leant over the desk towards Anselm. "I will be a great alchemist one day," he whispered confidently, confirming Anselm's thoughts, "restoring the name of our city to the minds of the Americans for all the right reasons. You wait and see."

Anselm nodded. He didn't doubt Renfred Rolandsson would try.

"Of course," Renfred went on, glancing around to assure himself they were still alone, "the best alchemy is done in America. You know why?"

"The eggs," Anselm muttered. "The Americans have access to the eggs of the dragons. The shells are said to be great transmitters when they're rendered into powder. Master Hunfrith said as much last year."

"That's right," Renfred nodded, his eyes gleaming. "Father told me that Einar was a dragon-watcher, of sorts," he said.

Anselm felt himself blushing again: Einar, his fool of a father. He'd hoped the story that had plagued his first year at the academy had faded from people's memories, the same way he himself seemed to have blended into the walls of the academy over time, but apparently not: he wondered who else amongst his new classmates had heard the same, if Renfred himself might have been spreading the word amongst the first-years this week.

Yes, his father had been obsessed with the American dragons. Many in Arrowstorm were. It was the only city in the nation they flew across on their way to mate: the best biologists and zoologists from the capital all came here to take the brief opportunity summer allowed for them to see such creatures passing overhead. None of them were as enchanted by the dragons as his father had been, though—a mere electrician and voluntary neighbourhood fireman, who'd actually snuck into the forbidden desert to spy on them when they came, according to some of the more florid gossip Anselm had had thrown at him last year.

"I bet he'd have agreed with me," Renfred whispered. "It isn't fair that the Americans alone have access to such things. Why, the eggs are even made *here*, on our land! Does that not make them *our* property, not theirs? We are supposed to be kin with the Americans. Their ancestors sailed west and found a new land, making alliance with the dragons. Ours trekked south and made a home here. Surely even basic goodwill and brother-hood means they should at least share their wealth a little?"

Anselm had never heard his father express such sentiments, so close to those of the anti-American zealots in the city, but he nodded now, a little hesitantly, and this seemed to encourage Renfred.

"You must have learnt a lot about them from him," Renfred said, his eyes wistful but somehow cold all at once. An odd and fervent air hung about him, as though he'd finally chanced upon something that had caught and held his interest at last.

"A little," Anselm admitted. He didn't wish to tell Renfred that he had thought his father an errant dreamer. Nor that the rumours were true: his father had, indeed, gone out of the city to illegally observe the dragons.

"This is what I'll do," Renfred said, sitting up again, "to make amends for my harsh words just now. I will help you. In one year's time, if alchemy is still not crystal clear to you, I will help you. With my father in a coma, I am head of household —much as you are head of yours. The prestige of association with my family would open many doors for you in Arrowstorm."

Anselm swallowed. "Why?" he asked. He cleared his throat. "Why will you wait one year?"

Renfred looked back at him as though the answer should have been obvious. "So you will have time to bring me an egg next summer, of course," he said. "I want one for my work." He picked up his book again. "It's a simple equation. You want my sister. I remember. You always did. Well, I want an egg. One egg equals one sister. If you and she were to form a union you wouldn't need to bother with all this," he tapped a finger on the rest of his books. "Bring me an egg and I will bless such a match."

And, with that, Renfred opened his book and returned to his work.

III

After his father's funeral Anselm had found some things in a box in the study. His mother had given him the key to this room—his father's former haven—admitting that, whilst Anselm was now ostensibly the head of the household, his territory was, in fact, circumscribed by the walls of that room, much as Einar's had been.

"Whatever is in there is yours," she'd said, "but that's it. Your sister and I are both busy women. We've no time for a boy's interference and what little money there is belongs to us all equally."

Anselm had accepted this. It was fair. Dowsabel and his mother both knew how to make a penny stretch like it was copper wire. His allowance, on the other hand, tumbled out of his grasp like water. And men had had disastrous impact on both his mother's life and Dowsabel's, he knew: his sister had been affianced four times and each union had broken up because Dowsabel had discovered fault with her suitors. His poor mother had suffered life with his daydreaming father.

"Living with a man like me is in itself a sellable skill," even that fellow had concurred.

The discovery that had excited Anselm most had been his father's secret stash of American magazines. He'd had no idea his father collected such gossip-sheets and scandal-rags. There were at least twenty of them, each packed with pictures of teenage witches as rouged and coiffed as strumpets; vampyr-slayers with defiant, beseeching glares; barbarian warrior-women on horseback and blousy princesses stumbling out of limousines. Anselm was on the cusp of thirteen that year and the sight of all that tight denim and enthralling beauty had been as giddy-making as a goblet of wine. He hadn't wanted to flick through Einar's collection of faded and oft-thumbed copies of *Supernatural Geographic* once he saw the American magazines tucked beneath. Full of the petulant nonchalance most teenagers in the city felt for the yearly appearance of the creatures in Arrowstorm's skies, he'd been much more taken with America's legends and lays.

He went back to this box of magazines and journals after his talk with Renfred, taking out the supernaturalist periodicals and putting them to one side on the study's desk. Beneath them were his father's journals, the log-books of his trips into the desert. Such trips were long restricted: hence the checkpoints and the watchtowers; the international negotiations every winter (where the rights of the desert cities and the demands of the Americans were in a constant state of flux, subject to internecine brokering); the simmering resentments

in the city. His father had rejoiced when Dowsabel found work
at the American Embassy, though. Not many men of Arrowstorm would have been so pleased, but Dowsabel's job meant
she had access to inter-province travel passes that their father
could display in his car when he went out of Arrowstorm to
look at the dragons.

Anselm took out the topmost journal (he had never
looked in any of them before) and opened it, half-wondering
if he might find some simple plan inside that outlined how
one could casually walk into a dragon's lair and come away
with an egg. He had no intention of doing as Renfred had
suggested. Going into the desert and risking the wrath of
either the dragons or the Americans was sheer lunacy. Still,
he was curious. Had his father known how to do such a thing?
If he had known he would surely have recorded it in one of
these books.

But instead of any kind of factual account Anselm first
found only a story Einar had been attempting to write:

*"The first dragon to reach America was called
Mayflower, or* Flor de Mayo *in her native tongue. It had taken
her a week to cross the Atlantic, a hopscotch journey that had
seen her land in Orkney, in Iceland, once on an iceberg and
twice in Greenland. It was a desperate journey, one that would
never have been undertaken if her riders had not been subject
to dire privations and persecutions in their native land,
England. The year was 1620 and those riders were the wizards
who had opened a gateway between our world and the world of
the great reptiles . . ."*

Anselm knew enough history and geography to know
that this was pure fiction. A list of imaginary places and made-
up words. Was this the kind of thing that had drifted down to
his father as he watched the dragons year after year? Was this
the source of his fascination with them? Anselm had not known
Einar's imagination could be quite so deft: no wonder his heart
had been ensnared out there in the hot-lands, if this was an

example of the dreams that came to him when he was under the spell of the American dragons.

He flicked through further and saw this journal was full of notes for the same tale and so he set it aside. The next book was more illuminating: there was a list of names *("U-Ta," "Gol-O-Rad-O," "Ay-O-Wah," "Kan-Zaz")* under a heading *"Are These Clan Names? Or Their Actual Names?"*: descriptions of habits; hand-drawn maps and, lastly, the secret of how Anselm's father had managed to get so close to the dragons of America to observe all of this. Anselm looked at the last paragraph on that page more thoughtfully than he had ever looked at his school books:

"I shall mark these entrances with glimmerfoil seeds this year and hope that they will be covered next year by this weed. I shall then know where to find them again. Glimmerfoil is a hardy plant and self-protective. Nothing in the desert eats it and even Americans know to avoid its stings."

Tucked into that last book Anselm found two travel passes, both of them undated.

"Lunacy," he muttered to himself, putting the books back in the box.

His father had always said great men were touched by a little madness, though.

The months passed and the secrets of alchemy continued to elude him.

He did not speak again with Renfred, but he saw him often in the corridors between classes. Night after night the dragons of America began to fly, unbidden, in Anselm's dreams and, day after day, he would look up as he moved from one lecture to the next and see the eerily calm eyes of Renfred Rolandsson surveying him from somewhere, a slight smile on the boy's narrow face. Occasionally the other boy would incline his head in acknowledgement he had been caught out, constantly keeping fresh in Anselm's mind the offer that was on the table.

At year's end Anselm's grades hadn't improved from the year before. In the spring assessment tests he actually managed to drop a grade in his practical exam. Master Hunfrith called him to his office to discuss ways Anselm could better organize his study time:

"For you're surely in need of something radical now," the old alchemist muttered. "If you don't wish to remain an eternal student, that is."

A radical solution?

Everything he needed to concoct such a thing was there, in the meagre legacy of his father's estate, he began to think: maps, notes, travel permits. As an added fillip, Anselm thought, he wouldn't mind seeing the look on Renfred's face when Anselm, the great failure, presented him with a priceless dragon egg.

The week before the dragons came he decided he would do it. He would go and steal an egg. All he needed now was some superficial reason he could give to Dowsabel to explain why he needed to borrow her car for a night and day.

In the end, he spun out a story of a study session at the home of one his tutors in north Arrowstorm—an all-night session with a meal and tents in the garden. Remarkably Dowsabel bought this tale from him wholesale and agreed that their mother could give her a lift to work the next day. It was established by all that Anselm was in sore need of the extra tutelage and, since it was free, it was worth doing. He felt a certain shame for this lie as the day ended, but that shame was not what kept him awake nor was it what coloured his dreams.

The dragons of America filled the sky in squadrons, flying into the fiery east without hesitation, just as surely as missiles fired from a distant kingdom. He watched them for hours, remembering Tamasine's lips against his; her determination to kiss him; the hot thrill he'd felt at being wanted for something. He imagined the kind of wife she'd make—dutiful and useful—and he watched the dragons, plotting, planning: telling himself the tale of what he would do and how.

IV

The American soldiers asked where he was going. He told them he was driving to Sea-Halls, the province to the north, where the Museum of Shipwrights was: he had an exam on the history of his people soon. The pass tacked into his sister's car window verified that he came from a family known to be co-operative and he'd taken great care to bring nothing outwardly suspicious with him. He had a packed lunch and some water: a little first-aid kit; a torch and a flare. Anyone driving through the desert would take at least that much, as the soldiers would have known. He had no camera to record anything, only a pen. He grew a little shaky when one of the Americans lifted up his father's journals from the back seat but the sentry must have simply thought these were the boy's own notebooks. He weighed them in his hand but did not open them.

"I'm staying the night there with family friends," Anselm blurted out.

The American put the journals back on the seat and nodded to his colleague. The barrier went up and Anselm was curtly waved through. On the wrists of the Americans gold watches gleamed in the afternoon sun. Their uniforms were greener than the desert had ever been. Bulletproof vests, grenades clipped on bandoliers, binoculars resting on bulging stomachs, all khaki: the Americans were pinker than the TV made them seem on the nightly news. Anselm gave them a small wave and drove out into the heat and the dust, heading north, parallel to the black horizon, stopping an hour later to wait and see if he had been followed. Nothing came along the road. He turned the car east, onto the flat desert, wending southwards.

Einar's notes recorded that certain ravines, where the dragons had burrowed fissures for egg storage, had smaller entrances on the far side of the gullies where they mated. In his books Einar guessed that this had been the result of some process that the newborns went through— possibly as they hatched, though he wasn't sure—that wracked the ground, splitting the dry earth at the back of the fissures. He further speculated that those caverns were the ones where the newborns had not survived, for the dragons seemed to avoid them.

Anselm's father had been able to burrow through these narrow openings and wriggle his way up to watch the dragons from within the unused chambers. There were several maps that noted where to turn off the road, what shape the land was, and where it was sensible to leave the car and continue on foot to get to these places.

Einar had written that early evening was the best time to approach the mating grounds. The path he'd followed was out of the sightline of the dragons on the ground, but there was no cover from any in flight: twilight was a time of day when they were not inclined to eat, he'd written—though the looping track he'd marked out to their mating grounds kept one away from the direction the dragons went when they hunted in the mountains, anyway. He marked the entrances to the tunnels he felt for certain were no longer used with the glimmerfoil, his later diaries noting that this had been a success: the tough weed had grown plentifully, obscuring the holes that led to the tunnels through the rock.

At sunset Anselm stopped the car where the map suggested, in a narrow valley about two miles from the first ridge of the hot ravines. Stepping out of the car he realized for the first time just how hot it actually was without the temperamental air-conditioning in Dowsabel's car on full. He was used to the heat of the city, but this was different. He was beaded with perspiration in a few moments. Shouldering his pack, he kept one of his water canteens at hand as he stomped across country towards the breeding grounds.

The sun was gone by the time he spied the first of the glimmerfoil clumps on the sloping land ahead. Behind it, barely visible, was a split in the earth, no bigger than a beach ball in diameter. He carefully pushed the tangled glimmerfoil bush down with his boot and leant into the hole.

It turned out the torch he'd brought had a weak battery, but its paltry light was just about bright enough for him to see how the hole became a tunnel within a few feet. He wriggled in and pulled himself forward, pushing his pack ahead. After a few feet he emerged into a space big enough to stand up in. The dim sky was visible not so far ahead, along the steep slope upwards, so he turned out the torch and felt his way along, his fingers running over seams of the desiccated rock. As he went along he felt the earth shaking lightly beneath his fingertips, while dusty downfalls of sand speckled his arm and head. He heard roars and saw the hole before him flare with flame.

When he came closer to the lip of the cave he went down on his belly and crawled slowly forward. The grotto of hard rock opened out quite high up over the deep ravine: looking out and down he saw a small grouping of American dragons.

The ravine was horseshoe-shaped. Its rough sides surrounded a bowl of the desert, marked only by the occasional boulder. There were five dragons in sight. With a sudden and thumping realization of the danger he was in, Anselm watched as a huge female emerged from another cave and slid down the rock into the bowl, sending shale out before her in a tiny avalanche. Two newborns, each walking with a floppy gait, leapt out of her way, barking weirdly, their wings shaking: another female shepherded them aside. A smaller dragon slumbered on ground close to the cave Anselm hid in. Another newborn, he guessed.

The solitary male, lounging on his back, rolled over to watch the sliding female as she steadied herself. With phenomenal speed he flipped up onto his four feet, shooting her a questioning look. She purred. The male took to the air, sending a swirl of dust and sand around the ravine. Little rocks skittered towards Anselm and he ducked back down, squinting his eyes tightly. The stirred air carried with it that smell of magic and the far-off: pretzels and bagels and endless prairies. Liberty. Doughnuts and apple pie. Democracy and skyscrapers. Steak. Grilled cheese.

As the evening darkened he simply watched them, giving no thought to what he had come to do, as fascinated as his father must have been. He just wanted to watch these creatures. Even the blundering newborns were a source of delight but, truly, it was the huge adults that hypnotised him. They seemed to flow with every movement in Anselm's eyes. He was his father's son in those hours; his face streaked with dirt, more deeply transformed by the joy that sat there after so long absent. Fire billowed out in the air below. Anselm felt the heat of it on his face. Soon the male returned, his jaws clamped around a mountain lion. He flung it at the feet of the female he had been eyeing up and she ate so haughtily Anselm almost laughed aloud, seeing the male's chagrin. But when she was done she consented to be mounted and Anselm watched, intrigued, as her tail lifted and the male writhed around her on his side, batting the air with one wing, in cautious approach. When he had penetrated her, his eyes closed and little flames and smoke puffed up from his nostrils. The female let out a sweet sound as the male thrust deeper and deeper and her wings went up and down languidly as they both dragged over the ground. The newborns skipped around them until their mother batted them away with a scowl. The male let out a huge roar and flipped up, detached from the female. He strutted around her and then took to the air again. Anselm craned up to watch him rise into the night, marking his presence through the black air by the spurts of fire he sent across the sky.

The ground shuddered close to Anselm. He looked sharply to the right and saw the slumbering dragon he had taken for a newborn was, in fact, an adult, after all: a female, smaller than normal, now approaching the tunnel he was in. One of her back legs dragged and Anselm saw a single working eye. The other was milk-white. The two newborns barked up at her, sounding amused. She mewed in protest at their mother, but that dragon had wandered over to the now-reclining female who had just mated. Anselm slipped back into the darkness of the tunnel. A moment later the silhouette of the lame dragon blocked the front entrance.

She stayed there the whole night, making terrible noises. Anselm decided to simply wait it out. At dawn, perhaps, he would be able to sneak past her and into the ravine. His father had written that the dragons slept so deeply, well into the day, that one could walk near enough to them to almost touch. Anselm had decided that was when he would make his attempt at snatching up an egg.

He settled against the hard wall of the cave and drank some water.

Something smooth and heavy hit him gently in the face and he woke up, momentarily confused and annoyed. Alarmed, he saw that dawn had come and gone. A white, mid-morning sky was framed by the entrance to the cave. The lame dragon must have moved off at some point whilst Anselm slept. He heard and felt movement outside. The dragons of America were awake. He had missed his chance.

But then he looked at the thing that had woken him and saw it was, in fact, a small egg. He gave a little laugh of delight at the improbability of this good fortune before reaching out to pick it up.

He realized instantly that something was wrong with it as his eyes cleared of sleep's fuzziness. The egg was cold, and a simple white colour. His father had written that dragon eggs were warm to the touch and either a white colour striped over with red striations or a shade of deep blue, speckled with little stars: either kind were at least two foot long.

This egg sat in Anselm's palm easily, no bigger than a grapefruit, but certainly heavier. He guessed it was some kind of stillbirth: its mother had not looked or sounded strong. Would Renfred still want it? Whatever the condition its insides were in it would still give Renfred enough shell to last him through years of studying, even practicing, proper alchemy.

Anselm thought about it. It would simply be suicide to go outside into the bowl now. And surely Renfred Rolandsson had not been expecting an egg that would come to term? Now Anselm had such things in mind he apprehended that Renfred must have been planning to terminate a birth from any egg Anselm brought him, somehow. Well, this saved him that bother, too.

Anselm put the egg in his pack and clambered around to the small gap that led out of the cave, glancing back just once: part of him wanted to look at the dragons for one, final time. Another part urged him away: he had done what he was bound to do.

Mission accomplished.

When he came out, pushing the glimmerfoil bush aside again with caution, the air on his face, though warm, felt fresh and invigorating. A kind of appreciation for his own daring began to bloom in him as he stood and stretched. He had seen what few men, even American men, had seen: the mating of American dragons. Furthermore, he had taken what no one in his own land had ever had from the creatures.

He clapped his hands together and looked about him. To the right, not far-off, was another clump of glimmerfoil. There was something dark tangled up in it. Piqued, Anselm walked over. It was a shoe. It was his father's shoe. The left, from a pair of brogues. The one that had been missing on the day Einar had been found in the middle of the north road, his old car pulled over onto the sand. It had been mating season then, too. The American soldiers who brought Einar's mangled corpse back to Arrowstorm had told Anselm's mother that they thought her husband had got out of the car and been hit by another vehicle on the road. Maybe he was flagging it down for aid, they'd suggested, though there was nothing mechanically wrong with his car as far as they could tell. She could collect it from their compound whenever she liked, they said. The battered body, too.

Anselm lifted the shoe out of the glimmerfoil cautiously. There was a brown stain on the inner heel. Dried blood, maybe. He looked past the briary weeds and saw that the entrance to the tunnel behind them had collapsed. Further up the ridge four cracked indentations buckled the rocks.

It was easy to imagine an American dragon landing there, its feet thumping into the earth at great speed, causing the cave below to fall in. He discovered it was also dreadfully easy to imagine his father crawling, crushed, out through the packed hole; just as terribly easy to imagine his father stumbling or dragging himself across the desert and back to his car, desperate to get back to Arrowstorm and help. Had he even wanted to pull over that day? Or had he done so in some delirium of pain and stepped out of the car in a panic and then simply fallen down dead, his wounds later takenas collision wounds? It was impossible to say, but Anselm was suddenly certain that was what had happened, nevertheless. He felt sick and sad and hot and cold all at once. This was something that could belong to him only, and forever. Dowsabel could not be told. His mother should never know; not even that such things were a possibility. He put the shoe back in the weeds, as though it were its own kind of marker.

Testament that a man had been there.

For some reason he knew he would be breezed back through the checkpoint when he got back to Arrowstorm. This confidence was new to him, and strange, but he trusted it unthinkingly and he was right to do so: as he stopped at the city gate the American soldier who'd beckoned him past the barrier yesterday merely peered in and nodded before turning to his comrade and shouting:

"It's the kid from yesterday. The student."

The barrier went up and Anselm went in.

He felt like the homecoming king.

V

The dead dragon came to him that night. No bigger than a dog, she wound about the struts that held the canvas over his rooftop bed, wraithlike and smoky and free from the shell where she'd died.

"Are you my mommy?"

Her voice was the cutesy, too-sweet voice of a child star.

"What?" Anselm sat up. The dead dragon put her front claws on his stomach and looked up at him with entreating eyes.

"Are you my mommy?" she repeated.

"No," he said. He looked into the little space beneath the platform his bed was on. He'd put his wicker laundry basket there with the egg hidden inside. Reaching over and lifting the lid he saw the egg was still there. "What's going on?" he muttered.

"What *is* going on?" the dead dragon asked him. She nuzzled up against his chest.

"Is this a dream?"

"*Is* this a dream?"

He gently pushed at the smoky creature and she swirled, becoming indistinct. He stood up as she coalesced back into her supple shape again.

"She is bonded to you," said a husky voice behind him. He spun around and saw that the dragon he had taken for a newborn in the desert, the lame female, was perched on the low, brick wall of the rooftop.

A little bit of piss spurted out of Anselm. She was here to punish him for his theft, he thought: What else could it be?

But then the female dragon puffed smoke from her nostrils. "I am glad," she continued. "It broke my heart that she could take no life from me and I could not bear to be the guardian of her spirit. The others have exiled me for it, but I was already as good as an exile to them." She looked at him pointedly. Her good eye was hard, full of bitterness. The dead dragon capered around Anselm, her tail whipping him without sensation.

"What am I to do with her?" Anselm whispered.

"You will know," the dragon said, looking with pain at her dead daughter. "It was men that made us magic in the first place." She spread her wings and, tentatively, rose up to balance precariously on her one, working back-leg.

"Where are you going?" Anselm asked, alarmed.

"Somewhere else," she said, in her rasping voice. She beat her wings, sending Anselm staggering back on his bare feet. He looked up and saw the sky was full of dragons. The mating season was over.

The dead dragon leapt onto his bedding and settled down.

"Who are you talking to?" she asked.

* * *

Renfred smiled slightly, seeing Anselm approaching him along the corridor.

"I'm afraid I cannot give you an egg—" Anselm began.

Renfred laughed. "Did you really think I expected you to? Nearly a year now I've watched you sweating, your fervid little dreams coming off you in waves. Most amusing!" The humour fell from his face. He leant close to Anselm. "You do not deserve Tamasine. You never did." He stood up straight again, clearly anticipating a look of sweet pain and confusion on Anselm's face.

But Anselm only smiled. "If I wanted her I'd have her," he said. And then Anselm Einarsson laughed. He turned back to carry on his way, the dead dragon bounding ahead of him silently.

"Where are you going?" Renfred demanded, sounding irritated. "We've got classes now."

"Not me," Anselm called back breezily over his shoulder. "I just dropped out!"

Despite newfound powers of persuasion and tangible confidence this move did not go down very well at home. Eventually he persuaded his mother that if he did not have a job by the end of the week then he would allow her to try and persuade the governors of the academy to take him back, passing off his recent decision as something hormonal. He found an unexpected source of support in Dowsabel, who loudly pointed out to their mother that it was about time her brother contributed something to the household: he already owed her for petrol and a car wash, she averred.

He found a job the next day loading crates at a depot uptown. It paid just a smidge under what his mother earned at her hospital job and, outmaneuvered, she condescended to allow him his whim. The job would have been deathly boring if the dead dragon had not been at his side, an invisible companion. At night he tutored her in the ways of the world:

this was how he discovered he had a voice that could tell tales well. By day she began to tell him the secrets she discovered she knew. She lost her saccharine voice quickly.

When winter came again he put the egg in his father's box in the study: now the dead dragon had emerged from it the egg felt brittle, light, useless. As he was just about to put the lid back on the box his eyes fell on the journal where his father's odd curate's egg of fiction was written. He slid it out again and sat at Einar's desk, reading it. The dead dragon crawled onto him. Anselm began to read it aloud and comment upon its merits, the strange flavours and resonances he suddenly realized were there. Shortly after, the dead dragon began to comment, too—making suggestions for changes and improvements: outlining possible routes of progression.

Anselm took a pen from a little clay pot on his father's desk and twirled it between his fingers.

*D*ragons of America was a huge and unexpected success: The dispirited literati of Arrowstorm hailed the novella as the emergence of a bold, new voice in a listless kingdom; politicians quoted from it, citing it as evidence of the feelings of their people, especially the young and the despondent. Anselm was interviewed on TV and radio both. Journalists made headlines from certain phrases in the book. Academics called it a polemic, an entreaty, the heartsong of a nation. Reporters from American magazines flew across the Atlantean Ocean just to interview Anselm Einarsson and take his photograph before flying home again, often on the same day.

VI

He was in the market when he saw Renfred Rolandsson coming along the lane. Anselm stopped to watch him cross the road and approach, suddenly remembering it was the day the academy's year's end exam results were posted. He murmured a greeting when the student stopped.

"How did you do?" he asked his former classmate, nodding towards the sheaf of certificates Renfred held.

Renfred shrugged, his face sullen and his mouth set. "I took five prizes."

"Must feel good," Anselm commented. Behind Renfred a tall and skinny girl had stopped to stare at Anselm. It had been happening more and more of late. Anselm still hadn't quite got used to this phenomenon of his newfound fame, though. He smiled at the girl faintly, taking in her straggling hair, the blinking eyes framed by her thin, gold-rimmed glasses, and her staid, traditional dress, before turning his attention back to Renfred.

"No," said Renfred. "I feel robbed. Cheated." Renfred's face was a caricature of the spoiled child, the thwarted kid. The dead dragon ran around the young student, standing up on her hind-legs and putting her front claws on Renfred's shoulders. She peered back at Anselm, pulling faces. Anselm chuckled.

Renfred looked at him suspiciously. "You know," he said, "my sister," he jerked his thumb over his shoulder at the tall girl, and Anselm realized with a start that the young woman was Tamasine Rolandsdottir, "has become a very respectful young woman now Father has passed, honouring old ways." He lowered his voice. "An arrangement could still be made," he said.

Anselm shrugged and said nothing. Renfred's mouth turned down. He sketched a bow and turned to walk away, oblivious to the fact that his sister had lingered: as the head of their household he more than likely expected her to walk a few paces behind him, anyway.

"I read your book," Tamasine whispered to Anselm. "You are altogether too forgiving when you write about the imperialists." She shook her head, sorrowfully, snatched her hand from Anselm's arm and moved on, head down again.

"What peculiar creatures!" the dead dragon exclaimed.

Anselm nodded. "But without them I wouldn't have you," he whispered as he watched Tamasine walking away.

He was in Sea-Halls the next summer, giving a series of talks at nascent writer's workshops in the province, when he heard the news: a young woman, a fierce patriot dismayed by the American presence in her homelands and their swaggering claims about the dragons and the desert territories, had immolated herself outside the American Embassy in Arrowstorm.

He seemed to know immediately it was Tamasine.

Renfred was shot dead later the same day, bound for the checkpoint out of the city with a homemade bomb strapped to his chest. The group Anselm was with had a radio brought to their meeting hall for his benefit. They sat huddled around it, listening. American alchemists had dismantled the boy's bomb, concluding it was a dud, lacking vital components.

Anselm came home. The city felt tense. More troops had been sent from the west to man the checkpoints and the streets. The young writer was invited to the embassy. At the end of Linden Avenue he saw the blackened flagstones where Tamasine Rolandsdottir had sat down, dousing herself in petroleum and making her proclamations. People had been placing red rocks around the charred spot in memoriam. The dead dragon skipped ahead of him and ran around the place. She did not grow, that dead dragon, but her smoky form now seemed shot through with colours in Anselm's eyes: the greens and oranges of the national flag.

Inside, at the ambassador's table, he was served ice-cold soda, as Dowsabel had told him he might be. Bowls of tortilla chips, guacamole, and salsa were laid out; plates of black and white biscuits and soft sponge fingers filled with cream. The ambassador, a black woman in an expensive pantsuit, asked after his work, saying she had read and admired his novella. She wondered if he was working now. Anselm told her things were certainly stirring. She asked the question he had been asked a hundred times in the north and he told her he got his ideas from ghosts, just as he'd said in those dusty community halls where he'd sat with the nation's next generation of poets and playwrights, novelists, and essayists. He sipped the cold soda and smiled at her. The dead dragon sat, as still and attendant as a watchdog, next to his chair.

"I wondered . . . that is to say," the ambassador began. She lifted some papers from a file she had brought to the table. "I've been sent a letter from the dean of one of our universities," she said. "He asks if you would like to visit his campus and speak to some of the students there. Would you . . . I mean . . . "

Anselm told her he would certainly think about it.

The ambassador walked him back down to the gatehouse at the end of their appointment. At the open gates she looked out, back along Linden Avenue.

"Such a waste," she said, when she saw Anselm's eyes had been drawn back to the blackened stones. "Don't you agree?"

"Oh, yes." He nodded. He wasn't actually sure what he felt about what Tamasine had done yet.

"I understand you knew the family?"

"We weren't close," Anselm Einarsson said. He shook the ambassador's hand, dimly aware he was being photographed by a guard at the gatehouse. The photo would be published in the following day's papers. The ambassador's thumb rested on the flesh between Anselm's thumb and his forefinger. He thought about the way life glanced off him, the way he seemed to simply absorb events of late in the hope they would make sense eventually; and he felt, for a moment, like he was again in his hiding place in the desert, staring down into a bowl of fire and danger, his eyes wide and his heart open: terrified and elated.

"And you'll think about our offer?" The ambassador asked him.

"Most definitely," he said.

He walked home along Linden Avenue, silent and thoughtful. He went though the house to the rooftop.

He sat looking west, turning the egg over and over in his hands.

"Will we go?" asked the dead dragon.

"*Can* we go?" Anselm asked.

"Oh, yes," she answered. "Most definitely."

He nodded, seeing she wanted to fly.

"Maybe we will make a name for ourselves there," he said.

"I already have a name," she said.

He looked at her.

"I am A-Ra-Ztam," said the dead dragon. She flowed through the air to Anselm Einarsson and settled down against him. She smelt like his mother's cooking, his father's favourite dishes: fried doughballs, spicy and piquant; hot raisin bread and olive oil.

She smelt like change and she smelt like home.

That night they dreamt of America.

WHERE SHADOWS GO AT LOW MIDNIGHT

John Grant

The party was still going at full swing when Kursten and I slipped out into the street. Light and sounds spilled from the upstairs windows and pooled around us, attempting to kid us the night wasn't as cold as it was. The pair of us laughed quietly together as the plumes of our breath in the freezing air frustrated the deception.

I pulled down a brand from the doorway and held it up above our heads.

Kursten shivered, her dark coat moving on her shoulders in a complicated dance, and broke her gaze away from mine, turning to look toward where Giorran lay in the distance and the darkness. Her home was there, and so was mine. On this cold night Giorran seemed a very far way away. I was tempted to suggest we went back to rejoin the party and stay making noise and merry until the daylight came. What stopped me was the comfortable nervousness that hung between us, the shared awareness of two people that they may soon become lovers.

"We take the roads or we take the fields?" she said.

The journey was shorter across country, but in the unreliable light from the brand it could be hazardous. We'd come here from Giorran by road through the twilight, taking our time as we ambled. Now that it was full night, though, we just wanted to get home as soon as we could.

Neither of us said anything about Ghosts.

"The fields should be safe enough," I said. "There hasn't been rain in a week. Besides, the ground must be hard as stone."

She nodded. It was so cold tonight even the air seemed solid, like flakes of mica, scraping our throats as we breathed it.

We began trotting down the cobblestones of the crooked main street of Starveling. The flame I carried had no purpose here. This was the night of the year's turn, and not even the youngsters were in their beds. Every window was lit, giving its brightness to the street. The cold kept most everyone inside, though. On our way to the edge of the village we met one or two folk braving the cold as we were, and muttered greetings as we passed. It was almost disconcerting, the emptiness of a street we were so accustomed to seeing filled with jostling friends and strangers.

Soon we were leaving Starveling and its lamps and revelry behind us. We stuck to the road for a short while, then climbed a bank and started to cut across the fields. Above us there were more stars than ever a person could hope to count. I fancied that the misty pathway of light meandering from one side of the heavens to the other, plunging to the horizon amid the darkness ahead of us, was a reflection in the sky of the course Kursten and I were taking to our homes. Spiky red reflections of my burning torch from ice crystals clinging to the grass completed the illusion. We were speeding across a swathe of fallen stars.

The image made the night seem even colder, and I said so to Kursten.

"*Think* yourself warm," she said with a chuckle, bumping my shoulder amicably with her own.

"I don't—"

"I said you should *think* yourself warm, Rehan."

"I know you did. I just don't know what you mean."

She laughed. "Whenever I'm soaking wet in torrents of rain, I think of myself being in the middle of a desert, and that way I can make myself sort of part-believe I'm dry. Sometimes it works so well I actually get thirsty. Tonight I'm telling myself it's broad daylight at the world's bulge."

"And the height of summer," I said, getting into the spirit of the game.

She inclined her head. "Oh, quite definitely the height of summer. No one ever go outside if they don't have to in case of being fried where they stand, or eaten alive by scorpions. They just stay indoors drinking cold water a lot and fanning themselves with long brightly colored feathers tugged from the tails of exotic birds that no one's ever given a name to."

"Because of the heat," I said.

Kursten glanced at me.

"Too hot to be bothered to name all the birds," I explained, answering the question she hadn't spoken.

"You see, Rehan? You're feeling warmer already, aren't you?"

I couldn't say that I was, but I was enjoying so much jogging along here in the starlight with Kursten by my side that the cold seemed to have decided to retreat a little distance from me. Yes, she and I were going to be lovers all right, perhaps even before the next dawn.

"What's that?" she said suddenly, faltering in her stride.

"What's what?"

"There." She pointed.

"I can't see anything."

"Neither can I, now." She pressed closer against me, seeking reassurance.

"What did you see?"

"Just something moving."

"A deer?"

She shook her head. "Something that looked as if it shouldn't have been there—that's the only way I can describe it." She shivered, but this time it wasn't the half-joking shiver of sharing a cold night. "Come on, Rehan. Let's get ourselves home to Giorran."

A thought hung in the frosty air that neither of us wanted to put words to. To talk about the Ghosts was to draw them to you, so people said, and while neither of us was so backward as to be superstitious we still didn't want to tempt fortune. The Ghosts built the world, so everyone knew, and they built Starveling and Giorran too, one on top of the other up here on the table mountain. Time and the winds had crumbled the center of what was once a mighty township so that now there remained only these two separate, distanced fragments, one called Giorran and the other called Starveling, as if by giving them the two old names people could pretend it had always been meant to be this way. Ghosts built the house where our friends were still celebrating the year's turn, and Ghosts laid the stony streets we'd clattered along after we'd left those friends there. Ghosts had done so very many things for which we were all grateful, but then they'd departed, and departed was the best place for them to stay. They didn't belong here in the world any more.

"Home across these desert sands?" I said, puffing my cheeks, trying to distract her from her fears. "My throat's parched from the heat already and I've hardly taken a step."

"I've heard tell there's an oasis somewhere near, a place we can get shade and water while we wait for the worst of the day to subside."

"But will the water be bright and cool?"

"Cooler by far than the sand."

"Then it'll do for me."

"I wonder," she said as we resumed our steady pace through the darkness, "what it's really like there."

"In the hot lands, you mean?"

"Yes."

"You've seen the pictures, heard the stories."

"But I've never met anyone who's actually been there to see for themselves."

"I have," I told her.

Kursten gave me a look of frank disbelief. "You've been there?"

"No. I've met someone who has."

"When?"

"She came to Starveling a few years ago. What was her name now? It escapes me. But she'd been on a ship that had floated—"

"Sailed," said Kursten firmly. "Ships don't just float when they're going somewhere, they sail."

"She was on a ship that sailed far to the south, taking metals scavenged from the ancient places here to trade for musical instruments carved and shaped from the tusks of vast creatures that roam the baking plains—"

"You're making this up, aren't you?"

"Some of it," I admitted. "What good's a story if it doesn't want to turn itself into a song? But it was true this person had floa . . . sailed aboard a ship which took her to the world's bulge, and it's true she told me some of the things she saw there."

Kursten shrugged. "I was beginning to like the big tusked beasties," she said. "Do say they were for real."

"If they were, my friend never saw one."

"Oh." Kursten's voice was wistful. After a moment she said, "So tell me something true."

"What she—"

I began telling Kursten as much as I could remember. It was difficult not to embellish the account with inventions of my own, but she'd caught me out once in a fabrication and I didn't want to risk the same happening again. Besides, there'd been plenty of marvels in the stories Anya—that had been her name, Anya—in the stories Anya had told the evening a pack of us had spent in the tavern down by Giorran's small harbor. There were spiders bigger than a person's head, dwelling in forest places where the undergrowth was so thick no one dared venture in for fear of never finding a way out. There were creatures resembling tiny Ghosts that swung high overhead in the branches or scampered like squirrels from one tuft of dry scrub to the next. There were rivers so wide no one could see across them, and giant lizards that dwelled in those rivers and could eat a person up in a single gulp. And in other parts there were no trees and no rivers and no lizards and nothing at all except endlessly drifting sands, an ocean of them with its own waves and even, so Anya had told us, tides. I'd found that last part hard to credit.

"And there are no shadows," I said.

"No shadows?" Kursten glanced downward. The flame I was carrying was making her own shadow dance on the stunted silvery grass.

"Not all the time." I hurried to correct myself. "Most of the daytime there are shadows, just like here. But at high noon the sun isn't just high in the sky, it's directly overhead. Its light is shining straight down on top of you. If you stick out a leg you can see a shadow beneath it, but that's all. There isn't a shadow loping alongside you as you walk. For a while, Anya said, you don't notice your shadow has . . . escaped. As soon as you do, though, it becomes nearly impossible to notice anything else."

"A place without any shadows," said Kursten softly, more to herself than to me. "I wonder if—"

But then we suddenly found ourselves venturing into an area where the going was treacherous underfoot. The long rains of the autumn must have turned this corner of the field into a lake of mud, and cattle or sheep had churned it with their feet into a miniature landscape of sharp peaks and narrow chasms. Frozen as hard as rock by the winter, the ground presented a million opportunities for twisting a foot or even breaking a leg. Kursten and I slowed down to a cautious walk, picking each new step carefully in the brand's unsteady illumination. After a few moments of this, I put the shaft between my teeth and went down onto all fours, as Kursten had already done. The heat scorched the side of my face, and the stars in the night sky vanished from my sight.

At the far end of the patch of frozen mud was a low hedge that we leapt over, its leafless twigs grasping for our bellies like ancient claws. What we landed in was another tract much like the one we'd just left, and every bit as perilous. By the time we'd safely negotiated it, several minutes must have passed since last we spoke, and Kursten's mind seemed to have wandered to other concerns.

"It's strange the Ghosts should have organized the days so well and the nights so very poorly," she sighed as she rose again to her hind legs.

I shook my head, grinning, and looked at her. Her eyes were red from my brand's glow as she gazed back. She was grinning, too.

"What I mean," she said as we began to jog across more level ground, "is that the Ghosts created daylight so we could move around safely during the day. Why didn't they create nightlight so we could do the same at night?"

"But if the sun was in the sky at night it wouldn't be night, would it?"

"It wouldn't have to be the sun—nor anything as bright as that. Just enough of a light in the sky to let us see where we're going . . . and to give us shadows, Rehan. I think that'd be very important if I were the one in charge of redesigning the world. It isn't *right* for people to be without their shadows."

So her attention hadn't drifted after all. She was still thinking about the stories Anya had told.

"There used to be something like that," I said.

"There did?"

"At least," I qualified, "we think there was. It's hard to be sure, but . . ."

By day I assisted an old person called Lesor who was trying to construct an archive in Giorran of anything we could salvage from what the Ghosts left behind. So much had been lost, of course—used as fuel or destroyed by the elements or sunk unfathomably far into the ground, likely never to be seen by living eye again—but still there was more than enough that had survived to keep Lesor and myself busy for many lifetimes. While he catalogued and stored, it was my task to scavenge in the hamlet and the surrounding countryside for anything that might be worth adding to the hoard. There were devices galore, of course, but these were useless to our purpose; nobody could figure out how to get the things to work. Just by having once been there the Ghosts had made us like themselves—not in body but in mind. Even so, I believed no one ever *would* be able to bring those contraptions back to life. But pictures—these we could sensibly archive. Together, after a day's gathering and cataloguing had been done, Lesor and I would often sit late into the night in his library struggling to understand the pictures the Ghosts stamped and painted on metal and stone and anything else they could find. There were also strange pictures they made which Lesor believed were pictures not of objects or creatures but of *ideas*. He dreamed of one day being able to interpret those ideas, to decipher the Ghosts.

As for me, I confined my interest to the pictures of things I could recognize. Every now and then there was one that showed the night, and in a few of these there were two brighter lights in the sky than the stars—two suns that were paler than the day's sun, and made of silver rather than gold.

"No one knows where they went," I said, "if ever they were really here at all. But when there were these paler suns in the sky at night, they would have given you the nighttime shadows you want, Kursten."

We'd come to another hedge. This time we ambled alongside it until we reached a gate, which I opened to let Kursten and myself through, and then closed behind us. It was good we were close to home, because my flame had almost burnt itself out. The frozen grass squeaked as we walked on it.

"Where are they now?" she said.

"The lights?" I put my head to one side. "Like I said, no one knows. Things change. There aren't always good explanations."

"Or maybe you just made them up?"

"No. I didn't do that. Ask Lesor. We don't *know* they existed but we're sure, if that makes sense."

Kursten pursed her lips. "It does. It does for me."

We passed a few paces in silence and then she spoke again, once more in that dreamy way that made me feel I was eavesdropping.

"So here we are at midnight in winter's dead, and all the light we have aside from what we've brought is the starlight, and everyone knows the stars will never cast a shadow no matter how many of them you gather together. Somewhere on the other side of the world, though, it's the hottest part of summer, and right at this very moment the people who live in those parts are suffering the rigors of high noon . . . and they don't have shadows either. Where are all . . . ?"

Her voice grew firmer, as if she'd just realized I was there as well and had decided to draw me into the conversation.

"Where do all the shadows go, Rehan, at someone else's high noon and our low midnight? They can't simply stop existing, or be losing themselves. Like those paler suns of yours, they must have found somewhere to go. So where are they?"

I started to explain once more about the sun being directly above, and the shadow being directly under, but I hadn't gotten more than a few words out before she waved me to silence.

"I understood the first time, Rehan. You don't have to tell me again. The sun pushes the shadows straight down into the ground. But what happens to them once they're there? And where *at all* are our shadows tonight?"

"We haven't any shadows at the moment," I said pedantically. "There isn't a light in the sky to give us them. Long ago—then it was different. Then there were silver nighttime suns to give our untamed, uncomprehending forebears shadows."

Not just to give them shadows, I thought, for I knew something in my bones even though the pictures Lesor and I pored through had never shown anything of this. *Long ago the lights in the starry sky were there for people very like us to howl at.*

"You understand so little about shadows, Rehan," Kursten was saying as we ran toward the yellow windows of Giorran, which at last were visible around a swell in the land. "Don't you see the symmetries the Ghosts created? There's the turning of the year in the icy cold of midwinter, and in the middle of summer there's the fiercest heat of all. There are cooler parts of the world, and warmer. If the noon is high on the other side of the globe right now, then it stands to reason it must be low midnight for us. All these opposites in perfect balance, Rehan. Don't you see it? And the shadows—the shadows that are lost both there and here. You've told me where the sunlit people's shadows go, but—"

Her words pulled my mind like a kite being tugged into the wind.

"I know where the shadows hide at low midnight," I said, throwing my brand away from me so the fading fire went turning and tumbling through the darkness like a fugitive piece of sun.

Kursten bared her fangs, and, tail high, broke into a full dash towards the homes the Ghosts had built for themselves and that our wild ancestors had, sometime back in the infinite past, come in from the forests and steppes to inherit. It took me a moment to realize she'd gone from my side, but when I did I began to race after her along the pathway that was leading to our lives together.

And, all around us, the countless shadows we created as we ran rose silently from somewhere under the ground, fleeing into the sky to lose themselves amid unknowing stars.

LINEAGE

Kenneth Schneyer

*A*nd yet I know so little. I feel the soil of a hundred lands under my feet, look into ten thousand frightened eyes, grasp uncounted brittle strands of hope between my fingers. But I cannot answer so simple a question as this:
  What am I, when I am not one of them?

Mathilde:
  I think your excitement is premature. If I understood your report (and it could have been clearer) there is a lot of work to do before you can approach the conclusions you're suggesting.

  Let's stick to the facts. I'll accept your statement that you've found identical resonance patterns in seven different artifacts from disparate periods and points of origin, representing four continents and more than three millennia. Having said this, and understanding that I don't doubt your word, please run the resonance tests again.

I will also accept your assertion that each of these artifacts appears to display a similar visual marking or design—although, to my eye, the similarity could be coincidental, and the pattern is so rudimentary (even childish) that one could imagine it arising by chance.

Even if both of these statements are true, it is an heroic leap to infer that somehow the artifacts are associated with the same individual. You admit the extreme improbability that this is true; why bring it up at all?

However, I think that we can settle the matter easily. You did not mention running a DNA echo series on any of these artifacts. Do so now. If there are traces, and they're similar for two or more of the artifacts, then you'll have something meaningful to say. Otherwise we need to look for other (more plausible!) explanations.

Don't worry; everybody leaps to conclusions early in her career. If we didn't get excited about this work, why would we do it at all?

Leo

Raisl had nearly calmed the baby to sleep when Jan slammed open the door. The sudden noise and light frightened Bella, and she started whimpering all over again. After a weary evening—Bella was cutting a tooth and keeping the two older children awake—Raisl's first urge was to snarl at Jan, if Moishe didn't take his head off first.

But Jan's grey, sweaty face told her that he hadn't intruded needlessly in to their cramped, musty alcove. The balding little man's agitation was clear even in this bad light. His eyes bulged; he was out of breath. Raisl knew what he was going to say before he spoke.

"They found out; they're coming," said Jan, looking at Moishe, not at Raisl. "I saw them coming down the street, a whole squad of S.S. I ran back, they didn't see me, but they're not far off. It won't take them long to get here."

Moishe, dazed, rose slowly from his chair; Yakov and Dvora sat upright on their cot. "How?" asked Moishe. "How could they find out?"

Jan bent over and took Raisl firmly by the elbows, impelling her and Bella up. "It doesn't matter *how,*" he said. "Go. Go in the next ten minutes or you'll all be in Oœwiêcim by morning. Get out of Krakow, however you can."

"But the plan won't work on a Sunday night," said Moishe, yanking clothes onto Dvora as Raisl wrapped the baby. "The children can't—"

"Forget the plan," Jan said. "Go. I recommend north, then west, but *go.*"

"They'll be right behind us!" said Raisl, her own eyes as wide as Jan's, her legs wobbly.

"No, they won't," said Jan. "I can stall them, talk to them, maybe as long as ten more minutes. If you hurry, if you're lucky, you'll slip by."

"You can't stay and stall them," said Raisl. "They'll kill you!"

"Maybe. It's been done before," said Jan. All of a sudden he grinned—and he didn't look like Jan anymore. The grin was feral, like a madman or a criminal; it transformed him from the timid clerk Raisl knew into something fey and reckless.

Then she saw that he had scratched something onto his forearm, with a pin or a knife. It looked like three circles in a row and it was very recent: blood welled from the shapes. She was afraid of him.

"Done before? What are you talking about?" demanded Moishe, who hadn't noticed Jan's face or arm, jerking on his thin coat and checking Yakov's buttons.

"Never mind," said Jan with a stranger's cheeriness. "I wish we had some apples, though. I have a taste for yellow apples right now."

"Apples?" said Moishe, his voice now rising in panic. "*Apples? Are you out of your mind?*"

Jan set his hand on Yakov's small shoulder, his mad eyes on Moishe and his face still in that weird grin. "Moishe, this is my house," he said. "Get the hell out of it and let me do what I want with the trespassers." From his gay tone, he might have been asking to stay a little longer at the card table.

That was the end of the discussion. In the next three minutes, Moishe, Raisl, and the children grabbed the few extra clothes, supplies, and precious things they could carry, embraced Jan in fear and confusion, and stumbled down the back stairs.

So began the first of many dreadful nights, the twisted dream of flight, starvation, and exhaustion that lasted for more than a year. Somewhere in those bitter forests and barren fields, Yakov died holding his father's hand; somewhere else Raisl let in the chronic, painful illness that would never leave her. She was still wincing from it, an irritable old woman in a stupid pink suit, when she watched Bella's youngest daughter stand under the wedding canopy in Ohio.

Jan outdid himself in wit and misdirection, clowning and practically singing to the soldiers for not ten minutes, but twenty. He was still grinning his infuriating grin when Lieutenant Haupmann gave the disgusted order to shoot him.

A gain and again, like a banquet, comes the heady inhalation of destruction. The choice, the leap, the delicious farewell, the sweetness of oblivion. Greater love hath no man than this. Dulce et decorum est pro patria mori. Hear, O Israel: the Lord thy God, the Lord is One. Come on, nobody lives forever.

But I am still here. If this is somewhere.

L eo:
I'd already run the resonance tests three times before I made my report; I understood how unlikely the data seemed. Nevertheless I ran them a fourth time per your instructions. The results were consistent: each of the seven artifacts has the

same resonance pattern, the identical sequence over all eight reference points, each point similar to four decimal places (data analysis attached).

I understand what you're saying about the design, and yes, I suppose it could be "in the eye of the beholder." But that peculiar pattern of three circles in a row, each with its own perpendicular "arm" or "stem," just seems too regular to be coincidental. It was the design, after all, that drew me to these artifacts to begin with; I saw two with the same device, then a third, and that persuaded me to run the resonance test and look for similar items. Also there's the fact that each of the designs seems to have been added hurriedly, not using optimum materials or craftsmanship. If I were at home and these objects were contemporary, I'd say this was a gang sign.

As you requested, I ran the DNA echo series. There are distinguishable echoes on all of the artifacts, but none of them match. The people who left genetic residue on these objects had no common ancestors for at least six generations (full report attached). I realize that this datum may seem dispositive.

But looking at the literature, I can't find a single recorded case where two different individuals left the same resonance pattern. Not one. The energy signatures are supposed to be more unique to the individual than fingerprints, retinal patterns or voiceprints. If you can find a confirmed exception, then please show it to me; I know I'm relatively new at this, but I think I know how to read.

Mathilde

From inside the still, musty storehouse, the noises outside were strangely louder, as if they thought he was hiding and were calling to him. Thomas heard every mournful, futile whisper of the breeze, every restless complaint of the birds. Naturally he couldn't avoid hearing the groans and thuds of the wagon and its two horses as they drove up the hillside from the west.

Squinting with his bad eyes in the painful sunlight, he saw a straight grey blur with spots of cream and a coppery halo atop the wagon. It was Anne, her fiery hair under a cap. Though he couldn't make out the details, something in her posture told Thomas that she was holding the reins with more force than was necessary. The horses shook their heads nervously.

"Not the usual time for you to visit the storehouse," Thomas said, wondering what the horses knew that he didn't.

Without introduction or greeting, Anne's flat, practical voice said, "I'll need you to give me as many of the food stores as you can, Thomas."

"Give?" He shaded his eyes with his hand. "Give, for charity?"

"Aye, it should be for charity, you hard man, but I know you'll not give a crumb unless it's paid for. So here." She threw something at him; he had to stumble forward to catch it in his hands with a heavy *chink*. It was a bag of coins—a lot of coins. He counted them quickly with his fingers, his eyebrows lifting to his hairline.

"This would buy all that's inside," he said. "It won't fit on the wagon, all that." Anne's farm was no smaller than anyone else's, and she had no family to feed, but these coins must represent nearly all she had in the world. It made no sense.

She answered, "Well, then consider it your best bargain of the season. Lord knows you need all the help you can get."

"There's no need to insult me, is there? Tell me, what'll you do with what you've bought so dearly?"

There was a pause. Then she said, "Drive to London."

Involuntarily Thomas stepped three paces forward; now he could see the expression on her face. But it did him no good; her face told him as little as her voice. "London? You'll drive a cart of food into the middle of a plague city?"

"Aye, if they'll let me in. They're starving."

"They're dying of the Black Death, woman! You'll have no trouble getting in. It's *out* that'll be the problem."

"The ones who aren't dying of the Black Death are starving. No one will go into the city."

"And for good reason! Those that go in don't come out."

"We'll see."

"Will you throw your life away?"

"I'd not call it 'throwing away,'" she answered. Then a strange, wide grin came over her face, a grin that he'd never seen on her before, reminding Thomas of a wolf on the hunt. It made him draw back, so that she was a comforting blur again. "Besides, it's been done before," she added.

"No doubt," he grimaced, moving into the storehouse.

"Have you any apples in the storehouse?" she called after him.

"Apples? No, they were gone a month ago."

"Pity, that. I have a real craving for a yellow apple; came on me all of a sudden."

Thomas found that he was reluctant to emerge again from the storehouse. When he came out with the goods, Anne had dismounted and took the first sack from him. So close as that, he could smell her sweat and the rosemary on her breath, and could see that she still wore that weird smile.

As he came close enough to hoist the sack, Thomas saw that there was a sign scratched on to the wagon's side, using a bit of chalk or stone, or possibly a metal tool. It was three circles in a row, each with a tiny stem over it. It hadn't been there when Anne drove up, he was sure. A witch's mark?

He did not have long to ponder the question. She gave him an unexpected kiss on the forehead with her dry lips before ascending again and geeing up the horses. Back inside the building he couldn't avoid the odd, foreign melody of her whistling as the cart rumbled back down the hill.

It took a long time before the sounds were gone.

For the rest of his life, Thomas listened half-hopefully for the sounds of Anne's horses. But they never came.

Instantiation, substantiation, manifestation, possession? I am no one, if more than nothing; years pass, but not for me. Then I feel, like an embrace, the fear and devotion—the lifeboat overflows, the enemy surprises the patrol, the burning wall begins to collapse, the asteroid approaches the shuttle, the dike bursts.

And I walk the earth again.

Mathilde:
You have no call to be offended. You are presenting unusual conclusions to the principal investigator with very little to back them up. You have to expect to be pressed on your hypotheses if you're going to stay in this business.

Yes, I do find the disparate DNA echo evidence "dispositive." If the same individual actually handled all seven objects then that individual would have left an echo on each of them. Maybe it wouldn't have survived, but *somebody's* echo survived, since you found it on the artifacts. The fact that it shows seven distinct, unrelated individuals seems to decide the matter.

As you say, I don't know of any recorded cases in which different individuals left the same resonance pattern. Perhaps we've found the first one. Or perhaps we've found evidence that resonance patterns normalize or disorganize under certain conditions. Each of those would be a meaningful discovery, would it not?

Let's not forget that our object is to collect meaningful data and find the explanations that most satisfactorily explain it. We're not after ultimate "truth."

Leo

* * *

Nicander could still smell the smoke from the campfires that had been put out. Pacing steadily over the cold, rocky ground, he saw the faintest blue traces over a few remaining spots. He nodded with approval. The enemy almost certainly knew their position and their numbers, and so the men had been allowed a little warmth and a chance to cook some meat, but there was no point being reckless.

Now they were all at work, whetting swords or repairing armor. Any talk was so low he could barely hear it, which was as it should be. They knew their business. A full night's sleep, and they'd be ready for—well, perhaps not ready for what was coming, but readier than any other army would have been. The twilight would end soon, and the night would be cold.

Nicander stopped at his captain's tent, cleared his throat, and said his own name loudly enough to carry. There was no reply, which he safely interpreted to be an invitation to enter.

A single lamp lit the space, granting Alexandros the look of a shadowy giant. He was oiling the straps of his armor and humming to himself, that same annoying marching tune he'd had on his lips for a month.

"Yes, Nico?" said Alexandros, who hadn't looked up when his enomotarch came in.

"One of the men can do that for you," said Nicander.

"Yes, and they can do their own, can't they?" said the captain. "Have you urgent tasks to take me away from the work of an honest soldier?"

"No, sir."

"Well, then. How are the men?"

"Calm, sir, for the most part. Some are edgy because they don't like the terrain."

"Ah now, the terrain is perfect." Alexandros spoke as if he were a connoisseur tasting a rare wine. He set down the armor, rubbed the excess oil on his arms, and picked up his sword like a father holding his infant son. He took out a whetstone and began to sharpen the blade, beaming at his handiwork.

Nicander said, "Gates of Fire."

"Delightful name for a battlefield," said Alexandros. "Makes you feel like you're already doing something great."

There was a pause. Alexandros seemed to know that Nicander had more to say, but he didn't ask him to continue. He ran his finger along the blade, nodding. Then he blew the iron dust off it; but he did not set down either the sword or the whetstone.

Nicander cleared his throat again. Alexandros looked up, amused.

Nicander said, "Sir, what in name of the Dog we are doing here?"

"Obeying the King."

"And what is *he* doing here?"

Alexandros seemed to consider whether this was insubordinate talk. Then he answered, "Having a drink with the Persians."

"Sir—"

"What is it you want to know, Nico?" The captain paused, glancing over at a bowl of golden apples on a small table. "The tactical situation is obvious. When you have a small force and the enemy has a large one, you choose the narrowest place possible. Can't get any narrower than this." He looked pleased with himself. "We'll hold them off all day. Several days, maybe."

"And then?"

"One of two things happens: either they'll go away, or we'll get to meet Charon face to face. Prissy fellow; he's probably Athenian."

Nicander ignored the blasphemy. The captain delighted in shocking him. "You think they'll go away?"

"Persians? They might. They dislike getting bloody noses."

"And if they don't?"

"I just said."

"But if we know we're going to lose—"

"It's not a loss. Lose a few hundred to save a few hundred thousand? Any trader in the market knows what a bargain that is."

"And we just make the trade?"

For no apparent reason, the captain's whole demeanor changed. He grinned, the wild, hungry grin of battle that Nicander knew so well. Using the whetstone, he slowly scratched three circles on the blade of his sword, near the hilt. Then he finished with a tiny line on each of the circles. Finally he lifted his sword to his face and kissed it.

Alexandros asked, "You were saying, Nico?" His voice had changed too, becoming hoarse; his eyes were dilated and the irises looked darker. Nicander fought an unreasonable urge to flee.

"I was saying, sir—I was saying, will we just make the trade? Give up all our lives without even a victory?"

Alexandros picked up one of the golden apples from the tray, tossed it into the air, caught it, and brought it to his mouth.

"Why not? It's been done before," he said, biting into the crisp, sweet fruit.

For a moment, I am Anne; for another, I am Krikor. I am Dzuling, Juan, Mbogo, Alexandros. There are a thousand crucial moments, but always the same choice. I do the only thing I know how to do.

Do I change anything? Brave men and women who never met me nonetheless offer their last breaths at the feet of their friends; I have seen them do it. So too Dzuling might have given herself for the shuttle unaided; maybe Jan would have faced the S.S. alone. Perhaps I do not forge their courage.

Perhaps the only gift I bring is joy.

MURDER IN METACHRONOPOLIS

John C. Wright

16

Third beginning:

    I woke up when my gun jumped into my hand. It was an Unlimited Class Paradox Proctor Special, and it was better than any alarm, better than any guard dog.

    I relaxed my eyelids open just a crack. It was dark. My balcony windows were fully polarized, so the glow from the golden towers outside showed only as faint, ghostly streaks reaching from pale mist below to black sky above.

    The door, the creator, and the dreambox all showed like blocky shadows in the gloom. I couldn't see more. This was one of the rooms in a lower tower, a pretty shabby affair, not far above the mist, and the towerlight from outside would have been dim even if the windows had been dialed to transparent.

    There. A silhouette against the glass. It was tall, with some sort of wide headgear, perhaps with a plume above.

I raised my arm very slowly, careful not to rustle the sheets.

I said, in the Control language, "Lights!"

The lights came on.

He didn't look surprised. That is a bad sign.

The joker himself was dressed like a French Musketeer from Cardinal Richelieu's time, complete with ruffles, lace, tall boots, swordbelt, and pig-sticker. There was something about him that made me think he was real, not repro. Maybe it was the battered, used look in his hilt and scabbard; maybe it was the battered, used look on his face. Maybe it was the smell. Usually you can tell pre-industrial from postindustrial types in one whiff.

One anachronism was the skull-plug clinging like an insect to the base of his neck. And that was wrong, all wrong, if this guy was a party-killer. There's some strange types wandering like ghosts in the Towers, from every spot of history that ever was, and a lot that never were, drifting from party to party, if they still got luster, or just drifting, if they don't. Some of the strangest are the party-killers, the kinds that do murder just to see who is going to be resurrected by the next day, and who'll be forgotten.

But this guy was all wrong for that. Real party-killers never used brainjacks to record their sensations. For them, death had to be live, or else it was nothing.

Second, this guy didn't look nervous or scared. He had the not-surprised look of a bad actor going through a flat rehearsal.

Third, he recognized my piece. And not many people have seen the three-dimensional cross-section of an Unlimited Special. What I had in my hand wasn't the whole weapon array, arsenal, detection and tracking gear, etc. That would fill up a room, or even a warehouse. No, all I had in hand was the aiming-guide, firing mechanisms, and the shielding unit which protected me from backscatter.

Still. Not many people know what it's like to look into the business end of an Unlimited Special. Not many at all.

"You're a Time Master," I said.

"Very good, Mr. Frontino," he said. His voice was blurry and harsh, as if he were not used to using the vocal cords he was using now. "That is the quickest you've ever come to the correct conclusion—this time around."

"And you're going to pretend I don't remember the other versions, because of—why?"

He spread his hands awkwardly, a gesture like a puppet with a clumsy puppeteer would make. "That should be obvious, Mr. Frontino."

"My other versions are being killed. And I suppose that if I pulled this trigger, your alternates won't remember this version we're in now either, eh?"

"Unless they were monitoring, no. They say the only way to kill a Master of Time, a careful one who looks into his past and future, is to wait for him to kill himself. But you flatliners don't have that privilege, do you?" He smiled, sort of a sickly impersonation of good humor.

"Yeah. But we don't have to sneak around, so afraid of paradoxes that we can't even show our own faces in our own city that we allegedly rule. And we don't have groups of phonies and crazies out and about pretending that they're us when they're not."

I reached up with my other hand and made an adjustment. Dots from aiming lasers appeared on his groin and chest and the wrist of his right hand, which was a little too near the hilt of his sword for my taste.

(Think it's funny, guy like me, armed as I was, afraid of his old-fashioned weapon, eh? People who think swords are quaint, not dangerous, never saw one used by a pro who knows his business. And the business is death by laceration, evisceration, impalement. No, swords are not quaint at all.)

I said: "There's one on the spot between your eyes, too. You can't see it."

"I'll take your word for it, Mr. Frontino."

I eyed him up and down carefully, looking for blurs or distortions which might indicate a timeshift. Nothing. Maybe he was actually all the way here, in this timespace, flying blind. But why? Most Masters kept a version or two of themselves posted a minute or so in the future to give themselves plenty of warning for any surprises coming. Not him though. Why? Didn't make sense.

He was still waiting for my next line. He didn't just sit there and tell me what I was about to say, like most Masters I'd met. Maybe he was less rude than most; or maybe he was just waiting for me to say something to let him know he was in the right version. Or, most likely, maybe he wasn't a Master of Eternity at all.

Whatever. "Spill it. Whatever you're here to say. Say it. Then get out."

"I'm here to hire you to solve a murder, Mr. Frontino."

"And you're pretending to be a Master? Walk back into the past and look for yourself."

"It hasn't happened yet." Again, the crooked smile.

"Cute. And are you going to stop it if I solve it?"

"Not me. Not that I foresee." Again, the smile.

"Solve a crime and let it happen anyway, is that the plan? Sorry. Not interested. I'm retired. 'Bye."

"Retired? But aren't you the only Private Investigator in Metachronopolis? You've even got a fedora and a trenchcoat!"

"Everyone dressed like that when I'm from. And I'm retired as far as the Bigwigs are concerned. Some Time Master wants to solve a crime? Step into the past and watch it happen or the future when it's already been solved. Look it up in history book. What do you need mere mortals for? Manpower? Double yourself up a hundred times."

"There are limits to the powers of the Masters of Eternity. Grim limits. Though, sometimes, where exactly those boundaries lay are . . . misty."

He seemed to think that was funny. Before things got too humorous, I decided to cut things short. I opened the firing aperture with a twist of the wrist to maximum cone-of-blast and let him see me set the timer. The timer started beeping a countdown.

"I don't take cases from Time Masters, see? All you guys are the same. The murderer turns out to be yourself, or you when you were younger. Or me. Or an alternate version of me or you who turns out to be his own father fighting himself because for no reason except that that's the way it was when the whole thing started. Which it never did, on account of there's no beginning and no reason for any of it. Oh, brother, you time travelers make me sick."

He drew himself up, all smiles gone now, all pretense at seeming human. My guess was that that was not even his real body, just some poor sap he murdered to have his personality jacked into the guy's brain. Perfect disguise. No fingerprints, retina prints, no nothing. Just another flatliner dead for the convenience of the Masters of Eternity.

"Why did you retire from the service, Mr. Frontino?"

"Let's just say I was tired of cleaning up after all the messes you guys leave all across your past and future. You'd think when you were done, you'd at least have the common decency to put everything back the way you found it."

"Everything? Absolutely everything?" His eyes were glittering now. "Be careful what you think, Mr. Frontino. Thoughts have consequences."

The timer on my gun was entering its final cycle, chiming like a little tiny bit of doomsday. "My friend here says you have about thirty seconds to leave. You have just enough time to try to scare me into taking the case by saying someone is knocking off these so-called 'other versions' of mine to stop me from taking it."

"No need for me to say it, Mr. Frontino. You're performing admirably."

"Twenty seconds . . . Unless you want to admit you're not a Master after all and tell me what this is really all about?"

"No, Mr. Frontino. You will be convinced I am a Master. And, before I forget to mention, you yourself will be the murder victim. I trust your interest in the case has increased? And should you still doubt my bona fides, here. I will leave a card."

And then he was gone. Something glittered in midair where he had been standing, the size of a playing card made of crystal, and fell with a chime of noise to my floor.

0.

Stories about Metachronopolis, the shining city outside of time, have many beginnings, they say. And I say that they all come to the same miserable end. If you ask me. If there is anyone out there left to ask me.

29.

Let's start with the ending. I want you to imagine tumbling end over end in a featureless gray mist, no gravity, no nothing, watching in horror as your fingers dissolve.

You don't remember what this means or how you got here, of course, unless you've got special memory like mine. Hardened memory. It lets you remember things that didn't happen, not in your timeline, anyway.

If you've got hardened memory, like mine, you can torment yourself to ease the boredom while you get erased, by going back over and over the stupid things you'd done, telling yourself that if you had the chance, just one more chance, you'd do it all differently next time around.

And if you're not too bright, it won't even occur to you that that's exactly the kind of thinking that got you into this mess in the first place.

(Except which place is the first place, anyway?)

1.

First beginning:

I regretted the words the moment I said them. But there are some things, once said, you can't take back.

I was opening my mouth to begin to apologize when she slapped my face. She leaned into the blow and gave me a good wallop, for a girl. Then she stood a moment, watching me with those beautiful hazel gray eyes of hers. Beneath half-closed lids, her eyes were like sparks of luminous fire. She stood, lips pouted, or sneering, coldly studying the effect on me.

I raised my hand to rub my aching jaw. Maybe I didn't look sorry enough, or maybe I looked too sorry. Never can tell with women.

She turned on her heel and swayed over to the door. She gave me one last burning look over her shoulder.

"Baby-doll, come back," I said. "I can make it right between us. Like none of that stuff ever happened. Like none of it ever had to happen . . . "

Maybe it sounded like I was whining, or maybe it sounded like I wasn't whining hard enough. Whatever, it was the wrong thing to say.

A faint look of disdain curled her perfect red lips. "You're a smart boy, Jake," she said, her voice husky and low, dripping with carefully chosen notes of contempt. "Smart enough to weasel out of some things. But not smart enough to know you can't weasel out of everything. Actions have consequences. Like this one. Watch me. Good-bye."

She swirled out the door, graceful as a lynx, and slammed it shut so that the glass rattled. I saw her slim silhouette against the glass for a moment, and heard the bright clatter of heels against the floorboards, down the hallway toward the elevators.

Then she was gone.

17.

There wasn't any real government in this city, except for the hidden Masters. But some of the important statesmen, Jefferson and Machiavelli and Caesar and guys like that, had thrown together a militia. Sometimes the militia circulated papers on unsavory characters, from petty thieves and party-crashers, up through to the odd rapist or kidnapper who molested one of the famous women from history, Helen of Troy, or Cleopatra, that some of the Masters supposedly kept around in their harems.

And then there was me. Jacob Frontino, Private Eye. Since there were no regular cops among the glittering towers, there was work enough for me to do. Except when there wasn't. People paid in favors, big or small, or in foodstuffs, ever since my Creator Box went on the blink. I got by. Why hadn't the Masters of Time shut me down long ago?

No one knows why they do anything.

I pulled on my trousers and tucked in the tails of the shirt I hadn't bothered to take off when I sacked out on the couch. I whistled a command-code toward the wardrobe, and serving-beams draped my trench coat around my shoulders. Not that I expected to be cold in my own apartment; the fabric is woven with defensive webbing, and detection-reaction cells. My own shabby version of shining armor.

And the wardrobe slapped my hat onto my head. It must have thought if I needed my coat, I needed my hat, right? Like I said, this was a low-tower apartment, and the circuits here were kind of dim.

I walked over slowly to where the Time Master had been standing. Something was shining on the floor.

The card lay between my feet, glittering like a lake of deep ice. Distant shapes, like drowned buildings seen at the bottom of a clear lake, hovered in the cloudy reflection. I reached down . . .

18.

Perhaps I wasn't thinking. Perhaps it was what flatliners call a coincidence. Only I don't believe in coincidences. I know there are Time Masters.

I had actually bent over and was reaching my hand down toward the damn thing when my smartgun emitted its shrieking chronodistortion alarm, and jumped out of its holster and into my hand. The grip tingled where the energy field had to grab my fingers and fold them around the stock.

By then it was too late. My eyes had focused on the image floating deep below the mirrored surface of the card. This one was attention-activated.

Whenever a human brain pays attention to any event, the possible timelines radiating from that point multiply, since that observation might affect the human's actions. There are circuits which can detect these multiplications, though I'd never heard of one being focused through a destiny card.

You look. You're trapped. Very neat, very tidy.

It was a picture of a wide, high place surrounded by pillars. Of course I recognized it. The Prytaneum of the Masters of Eternity. And then I was there.

19.

"Welcome to the crime scene, Mr. Frontino."

3.

Second beginning, this one brighter than the others:
I recall my first view of the city.

I thought it was a job interview. I had no other work, no future, and the best woman I had ever laid eyes on had walked out on me the night before. I wasn't in a great mood, but, at that point, I was willing to listen to anything.

Almost anything.

"Time travelers?" I said, trying to look chipper. I was trying to think of a polite way to say good-bye and get lost.

He didn't look crazy. (The real crazies never do). Mr. Iapetus was a foreign-looking fellow in a red long coat of a fabric I didn't recognize. He had dark, magnetic eyes, high cheekbones, and wore a narrow goatee.

The office was appointed with severe and restrained elegance. To one side, a row of dark bookshelves loomed; in the center was a wide mahogany desk, polished surface gleaming; to the other side, heavy drapes blocked a hidden length of window. I did not think it odd at the time to see bright sunlight shining from the carpet at the lower hem of the window drapes. It had been raining when I had come into the lobby just behind me.

Mr. Iapetus was standing by the window. He took up a fold of drapes in his hand. "I believe in what you might call the shock-therapy method of indoctrination. It helps make the tedious period of disbelief somewhat briefer."

A wide yank of his arm threw the drapes aside. A spill of blinding sunlight washed around me.

Blinking, I saw I was high up, overlooking a city of towers rising from clouds. It had been overcast, a dark day, on the ground floor when I came in. I had trudged up two flights of stairs. Now, I was miles up in the air. And glory was underfoot.

4.

"Behold Metachronopolis, the city beyond the reach of time!"

Towers made of gleaming gold, taller than tall mountains, rose in streamlined ramparts all around me, like swords held up in high salute. Far underfoot, in the canyons and gulfs between the towers, cloudbanks drifted, stained cerise and gold from the light shed by the towers. I could not see the ground.

Great bridges, elfin-graceful, arched across the miles from balcony to balcony of the gleaming structures, with giant statues placed at even intervals, sentry-like, along their tremendous length. The balconies were thickly grown with hedges and arbors, and the bridges were like parklands suspended in the air, with figures dimly glimpsed strolling among the greenery. Or flying.

I thought they were seagulls at first. They rose from the clouds below. Bright figures rose and soared past the window, comet-swift, and I saw that they were manlike beings, robed in cloaks of light which fanned out like angel wings to either side of them. Up along the wind they fled, swifter than rising sparks, handsome men, and women with faces like young girls, heads thrown back and eyes alit with pleasure. They were dressed in the costumes of all ages.

Among the flock were monsters like satyrs and chimera and animal-headed people, like the gods of ancient Egypt, jackal-headed or hawk-headed.

The air was alive with fliers, darting from window to window, or from minaret to minaret, balcony to balcony, bridge to rooftop-garden.

And, dimly through the glass, I heard the air was filled with music.

Iapetus' voice rang with pride: "Many histories have many strange beginnings, but time travel is inevitable in every time line, and, from time travelers, the Masters of Time come forth, the Masters of Eternity, and all come here, one and all, their mighty monuments and towers to build. Yes! Metachronopolis has many beginnings, but all timelines lead to her!"

I was impressed by the sights. "When do I get my chance to sign up?" I said softly.

Iapetus opened the window. I smelled the scent of wind-blown petals from the far gardens, and heard the flourish of trumpets, and the tolling of deep bells. "In a sense," he said, "You already have. Examine your memory."

He took a gun out of his pocket and shot me in the leg. I fell screaming, blood pumping through the fingers I clenched onto my shattered knee . . .

And then he hadn't. Never had. No gun, no wound.

The shocking memory of having been shot, horribly wounded, was already beginning to fade, like a bad dream.

But I didn't let it fade. For one thing, it was impossible for me to have two separate and distinct, mutually contradictory memories of the same event. I was so shocked by the blatant impossibility that I clung to the memory, forced it to stay in my head, just so I could look at it.

Because I somehow had seen both: his fingers were momentarily blurry, as if I were seeing them through a thin mist. His right arm somehow seemed to be both hanging at his side and bending at the elbow as he put it in his pocket.

For another, I wanted to remember the look on Iapetus' face as he shot. Just for a second, as he raised the strange pistol, he wore a look so inhuman and expressionless, that I would have called it cruel, if he hadn't seemed so cavalier and nonchalant . . .

"Déjà vu is a milder form of the same phenomenon," he continued in the same bored, dry tone. "Some people have a naturally hardened memory. Our training can increase the talent. It is, of course, a talent utterly useless except when there is a Master of Eternity nearby, manipulating the chronocosm. Then it is precious. Useful to us. Our instruments show you have a strong natural hardness of memory; a stubborn streak. Being able to remember alternate versions after a time-change does not make you a Time Master, of course. But, still, it's better than being a flatliner. We call it pawn memory. I trust you see the humor? Pawns cannot leave their own files, their own timelines, so to speak, unless a major piece is near. And, yes, some pawns reach the final row."

20.

So of course I recognized the place. Highest tower in the city, biggest, brightest. A vast floor of shining black marble, inset with panels of mirrored destiny crystal, stretched across acres toward wide balconies, which looked down upon the titanic gold towers far below. The place looked like it was open to the air on every side, but between the tall pillars must have been panes of invisible glass or some sort of force field to maintain the pressure at this altitude. The sky above was so dark blue it was almost black.

I think I saw the curve of the horizon.

Standing near one of the thrones that formed a semi-circle embracing the floor, was the smirking smart-alec who talked like a Time Master and dressed like d'Artagnan, floppy hat, boots, rapier and all, who had so neatly sucked me into what he called the crime scene. We were not alone. Standing near me was a cataphract in power armor, circa A.D. 4400, the era of the Machine Wars. He had his faceplate up, and I could see the cold, no-nonsense look in his eye. The armor was throbbing on standby; I could hear the idling hum of the disrupter grids and the clicking of the launch-pack warm-up check from here.

There was a whine from his elbow servo-motors when he folded his arms, putting his fingers near the control points on his chestplate.

I was fast with my smartgun. I didn't think I was that fast. I put it back in the holster, slowly, like a nice little boy who didn't want to get flattened.

At his nod, an aiming monocle clicked out of its slot on his helmet visor and fell over his eye. Little red dots appeared up and down along my chest, just to let me know he was thinking of me.

I turned to d'Artagnan. "Cute trick with the destiny card," I said.

"You didn't want to be here. Well, now you are."

"What's the big idea with the tin can here?" I said, hooking a thumb at the cataphract.

"That should be obvious, Mr. Frontino. We want you to solve a murder, not to prevent it. Even highly trained Paradox Proctors get uncertain about their oaths if ever they look into the circumstances of their own future deaths. They always wonder, can't the universe stand just one more small strain? Surely one more tiny fold in the fabric of time won't unravel the whole web? And what does it matter to me anyway, if the chronocosm dies, so long as I myself can live?"

He chuckled, then added: "If that's what loyal Knot-cutters think, well, well; what are we to expect from one who is retired? Especially since he did not ask our *permission* to retire, did he?"

I turned away. I wasn't sure what I would say, so all I did say was: "And where's the body?"

"I have composed a null-time vacuole to bracket the event," he said, drawing a mirrored destiny card from his doublet. "You may examine it at your leisure."

First clue: why did d'Artagnan here bother saying so much? Time Masters are only talkative in virgin time. When they've been through the same scene a dozen times or so, they usually get right to the point. He had been acting the same way last night, when he interrupted my beauty sleep. Was there such a thing as a Master of Time who didn't like to time travel?

Clue two: why me? Why these high-pressure tactics to herd me into this thing? They had other paradox-killers. Plenty. One of them was looming behind me right now, dressed in his happy mechanical-man suit.

D'Artagnan slid the destiny card into the crystal material of the nearest throne-arm. The throne itself was made of a block of the same "substance" as the card: an area of frozen time-energy. The surface was time-conductive, so it reflected the image in the card. (I've always wondered why they make their chairs that way. I guess nothing else is good enough for a Master of Time to warm his butt on. On the other hand, no one could monkey around with any of these throne's histories, not made of what they were made of, or go back and have had built bombs or bugging cells inside them or whatnot.)

And the strip of the floor leading from the throne to where I was standing was also made of the same substance. I saw the new scene too clearly to deny it. And I was there.

21.

I saw a single, still moment of time.

Everything was "lit" by the weird non-glow of null-time. Any object grew bluer and dimmer the longer you stared at it. I was used to the effect; I kept my gaze swinging back and forth as I stepped into the scene, always moving. D'Artagnan and the cataphract stepped in behind me, the leg-motors on the power-armor humming with understated strength.

There were only two figures frozen in the moment of the murder scene. One was motionless on a throne, armored in ice and cloaked in mist; his face, a mirror. The other was a tall guy, not so good looking, trench coat scarlet with motionless flame, stylish fedora suspended in mid-air to one side of his head. He was in the middle of getting shot, impaled on an energy-blast.

Yours truly. Of course. And to think that one of my goals in life had been to leave a good-looking corpse.

I looked at the blast first.

It originated off to the left. Near one of the pillars, about shoulder-high, a small puff of mist was frozen. Trailing out from it, motionless, like a worm made of flame, was a line of Cherenkov radiation, and knots and streamers of cloud where the atmosphere couldn't get out of the way fast enough to avoid being vaporized. Little glowing balls like St. Elmo's fire dotted the fiery discharge-stream, where ionized oxygen molecules were being turned into ozone. Brighter crooked lines paralleling the discharge-path indicated atoms split by the force of the passing bullet.

At the other end of the discharge-stream was me, also ending. I looked at myself hanging in mid-air, caught in mid-explosion and mid-death. My smartgun was leaping like salmon trying, too late, to get into my fingers. It hung, frozen, a few inches above my out-flung hand. Not smart enough, this time, it seemed.

I (the me version of me, that is) stepped through clouds of blood and flying steam to get a closer look at me (the becoming-a-corpse version of me). The exit wound was enormous, as if half my chest and all of my left arm had been drawn in hazy red chalk-smudges by an Impressionist artist.

The smell was terrible. I know the textbooks say you're not supposed to be able to smell anything in null-time. But, I figure, that if my eye can move through a cloud of frozen photons and pick up an image, then my nose can move through a cloud of motionless me-molecules and sniff roasted flesh.

There was no visible entry wound. Of course. The bullet must have been ultra-microscopic, perhaps only a few molecules wide, in order to be small enough to slip through my smartgun's watchdog web. And it must have been traveling fast enough, a hefty percentage of the speed of light, to be quick enough to get me before my smartgun could react.

And the bullet was programmed, somehow, to drop velocity and transfer its kinetic energy to my body in a broad, slow shockwave once it struck.

Somehow? A time-retardation wave could do it. The relative velocity would change once it left the field. Just another application of the same technology which made my smartgun.

Heck. I could have this done this myself, with a smartgun just like the one I had. I already thought of two ways to reproduce this effect just with the programs I presently had loaded.

I straightened up and backed away, brushing anachronistic drops of blood off my coat.

23.

After I was done looking at the figure on the throne, I turned and said to d'Artagnan, "I need to take a reading of the time depth and energy signature of the discharge wave with the sensors in my smartgun. I'm going to draw it nice and slow, so your steel gorilla knows I'm on the level here. That all right with you?"

D'Artagnan spread his hands. "That's fine."

For the first time I noticed a slight blur of mist around his fingers as he made the gesture.

He had time-doubled. It looked like a Recursive Alternate Information shift; but I wasn't sure. There was an alternate line out there somewhere where he had done something else with his hand. Maybe touched a control or given a hand-signal to the cataphract. Or, if it was actually a Recursive Anachronism shift, he might have handed something forward or backward to himself.

Or he might not have done anything at all. With a Parallel Displacement shift, a Master of Time, a real one, maintaining position a few seconds away and pacing us, could have handed him something.

I drew my smartgun slowly.

25.

And I was thinking: Why not?
          Why the hell not?

Hitler's mother, at sixteen years old, looked up at me with eyes as wide and trusting and innocent and hurt as any you'd ever dream of seeing. She hadn't done anything wrong. Maybe she would have said something, but the slug had torn out her throat. She got blood all over my pants and shoes when she fell toward me. It had smelled then the way it smelled now.

Stalin's mother was a sad and overworked washer-woman, living quietly and harming no one when the Masters decided to abort her future. They had me shoot her in the stomach twice more after she fell, burnt and screaming, just to make sure the helpless baby would be dead.

Why not? They can all make it undone again. So they told me.

And then one Time Master or another took a dislike to the atomic wars of the 2030s. Einstein was a little boy playing with mud-pies in a backyard garden when my misplaced scattershot tore off his arms and legs and left him blind, bleeding and screaming until I could reprogram and fire a particle beam to put him out of his misery.

When I asked to be allowed to go back and do that ass-assination again, the Masters' representative told me that chronoportation should not be used for frivolous reasons. He sternly warned me that paradox weakened the fabric of timespace.

Why not?

I won't even tell you who I had to kill to let a curious Master of Time explore the alternate line where Christianity never rose to dominance in Europe. At least that one was done with one clean shot to the head.

Why not?

If I could set out to kill pregnant women and innocent girls and little boys and the nicest guy I'd ever met, why not set out to kill me?

22.

I looked around to see who I had been (was going to be) talking to, when I was (would be) shot.

Only one of the thrones was occupied. There he was in all his regalia. A Master of Eternity. His armor was made, not of metal, but of destiny crystal, gleaming like ice. From his shoulders depended a cloak of mist, created, allegedly, from a single thread vibrating backward and forward across several seconds. This cloak of distorted time fell from his shoulders in streamers of vapor, dripped across and down the chair arms where he sat, and hovered in curls around his ankles.

I could not see his face. His crown was projecting a forcefield like a mirrored helmet to protect his head from the radiation of the murderous discharge in front of him.

Clue three: why did the Master's armor have time to react to the assassin's bolt when the victim's smartgun did not? Coincidence? But I didn't believe in coincidences. What people call coincidences are arrangements by the Masters of Time as sloppy make-shifts to put broken timelines back on track.

And I sure as hell didn't believe in Masters any more.

5.

Iapetus leaned past me and opened the window. He paused a moment, allowing me to savor the smell of the high gardens, the deep chime of distant bells, to hear the calls and cries of delight from the winged fliers.

He spoke: "There needs be no further interview nor testing. Any Master dissatisfied with your future performance would have already retroactively informed me. The choice is now yours."

He straightened, looking me in the eye, smiling, and saying: "The rewards of loyal service to the Masters of Eternity are many . . ."

1(a).

I didn't say anything to her, this time. I bit back the angry confession which sprang to my lips. There are some things which, once said, can never be taken back.

Instead, I put my hands on her shoulders, and drew her closer. "Baby-doll, there's no other woman. There just is no one else . . . " I lied smoothly.

This time, my past didn't catch up with me. I could always outrun it, always stay one jump ahead of the game.

I smothered the pang of guilt I felt at the thought as I lowered my head to kiss her.

6.

"...including material rewards, without limit . . . "

10.

While I was waiting for the croupier, and the manager, and the manager's assistant, to collect my winnings into a large suitcase, I stepped into a telephone booth, with a copy of tomorrow's stock market under my arm, to make a call to my broker.

I yawned while the phone rang. It all seemed so tedious, so safe. Maybe this time around I would walk into the ambush the thugs hired by the manager were planning.

7.

"...as well as the knowledge that you are doing good and useful work to preserve both past historic treasures and the integrity of the time-space continuum . . . "

11.

The Roman legionnaire stood there, shaking and sweating, eyes rolling wildly, unable to move, numb in the grip of my paralysis ray. I would have preferred to shoot him, of course, but orders were not to chance future archeologists puzzling over slugs found in one of Caesar's troopers. I could tell he wanted to scream when I pulled his short-sword from its scabbard, put the point under the belt of his armor, pushed.

He fell down the steps of the Library at Alexandria, and I kicked the torch he had held down after him, safely away from the precious scrolls and papyrus.

There was blood splashed all over my coat and trousers.

I was doing good work. Why did it make me feel sick to my stomach?

A half a score of legionnaires trotted around the corner at a quickstep, shield and pilum in hand, led by a decurion. They let out a roar when they saw their dead comrade, and shouted vows of vengeance to their gods. Then they lowered spears, formed ranks, and charged the stairs.

I laughed. Did they expect me to wait around for their vengeance? For the consequences of my actions to catch up with me? They would never catch up.

A twist on the barrel of my smartgun opened the paralysis induction beam to wide-fan. They fell and waited, helplessly, for me to slaughter them. I tried not to look them in the eyes as I moved from one to the next with a knife.

8.

"...and, since the Masters of Eternity are all-powerful, no one can oppose them or stop them. They have no enemies . . ."

13.

When I woke up, I was slumped in a heavy, high-backed chair of dark red leather, at the end of a long conference table of black walnut. Nine hooded figures sat around the length of the table.

Light came from two high candelabrums, burning real candles and dripping messy wax like stalactites down their sides. The room around me was dim; I had the impression it might be a library. There were no windows, no clocks, nothing in view like a calendar. I could hear no noise from outside. It may have been day or night of any season, any year.

The robes, likewise, could have been from practically any date or era. They all wore gloves; I saw no rings or jewelry.

"Do not be alarmed," came a polite tenor from my left. "I know you do not recall this, but you volunteered to have a small part of your recent memory blotted out. It was a condition our anonymity required to make this conversation possible. You wanted to speak with us."

"And who are you supposed to be?" I asked, straightening up, my fingers pressed against my throbbing temples. "And why the hell did I—you claim—want to speak to you so badly?"

The hooded figure at the other end of the table leaned forward slightly. He had a rumbling, bass voice: "We are the eternal enemies of the Master of Eternity, Mr. Frontino . . . "

24.

I drew my smartgun slowly, so as not to startle d'Artagnan or Ugly Boy in the fancy steel suit. Idiots. They might have stood a chance if Ugly Boy had had enough sense to keep his faceplate down. As it was, I gyro-focused an aiming laser to keep a dot right between his eyes where he couldn't see it, while taking a reading on the energy discharge which killed (was going to kill) me (future-me). I didn't have to point the gun-barrel at Ugly Boy to do it; my gun was pretty damn smart.

The formation readings did not surprise me. The energy signature was the same as that generated by the gun held in my hand. Not the same make or model, the exact same gun.

Of course. Obviously. I was going to shoot myself.

Means I could see; what about opportunity?

The time-depth reading on the spot of mist from which the murder-discharge radiated did surprise me. It was a matter of a few minutes, positive or negative. Something was going to make me shoot me in a moment or so from now.

And that left only motive. And I couldn't imagine any motive, at first.

But then I thought: Why not? Why the hell not?

26.

I swung my barrel to cover d'Artagnan.

"OK, fancy boy," I snapped. "Charade's over. Do I need to shoot you to make the real Master show up?"

"You think I am not a Time Master?"

I shook my head. I could have explained that I hadn't seen him chronoshift but once, and that, since he wasn't wearing a mist cloak like a proper Master of Eternity, such shifts would have been obvious. A Master who did not have other-selves as bodyguards? Who lived through all his time lines in blind, first-timer, unedited scenes? A time traveler who didn't time travel? But all I said was: "You talk too much to be a Master."

"You might as well put your gun away, Mr. Frontino, or I will have my . . . " he nodded toward the cataphract and his sentence choked to a halt. He saw the aiming dot punctuating Ugly Boy's face.

"I don't know if you can see my settings from there," I said.

He nodded carefully. "Your deadman switch is on."

"And the change-in-energy detector. Any weapons go off near me, and my Unlimited friend here goes off and keep on going long after I'm dead. Well? Well? I want some answers!"

The cataphract's launch-harness unfolded from his back like the legs of a praying mantis opening. Tubes longer than bazookas pointed at me. He raised his hand toward me. With sharp metallic clashes of noise, barrels came out of the weapon-housings of the fore-arms of his vambraces. I was standing close enough that I could hear the throbbing hum of his power-core cycling up to full battle-mode. The mouths of his weapons were so close to my face that I could smell ozone and hot metal.

My nape hairs and armpits prickled. I could feel my heartbeat pulsing in my temples; my face felt hot. Standing at ground zero, at the point-blank firing focus of a mobile Heavy Assault Battery, really doesn't do a man's nerves much good.

"Well?" I said, not taking my eyes from d'Artagnan. "Things are going to start getting sloppy!"

Even d'Artagnan looked surprised when the frozen image of the Master on the throne stood up and raised a hand. Of course the time-stop had meant nothing to him. He had merely been sitting still, faking it.

"Enough!" His voice rang with multiple echoes, as if a crowd of people were speaking in not-quite-perfect unison. "You have sufficiently passed our test, Frontino. You were brought here to assume the rights, powers, and perquisites of a Master of Eternity. You may assume your rightful place at my side. There is no need for a coronation ceremony. Here I give the reality of power."

With a casual toss, he threw a packet of destiny cards at my feet. A full pack: every iris into every epoch Meta-chronopolitan time-engines ever reached, no doubt. The pack fell open as it struck the marble floor. Shining mirrored cards fell open, glittering.

Like my smartgun, the crystal surfaces were merely the here-now interface connected through higher dimensions to the gigantic chronoportation machinery which filled all the golden towers. Rumor said the whole city of Metachronopolis, from stratosphere to misty sea, the gold substance of the towers, the crystal windows, was one titanic time-distortion engine.

These were the real things. The glassy depth held images from history, ages past and future, eras unguessed: castles, landscapes, battlefields, towers, all the cities and kingdoms of the world.

All I had to do was stoop over and pick them up. If I just bent a little, it could all be mine. Me, pulling the strings for once; the puppet-master, not the puppet. Not the pawn.

9.

I stood at the window, watching the golden city of glory with eyes of awe. I asked Iapetus. "I still have some questions. May I ask . . . ?"

"Certainly, Mr. Frontino."

"How can it be possible? Time travel, I mean? What happens to cause and effect?"

Iapetus' smile was sinister and cold. "Cause-and-effect is a delusion of little minds. A cultural prejudice. The ancient wisdom of the prescientific ages recognized that the workings of the universe were in the hands of unguessable powers. They called them gods instead of calling them the Masters of Metachronopolis. But it is all one."

I asked: "So what happens if you kill your grandfather?"

"Nothing truly exists," explained Iapetus impatiently, "Except as a range of uncertain probabilities. Normally this uncertainty is confined to the subatomic level, creating the illusion of solid matter, life, causality.

"If you killed a remote ancestor," he continued, "the uncertainty of the events springing from that would increase, since your likelihood of existing in your present constitution would decrease. You might possibly survive having a remote ancestor killed; there is a small chance that some of your genes and elements might pop into existence without any cause;

certain subatomic particles do it; it is unlikely that trillions of particles would leap together spontaneously to form you, but it might happen. Killing your father is remotely unlikely, however; the uncertainty there would become macroscopic. Visible to the naked eye."

"Visible as what?"

"Mist. Photons bouncing from you become randomized in their paths as your exact position becomes uncertain. It looks like a blur of mist stretching between the various points you might affect. Gravitons likewise become uncertain."

But then he smiled and made a casual gesture. "But why dwell on such an ending? Rest assured that if there is any possible timeline which avoids such an appalling end, any at all, the Masters of Eternity will gently lead you into it. There need be no end."

"But won't that shunt itself create more uncertainty? Another paradox?"

"Perhaps," he said with an airy wave of his hand and a snort of disdain. "But why worry? The results of that paradox can be postponed by means of additional paradoxes."

"Doesn't sound quite right," I said. "Like borrowing on credit to pay off bad credit. What happens tomorrow, when all the bills come due? What happens when the loan shark comes to collect? There is always a loan shark."

"For a time traveler, tomorrow does not exist unless he walks into it. And, if you are loyal to the Masters of Eternity, you may, one day, be exalted to that high position yourself, and have all the past and future as your plaything. Well? What do you say?"

27.

The cards lay shining at my feet on the marble floor.

"Well?" came the many voices of the Master. "What do you say?"

14.

"Am I supposed to be impressed?" I asked the hooded figures seating around the dark table. "Enemies of the Masters of Time? How? How can you fight them? Use time travel? Manipulate the timelines, play games with eternity? Then you are Time Masters yourselves, whether you admit it or not. And if you don't or can't time travel, you're sunk. So what's the gag?"

"We are, indeed, the enemies of the Masters of Eternity," said the deep bass voice, "but we do not fight them. Why bother? Masters are creatures of unreason. They deny cause-and-effect; they act without heed for the consequences of their actions. We need only stand by while they destroy themselves. The only thing we really need to do is warn their victims before they too fall into the same trap."

"Which victims?"

"You, for one, Mr. Frontino. Drug users often become drug pushers to afford their habit. Likewise, Time Paradox Patrolmen must often become Time Masters to protect their own personal past from being snarled or destroyed by Masters."

"Me? A Master of Eternity? They're going to make me one?"

"Perhaps someday."

"And this is what you want to protect me from?" I had to laugh. "Why not 'protect me' from becoming a millionaire? Why not 'protect me' from becoming a god?"

The tenor voice from the left spoke. "Say, rather, we want to protect you from playing at God. Don't you recognize that time travel, by its very nature, is and must be insane? Immoral?"

I stood up. "Very dramatic. Look, I don't know what kind of crackpots you are, but if it comes down to a show down between you bunch of flatliners and the Time Masters, I think

I want to be on the winning side, thank you. So where's the exit to this madhouse, eh?"

I slid my hand into my coat as I stood. I was expecting my shoulder-holster to be empty. Instead, my fingers closed around the streamlined grip of my smartgun with a familiar magnetic tingle. I felt warmth in my palm. The circuits were active.

That stumped me. Why the hell would the self-proclaimed Enemies of the Time Masters let me go fully armed in their midst? One of the robed figures spread his (her?) gloves, and spoke in a light, soft voice: "Please, Mr. Frontino. Allow us a moment to explain ourselves. Perhaps we seem zealous. That does not necessary mean that our conclusions are wrong, does it? Let us have our say, then you can judge for yourself. Your powers of reasoning are good. Use them."

This had not been the way Lord Iapetus had spoken, way back when I had been first recruited. I sat.

The one at the head of the table—the bass voice—spoke: "Time travel (and I do not include harmless sightseeing) means using future knowledge to change the past. It means an attempt to elude the consequences of reality, without caring whether or not you cause the paradoxes that unmake reality. Consider also that morality judges the goodness of acts by their intentions and consequences. Time travelers deny consequences are related to intentions, or even that consequences exist at all. Is it moral to kill an innocent young girl who will one day become Hitler's mother? Be careful before you answer; you yourself do not know what tyrants you may one day father, do you, Mr. Frontino?"

"Maybe it's not so moral," I said. "But so what? Flatliners can't fight Time Masters. They're all-powerful."

There was a murmur of laughter around the room at that. One amused voice said, "All-powerful? They are as helpless as condemned criminals on death row. The Masters of Time are living on borrowed time. They know it. Don't you?

You've seen what's at the bottom of their towers, haven't you? Tell us, Mr. Frontino, what is at the foundation of the city of Metachronopolis?"

12.

Some hidden Master or another wanted to reward me, and the other Proctors in my squad, for the work we had done destroying the technological progress of civilization circa A.D. 2300. It had been a delicate bit of work, since we had to eliminate the society's ability to investigate temporal mechanics—can't have a bunch of flatliners developing time travel on their own, after all—without eliminating the technological progress leading to the development of some of the Time Masters' favorite toys from later eras—including the multidimensional matrix formulations involved in smartguns like mine, or cataphract-style armor.

But we had done well, killing all the right people at the right time, and the Master invited us to his tower for a party. Everyone who still had luster to him was there then, including a dozen versions of Keats, each reading a slightly different variation of his completed poem, *Hyperion*, and an older and a younger version of Agamemnon, which some Master had brought as a joke, to watch the older version trying to convince the younger not to go to the Trojan Wars. There was also a confused version of Thomas Jefferson talking to descendants of Shaka Zulu from an obscure timeline where the blacks kept the whites as plantation slaves in Virginia. Richard the Lionheart and Saladin had been given antigravitic power-armor, and were flying around the party scene, blowing huge chunks in the scenery and unwary guests while trying to get each other. All great fun.

I kept noticing the servants. There were so many people who lived among the towers whose memories were not hardened enough to remember who they were or where they came from: People forgotten by the Masters once they were no longer amusing. Young versions of Cleopatra and Semiramis were both working that evening as cocktail waitresses, trying to earn a little extra money to keep their rooms in the lower towers. They had been queens, in other worlds, once, but their time-periods were apparently not in style any more among the Time Masters; they were no longer invited or received, but they knew too much about the future to be allowed back home. I saw Cleopatra serving a drink to a Marc Antony who either was a version who came from a timeline who didn't recognize her, or just a jerk who pretended he didn't. Sad.

Since she lived in a bad section of the towers, I walked Cleo home after the main part of the party was over (more famous parties became part of the History Circuit, could always be revisited, and never ended), and, seeing how dark and misty things were here, and since I still had the security all-pass which had gotten me into the Masters' floors of the tower to begin with, I wondered if I could get past sentries and gates of the lower areas and see what was at the very bottom of these towers. From the sound which sometimes came up from down below, I had for a while now started to wonder.

I knew it was forbidden, but I was in a pretty glum mood and didn't much give a damn anyway, so . . .

15.

In a queasy voice, I answered the Enemies of the Masters of Time: "Mist. Mist and uncertainty. There is no bottom. It just gets more and more misty the further down you go . . . "

I shivered at the memory. The lower bridge had been invisible beneath my feet, swaying, soft and marshy, mutating in shape as I walked. The gargoyle statues looming on the railings had worn one face, then, after the mists blurred past, another. It had been dark, with muddled images of tower-roots fading and swaying around me. The thick tower walls were nothing but streams of smoke. From the abyss underfoot, a screaming voice had begged me not to pick up the white cards. The voice sounded familiar. I shouted back, but there had been no answer . . .

"The towers don't have any foundations," I said.

More laughter. A young man's voice came cheerfully from the right, "An apt metaphor for the Time Masters' whole system of thinking, I deem."

The laughing all the time was beginning to get on my nerves (maybe because I had almost never heard a Time Master laugh. Not nice laughter, anyway).

"What do you guys want from me?" I demanded.

"We would like you to withdraw your loyalty from the Masters of Eternity, not just the present group, but from the whole concept of time travel; to avoid time travel as much as possible; to prepare your memory for a massive shock. Major timeline changes are due, once the Masters are overthrown."

"You are talking about the elimination of time travel altogether?"

"Is there any other position we can take, given our philosophy?"

"Eliminate how?"

"By letting nature take its course."

"You talk as if it is . . . inevitable."

The robed figure shrugged and spread his gloves. "Suppose you were a Master of Time, Mr. Frontino, and all of time is yours. Another Master has gone back to do something which might affect your past, something that may alter the circumstances of your culture and history, or even redact your birth. Whether his meddling is deliberate or not, what is the safest way to neutralize his interference? Safest, quickest, best?"

That was an easy one. How did Time Masters solve all their problems? "Retroactive murder. Eliminate him."

"Just him? Remember that you cannot really reason with the other Masters of Time. If they were people who listened to warnings about the consequences of their actions, they would not be time travelers in the first place."

"So if time travel necessarily—you claim—and inevitably—you claim—eliminates whoever does it," I said, "what happens after everything collapses?"

The bass voice said, "Our research indicates that there is one core timeline, the line where time travel was never invented, and never will be. The whole unwieldy structure of multiple branching timelines and time loops manipulated by the Masters of Metachronopolis is a temporary shadow or reflection of that core line into the surrounding chronic ylem. Our chronocosm is temporary and unstable, like the creation of certain virtual particle pairs in base vacuum, which exist for a brief time before they eliminate themselves. But some of us remember the core line. Surely you recall what your life was like before you meddled with time travel."

I shrugged. "My life wasn't so great."

"But better than this."

I shook my head. "I don't need to listen to any more of this. Look: your whole notion is based on the idea that Time Masters are all some sort of criminals or infantile maniacs. That they will keep meddling and monkeying with the past until they eliminate themselves. I don't buy it. Aren't some of them reasonable? Don't some of them listen to reason?"

"That is always our hope, Mr. Frontino. We would not bother talking to you if we did not have that hope. Here."

There was a mirrored glitter as he took a dark card from his robe. Then, with a flick of his gloved fingers, he slid it across the table toward me.

I did not reach for it. "What is this supposed to be?"

"Think of it as the Final Destiny Crystal. It is a destiny card attached to the core line. Naturally, you can only use it

once; since, once you are in the core line, where time travel is
impossible, and you cannot come out."

I looked down.

The surface of the card was completely black, with no
image at all inside of it.

It might have been my imagination, but I thought I felt
a sensation of immense cold radiating from the dead-black
surface.

"No thanks," I said leaning slightly backward from the
absolutely featureless, dark card. "Me go back to being a
flatliner: blind future, irrevocable past, trapped in a present I
can't change? Sorry. Let me out of here. Unless you got
something more for me to hear?"

They didn't.

One of them—I think it was a woman—got up and held
a candle near a mirrored frame on the far wall. Except
it wasn't a mirror; inside the depth, I saw a picture of one
of the bridge-top winter gardens near the Museum of Man,
in the mid-upper levels not far from the center of the city,
shining with golden towers. The picture surged into my
imagination . . .

I suddenly had another question for them, and so I
turned around, but there was only more golden bridge-way
behind me. They were gone.

28.

"Where are the other Time Masters?" I asked the
mirrored figure on the throne. "Or is elevating me
to Mastership just something you decided all on your
lonesome?"

An eerie, bubbling noise like many disjointed voices
laughing came from the mirrored mask. "Other Masters? Why
should there be other Masters? How would you expect us to
govern ourselves?"

That one stumped me. I squinted. "Don't know. I always thought you guys had a leader, or you took a vote or some-thing . . ."

Again, the weird blurred laughter. "Why should I tolerate to abide by the outcome of any vote, when I could play the scene again and again until the vote came out as I desired? How much less would I brook the commands of a leader! Why should I tolerate any difference of opinion of any kind whatsoever! If I know a man's birthdate, or his mother's, then he exists at my sufferance only for so long as it should please me!"

"Yeah, right. What are these other thrones for, then?"

"Meant for other versions of me!"

"Pretty empty now, aren't they?"

A terrible silence hung in the air.

I said slowly, "You're becoming more and more unlikely now, is that it? There are fewer and fewer alternates because you've eliminated other possibilities. You've mucked around in the past so much you've edited yourself out of the cosmos, haven't you? And you couldn't stop meddling in history, even when you knew it was destroying you . . . "

"You will meddle when you become a Master of Eternity also. It is our nature. Pick up the cards, my brother Master! I command it."

"And if I say no?"

He stood up, his cloak of mist writhing and billowing around his glinting mirrored armor as he stood. The voices from the mask were blurrier now, shouting: "Then you die!"

I don't know who fired first, me or the cataphract. The Master threw his mist-cloak up, so that my shots and lines of hissing energy went into the mist, became uncertain, and vanished before they even reached the Master.

Without thinking, I switched to a special program, something small enough and fast enough—a few molecules wide, accelerated to light speed—to make it through the uncertainty mist of the cloak without being affected.

He must have known it was coming. The Master shrugged his cloak open and spread his arms wide, trying to catch my bolt on his chest. He had been ready even before I shot; he was right in the way, in the exact spot, even before I aimed.

Of course he was manipulating the chronostructure, playing probabilities and possibilities like a musical instrument.

It was not until after my shot was absorbed into the surface of his breastplate that I realized what a fool I had been. Time Master armor was made of the solid time-energy we call destiny crystal. He could focus the surface to open into whatever timespace he had potential to reach.

And I knew exactly where and when that bolt would come back into normal space, and who it would shoot.

I had even jumped forward as I was firing, so that I was standing in the spot where, later/earlier, I would find traces of the body.

Looking over my shoulder, I wondered why the cataphract's million-cycle energy bolts hadn't landed yet.

Of course. Ugly Boy was frozen. A hundred arms of flame and energy, bullets and bolts, were motionless, radiating from him toward me. He had made movement enough to startle my gun into firing, but now he was wrapped in the deep red Doppler-shift of a time stop.

He faded into darker reds and disappeared in a swirl of mist.

The Master had only needed the cataphract to get me to fire, and, out of the whole arsenal of my gunplay, he had only needed that one special projectile—the one with my name on it. With the precision of a master surgeon, he had plucked that one super-bullet out of the hails and streams and storms of weapon-fire I had expended, and sent just that one merrily on its way to kill me. As predicted.

And this whole heavy-handed approach, breaking into my room at night, pushing me, getting me riled, was all just to make sure I was mad enough to have my smartgun drawn and set on reflex. Very neat. Very nice. And I was the goat for having walked into it with my eyes wide open.

The image of the corpse had vanished with the cataphract. Pieces on the chessboard no longer needed. But for some reason, the d'Artagnan body was still around. Being remotely teleoperated from inside the Master's armor?

I turned to the Master. "Open your faceplate. You're me, aren't you? That's the way these damn time travel things always work out. I've been trying to think of what could make me change my mind—in the space of a few minutes—to make me want to join up with you and your rotten crew.

"And the only reason I could think of was that the choice was join up or die.

"If I stay flatline, I've just shot myself. The only way out is to create a paradox, change the past. The only people who can change the past are Time Masters. So therefore the only way to save myself is to become a Time Master. Q.E.D. So now you've forced my hand. My only question at that point was: why bother?

"Why go to such effort to create a Master, a possible rival, a possible enemy? Answer: You had to. Not another Master. The same Master. You had to make me a Time Master or else you would never come to exist. And, then, once I'm you, I'm stuck. I'll have to play the same crooked tricks on my younger version when it's my turn, or else I'll get edited out into the mist myself. Everything justified. Every step rationalized away. Because whatever you have to do to survive is OK, isn't it? Necessity excuses everything, you think, right?

"Except—" I said slowly, "Except that it doesn't. The one piece of the machine you need to make all the rest of it work is my cooperation. You've got to assume that I'd do anything, no matter how rotten, just to stay alive; because you are just the version of me who did just that.

"But what if I throw a monkey wrench into the whole works? What if I just stand here and take it? Maybe I deserve to die. I killed a lot of innocent people in my day. I'm sure it won't hurt me any more than it hurt them, and probably a damn sight less, judging from the size of the blast that does me in. Better than I deserve, maybe.

"And it will all be for the same reason, won't it? Killing someone before he commits the crime.

"But I'll die happier than those poor flatliners I killed for you. At least I'll know why I'm dying. And I'll know I'll be taking you to hell with me."

And I just stood there.

The blur of voices echoed from the helmet of the Master of Eternity: "Nobly spoken! Nobly spoken but sadly mistaken. You are not so important as that. Not to me, nor, I think, to anyone. I am not you, I am not your son. You are nothing to me. But I! I am everything to you!"

"You're lying," I said tiredly. "Who are you? This is just a trick to get me to pick up those damn cards. Show me your face."

He opened the faceplate with a slow gesture.

And there was nothing behind it. Nothing solid.

I saw a horrible blur of half-formed faces, multiple overlays of translucent features, crowned with a weightless, shifting mass of floating hair. The only thing clearly visible was the skull beneath, half-glimpsed through the misty vibrations of face crawling over it. Perhaps the skull-bones had a smaller range of motions, a less uncertain future, than the rest.

I stepped half-backwards in disgust and shock. Something in the narrow angle of the jawline seemed familiar. "Iapetus?"

From the mist came many voices. I could see the muscles of the tongue and throat writhing snakelike through translucent layers of throat, the knobby ridges of the neck-vertebrae looking like a black tree-trunk behind. "So you call me. Fitting, is it not? Father of Epimetheus and Prometheus, past and future! A titan!"

"Who are you?"

"I am the Inventor. The Crystal-Smith. The man who synthesized the first destiny crystal out of the subatomic substance of folded time. The first time traveler. No matter whether you wish it or not, once you are a Master of Time, you must go back to sustain my existence, lest no Time Master at all ever will have had existed. I am the First. Upon me, all depends. Perhaps, yes, I created the universe. Certainly my probes into the ultimate dawn of time had sufficient energy to trigger the Big Bang. But you—you are one candidate of many. Many! Your death causes, for me, inconvenience, no more. Does it seem so noble now, waiting passively to die? No? Then pick up the cards! Pick up your destiny! Become a Master of Eternity! It must still be a possibility, or else you would not still see me!"

For some reason, at that point, I glanced over at d'Artagnan.

There he stood, still looking calm and amused and aloof, watching us with a remote disinterest, like a scientist observing an experiment in whose outcome he has no particular stake.

Why so calm? I thought this guy was the brain-slave of the Master, or else another version of the Master himself; an earlier version, I supposed, because, as blurred and as uncertain as the smoking skull in front of me was, there weren't any future versions coming.

Was he looking at his own future dissolving? Or was he . . .

Or was he not related at all?

Seeing my eyes on him, he nodded politely, and opened his hand, the same hand which, earlier, I had seen blur in a timeshift.

He held up a destiny card in his fingers.

It twinkled like black ice when he turned it over and over in his fingers, toying with it, making sure I saw it. It was entirely black, with no images at all in its depths.

Then, with a smile, he tossed the card so it tinkled to the floor to one side of the pile the Master of Time had thrown.

There they lay. On the one hand, was a pile of flashing white cards, glittering like diamonds, with all the kingdoms of all the ages shimmering in their frozen hearts. On the other hand, lay a single, blank, black card.

I looked up at the Master. There was nothing but a trickle of mist hovering in the blind sockets of his eyes. His hair was floating weightlessly. He was already in the mist, already falling through the endless end, cut off from gravity, cut off from reality, more dead than a ghost.

His voices: "I do not hear a response!"

Many other candidates, huhn? I didn't see anyone here but me. So I spoke up: "If I were a nice guy, I'd wish you to go to hell. That'd be warmer than where you're going."

Even to the last moment, he did not seem to admit or recognize that what was happening to him was irrevocable. He kept shouting at me, and there was dozens of other voices saying slightly different versions of the same sentences, all at once, a garbled mess. No doubt he was replaying the scene several times, trying different words, hoping one would reach me. "It matters not! I have always relied on the weakness of mankind to do my work for me! They will always want to elude the burden of reality! I promise them action without reaction, motion without consequences! Everything done can be undone again! And . . . as soon as I am whole again . . . I will go back . . . not recruit you . . . this time . . . different . . . Destroy you! . . . I will never die . . . I can never die. . . Destroy you all! My power is endless . . . I . . . "

And so on like that for a moment, about how great he was and stuff. And whatever his last words were supposed to be, they trailed off into a pathetic whisper of garbled noise as his lower jaw dissolved. Then his helmet was filled only with mists and shadows. Then, nothing.

Empty armor clattered to the floor, full of hollow noises and echoes. Then it wasn't there and never had been.

While he had been talking, I had stooped over and picked up the Final Destiny card. Maybe that was the turning point. Maybe once it was in my hand, the percent chance that I would change my mind and become a Master of Time after all wound down to around zero.

I said to d'Artagnan, "That was Iapetus. He made me a Paradox Proctor. He's the guy who hired me, back when. Am I going to fade away too, now that he never did that?"

"No." D'Artagnan smiled. "Much more likely that you'll get shot. That bullet manifests itself in a minute or two, and you know you smartgun's shields can't deflect it, and you know the bullet's hunter-seeker program will chase you however you try to dodge. Better use the Final card."

"You're one of the anti-Master group?"

"Of course." He reached up and pried the false skull-box off his neck. It was just the back half of a box, held against his neck with a traction field, or maybe just epoxy. When he tossed it aside it clattered, hollow, with a noise like cheap plastic.

"And he's not the real Inventor, is he?"

"There is no Inventor. Time travel cannot be invented—how could it be? Illogical things cannot be discovered by the orderly process of science. He's just one of many who went back in time and gave a set of destiny crystals to his younger self, who would then go back and give them to himself again, in turn. We suspect that he was no more 'first' than any of the others. He was just a little more ruthless about tracking down and eliminating the competition. But there was never a first inventor. Time travel, by its very nature, can have no cause. It is spontaneously created in the flux of nothingness surrounding the core timeline, and, if men do not seek to exploit it, it vanishes just as spontaneously."

"But—isn't there some way, any way at all, to put time travel to a good use?" This was the question that I had wanted to ask them before, but hadn't thought to ask. "Like—what if everyone had it? If we made everyone into Time Masters, they could . . . "

"You are assuming they all would not immediately go to war? That they would have some sort of government or civilized process for handling differences of opinion?"

"Sure."

"But such a government could exist if and only if they all abided by an agreement not to interfere with each other's pasts, correct?"

"I guess."

"And that would require that they could not change even their own pasts in any particular which might ever affect another person, correct? Since every event affects every other, the range of this prohibition would have to include all external events, no matter how small or private. And to enforce this agreement, they might have to resort to an amnesia block (not unlike the one we gave you the night you visited us in our headquarters). This block would make all memories of alternate timelines seem like daydreams, but all memories of the future seem like forethought, good judgment, or prophecy. Correct?"

"I suppose so."

"Everyone would be a Master of Eternity, infinitely powerful, but at the cost that they can never know, never reveal it, not even to themselves; because they all agreed to forget. Can you think of any other fair way of doing it?"

"Not offhand."

"But, my dear boy—what else do you think the core timeline is?"

That was good enough for me. I looked at the black card, tossing aside my smartgun as I did so, glad to be rid of the weight.

Deeply, deeply, I stared past the surface, and my imagination went blank for a moment . . .

2.

This time, she slapped my face. And maybe I leaned a little into the blow. After all, I did deserve it.

I saw her slender shadow against the glass of the door after she slammed it.

She packed quite a wallop. I rubbed my jaw ruefully, knowing I'd never see her again. There was no way to turn back time and undo what I'd done, no way to unsay what I'd said.

I looked up. I heard her heels clashing against the floorboards, receding.

On the other hand—why had she hesitated just outside? And why was I so quick to say "never"? It's not like anyone knows what tomorrow brings. We can't change the past, but we sure as hell can try to change the future.

I ran toward the door, calling out.

Maybe I could catch up with her before she reached the elevators.

30.

In the other ending, the one I'd rather not dwell on, I had no breath to scream when I saw the world dissolve into mist, the golden towers falling. For I had stooped, not toward the one black card, but toward the many shining ones. They seemed so bright, and I thought I'd always have time to change my mind later.

I hope this warning reaches you in time.

An End

TO SEEK HER FORTUNE

Nicole Kornher-Stace

I.

In the land of black salt and white honey, the Lady Explorer bartered a polar bear's pelt, a hand-cranked dynamo, her second-best derringer, and three bolts of peach silk for her death.

"You stole the map that brought you here," said the witch who was waiting at the shoreline when the Lady Explorer had hacked her way out of the trees. At first the witch had said nothing, sitting on her heels, skinning iridescent fish into an ebbing tide. She didn't watch, though the Lady Explorer did, as the sea bore each raft of scales, like chips of ice and fire in the setting sun, away to sea. To all appearances the witch expected the Lady Explorer to recoil in horror when the guts followed. The grunt brought on by her failure to flinch could have signified anything from approval to cramp.

When the witch spoke, however, the Lady Explorer glanced up from the water, startled. "I *beg* your pardon," she gasped, hand to mouth in her best well-I-never pose, while behind it her mind worked into a lather.

"It's not surprising. Seeing as the crew you fly with stole that ship as well."

The Lady Explorer froze. A sudden terror seized her in its teeth and shook. If the witch knew that, then what else could she see? That she'd been nothing but a stupid factory girl, upswept on the wave of a rebellion and rejoicing even through her fear? That she'd had to pay her way to the factory-workers-turned-airship-crew with the only currency she had? And what she'd had to do to in the end to earn their respect?

She remembered the tools in her hands, her skirt in her hands, the gun in her hands, and was ashamed.

The boy peering out from behind the Lady Explorer's hip looked up at her, one hand fisted in the sailcloth of her slapdash trousers, gauging the tension radiating off her. One good startle from fleeing back into the jungle, or perhaps into the sea.

The Lady Explorer gathered herself. *Well, I did not come here to gawk at the sights like a schoolgirl at a cathedral. I came here for answers. Before it's too late.*

She said, "I *assure* you, I did nothing of the—"

"That contraption up there tells me different."

Bewildered, the Lady Explorer looked over her shoulder to follow the witch's gaze up and up to where the airship perched with its improbable delicacy on the lip of the caldera. As the Lady Explorer watched, it roused and settled, preening like a nesting hen the size of a four-story brownstone with bat wings and rose windows for eyes. She blinked and looked again and it was still.

Water. She needed water. And she'd eaten nothing but the hardtack pilfered from that scuttled pirate outrider for the best part of a week. Nor slept: the last scraps of dried meat and fruit she'd squirreled in the boy's bunk, then sat the door daylong, nightlong, rifle in her lap. The crew would mutiny,

and soon, she guessed, but hadn't chanced her yet. If she had
to cut off her arm and roast it over the combustion engine, the
boy at least would eat.

She steeled herself. Her chignon had exploded in the
heat; sodden squid-arms of it slapped her face, her eyes.
Irritably she shoved it back, drew herself up, set her shoulders
and her jaw to hide her apprehension. She'd not come this far
to be toy for some rootwitch, regardless what she knew.

She affected the disdainful drawl the foreman used to
use, days when she'd beg early leave from the factory with a
migraine from the eyestrain of the close work, or a roiling in
her guts while her womb built a person even as her hands built
a ship. "Is that so? I see you two are great friends already.
What else does it—"

"It remembers the place where it was born," the witch
interrupted, her voice gone dreamy like a child's half-asleep,
like some seer's in some cave. The Lady Explorer snapped to
attention, for she had heard that tone of voice before. "It
smelled of grease and sweat and metal there. Men and women
hunched at benches, piecing up its bones, its skin. It came
awake like a whale rising from the dark depths of the sea.
When they set its heart in place, the joy leapt up in it, flew out
of it like lightning: the discharge of it killed three men. Just
fried them where they stood, like a basketful of eels. The
smell—" She chuckled. "You should see your face. It remembers the taste of you, as well. Blood and bone."

Before the Lady Explorer could react, the witch seized
her bad hand, held it up so that the empty finger of her glove
fell slack.

Instantly the sense memory flooded her, despite the
intervening years: a stab of panic as her hand caught in the
struts, a snag, a drawing-in. The other workers' shouts. A
sharp wet crunch.

She jerked her arm away.

"It says it never meant to hurt you."

She still felt that finger sometimes, or its ghost. Hoisting the boy to her shoulders. Hacking through brush. Burying her people. Unburying other ones. Sighting down the rifle's length. It still knocked her aim just out of true, if she permitted it, which she did not. Only by pulling well more than her weight on the crew's endless expeditions would she maintain their fragile tolerance of her own infrequent ones, and she'd be damned before she showed those bastards any weakness.

"If you know all that, then you know why I'm here. I didn't come to fence with witches."

"Did you not?" Her face cracked along its fault lines into a quiet smile. "A pity."

As the barter was brought down from the airship and the Lady Explorer disappeared inside the witch's little house, the boy drew cities in the white sand with a stick, shell-fragments for carriages and leaf-spines for streets. By now he was good at waiting. It took much longer to make a city than to have a card revealed to you, even if it was a fortune-telling card, as his mama had explained; an answering card. A card that tells you secrets. He couldn't count high enough yet to know how many secrets his mama must've been told by now. A great many, he was sure. He imagined her as a Mama-shaped penny-candy jar, each secret a bright sweet bauble nestled behind the cold glass of her skin.

He picked the biggest shell-carriage up and marked it with a charcoal from his pocket: one messy-haired smiling face that was his mama, one smaller smiling face that was himself. Turning, he tossed the shell into the sea and watched as it skipped four times and sank. He knew from his mama's stories that there were cities down there too.

When the Lady Explorer emerged from the little house she looked paler, greyer, older; lighter and heavier at once. But her arms were still strong when she picked him up and swung him. "It's time to go," she said, and he rode her shoulders back into the treeline. When the jungle shut its curtains at their backs the sun went out like a lamp, so that when he closed his eyes against his mama's hair, the wet sweet smell of rot was all he knew.

The vast dark stingray of the airship stirred and lifted, and as it rose above the canopy the Lady Explorer held her son up to one of its eye-windows so that he could wave goodbye to where they'd been. Offshore, a thrashing in the water caught her eye, which her fieldglass soon revealed as a pod of dolphins harrying a shark. *My sins,* she thought, and smiled grimly down at them; *my sins.*

II.

In the land of silver trees and golden fruit, the Lady Explorer bartered a case of tawny port, the captain's quarters' folding screen and rolltop desk, a sterling filigree tea service, and the airship's only drop glider for her death.

"What's the vintage on that port?" the scientist inquired, almost before the Lady Explorer, her son, and two of the airship's roustabouts had unpacked all the crates. Still breathless from the climb to the laboratory, the Lady Explorer stuck a hand in blind and rifled the excelsior. It had gone damp with the temperature shift to the glass, and the bottle that she grabbed was cold to the touch and slippery. She hefted it and squinted: half because her eyes betrayed her, half to hide the twinge her back gave as it straightened. She couldn't help conflating her bones with the airship's bones: each joint gradually tarnishing, gradually grinding down from shiny brass to verdigris.

"Eighteen—sixty-six," she read aloud, and improvised: "A fine year for the—"

The scientist sneered. "You wouldn't know a fine year if it bit you in the leg. The not particularly well-turned leg, I don't doubt. Just look at you. Bristling at me like a mad dog.

Your stance—your hands—you're utterly transparent. Rings on your fingers and engine grease under your nails. That corset's the only thing keeping your spine from snapping under the weight of that vast empty skull. Feigning at *quality*, madam, suits you ill."

Hating herself for it, she dropped her gaze. Snickering at her discomfiture, he crouched beside the crates, and as he did so a light glanced off his ankle, catching her eye. From there, a slender silver chain ran a few yards to the leg of a long table laden with flasks and beakers and the disassembled skeletons of automata. The table, she now noticed, was bolted into the floor. The skin where the chain had bitten was greenish and suppurating.

When she looked back, the scientist was staring out a window no wider or longer than her forearm at where the airship waited, quiescent, mantling a lane flanked with marching rows of pomegranate trees.

The look on his face reminded her of the look on her own, back when it was someone else's airship and she and fifty others were working themselves half-dead to build it.

The sudden sympathy she found she felt slowed her reaction to a staring inutility when, beside her, her son drew a long pistol and brought it to bear between the scientist's eyes.

"Speak to my mother in that way again," he said airily, "and you'll be scraping that smug look off the wall."

"I suppose," said the scientist, "I may as well be charitable. That—" he pointed at the crates— "is utter swill, but I can take it off your hands. Perhaps it will serve to degrease the hydraulic fittings. Now then. Shall we get this over with?"

Long accustomed to this dance, her son left the laboratory before being asked to, ushered the roustabouts before him, and had the grace not to slam the door at his back. Nonetheless his gut clenched with the certainty he'd seen the scientist—who was readying some vibrant fluid in a crucible that was a clockwork raven's head, over a flame that was its heart—cast him an ugly smirk as he went out. His mother was occupied in inspecting a half-clockwork, half-organic specimen, which bobbed in its pickling jar amid threads of its own flesh and flakes of its own rust. She'd seen nothing.

The three men sat in the hall (he counted himself a man now, for his voice had nearly stopped cracking—ah, now *that* was an embarrassment he wouldn't miss!) and gambled rifle-cartridges and chores and coins upon a weathered pair of ivory dice that lived in the pocket of one of the roustabouts, the story behind the acquisition of which was subject to its keeper's whim. Today he'd cut them from the belly of a black wolf in a pinewood by a lake, along with an ell of scorched red velvet, a flintlock pistol, and a mismatched scattering of bones.

"Three scapulae and five clavicles," he pronounced grandly, "but no mandibles or frontal plates at all!"

At this point the Lady Explorer's son knew the roustabout had been practicing his reading with the Lady Explorer's medical journals again (while tempering his learnings on human anatomy with a blithe disregard of the respective sizes of a wolf's mouth and stomach) and immediately decided to outgrow his long-lived fear of the roustabout's yarns.

The dice had earned him a week free of maintenance duties and a tidy heap of coins—round, ringed, hexagonal, octagonal, brass, copper, silver, lead—by the time his mother emerged from the laboratory, flushed with agitation and worrying at a sleeve. When she forced a smile and reached a hand down to help him up, he did not quite disdain to take it.

Most of the coins he left on the floor in a sudden fit of apathy. His favorite only, which he'd been palming as a good luck charm throughout the game, he pocketed. Its reverse was obliterated but its obverse bore the likeness of a very young girl with cornsheaves in her hair beneath a coronet of seven-pointed stars. The tears she wept looked oddly dark.

Leaving, he could not help but notice the utter silence from beyond the laboratory door. He cast a furtive glance over his mother but could discern no bloodstains on the skin or cloth or hair of her. Besides, he reassured himself, he would have heard the shot.

III.

In the land of violet storms and crimson seas, the Lady Explorer bartered the spare canvas for the airship's wings, five phials of laudanum, the last kilo of salt, and the auxiliary power supply for her death.

Her eyesight failed her in the rain, so her son read out the water-warped, mold-furred tavern sign to her: The Rotting Shark.

He hoped she also could not see the look of surprise, half-tender, half-annoyed, that he found himself wearing at this admission of her mortality. Up till now he had fancied her close kin to the automata: ageless so long as her clockwork was wound or her engine was fed.

For a moment he looked as though he was about to speak. Then, noticing her utter absorption in the door, he sighed and fiddled with his cuff instead.

The noises from within the building were what they'd by now come to expect of such places: drunken shouting, and below it, lower-keyed tones from what cardsharps and cutpurses and gunslingers took delicate advantage of that drunkenness. Someone wauled a marching song from one war or another on a flute. A crash as of a flung chair followed, and the music stopped.

In a moment, two men stumbled out the door, bearing up a deadweight third who bled heavily from one temple.

"This time I stay with you," the Lady Explorer's son informed her.

She looked away over the rumpled crinolines of mead-
owland, lying as if discarded at the trackless flyblown foot of
seven gangrene-colored hills. As she watched, a dark bird
stooped and hammered down on something unseen in a
stubbled field.

Then she shrugged and shouldered through the door.

A figure hailed them at once from a far table; they
crossed the room and sat. The shape across from them was
hooded, but the voice had been a girl's. When she pulled
the hood back, the Lady Explorer's son nearly shouted in
alarm.

The girl was two girls, bound together as in the cases of
some twins he'd seen in the medical journals—but by some
kind of ivy, not by flesh. Green tendrils had grown through the
trunks and necks and heads of both, binding them together like
a corset, hip to temple. A thick finger of ivy had crooked itself
through one girl's eye, just missing the other's where it
threaded through her socket, squashing the eyeball sideways
but not quite bursting it.

"We were expecting you," the ivy-girls said, their voices
tightly harmonized and not unpleasant. The Lady Explorer's
son wondered by what perverse whim of nature the ivy's tithe
had been no greater—and no less—than a certain fraction of
their loveliness. The Lady Explorer wondered whether they'd
ever been able to climb, or dance, or run, or keep a secret.

"From a long way off we saw you. We saw a woman
who escaped the slow grind of a wretched death only to
become obsessed with it, stalking it as any starving hunter
stalks his prey, and wasting as acutely every time it flees his
snares. A grail quest, a fool's errand, a dog chasing its tail,
and yet she persists. Before we tell her fate, we would
comprehend her folly."

The Lady Explorer glanced over, but her son was sitting
with arms crossed, gazing back at her with defiance. She
sighed.

"When we built the airship," she began, "one of my tasks was to hold the tray of wires and electrodes when the master engineer connected her controls up to her heart. I could barely hold it still. I couldn't feel my hands. The calluses from stitching wings—every night I'd go home and touch my stomach, where the baby grew—" a sidelong glance at her son, who flinched away, embarrassed— "and every day I felt it less and less. As if he was slowly disappearing. Or I was."

She flexed her fingers, staring as though she expected to parse sudden revelations from the caked grime of her gloves.

"And so all the workers bided their time until the airship was completed? Tell us, were the first whispers of rebellion yours?"

She almost laughed full in their faces, remembering how near she'd come to pissing herself when the shooting began. How another worker had thrust a gun into her hands and she'd stared at it, aware only in a vague sense of how it fired. How she'd hidden under the workbench with her belly to the wall, so the bullets couldn't reach the baby without passing through her first. How she'd stayed there until the sounds of shooting turned to scavenging as the workers loaded up the ship they'd won with anything they'd found to hand, and she was dragged out by the apron-belt and tossed aboard, a spoil amid spoils.

What she said was: "The airship's switchboard was full of dials and toggles—the only intermediary between the captain's will and the ship's. I watched the engineer set each piece into place and wondered whether somewhere inside me there was a switchboard just like hers, with dials to show all my potential fears, potential loves, potential deaths. Who knows what becomes of us in the other world? Why might we not have a choice? Might it not be that each time my death is told, that that dial stops, and where it stops becomes the truth? And if I reject the death it tells, maybe I can start the dial spinning once again."

"Until it stops."

"When someone tells a death I can accept, I'll *let* it stop. I'll keep on searching until someone does."

The girls eyed her closely. "But what the ivy tells us," they said, "so shall be."

"That's what you all say. You tea-leaf-readers, card-turners, guts-scryers, hedgewitches, table-tappers, you're all the same. So far I should've been shot, drowned, stabbed in an alley, run down in the street, fallen off a widow's walk, been shipwrecked, hit by lightning, and perished of consumption in a garret. And yet I am here and asking."

Once they'd given her her death on a folded slip of paper and she had gone her way, the ivy-girls went hooded out into the rain, watching the airship shake the water off its back like a dog, bank hard, and vanish oversea.

"Lies of omission are still lies," said one mouth, while the other one said: "She really ought to tell that boy the truth."

IV.

In the land of blue ice and red lichen, the Lady Explorer bartered half of the phosphorous matches, a foxfur waistcoat, the least mildewed of the down quilts, and the airship's rudder for her death.

The whaler had been stranded on the ice shelf some twenty-odd years when the airship touched down and hailed her—more as a formality than anything: she was tatter-sailed, barnacle-encrusted, glazed with ice, and the Lady Explorer half-expected to see *Mary Celeste* or *Flying Dutchman* emblazoned on her stern. What was there, however, was a palimpsest of christenings: something unintelligible overpainted with *Lydia* in what looked like long-dried blood.

Someone's sweetheart, the Lady Explorer surmised in the wan scraps of her worldliness. Some woman out of widow's-weeds two decades gone, and taking solace where she may. She wished her well.

For half an hour, the airship's crew signaled to the *Lydia* with flags and phosphorus flares while the Lady Explorer checked the navigational instruments against five different maps and shook her head at each of them in turn. At last, the Lady Explorer in a white rage and the crew jubilant, they readied the salvage gear.

Just as a few of the men were beginning to swing grappling hooks over their heads, and others to cheer them on, the engine-tender spotted a group of figures approaching across the shelf, each dragging two or three frozen ringed seals behind him, bound together by the hind flippers in strings like sun-dried fish she had seen once in a market on the bone-white shore of a blood-warm sea.

Later, over the last of the airship's Darjeeling, they sat around the *Lydia*'s reeking try-works, the earthbound ship's crew and the winged one's, and the *Lydia*'s bosun read the Lady Explorer's death in the swirling oil of the try-pot.

When the bosun whispered what he'd seen into her ear, the Lady Explorer set down her tea, clambered down onto the ice shelf, and began to walk. Slowly, faltering: her legs leaked strength like water through cupped hands these days, and her joints screamed every time a foot shot sideways on the ice.

"She'll come back," the bosun told the Lady Explorer's son when he hissed a curse and stood, brow creased with equal parts concern for her frailty and anger at her stubbornness, to follow. "They always do."

"How will she find her way?"

"The ghosts'll show her. Old flensing trails." The bosun pointed out across the shelf, where, some half-mile inward from the *Lydia*'s berth of ice, a vast red stain bled up out of the endless white like overdilute watercolor paint. It spread, growing tendrils that stretched out in turn and doubled back and looked, as the Lady Explorer's son's field binoculars and the last late light informed him, very like the wakes of bloody booted footprints tacking back and forth around the suggestion of some hulking shape he could not see.

"What did you tell her?" he asked at length.

The bosun's eyes went misty. "That she'd go out in a blaze of glory in a dogfight with a man-o'-war, all hands lost, and she'd plummet from the sky like Lucifer aflame—"

The Lady Explorer's son sighed.

"Well, what d'you want me to have said? It's what I *saw*."

"I don't know. Something." He tipped his head back, watching as the first pale stars came out. "She's like an old man sleeping in his coffin to get used to the idea. I wish one of you would tell her something that would make her send it off for kindling and get back in her goddamned bed."

"Nothing wrong with preparing to greet the spirits on the far side of the river," said the bosun primly, picking tea leaves from his teeth with a whalebone pin.

"Not unless when you do greet them," the Lady Explorer's son retorted, "you find you have *nothing at all to say*."

Returning along a strange red path she hadn't noticed on her journey out across the shelf, the Lady Explorer found the *Lydia*'s crew trying to force the airship's rudder to fit where the *Lydia*'s once was and the airship's crew strapping a new rudder in place with an elaborate harness that put her in mind of a spiderweb. The harness was seal-sinew and her son had carved the rudder with the tools they'd salvaged from the factory from a single block of ice.

"Almost pieced back together," the grinning bosun told her as she passed the *Lydia*. "Patched the hole in her hull with some pitch off a merchantman gone astray a few years back. A few dozen more seals, and we'll have enough skin for a sail."

Her nerves were still raw from mediating the barter for the rudder, and her heart still kicked her every time she recalled how her son had come to her aid against their crew and vowed to get the ship back in the air, and though she'd tried ten times since then to catch his eye and smile, he had never looked her way.

Coming round from the prow, somewhat stung at her son's apparent scorn, it nettled her to discover that, for her part, she could not quite meet the gleaming violet placidity of the airship's regard. She made a shy-eyed gesture at the makeshift rudder, then held up her bad hand for the benefit of the airship's compound gaze. "Now," she said, finally hazarding its stare, her face unfathomable, "we're even."

The new rudder took them eleven degrees south before it began to melt. When it had shrunk from an outhouse's size to a steamer trunk's, then to a tabletop's and a sawblade's, the airship's crew set her down on the water and took shifts paddling with whalebone oars, following their collective guesswork of unfamiliar constellations south.

Four days' cruising from its landing, a hunting pod of orcas surfaced around the airship and chaperoned it straight to landfall some six hundred miles on. During this leg of the journey, great clumps of kelp and cairns of fish were given to appear on deck, always at night, always when nobody stood watch, and by no agency that anyone on board could later rationally explain.

V.

In the land of grey houses and grey streets, the Lady Explorer bartered the greatcoat off her back, the machete and flensing knife from her belt, the copper honeycombs and amethystine glass of the airship's compound eyes, the compass round her neck, the rainwater cistern, and the shorn iron-grey length of her hair for her death.

She tired quickly here. She told herself it was the sullied air, the oppressive angle of the light, the smell of dust and gin and desiccated violets coming off the flocked wallpaper of the medium's salon. But her hands were veined and mottled, her memory and bladder failed as often as they held, and she did not believe her own lies.

She flew a ghost ship now. The crew had pooled what they had gained and kept over the years to purchase a retrofitted washbasin of an airship from the shipyard outside town, which they'd (somewhat amusingly, she thought) renamed the *Swan*. They would break the bottle on her bow within the week, and then she would take wing.

Her own airship, or what was left of it, rested in the yards, lonely as a boat in drydock, while she and her son paced the warren of its rooms like restive ghosts themselves.

In what her quest had not ransacked from the captain's quarters of the airship, the Lady Explorer's son sat her down on a rotten chaise and took her hands, more to pin her in place when he stared her down than out of any outward tenderness.

Reflected in her dulling eyes he saw a figure trapped as if down a well and glaring out at the world it could not reach. With a mild shock he realized that it was himself.

He forced his gaze back to her. "Look at you," he sneered. "Have your damnable dials stopped yet? You've one foot in the grave already, and what do you have to show for it? Has it never crossed your mind that none of your precious mountebanks can tell your fate any better than I can? Look here, at the scuffing on my boot. There—*that* looks like a swarm of bees, and *there*'s the river you jump into, trying to escape them. These pebbles stuck in the mud on the sole signify the rocks you forgot you had in your pockets, and sadly you drowned." He paused, trying to collect himself. "You look me in the eye and tell me that this—" he gestured at the room, once fine, now as though ravened at and left for dead—and at her, once strong-armed and sharp-eyed, now rotting like a windfall full of wasps—and at himself. "That any of this was worth it."

She eyed him very closely. "Do you honestly think that this—that any of this—has ever been about *me?*"

Not waiting for an answer, she shook her hands free of him and left.

In her absence, he took a deep breath, counted to ten, let it out slowly, and when this failed to have any noticeable effect on his level of serenity, he took four long strides across the room, and swept a shelf full of framed daguerreotype and conch shells and hurricane lamps to the floor. For a moment the crash appeared to satisfy him. He turned halfway. Then spun on his heel and punched the wall.

From the wall came a whirring and a series of reproachful clicks, and then a panel in the wainscoting slid free, releasing a bloom of mildew and two folded sheets of paper. Both were yellowed with age and buttery soft with re-reading.

The softer and older-looking of the two he recognized. The words were centered on the page in a clump, outlined by a long-armed globular shape, which, in turn, was flanked by smaller outriding shapes. A few squiggles off to either side of the central mass suggested waves.

Mama,

Because you always have your Nose in your Book of Maps, I will Hide this Letter there, Disguised as a Map. If you are reading this, I have Tricked you, and I am Sorry, so please do not be Angry.

I met some Boys and Girls on the Beach yesterday, when you told me to Go Play while the Grown-Ups Sold some Things at the Docks. I tried to Play with Them, but they laughed at me and kicked Sand on my Trouser-Legs. They said that Real Boys and Girls live in Houses and have Pet Cats and Sunday-Shoes and Governesses. They did not Believe that I could live in the Sky and still be a Real Boy. One bigger Boy said that I must be a Gull-Boy or a Crow-Boy and my Mother a Bird. I struck him in the Nose. It bled. A lot.

Still I think I should like to Live in a House. I do not know what Sunday-Shoes or Governesses are, but I did like to Play with Jacob's Cat, before we had to Put her in the Stew.

P.S. I am also Sorry that I spilled your Ink, but I needed a Shape to draw my Coastline from. I told you that little Cora did it. That was a Lie. Please do not be Angry about that too.

The other was unfamiliar.

My darling Child,

Oh! I cannot Call you so anymore, can I, for you are a Grown Man now and I an Old Woman, and much like a Madwoman in an Attic, I fear, as far as our Fellows are Concerned. I do not doubt your Sentiments toward me are similar. Well do I deserve Them!

To my Shame, I have not been wholly Frank with You. I cannot Undo my Errors now, but I can, perhaps, patch up some few of the Holes that they have Rent between Us.

When we stole the Airship, I was but a Girl—a Working Girl of Twenty, with Engine Grease in her Hair and all over Bruises, Cuts, and Scars from her own Labor. A Girl just Strong enough to stay aboard the Ship, give Birth to You, and there fight to Remain; but a Girl just Silly enough that when we Stopped outside a Town to Make Repairs, and a Travelling Circus joined our little Camp, and those of the Crew with a Spiritist Leaning asked the Circus Fortune-Teller to tell theirs, I went along.

What the Fortune-Teller told me was that our Airship would be Crippled by a Broadside with a 'Ship-of-the-Line and drift through Equatorial Waters, deadlocked as a Clipper on a Windless Sea, and that I would Perish of Starvation, along with most of the Crew—and my only Son.

It was in that Moment that I became the Person you have always Known me as. After a Life of Hardship, which until Then I had Accepted, I resolved that I would Fight—an unseen Enemy, and a Formidable One, and perhaps One who cannot be Defeated, it is True—but I could not leave you to that awful Fate—or to any of the Others, prescribed to me over the Years.

Because, as perhaps by now you will have Guessed, each Death that I was told was Mine—but it was not Mine Alone. I have seen you Shot, Drowned, Stabbed in an Alley, Run Down in the Street, Fallen off a Widow's Walk, Shipwrecked, Hit by Lightning, and Perished of Consumption in a Garret—and it haunted me. But what Haunts me more is this: would those Deaths have been Mine Alone if I had not Sought to Keep you Close? Will my Attempts to Rescue you lead you to your Doom instead?

Though I fear I shall never have the Courage to Say it to your Face, it is my one remaining Wish that you get out, get free of this, and live your Life as best you can—and perhaps, one Day, find it in your Heart to Forgive one Foolish Old Woman, who sought to Protect you by keeping you—by keeping Both of us—Encaged.

And now I am off to Deliver this Letter before I change my Mind. Lest I give the Crew Reason to think that a Woman who has Learned to Repair a Combustion Engine in Freefall or Shoot a Tiger between the Eyes at Ninety Paces is afraid of her own Son!

P.S. It turns out I am not as Brave as I had Hoped. It is Three Months since I Wrote this Letter. I will Show it to you this Evening, upon your Return from Treasure-Hunting with the Crew, and then likely Flee to my Room like a Child from a Strange Noise on the Stair.

The Lady Explorer's son stared at the letter for some time—at the shakiness of the penmanship, the smudges from re-reading, and the date at the top, some six years gone. Then he folded both letters back up together, put them back in place, and went to pack his things.

"The spirits sense resistance in your soul," the medium said to the Lady Explorer, as the table rose and sank and the chandelier flared and dulled and the curtains snapped against the panes in a gale-force wind localized specifically to themselves. After giving the Lady Explorer ample opportunity to admire these phenomena, the medium took up the mirror in which she'd read the Lady Explorer's death and swaddled it in black silk. "You're like a ship fleeing a storm with no sails, no bearings, and no port to pursue. I have dealt with spirits that did not know or accept that they were dead. You seem not to know how to be, or accept being, alive."

That evening, the Lady Explorer stood on her balcony, watching as the airship lurched, unmanned and blinded, up through the city's widow's-weeds of coalsmoke toward its maid's May-wreath of sun. Once it dwindled to a crow, a flake, a mote, she took herself back inside her newly rented rooms, threading her way between heaps of pelts and boards of butterflies and oddly fleshy potted flowers that would not survive the snow.

At her desk she sat, dipped her pen, and in rusty penmanship with a quavering hand began to write:

The Worlds within Us and without Us are the Same. In One as in the Other, We delude Ourselves that there are New Lands to discover, Virgin Territories awaiting Conquerors and Claimants, while in Truth there are only Lands to which We Ourselves have not been. Some Trepidation is natural, then, on the Final Approach to an Unfamiliar Landmass, looming with presumed Malevolence on a glittering Horizon . . .

Perhaps the airship would find itself a new batch of disheartened, wanderlustish souls to keep it company. Perhaps it would return for her, or for her son. Perhaps it would be grappled down by scavengers, flayed for parts, before it reached the sea. Or perhaps it would fly on, uncrewed and uncommanded, flaunting for the ghost-ship-hunters and the tall-tale-tellers and what children did not flee its shadow when it spread its wings against the sun—until the years dissolved it as they dissolved her, and it fell in clinker from its perch of air.

Her head grew heavy, and her pen stopped. As she dropped down into sleep she found herself smiling as she replayed in her mind how she'd returned to the airship from the medium's that afternoon to find that her son was gone, the thread she always kept tucked in the edge of the false panel in the wainscoting was on the floor, and on her pillow was a sheet of paper.

It was one of the recruitment broadsides the *Swan*'s crew had been passing around town, featuring a woodblocked airship folding her wings against her hull to stoop upon some hapless prey or other on a placid sea.

When she turned it over, penciled on the back she found the note.

I have seen Sunday-Shoes and Governesses, and I prefer the Sky.

FOLD

Tanith Lee

Jintha wrote letters from a tower. They were letters of love.

The tower itself was quite high, probably of thirty storeys, but Jintha had long forgotten. He himself resided on the fifteenth floor. He had forgotten this too.

Beyond his apartment there were always various sounds in the tower, which had made him fantasize that he lived in a sort of golden clock, inside the *mechanism* of it. All who lived there, accordingly, would have their own particular functions, Jintha's being, (obviously) to write love letters. This kept the clock accurate, made it work. Sometimes the clock *struck*. That was the silvery clash of the elevator doors. While the smooth ascending or descending purr of the murmurous elevator was like the movement of an intermittent pendulum. Birds often alighted on the broad sills of windows, or the elegant gargoyles which adorned the building. The clicking of their claws or whirr of their wings provided the clock's ticking—now loud, now soft, now stilled—and now restarted.

The gargoyle outside Jintha's main window, which was that of his living-room, was in the form of a long-necked verdigris lion's head, its maned forehead decorated by the horns of a gazelle. During or after heavy rain, water would fountain down from all the gargoyles. Especially at sunset this was very beautiful, the streams like strands of a disparate waterfall, luminous against the pale pink sky and slim darkening shapes of the city, which ended against the holy wall of an ice-blue sea.

There was another interesting feature of the main window. It was an optional feature; not every tenant of the tower had one. It possessed a binocular lens. Jintha had merely to press his hand or forehead against a certain area of the crystalline, self-cleansing window-pane to activate it, and so see straight down into the street below, at a magnification resembling only a few feet of separation from the subject. A quantity of the building's other binoculars, which Jintha's rooms did not have, directed sight all the way out to the esplanade that ran parallel with the ocean's brink. But Jintha had never required such a viewer. He remained intransigently enamoured of the glamorous sidewalk fifteen storeys—had he remembered—beneath his window.

It was such a lovely street. A wide road perfectly maintained by occasional noiseless machines, and along which rode the attractive city transports, was flanked by two pedestrian pavements, the nearer of which was laid with slabs like translucent marble. Several stores, spangled with alluring goods, opened on both sides of this thoroughfare. But oh—the people. They passed up and down, an endless pageant both day and night. For once the sun had set, the slender city lighted itself with yellow stars, and the most delicate street lamps, rounded lanterns on ornate iron posts, lit the concourse.

Although not a part of the clockwork of the tower, these passing people he saw seemed, to Jintha, another vital mechanism. *They* were the clockwork of *life itself.* And so he would perceive and stare deeply into the individuality of each. And one by one, always, he would find among them those with whom he fell in love.

Despite their transience, Jintha's love affairs with the passers-by below, were intense and, to him, entirely meaningful. They sustained him. They lit his days and nights like sun and lamps and stars.

And therefore, quite naturally, he wrote these persons love letters.

For example.

There had been a young man Jintha had seen every day for one whole month, who always walked across the vista at about 7 a.m., just after the dawn had painted in the street. The young man had hair like black silk, which fell below his shoulders. His skin and eyes were tawny. He was always smartly dressed, as if for some important clerical office, in one of three suits. One was pale grey, one dark grey, and one a mild grey-blue. His shirts however were always different. In the whole month Jintha believed he had never seen any single shirt repeated. Sometimes the young man wore silver hoops in his ears and sometimes copper hoops. He had beautiful strong hands that made Jintha think he might be also a musician. And on the twenty-ninth day of the month Jintha was rewarded by beholding, in the young man's grasp, a violin case. Jintha had already named him "Musician." After seeing the violin case Jintha wrote him a letter.

"Dear Musician," (it began)

"You fill my days with palpable if unheard music. Seeing you pass, for me the day begins to bloom, the sun opens fully her eye. She lights you to a splendour. What music you must make upon that violin you carry so caringly, like a kind father with a beloved child. If I listen very hard it seems to me I hear this music at last. How marvellously well you play. May your magnificence only increase, and your life blossom and bear fruit. I shall never cease to be happy for those glimpses I have had of you . . . "

But Jintha knew that seldom did anyone continually pass below the tower. And after eight further days had gone, the young man with the violin no longer went by. No doubt he had found another route, or another workplace, or had bought himself a personal transport, or become suddenly noted for his musical skills and so hurtled up the mountain of fame.

Sequentially then, Jintha took his completed love letter, which ended in this way: "I remain, dear sir, your obedient servant," and folded it carefully into the shape of a bird with two outstretched wings. Then, undoing the upper pane of the living-room window, he cast it free into the evening air. Down, down it floated, smooth as a white-winged gull. He always turned away at the last, not to see where it might fall, if any picked it up, what became of it.

A sad nostalgia lingered for Jintha for a little while. But soon enough a beautiful young woman began to come and go along the sidewalk. Her hair was the colour of fresh lemons, and she always wore a pair of dark trousers or a long dark skirt, and over these, tunics of twenty or more colours, belted in by a sash of violet or green, mauve or scarlet. Jintha named her "Rainbow."

"Dear Rainbow," (he wrote)

"'You are like a garden of flowers, changeably unchanging. Yesterday you carried oranges in a bag, but later, returning in the dusk, grapes and aubergines. I imagine for you meadows of poppies and heliotropes,

descending to a vast forest where peacocks spread their fans.
Yet always within sound of a sea . . . ”

Rainbow went by twice each day, passing from right
to left, and left to right on the way back, for five days. Then
Jintha did not see her at all for nine more. Then she
returned, but only once, and from that single journey (right
to left) at 11 a.m., she did not come back either way.

Jintha waited a further nine days, then concluded his
letter, “I remain, dear madam, your obedient servant.” He
folded the paper into a bird and let it fly.

But after another space of sad nostalgia, Jintha
beheld a wonderful old woman with long white hair and
a crooked back, like a carving from purest ivory. He named
her “Empress” and wrote to her three love letters in all,
one for each of the nights he saw her haltingly go by. (She
was not, of course, the only one to whom he wrote three
times.)

We do not know much of Jintha’s adult background. We
know very little of his beginnings. And that which we
do know, we have gained, (mostly) through a kind of
hearsay.

Apparently he was born a sighted child to blind
parents. He had been, it is generally thought, an accidental
baby, conceived without intention when the couple were old.
Even so, they loved him. Later, too, inevitably, they found
him useful.

Jintha, it seems, rather than resent this, derived
great pleasure from assisting them and successfully doing
for them what they could not. More than fundamental tasks,
he loved to describe for them the images and people he saw
all about him, themselves included. Naturally (one assumes),
they may have found his narratives puzzling, for both had
been sightless from birth.

One day they were to go to visit sighted relatives in a distant city. Jintha was then somewhere between eleven and nineteen years of age; the collected data cannot be made more precise. Having escorted his parents into the safety of the air transport, from which they were to be met, Jintha returned home, for at that time they had, with Jintha's sighted help, run either a flourishing café or library, depending on who thinks he has learned the facts and tells the tale.

Unfortunately the air vehicle carrying his parents on their journey malfunctioned, a very rare event in recent times, and crashed with total loss of life.

The bereaved child or young man that Jintha then was kept up the family business for several further years. But it is said, and given other evidence seems likely, that during this era he wrote a letter to his parents every month, detailing certain happenings, wishing them well and to be enjoying themselves, and reminding them of how he loved them, and of their great personal beauty. It is thought he compared them to engravings, or exquisite slender old trees clad in the platinum foliage of their hair.

Eventually someone else wanted to buy the café or library, and Jintha sold it. Probably in that case, this was what financed his life-purchase of an apartment in one of the fine tower-blocks of the city.

Once installed, it transpires he never again left his rooms. *Almost* never again.

The accommodation was simple enough. The large living-room, a spacious bathroom, a small kitchen and bedroom. Fully furnished and equipped with all expedient devices, the apartment could maintain itself, and also its inhabitant. It provided good food and selected beverages, heating, cooling, light, and clean water. As is usual too, such extras as the binocular, and so on.

Here Jintha seems to have lived, in calm and quiet, for some fifty or sixty years.

Though having no actual occupation, he appears never to have been unoccupied. Both his vocational work and his leisure pursuit were Humanity. This composite he studied, contemplated, examined, wrote of, and— undoubtedly—adored. It was not, presumably (demonstrably), that he beheld no flaws. It was simply (and here we use that word advisedly) that he fell in love with them. He *loved* them. He *loved*.

Most of the letters Jintha dispatched throughout this time in the tower, carefully folding them and casting them free as birds on the air, were never found, or *if* found, revealed. Of those that did fall, so to speak, into more talkative hands, none was said to have alighted either on the sidewalks or road below the tower, or in any closely adjacent area. Some were picked up, it seems, on other streets either deeper into the city, or further along towards the esplanade. Others were discovered on windowsills, in garden trees, and once (allegedly) aboard a small ship at anchor further along the coast.

In a very few circumstances, despite being sent out long after their actual objects had ceased to use the thoroughfare below the tower, they were recorded as having been found by the very people to whom, even under Jintha's invented names, they were—almost certainly—addressed.

An illustration: a violinist had reported that he saw "his" letter in a flowerpot outside his lodging-house. He was both extremely shaken and touched by it since, after several months of vicious bad luck and near penury, he had just then gained an excellent position with a prestigious orchestra to the north. That very day of locating the letter, he had resigned his ill-paid clerical job in a shirt factory. The only benefit had been the chance to "borrow" endless types of shirts.

Meanwhile the woman whom (very probably) Jintha had named "Rainbow" had been handed "her" letter one entire year after she had disappeared from the street below the tower. One year, that was, after she had, with no warning, met the love of her life, and immediately sailed away with him on his pleasure craft. (Her existence before had been both demeaning and potentially dangerous.) Only when the ship returned and lay briefly at anchor a few miles from the city, did her companion bring down to her a letter he had dislodged from among the rigging.

The old woman with long white hair and the crippled spine had never admitted finding any letter at all. A distant friend merely told her extraordinary story. Which was of one morning waking to discover her back entirely healed and flexible. Of course, in this instance, she may *not* have been the "Empress" of Jintha's letters.

One other, though, did lay public claim to a letter. He was, or had been, an impoverished and lonely student, a failure and outcast, unhappy to the point of suicide. He had, generally at that time, been reckoned unspeakably hideous, his features causing horror, while life had also cursed him with an incurable skin rash which, while not painful or contagious, persuaded those he met to turn from him in embarrassed revulsion.

The student, whom Jintha had named "Panther," was, on a particular evening, creeping along beneath the tower. His misery was so overwhelming that he barely glanced at the street before him to see his way, let alone up at any far-off window. Yet abruptly he felt, he afterwards said, as if a powerful (indeed Godlike) hand had gently but firmly lifted from him the smothering cloak of gloom and despair.

"It was," "Panther" declared, his eyes shining, "as if a storm cloud of enormous weight, which all my life had been dragging me to the ground, *dissolved*. Suddenly I saw the westering sun, the glory of the sky. I straightened up and drew in a single breath that was like the first I'd ever taken, and it seemed to fill me with light and possibility. I felt—how can I describe this?—I felt I too had the resource of bright and unconquerable abilities. I need not hide. I needn't be afraid."

That very evening he went to a cheap and popular café, and ate a meal and drank a glass of wine. He spoke confidently and courteously, even benignly, to those about him. He was not even startled when, after a moment or two, they reacted to him as to someone they could both respect and like. The next day he threw himself into his desired programme of learning, in which until then he had done poorly—and soon began to excel in every chosen field. In due course he had become eminent in that profession for which he had great talent, and also great love. He was a teacher both of the written word and of the sciences. Able to teach equally the brilliant and those thought unteachable, his students worshipped him. He had besides a mistress of unusual beauty and charm.

As for the letter written to "Panther," "Panther" had not come on it until nearly a decade after the burgeoning of his life. In fact, or so he said, he had drawn it from the pocket of an old coat he had worn off and on for years since last being on the street below the tower. For all intents and purposes it had never been in the pocket until that second. Certainly, till then, he had never put his hand on its folded shape.

"Dear Panther," (it began)

"You fill me with a passion of admiration. What a glorious face is yours—unique and nearly supernal in its power. A single glance shows me the generous line of your mouth, your nose like a noble fallen column of beautifully veined stone from classical times, your wise, magician's eyes;

one so wide, the other narrow as the slimmest polished blade. It is at once evident how the wide eye, fearless as a camera, looks out on the world, knowing instantly how to assess and to translate all it sees. While the bronze blade of the other eye looks *inward* to the hidden world of visions and the spirit. Are you a priest? A mage? Yours is a face that has met with the gods themselves, and as they infrequently do, they have let you keep some knowledge of them, that you may teach other men the way to all things fine and wonderful. You are one of the custodians to the gate of life. But oh, you are clad also in the pelt of a warrior beast, the white pelt of snow-panthers patterned in crimson, your insignia. This kingly garment, half animal and half spirit, demonstrates your *physical* power, and your inherent supernatural gift for enlightened rule in the hierarchy of mankind . . . "

A fter he had lived in the tower for the fifty (or sixty) years, Jintha rose very early.

It was before even the first blink of dawn could colour in the vertical sky, and the holy, ice blue wall of the sea, this distant view that was yet so clear, always, was like a painting on glass.

He bathed himself as ever, but did not dress. He made a pot of black mint tea. Then he drew from their place (some cabinet or drawer) a fine smooth pen and two flasks of ink. No paper, however.

What Jintha did then was to begin a very long letter.

And this he wrote out on his own body.

It began on his left foot, ascended up the left leg to the thigh, and so on to the left side of his belly. (Jintha was a lean, spare man, his skin largely, if untypically, free of wrinkles. That being so, his writing was perfectly legible.)

Having mounted his belly, he continued the letter upward until it had covered all his left side, after which he

wrote carefully along his left shoulder, and down the front of
his left arm. When this was accomplished, leaving only his
left hand bare, Jintha somehow wrote upward over the *back*
of his left arm, across the shoulder-blade, and thereafter
down his back itself to the left buttock, and below on to the
back of the left thigh, leg, all the way to the left ankle bone.

He *then* commenced to climb up the back of his right
leg to the right buttock, right side of his back, (leaving only
the ridges of his spine and the division of his buttocks to
tabulate the letter in two neat columns).

The rest of the process may, from this, be predicted.
Returning across the right shoulder-blade, down the right
arm at the back (exempting only the right hand), up the
front of the right arm, across the front of the right shoulder,
down the right pectoral and the belly—the central muscles,
navel and genital area serving here as the column
divider—and *down* the right leg. To finish up on the top of
the right foot, by the toes.

How Jintha was physically able to do this remains a
mystery. Perhaps he observed the process regarding his
back, and other rear surfaces, in the huge mirror with which
all the tower bedrooms were fitted. This presupposes he
could follow mirror writing, as well, of course, as himself
writing elsewhere upside down. Also that he was blessed
with an astounding agility and eye-hand co-ordination, to
which ordinary ambidexterity and double-jointedness were
nothing.

When everything was completed, he must have—as
throughout—allowed the ink on all his last "pages"
completely to dry.

Only the column-dividers to front and rear were
unused, and two long slender margins that extended from
below both armpits and so down both outer sides of the ribs,
over each hip and along each leg to the ankle—the same
margin being observed too on the inside of the legs, (and

arms) and, as previously explained, the genital and anal
preserves. The hands were quite bare, as were the soles of
the feet; also both the face and neck, front and back.

It would seem, (there is eyewitness evidence) that the
letter began (on the upper side of the left foot) "Dear Loves."
It ended virtually on the top of the right foot, phrased as all
Jintha's letters appear to have concluded: "I remain, dearest
Loves, your obedient servant." And, as ever, no name was
signed. Jintha's name was only finally obtained by inspection
of the tenancy agreement relating to his tower apartment.

About 10 a.m., when the tower was almost empty,
Jintha donned a light robe and left his rooms. He left them
for the first time in fifty or sixty years.

Outside his window he would have seen the gargoyles
dryly glittering. It was a fine sunny day. There would be no
rain. Jintha walked to the elevator and summoned its silvery
carriage. Getting in, he allowed the mechanism to drift him
purringly up to the roof.

If Jintha had ever been to the roof of the tower at the
very beginning is unknown. Maybe he never had. Besides, it
was so very long ago.

Apparently he stood there some while behind the
waist-high railing, gazing down and down, now thirty floors,
past the streamlined storeys and between the sparkled
greenish-copper hedges of gargoyles—to the vista he could,
lacking the binocular, only inadequately see.

The reason why all this is so minutely documented is
due to the curiosity (and redundancy) of a man who also
lived in the tower. Having lost his work only a week before,
this man, whom the authorities named Witness One, was en
route to quit the building in his usual search for
employment. (His subsequent celebrity would solve that
dilemma, at least, very nicely.)

However, having noted, as he said, "an elderly man of
some distinction, dressed in a loose cotton robe, and otherwise

covered in what looked like calligraphy" going into the elevator,
Witness One became intrigued. Putting his personal quest
from his mind, he checked where the cage was bound, and
raced up all the stairs of the remaining fifteen storeys. It may
here be noted his former occupation had been an athletic one.

To start with, Witness One opened the door at the
stair top softly, and surreptitiously peered out. Accordingly
he beheld Jintha for some while gazing down at the city
below. Jintha appeared, Witness One said, both "serene and
very pleased. His face was all smiles. It was—a tender face."

But then it seems Jintha undid his robe, neatly rolled
it up and set it by, giving it a "little pat—like a man taking
leave of a neighbour's dog he likes very much."

When Witness One took in the full extent of Jintha's
written-on body, nevertheless, the observer felt a pang of
fright. This old fellow was clearly insane. The witness
prepared himself, he said, for something truly horrible. He
suspected suicide, and was ready to tackle the madman, save
him from himself, or at least to be sure that self-murder was
the only recourse.

"I would have helped him the best I could. If there
honestly was no way out, obviously I'd have helped him end
it myself. But this poor old man, he should never—I
thought—have to do it in *that* way. Jumping from the roof!
And it was such a busy street. He might kill other people,
falling down on them."

What happened next, though, flung all idea of
intervention from the witness's brain.

Jintha had always folded each of his letters,
exquisitely and identically and flawlessly, to the shape of a
bird, its head pointed forward, its wings outstretched to sail
the air.

Now he began so to fold *himself.*

"If I hadn't seen this with my own eyes, I never would
have credited any of it."

The Witness, who willingly underwent the most contemporary lie-detection test, related his account many times over. He remarked later that, rather than anger or distress him, this process helped him find a sort of understanding joy in what he had seen. A true belief—a hope.

Jintha folded himself. He folded himself to the shape of a paper bird with outspread wings. Written on as a letter, he folded himself (exquisitely and identically and flawlessly) as he had folded all the other letters of love. *How* he did it is unanswerable. Yet demonstrably it caused him no pain and no overly strenuous effort. Naturally, it did dehumanize the very last of Jintha. It altered him from a man written upon to a written parchment, to a paper bird, to a *message*.

And when the last muscle and bone had noiselessly and calmly realigned itself, the Letter sprang upward, as a bird might well spring to launch its flight, and over the railing, and down, down through the shining air, toward the sidewalk and a concrete death.

Witness One, gagging with outrage, leapt across the roof. He was far too late.

He craned over and watched the initial fall. And so he beheld Jintha, who was now Jintha's Last Letter, turning slowly in the atmosphere, still unexpectedly near enough that the witness could read, upon the top of the left foot, the words: "Dear Loves, The time has come when I must go away . . . "

Before distance and shock cancelled rational sight.

It was for sure a busy street that morning. So many looked up, and saw.

They saw, they said (we refer here to a multitude of witnesses, labeled from Two to Seventy-nine), a paper pigeon, dove, or gull of unusual size, floating down through the upper air, quite slowly, sometimes fluttering and turning, revolving, dipping, dropping; even now and then swirled up again a little way by some current of the morning breeze.

Nobody was afraid or disconcerted. They were only interested, questioning or perplexed, and one or two quite enchanted, since it reminded them of pretty kites flown in childhood.

Of all the seventy-eight witnesses (the seventy-ninth, who was labeled One, being still on the roof), not a single man or woman did not catch a fraction of Jintha's last letter—a paragraph, three or four lines, a sentence, a phrase, a solitary word. There was too an overall conception, common to them all, of the placement and direction of the writing climbing up and down on Jintha's body.

From their recollections, which seemed to remain, indefinitely, fixed and fresh, elements of Jintha's earliest life, and his sole resultant purpose, have been pieced together. For in this ultimate letter he set out to tell the world—or the city, a world in miniature—how he had come to his vocational study and his passionate, obsessive love affairs; how much he had relished and valued them. The happiness and fulfillment they had brought him.

As he fell, light as feathers, dawdling as if in delight, such fragments as these:

"To see your faces in the loveliness of yourselves. Each separate, each connected, like precious jewels swimming inside a golden lake . . . "

"My food and drink—oh, my banquets of amethyst and stars and red rose wine . . . "

"My amber days, my days of azure . . . my nights of cinnabar and ebony . . . "

"My faultless loves. All, all of you. Your sweetness and your goodness pressed like myrrh inside your very bones, not knowing what you are and led astray by lies, made to think yourselves cruel and barbarous and, for the longest moment being, perhaps, cruel, barbarous, fulfilling an untrue prophecy—but never *never* either or any evil thing *at last* . . . "

"How I have loved you. My love can never leave you. How can it ever tear itself away?"

"Believe in the golden creatures that you are. I have *seen* you, blazing through, like suns through the cloud of night."

The general consensus estimates that about an hour passed, while the enormous paper bird or kite flew over and above them, all the while, if in interrupted stages, tending nearer and nearer the ground.

By then it was about midday. The solar disk stood centered over the peak of the tower that had been Jintha's home.

Away along the other road, the sea-paralleling esplanade looked white and clean, and behind was the holy wall of the blue, vertical-seeming sea, against the limitless glowing of the sky.

With no warning, Jintha's final letter dipped low. It passed just above all their heads, brushing—some of them later vowed—their hair, like a whisper, or a caress. The letter sped then very fast, horizontally off along the other road, straight over the esplanade, (where new persons, the very last witnesses of the seventy-nine) deciphered such fragments as "all ends in light" and "tomorrow is only yesterday." Until, in the closing seconds, a beggar, who presently became known as a writer of distinction, accessed the tiny postscript:

"My arms enfold you—until again."

Next instant the paper bird of Jintha struck—not the paving of the esplanade, but the vertical wall of the sea. Against the glass-painting ice blue holiness of it, the witnesses saw a vivid yet nonviolent flash, like an exploding pearl. From this, the most radiant yet translucent sparks poured away and melted into thin air. Harmless, silent, couth.

Nothing remained then. Nothing at all.

Everything.

PINIONS

The Authors

Marie Brennan is the author of five novels and over thirty short stories. *A Star Shall Fall*, the third installment in her series of London-based historical faerie fantasies (following *Midnight Never Come* and *In Ashes Lie*), will be out from Tor Books this autumn.

About "The Gospel of Nachash," she has this to share: "One night, while out at dinner with a motley group of friends, I discovered that one fellow—a friend of my husband's I'd never met before—was an Episcopal priest. Since he was also a folklore major in college, and I'm writing the Onyx Court books, I mentioned that I might want to pick his brain about the Church of England's eighteenth-century theology, particularly with respect to faeries. This resulted in him telling me about how eighteenth-century priests, inspired by developments in astronomy, began speculating as to whether there was life on other planets . . . and whether that life had been saved by Jesus Christ, or whether they would need their own messiahs.

"To which I said, 'That makes me want to write about a faerie Christ.'

"By the time my husband and I had driven home, I had the bones of the story, and a finished draft just over a month later. Many thanks to Rev. Devin McLachlan, my husband Kyle Niedzwiecki, Jessica Hammer, and Yonatan Zunger for helping me work out all my Old Testament/New Testament/Jewish Midrashim/faerie lore details. (For the record, this story is not background to the Onyx Court novels.)"

Tori Truslow was born in Hong Kong, grew up in Thailand, and studied in the UK. She has spent the last two years in Bangkok, working as writer-in-residence at an international school, directing experimental theatre, and researching for a novel. She travels as much as possible and could happily spend the rest of her life roaming the world, writing stories about stories about stories. You can find her online at http://amagiclantern.livejournal.com.

About "Tomorrow Is Saint Valentine's Day," she tells us, "Despite falling in love with Andersen's fairy tales as a young child, I never got on with the way the strange and magical world of 'The Little Mermaid' was funnelled into such a neat and didactic ending. When the seeds of this story's world were planted—simultaneously by Shakespeare's striking image of the 'moist star' and a collaborative exercise I ran for my old writing group—I knew at once that it was the setting I needed in which to try a new telling of the love between a mermaid and a man. A setting that would resist neat conclusions and morals; a situation that would resist straightforward sexuality.

"This is a story of gaps and overlaps, written after reading too many tales (both fictional and academic) that demand to be read in just one direction."

Georgina Bruce writes mainly speculative fiction. Her stories appear in various places, including *Dark Tales, Expanded Horizons,* and *Strange Horizons.*

About the writing of her story in this volume, she says "'Crow Voodoo' is mysterious. I had the first sentence for a year, but no idea what it meant or what to do with it. But it kept whispering to me, and one night I sat down to write and found the story at my fingertips. Writing is not usually like that, and most stories have to be built, shaped, carved, forced, and coaxed into life. This one was waiting to be found, its little heart already beating."

Michael M. Jones is a writer, editor, and book reviewer, which occasionally leads to some confusing moments involving books from the future, odd looks from the neighbors, and awkward encounters with the UPS guy. He lives in Roanoke, VA, with an extraordinarily understanding wife, a pride of cats, and a plaster penguin which once tasted blood . . . and enjoyed it.

Recent publications include "Claus of Death" (*The Dragon Done It*, Baen, 2008), "The Muse's Mask" (*Like A God's Kiss*, Circlet, 2009), and "After The Hunt" (*Like A Queen*, Circlet, 2009). Under his editorial guise, his first anthology, *Scheherazade's Facade*, is slated to come out from Norilana Books in October 2011. Visit him, and an ever-growing archive of book reviews, at www.michaelmjones.com.

About "Your Name Is Eve," he confesses: "This story came to me, and I almost hate to admit it, in a dream. Or perhaps in that twilight moment between dreaming and waking. The characters and their relationship sprang into my mind fully formed, already aware of who they were and the roles they were to play. While subsequent rewrites over the years may have changed some of the details and enhanced the emotional connections between Clancy and Eve, the ending has never changed significantly. Like all good dreams, it can be interpreted in a variety of manners. For the movie version, I'm hoping they'll get Crispin Glover for Clancy, or maybe a young what's-his-name. You know the guy."

Gemma Files has been a film reviewer, teacher, and screenwriter, and is currently a wife and mother, even though—like Yukio Mishima—her heart's leaning has always been for Night, and Blood, and Death. Her story "The Emperor's Old Bones" won the International Horror Guild's 1999 Best Short Fiction award. She is the author of two short story collections (*Kissing Carrion* and *The Worm in Every Heart*, both Prime Books) and two chapbooks of poetry (*Bent Under Night*, from Sinnersphere Productions, and *Dust Radio*, from Kelp Queen Press). Her first novel, *A Book of Tongues*—Book One in the *Hexslinger* series—is available from CZP Publications.

"Though it stands alone," Gemma writes, "'Hell Friend' can be read as a sequel of sorts to my novella 'The Narrow World' (*Queer Fear II*, Arsenal Pulp Press), which introduced the character of Grandmother Yau Yan-er. Other influences include vague musings about the sociological effects of Stephenie Meyer's *Twilight* series on modern-day teen girls and years spent watching movies from Hong Kong and similar quarters, which is how I first encountered the phenomena of Hungry Ghost Month, the Gods Material shop, and Hell items; Kelvin Tong's *The Maid*, from Singapore, is owed a particularly concrete research debt. Finally, though I've tried to add enough emotional realism to elevate this work beyond mere 'exotic' sensation fiction, I'm obviously playing with cultural cues that are not my own, and therefore apologize for any offense I may have unwittingly caused in advance."

C.S.E. Cooney grew up in Phoenix, Arizona and currently resides in Chicago, Illinois. In a garret. Her work has appeared in Subterranean Press, *Doorways*, *Ideomancer*, and *Goblin Fruit*. She has two novellas forthcoming in *Black Gate Magazine* issues 16 and 17, and a short story in *Pseudopod*. Occasionally, she will write a horrific theater review for *Killer-Works*, an online repository for all things disturbing, and a slightly less horrific theater review for *Centerstage Chicago*.

Claire (for that's how we know her) writes that "Braiding the Ghosts" was "one of those rare stories that shot out of my brain fully formed, like Athena in her brazen greaves, or maybe like a baby chicken. It has since been extensively rewritten. I also want everyone to know that I have a Mima, a Nana, and a Grandma, and they are all the loveliest grandmothers ever, and this story is no reflection on them."

Gregory Frost's recent duology *Shadowbridge* and *Lord Tophet* was voted one of the best fantasy novels of the year by the American Library Association. In reviewing *Shadowbridge*, Dave Truesdale called it "a creation unique, I believe, in fantasy." The two-book story was also a finalist for the James Tiptree, Jr. Award in 2009, and received starred reviews from *Booklist* and *Publishers Weekly*.

Greg's previous novel was the historical thriller *Fitcher's Brides*, a finalist for both World Fantasy and International Horror Guild Awards for Best Novel. Author of fantasy, science fiction, and thrillers, as well of short fiction, he has been a finalist for every major sf, fantasy, and horror award. *Publishers Weekly* proclaimed his 2005 collection, *Attack of the Jazz Giants and Other Stories*, "one of the best fantasy collections." Recent stories include "The Final Act," in *Poe: 19 New Tales Inspired by Edgar Allan Poe*, edited by Ellen Datlow; "The Comeuppance of Creegus Maxin" in *The*

Beastly Bride, edited by Ms. Datlow and Terri Windling; and "The Bank Job" in *Full Moon City*, edited by Darrell Schweitzer. He has taught writing at the Clarion, Alpha, and Odyssey workshops, and is the current director of the undergraduate fiction writing workshop at Swarthmore College in Swarthmore, PA.

About "Lucyna's Gaze," he says, "I give writing students in my workshops a lot of both in-class and take-home writing exercises. Every now and then I start thinking 'Well, how do I know this particular exercise is actually any good? It's possible that what seems compelling or interesting is in fact just something that sounds clever.' So on numerous occasions I've given myself the same exercise. Sometimes I write alongside the students in class. Sometimes I try it at home. I performed the latter twice recently. The first time, Ellen Datlow had just asked me to write a story for her Poe anthology. I'd been thinking about that, about what obscure work of Poe's I was going to ping off. And at about the same time as I figured that out, I was teaching a class where I'd given them an exercise that begins with the prompt 'Two people come out of a building . . . ' And I thought, 'What would happen if I took my idea for the Poe story and used this exercise as a launching point?' The result was a story called 'The Final Act,' which is as mean and perverse a story as I've ever written.

"A few months later, I was flipping through a book in search of another exercise and came across one that sprang from the premise 'Write a story about two people who are naked.' This time I had no project in mind, in fact nothing in mind at all. I read that, and went on to the next exercise, and then maybe a few more; but for whatever reason that premise had got stuck in my head, and within the hour I was working out what evolved into 'Lucyna's Gaze.' Thus have I determined that the exercise is valid—which means I'll continue torturing students with it."

Shweta Narayan has lived in six countries on three continents, read and loved folk tales and fables in all of them, and gotten pretty geopolitically confused in the process. The internal narrative within this story is based on an Armenian tale, "Clever Anaeet," which Shweta says she has loved since she was seven or so but did not recognize as non-Indian till much later.

Other stories of the clockwork bird have appeared in *Realms of Fantasy* and the Clockwork Jungle Book issue of *Shimmer*; Shweta's other fiction can be found in places like *Strange Horizons* and the *Beastly Bride* anthology, and her poetry in *Goblin Fruit*. She was the Octavia Butler Memorial Scholarship recipient at the Clarion workshop in 2007. Her Web site is shwetanarayan.org.

About "Eyes of Carven Emerald," she writes, "To me, this story's primarily about worldviews and motives. The events are adapted from history (for the outer narrative) and an Armenian folk tale (for the inner one); my part was figuring out the mind-games of two particularly ornery main characters. The rich real-world background made Alexandros' and the bird's verbal sparring a lot of fun to write—but getting their *reasons* onto the page involved a lot of hair-tearing and red pen. Turns out megalomaniacal geniuses only explain themselves in movies.

"A linguistic note: Michael Ellsworth, historical linguist extraordinaire, put a lot of work into figuring out period and language-appropriate names. He even derived some etymologies himself. This gave me a range of somewhat different sounds, which hinted at differences between the cultures without pausing the story to do so. In a couple of places, I even had the same character referred to by two names: for example, the man we would call Darius of Persia is called Dareios by Alexandros and Darayu by the bird. This is an early hint about their vastly differing points of view.

"Any error in historical accuracy is my own, as is the decision to use the Persian form Rokhshna rather than the Greek Roxane, and the modern form Anaeet rather than the probably-accurate Anahita (which sounded too close to Sanskrit.)"

S.J. Hirons (sjhirons@yahoo.co.uk) was born in Greenwich, England in 1973. Educated at Rugby and Cambridge, he currently resides in Leamington Spa, where he works for Warwickshire's Asylum Seekers Project. He has studied creative writing at the UK's National Academy of Writing and Birmingham City University. More of his short fiction can be found in print in: *Title Goes Here:*, *Subtle Edens: An Anthology of Slipstream Fiction* (Elastic Press), *52 Stitches: A Horror Anthology* (Strange Publications), and online at: *The Absent Willow Review*, *Pantechnicon* and *A Fly in Amber*. His current favourite listening is the Dirty Projectors masterpiece, *Bitte Orca*, though he usually mixes up the running order, and his preferred reading is a bit of Bolano.

He says that the idea for "Dragons of America" literally "fell out of a clear blue sky in front of me, like a piano in a cartoon. And, much the way it is with any piano that's taken such a tumble, putting it back together was no easy task. Fortunately our esteemed editor proved to be singularly adept at getting the ramshackle heap I presented to him to play in tune, and I thank him for that very much."

John Grant is author of some seventy books, of which about twenty-five are fiction, including novels like *The World*, *The Hundredfold Problem*, *The Far-Enough Window* and most recently (2008) *The Dragons of Manhattan* and *Leaving Fortusa*. His "book-length fiction" *Dragonhenge*, illustrated by Bob Eggleton, was shortlisted for a Hugo Award in 2003; its successor was *The Stardragons*. His first story collection, *Take No Prisoners*, appeared in 2004. His anthology *New*

Writings in the Fantastic was shortlisted for a British Fantasy Award. His novella *The City in These Pages* has recently appeared from PS Publishing.

In nonfiction, he coedited with John Clute *The Encyclopedia of Fantasy* and wrote in their entirety all three editions of *The Encyclopedia of Walt Disney's Animated Characters*; both encyclopedias are standard reference works in their field. Among his latest nonfictions have been *Discarded Science, Corrupted Science* and, in Fall 2009, *Bogus Science.* He is currently working on a book about film noir, on an investigation of Fundamentalist US hate groups, and on "a cute illustrated rhyming book for kids about a velociraptor."

As John Grant he has received two Hugo Awards, the World Fantasy Award, the Locus Award, and a number of other international literary awards. Under his real name, Paul Barnett, he has written a few books (like the space operas *Strider's Galaxy* and *Strider's Universe*) and for a number of years ran the world-famous fantasy-artbook imprint Paper Tiger, for this work earning a Chesley Award and a nomination for the World Fantasy Award. His Web site is www.johngrantpaulbarnett.com.

About "Where Shadows Go at Low Midnight," he explains, "The idea that shadows disappear at high noon on the equator has always fascinated me. The reason they do so is clearly no mystery, but that doesn't stop it seeming somehow a miracle to someone who's spent all his life in highish latitudes. A while back, while I was letting my mind play for the zillionth time with the notion of solar shadows disappearing at equatorial high noon, it suddenly occurred to me that it's less easy to say where they go at 'low midnight,' when they're equally nonexistent. In mundane terms, the sun casts no shadows at midnight for the thunderingly obvious reason that it's on the wrong side of the planet; but that's to attend only the surface meaning of the question. An image popped into my head that was at once deeply silly and, it seemed to me, very beautiful. Other ingredients were added to the ferment before the story told me it was ready to be written . . . and then it proved, damn its eyes, to be astonishingly difficult to write, I guess because I wanted coldness and warmth, wisdom and ignorance, and humanity and nonhumanity all at the same time."

Kenneth Schneyer resumed writing fiction in 2006, after a hiatus of twenty-six years. During that interval he acted with a Shakespeare company, practiced corporate law, taught in a college, managed IT projects, got married, had children. The fiction reboot provided an escape from the one-bedroom apartment his family shared during a home renovation, and has not stopped since. His work has appeared in *GUD Magazine, Nature Physics, Odyssey Magazine, Niteblade,* and the anthology *Misfit Mirror,* with more to come in *Analog: Science Fiction and Fact.* He is a 2009 graduate of the Clarion Writers Workshop. Born in Michigan, he now lives in Rhode Island with the ritual artist and singer Janice Okoomian and their strangely artistic children.

He details the origins of "Lineage" thus: "The thought of a recurring spirit, manifesting in different people at different times, has haunted me for a few decades now. At first I brooded on a revolutionary anima, one that would appear in singular and timely catalysts like Lenin or Robespierre, who likely would have been useless outside of the context of their historical moments. Later I was drawn to a sprit of self-sacrifice, a thing that willingly dies over and over, yet cannot die itself. Then the weird smiles and golden apples came to me one Thursday afternoon in the spring.

"Although the rotating narrative voices are now the most prominent (and, for me, the most fun) aspect of the story, they were not my original plan. The first draft, titled

'Done Before,' contained only the three historical scenes with Jan, Anne, and Alexandros. Friends told me that it needed more connective tissue, which led me to the debate between the archeologists Leo and Mathilde; this is when I changed the title to 'Lineage.' Then other friends said that the story lacked closure, that too much was left unexplained. This prompted the disembodied voice of the spirit itself. It often happens that way for me: the niftiest ideas don't pop up until the third or fourth draft."

John C. Wright is a retired attorney, newspaperman, and newspaper editor (details below) who was only once on the lam and forced to hide from police who did not admire his newspaper.

He graduated in 1984 from St. John's College in Annapolis, home of the "Great Books" program, and in 1987 from the College of William and Mary's Law School (going from the third-oldest to the second-oldest school in continuous use in the United States), and was admitted to the practice of law in three jurisdictions (New York, May 1989; Maryland, December 1990; DC, January 1994). His law practice was unsuccessful enough to drive him into bankruptcy soon thereafter. His stint as a newspaperman for the *St. Mary's Today* was more rewarding spiritually, but, alas, also a failure financially.

He presently works (successfully) as a writer in Virginia, where he lives in fairy-tale-like happiness with his wife, the authoress L. Jagi Lamplighter, and their four children: Eve, Orville, Wilbur, and Just Wright. His novels, all published by Tor Books, include *The Golden Age* trilogy (*The Golden Age*, *The Phoenix Exultant*, *The Golden Transcendence*), the *War of the Dreaming* duology (*Last Guardians of Everness*, *Mists of Everness*), and the *Chronicles of Chaos* (*Orphans of Chaos*, *Fugitives of Chaos*, *Titans of Chaos*). The first *Chaos* novel was a Nebula Award finalist, and the entire trilogy was short-listed for the Mythopoeic Award. His most recent novel is *Null-a Continuum*, a continuation of the classic and bizarre Null-A series created by A.E. van Vogt. His short fiction has appeared in various "Best of the Year" antholologies.

About "Murder in Metachronopolis," John says, "In writing a time-paradox murder mystery story, one has to keep in mind that the readers will expect the detective, the murder victim, and probably the murderer too, to turn out all three to be the same man; unless, of course, the murder victim turns out to be no one at all, as when the event is retroactively made never to have happened; or both.

"There is something about time travelers that always provoke my suspicion, if not indignation. Since the time travelers do not follow the law of cause and effect, why need they follow any law at all?" He says he wrote "Metachronopolis" in order "to examine that suspicion" and adds that "for the reader's convenience, the sequence of events is numbered according to its anachronological order."

"Metachronopolis" shares some elements of setting with John's story in the first *Clockwork Phoenix* volume, "Choosers of the Slain," making it the first tale in our pages to expand on a previously introduced multiverse.

Nicole Kornher-Stace was born in Philadelphia in 1983, moved from the East Coast to the West Coast and back again by the time she was five, and currently lives in New Paltz, NY, with one husband, two ferrets, the cutest toddler in the universe, and many many books. Her short fiction and poetry has appeared or is forthcoming in several magazines and anthologies, including *Best American Fantasy*, *Fantasy Magazine*, *Ideomancer, GUD, Goblin Fruit, Lone Star Stories*, and *Farrago's Wainscot*, and has been nominated for the Pushcart Prize. She is the author of one novel, *Desideria*, and her featured poems from the Summer 2009 issue of *Goblin Fruit* are collected in the beautifully illustrated chapbook *Demon Lovers and Other Difficulties,* available for sale at goblinfruit.net. For further miscellany, check out her blog at wirewalking.livejournal.com.

About "To Seek Her Fortune," she rather puckishly elucidates, "This story is the result of my taking the time-honored tradition of expanding a short story into a novel and running it in reverse. The novel in question is underway. (Mythpunk/steampunk/paranormal mashup! Now with about 900% more Sentient Airship!)"

Tanith Lee was born in 1947, in London, England. After non-education at a couple of schools, followed by actual good education at another, she received *wonderful* education at the Prendergast Grammar School until the age of 17. She then worked (inefficiently) at many jobs, including library assistant, shop assistant, waitress and clerk, also taking a year off to attend art school at age 25. In 1974 (curious reversal of her birthdate) DAW Books of America accepted three of her fantasy/SF novels, (published in 1975-6), and thereafter twenty-three of her books, so breaking her chains and allowing her to be the only thing she effectively could: a full-time writer.

Since then she has written seventy-seven novels, fourteen collections, and almost three hundred short stories, plus four radio plays (broadcast by the BBC), and two scripts for the British TV cult SF series *Blake's 7.* Her work, which has been translated into over seventeen languages, ranges through fantasy, horror, SF, gothic, YA and children's books, and contemporary, historical and detective novels. In 2009 she was awarded the prestigious title of Grand Master of Horror. She has also won major awards for several of her books/stories, including the August Derleth Award for *Death's Master,* the second book in the *Flat Earth* series.

Speaking of *Flat Earth*, Norilana Books is currently reprinting the entire *Flat Earth* opus plus two new volumes in the series. Also the *Birthgrave* series and the *Vis* trilogy—with one new novel that links both these stories together.

She lives near the south east coast of England with her husband, writer-photographer-artist John Kaiine. And two tuxedo cats of many charms, whose main creative occupations involve eating, revamping the carpets, and meowperatics.

About "Fold," she shared this note: "I'd just completed another, much much darker story, which also concerned letters written from a (very different) type of isolation. However, the theme of this one came—nor for the first—from an idea of my husband's. I rest my case . . . "

Choose one of the following: **Mike Allen** is (1) the editor of the critically acclaimed anthology series called *Clockwork Phoenix* (which, by coincidence, includes the book in your hands); (2) the editor of the poetry journal *Mythic Delirium*, which celebrated its tenth anniversary last year with the publication of a Neil Gaiman poem; (3) a Nebula Award-nominated short story writer with short fiction in *Interzone*, *Weird Tales*, *Cabinet des Fées*, *Pseudopod*, *Podcastle*, and the DAW anthology *Cthulhu's Reign*; (4) a three-time winner of the Rhysling Award for best speculative poem of the year, with more than two hundred poems published in places like *Strange Horizons* and *Goblin Fruit*; (5) the arts and culture columnist for his home city's daily newspaper; (6) a husband of more than eighteen years to his tolerant wife, Anita, and owner of more than six years of a goofy dog named Loki, all of whom are slaves to three psychotic cats; (7) a middle-aged white guy with a not-so-middle-sized paunch and a very manly beard. Take your answer, multiply it by 26, divide it by Planck's constant, round the result to the nearest real number, count down that many cards from the top in a Thoth Tarot deck, turn that card over and record the result. Wrong answers will be recorded as black marks in both the *Book of Life* and the *Book of the Dead*.

On passing the first test, you may be permitted to take the second: in less than two hundred words, describe the purpose of a clockwork phoenix. The subject of the first quiz attempted the second, and this is what he wrote:

"You could say it's my selfish attempt to build a better monster, since so few I encountered in the wild either frightened or seduced me. You could say I wanted a creature made from the baroque and bizarre that felt no need to make a statement about its parts, but would content itself with mere being. You could say that all the mutant's parts, gifted with sentience of their own, had to sing sweet poison in the key of beauty, spin tales rich in both what's said and how. You could say these explanations, like the phrase 'clockwork phoenix,' mean nothing at all."

Clearly, the subject failed. The consequences involved intravenous quicksilver, hand-cranked trepanation and concertina wire. Don't let yourself make the same mistake.

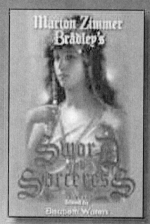
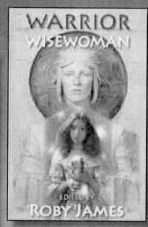

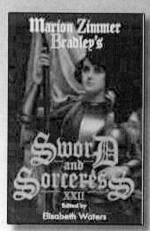

LaVergne, TN USA
26 July 2010
190949LV00008B/1/P